W9-CNQ-554

Keeper of

the Spirit

By Kim Mattson

Keeper of the Spirit

All Rights Reserved

All characters in this book are fictitious. Any resemblance to actual persons, living or dead, is purely coincidental.

This book is protected under the copyright laws of the United States of America. Any reproduction or other unauthorized use of the material or artwork contained herein is prohibited without the express written permission of Port Town Publishing, 1106 N. 8th Street, Superior WI.

Copyright © 2002 by Kim Mattson

<u>Published By</u>
Port Town Publishing
1106 N. 8th Street
Superior, WI 54880

<u>Web Address</u>:
www.porttownpublishing.bigstep.com

ISBN: 0-9716239-6-1

To my husband Jeff, and my kids, Travis, Trevor, and Kelsey,
for giving me the gift of time to follow my dream...
To my friend, Lee, who encouraged me to never give up...
And to Mom and Dad, for always believing in me.

INTRODUCTION

In the northern part of the United States of America, along the Canadian border, there is a place called Minnesota. It is a land of wild beauty to this day, with vast areas still untouched by modern man and his quest to modify and tame the wilderness.

The first known inhabitants of this state were Indians of the Lakota branch of the Sioux nation. It is from their tongue that Minnesota, meaning "cloudy waters", derived its name. But, even before the white man encroached upon these proud people of the land, another band, the Ojibwa of the east, pushed the Sioux further west and claimed their original lands. In 1854 and 1855, the Lakota were forced to relinquish almost the entire northern half of Minnesota, including the richest timberland in the region.

Minnesota was admitted to the union in 1858 as the thirty-second state, and shortly thereafter the first lumbering camps began operation in the area. Settlers from the east, as well as immigrants of Scandinavian and German descent, flocked to the area in great numbers. They were hardworking and self-motivated people, who sought a better life. These men hired themselves out to the lumber camps— lumber camps located in a picturesque territory that so resembled their homeland an ocean away.

Minnesota's rich timberlands were a mainstay for the state early on. The logging camps north of Duluth became a major supplier of lumber, not only for the United States, but also for our European neighbors. The men who had the foresight to establish themselves early on as entrepreneurs in the lumber industry profited greatly upon the logging of an abundance of pine. They set down permanent roots, and second and third generations followed in their footsteps.

The varied strengths of intermingling nationalities made the state what it is today. Those early Minnesotans consisted of men and women who were willing to suffer day to day hardships in order to create a better life for themselves—life in a land that meted out harsh conditions year round. But, they were able to laugh, too, and love, through struggles that, at times, seemed endless and overwhelming. Their inner strength, fortitude and lust for life though, carried them forward and, as the cold Minnesota night winds howled through the very trees that were their livelihood, they slept peacefully—knowing, with a sense of pride, that they had accomplished what they set out to do.

Keeper of

the Spirit

By Kim Mattson

Prologue

August 20, 1869
New York City

The hot rays of the afternoon sun followed a small red-haired girl as she crept silently down the path and glanced warily, first in one direction, and then the other. She crouched at the end of a brick wall and listened intently for any noise that would give away the whereabouts of her pursuer.

The muffled crack of a twig breaking nearby was enough to make the young girl spring to the leaf-covered path and run like the devil himself pursued her. An instant later, a hard object slammed into her shins, and she catapulted head first into a rosebush. The prickly thorns scratched the exposed skin of her face and arms.

Eleven-year-old Emma Sanders backed out of the bush and yanked her petticoat free of the branch that held her prisoner. She rolled over onto her backside, swiped at the first tears that welled in the corners of her eyes, then gritted her teeth with determination and stifled the flow. Emma would not give the older blond boy, who stood above her now and laughed wickedly, the satisfaction of seeing her cry.

A younger boy rounded the corner of the same brick wall a moment later. A concerned frown wrinkled his brow when he saw his friend mopping blood from her bruised knee.

"What happened, Emma? I heard you cry out."

She bit a trembling lip to hold back the forbidden tears and glared up at the elder of the two boys through venomous eyes. "Your nasty old brother tripped me on purpose, Evan, and I fell into the rosebush!"

The elder boy's shoulders shook with another wicked laugh. "That's the game, isn't it? I'm it, and I caught you fair and square."

"You did not!" she shot back. "You hit me on the leg with a stick, and that's not fair." The little girl inspected her swelling shin, which now turned color before her eyes.

"Emma's right," Evan replied. "You never play fair, Samuel. There was no need to hit her like you did."

He reached down a hand to pull Emma to her feet, and then brushed the grass and dirt from her dress. "Come on, Em, I think maybe we should get those scratches cleaned up."

Samuel snorted caustically in their direction. "Go ahead then, you babies. It's just like the two of you to make such an issue out of nothing. It's a stupid game anyway."

The older boy watched as Evan took Emma's arm and led her toward the kitchen door of the house she grew up in. Once again, he felt like an outsider.

The two of them made him sick. The good and kind Evan, always ready to protect the little witch, Emma. Samuel could not understand why his younger brother continually included her in their games and outings. She was a prim and proper pansy girl, who never wanted to play real boy games. He shook his head in disgust.

Samuel stomped off as the other two entered the house, then paused when he suddenly remembered the litter of kittens he discovered in the stables the day before. His pace quickened and a malicious smile touched his lips as he mentally devised new ways to torture the babies and their mama.

Chapter One

May 1, 1880
New York City

The handsome raven-haired man stood at the window of his hotel room and observed a lamplighter move from post to post across the dark sidewalk below. Once again, he noticed the litter and overall filth that covered the streets—dirty streets that were nothing like the pristine, tree-lined roads back home.

Tyler Wilkins arrived in New York City earlier that day from Minnesota—a place where the landscape was still green and unsoiled. What he had seen so far assured his tired mind that the "big city" was not to his liking. Only four days had passed since he left his home, but he missed the fresh air and wide open spaces already.

He had been born and bred in the beautiful Midwestern wilderness, where nature still reigned. He was forced to work hard for a living—work that resulted in a tall, rugged and well proportioned body.

A rueful smile touched his lips at his own thoughts. His brothers would be slapping each other's backs with glee at the idea that he was contemplating his own physique. They told him regularly that the ladies found him attractive and that he would be a fine 'catch' if he would just give some woman a chance.

For the life of him though, Tyler had never been able to understand the appreciative glances he received from the opposite sex, simply because of a few muscles derived from long days of physical labor.

He was just a man, like any other, and nearly thirty years old now–too old for women to consider him as a desirable partner, no matter what his brothers thought. True, not a strand of gray hair laced the thick curls that wound their way around his ears and past the nape of his neck, but he was still not getting any younger. His green eyes, which used to shine with a translucent sparkle, were now tinged with the redness of exhaustion and the pain of loss.

The long overland train journey, and then the final coach ride from the depot to his hotel had truly tested Tyler's thinning patience. He could still feel the lurching of the carriage as the wheels dropped into boulder sized potholes at every turn. Earlier, in front of the hotel, he informed the driver in no uncertain terms of how he felt about the local mode of travel. The cabbie, immune to the never-ending disdainful comments of his customers, merely shrugged off the complaints and told him to pay up. Tyler dropped some coins into the driver's hand, then resisted the urge to pull the other man from the driver's seat by the neck when he spat at his customer's feet. The cabbie slapped the reins across the rump of a sickly looking horse, and the carriage rolled away.

Tyler's long, muscular body had been crammed into train seats and bouncing carriages for too long. He was normally an active man, used to rigorous work, and the sudden inactive position he found himself in did not sit well. He flexed his broad shoulders to relieve the ache in the back of his neck, and then reached up to rub the offending spot. His chest rose and fell in a heavy sigh as he turned from the window, then retraced his steps to the bed to unpack the month's worth of clothes that lay in an open valise.

Tyler pulled open the top drawer of the cherrywood bureau and neatly stacked the starched and pressed shirts. A fleeting smile crossed his lips when he thought of Mamie, the old Negro housekeeper back home. She was excited about his trip and had stuffed just about everything he owned into the suitcase, from riding clothes to formal dinner jackets...

"You all jes never know, Tyla," she said on the morning of his departure for New York. "My mammy allus said 'be ready for anythin', Mamie, allus be ready for anythin', cuz you jes never know what be 'round the corner'." She moved between the bureau and the bed, where his bag lay open on the coverlet. "And you, boy," she reprimanded, "ain't been round no corners or done anythin' or gone nowheres 'ceptin that darn sawmill of yours nigh on two years now. 'Bout time you be vacation bound and be doin' some relaxin'. Yessiree!"

"It's not a vacation, Mamie," he replied absently. "I'm going for a business meeting with Mr. Sanders of New York."

The old Negress placed another shirt in the bag and turned to the bureau. Tyler lifted it back out again when she was not looking and dropped it on the bed.

"Business, business," she mumbled on. "Is that all you be thinkin' about?" She shook her head and smacked her lips, then had the audacity to walk up to him and shake a brown finger under his nose. She deftly returned the shirt to its place inside the bag. "You leave that shirt where I put it!" Her scolding words suddenly softened. "Listen here, boy. There ain't being a thing for you to worry 'bout back here when you're gone. Trevor knows how to handle anythin' comes up at that darn sawmill, and me and Carrie can handle Miss Janie jes fine. You need a time from this here place. It's been too long acomin' since you did anythin'."

"I know, Mamie." Tyler closed his eyes and fought for the strength to continue. "It's just that this is the first time I've left Janie alone since..."

The words trailed off in mid-sentence and his jaw hardened. He could not even finish the sentence aloud. Tyler spun on his heel, crossed to the fireplace and stared into the dying embers. He struggled to hide his emotions as the past years, and the pain he now clutched close to his heart, came back to haunt him.

Almost two years had passed since his beautiful wife, Sara, was killed when she jumped in front of a runaway carriage to save their five-year-old daughter, Janie. Witnesses said Janie darted out onto the street and Sara, who was a step behind her, grabbed the little girl by the arm and tossed her aside just as the careening carriage bore down on them.

Sara never had a chance.

Since that day, Janie had retreated into a silent world. Tyler took her to the best doctors and psychiatrists in the state, but none of them could coax the return of the girl's sweet, innocent voice or her former happy, self. The only prognosis was time and patience. She would speak again when she was ready, but her father was beginning to give up hope. He tried everything—and nothing worked.

Tyler had not left his daughter for more than one night since the accident, and leaving her now tore at his heart. He shook his head in silent rebuke and wondered for the hundredth time why he let his brothers talk him into this insane idea of going to New York.

Mamie reached out a warm hand and placed it over his, where it rested on the fireplace mantel. She gave his fingers a heartfelt squeeze.

"What's done, is done, boy," she spoke softly. "Now ain't the time to be livin' in the past. Go to that New York and be enjoyin' yoursef. It be time for you to start livin' for yourself, and not jes for Janie. That daughter of yours is surrounded by people who be alovin' her like crazy. She be jes' fine. You have to believe that."

Tyler turned to peer down into the craggy brown face of the woman who helped raise him from a lively young boy of nine, when his own mother died giving birth to his baby sister, Carrie. His brothers, Trevor and Cole, were only seven and four at the time.

The night his mother died, a part of his father left with her. Tyler remembered all too well Thomas Wilkins' retreat from society, and the ever present sadness and loss he wore like a cloak for the remainder of his years. Until the day his father passed away, probably of a broken heart, the elder Wilkins worked like a man possessed to establish himself as one of the richest timber barons in Minnesota. By the State's first anniversary in 1859, his efforts had created a logging dynasty for his sons. The hours spent at the mill though, robbed his children of the love and comfort they craved from him after losing their mother.

Tyler gazed at Mamie now and reflected on how the old Negro woman had always been there for him and his siblings as they grew to adulthood. Even after all those years, he could still remember the feeling of her soft, rounded shoulders and comforting arms on the day he was no longer able to keep up the pretense for his brothers that all would be fine.

She found him weeping with lonely pain behind the old smokehouse, held him close, rocked him, and let him cry out his agony. She promised him her life that day. She told him that she loved him and would never leave him—and she never had. She single-handedly took over their mothering, and her devotion was like an anchor for all of them.

Tyler had tried desperately to follow Mamie's lead during the past two horrible and lonely years. He continually strove to stay accessible for his daughter, always ready with a loving smile and secure arms for her to cling to—even when his own grief became overwhelming. Never did he want Janie to go through the pain he and his brothers did—the pain of losing both her parents, when only one had died.

Now, years later, except for a multitude of wrinkles on her face, curly dark hair gone white, and a slowness to her step, Mamie was still there for all of them. He collected her into the circle of his arms and gave her a loving squeeze.

"Mamie, Mamie," he sighed against the gray curls. "What would I do without you and your many, and I emphasize *many*, words of wisdom?"

The mood lightened and she playfully slapped him on the arm. "Oh, go on with you now, boy!" She stepped back and brown hands rested comfortably on wide hips. "Don't you be sweet talkin' me! You have a good time in New York. Mamie'll take care of everythin' while you's away."

"I know you will," he replied. "You always do." And Tyler hugged her once more...

A shrill whistle from the street below brought Tyler out of his reverie. He had not even realized he was standing at the window again. Thoughts and emotions tumbled over one another in his mind. Could he do what Mamie suggested? Could he simply allow himself to enjoy the sights of New York and take this time to reflect on what he needed to do to get on with his life?

He shook his head. It was so hard. He would turn thirty this summer. He was an adult with responsibilities, and yet he felt at loose ends. He had existed in a state of limbo for the last two years, and that condition took its toll emotionally. Excitement and genuine happiness had been missing in his life since the day of Sara's accident—a realization that he had not given the slightest thought to until that very moment.

His days were filled with work at the mill and seeing to Janie's needs; his nights were laden with an abject loneliness. He would never have survived the past two years without his child and his family. They were the ones who made it worth getting out of bed each morning, now that his beloved Sara was gone.

Tyler's main objective for the last two years had been to keep his emotions at bay until he retired at night to his own private hell. There, in his bedroom, he was alone. There, no one could see his suffering.

A small, sad smile curved his lips as he realized the extent of his siblings' support and love during the worst time of his life. The smile turned into a frown though, with the sudden awareness of the hell they must have gone through themselves upon Sara's death. They had put aside their own pain to take care of him.

Shame seared Tyler to the very core. He had not even tried to restore his life. He had simply existed, from one day to the next. His eyes filled with sadness as he gazed out into the darkness of the night, and an image of his beautiful Sara floated into his mind. The pain of loss knifed through him again, as deep as the day of her death.

It still did not seem real most days. Every so often, as he sat on the porch back home with Janie, Tyler still half expected to hear Sara call out to them that dinner was ready. Other times, he would hear her seductive voice in the shadows of their bedroom, urging him to hurry beneath the covers; she was cold and needed only him to warm her. He would always love her and would never forget her, but he knew deep in his heart that the time was at hand to move on...but how could he?

Tyler leaned his forehead against the coolness of the windowpane and closed his eyes. He envisioned her ready smile, the long blonde tresses that curled coyly about her shoulders, the complete trust and contentment in her eyes when she gazed at him. He could almost smell the fragrant scent of the perfume that clung to her silky skin. He could still feel her body pressed against his when they were making love—and the memory pierced his very soul.

His agonized whisper in the darkening room became a desperate plea. "Sara...Sara, please help me find a way out of this hell. I have to go on living." Tyler squeezed his eyelids shut and balled tight fists against the windowpane. "Please help me go on without you."

His forehead lolled against the glass. "I want to laugh again. I want to *live* again." The familiar ache filled his chest, then grew stronger. "What should I do? Please...you've got to help me...I'm lost and still trying to find my way."

His body sagged against the window as if it awaited an answer. The minutes passed and another image of Sara's sweet smile formed in his mind. Ever so slowly, a quiet understanding crept into his heart. She would always be with him—through Janie and the beautiful memories of the time they shared—and he was doing her an injustice by not living life to its fullest. It was his duty, as a father, to make life as meaningful as possible for their daughter.

For the first time since Sara's death, Tyler felt that he would not forsake her by living. His guilt—a heavy burden he carried because *he* was still alive—receded at last. It was the first time in two years that he acknowledged the guilt, only to finally grasp how foolish it really was.

Tyler would never truly love again, not in the way he loved Sara, but he would go on. He experienced something special with his wife; a closeness that few couples share, but Janie needed him now. He would survive for his daughter from this day on—really *live* and not just exist, as his father had done.

Tyler's weary eyes fluttered open, and the wetness on his cheeks surprised him. He was exhausted, he knew, and emotionally drained. He wiped the tears from a tanned face with the back of a shaky hand, then moved to the bed and tossed the valise onto the floor. He sank onto the rose-colored quilt and stretched out, reveling in the feel of its silky coolness through his shirt, then stared at the crystal chandelier that hung from the ceiling.

The jumbled thoughts slowed in his mind. *So many separate pieces*, he mused silently. *But when you put all the pieces together, they create a whole. My life needs to be like that. It's time to put all the pieces back together again; time to make a whole.*

He closed his eyes and, as the remaining tears dried on his face, Tyler Wilkens slept soundly for the first time in two years.

Chapter Two

Dust and gravel rose in a small cloud around the horse's hooves as it skidded to a halt in the stable yard. The young woman's laughter drifted through the air as she vaulted from the saddle, then turned to keep a close eye on the dirt lane behind her. A small, slender hand reached up to pat the mount's sweat slicked neck while she waited.

Emma's cheeks were pink from the cool morning air, and her green eyes sparkled with humor as she waited for Evan to catch up. She knew he would be chuckling too, even though she had won the race once again.

She watched him round the bend in the long driveway, then urge his horse on to a breakneck speed until he reined it to a dancing halt before her family's stable. He shook a fist at her amicably.

"Emma, one of these days you're going to break your neck riding like that!"

She tossed her head, laughed up at him, and rested one hand on a slim hip. "Oh, come on, Evan! I know exactly what I'm doing! Just admit it—I'll always be the better rider."

She reached to gently stroke her horse's neck again and casually watched as he struggled against his mount for control. Finally, Evan won out and the strong - willed animal calmed.

Her attention turned to her own mount and a happy sigh escaped through her full lips. "Isn't Bonnie beautiful? She runs like the wind!"

Evan shook his head in amazement. "I can't imagine what your father was thinking when he purchased that beast for you."

The young man knew Emma was a superb rider and that she was happiest when on the back of the spirited mare, yet still he gently reprimanded her. The two of them had ridden together for years and, not once, did he ever see her make a mistake while atop any mount. She handled a horse better than anyone—men included—that he had ever come across.

Emma cocked an eyebrow at his comment and continued to gently stroke the white mare. Her father presented the beautiful Arabian to her on her twenty-second birthday, just six weeks earlier. Horses had been her passion from the time she was a little girl. Her first horse had finally reached an age where it deserved to be let out to pasture and while away its days. Her father surprised her with Bonnie only a few days later.

Her gaze swung in Evan's direction again, and Emma shuffled her feet as she gathered the courage to speak to him about a subject that had weighed heavily on her mind since the two of them left the yard earlier that morning. It was a discussion she did not look forward to.

"I suppose our rides together are going to be cut short now that Samuel will be coming home." Emma tried desperately to make the statement sound nonchalant.

Evan had been expecting this conversation. He had informed Emma that his older brother would be returning home after six years of schooling, and he knew she would eventually have something negative to say about it. Samuel and Emma had never gotten along, even as children, and Evan silently vowed to do his best to end the friction between them.

"Em, there's no reason why the three of us can't spend some time together. Samuel's been gone for six years, and I'd like to get to know him again."

She managed to keep the look of disquiet from marring her porcelain features as she loosened the cinch on Bonnie's saddle with agitated hands. "I'm sorry, but you go right ahead and get to know him again. I, on the other hand, can't quite forget all the years of abuse."

He jumped down from his horse, placed his hand on her shoulder, and searched her familiar green eyes. "You're my best friend in the world, Emma. I would love to see you and my brother get along. Don't be such a ninny! People change—you know that. We've got the entire summer ahead of us to have fun, and I'd like to include Samuel."

He could see by the set of her jaw that she was not about to change her mind—at least not right away. It was a look he knew well due to their many years of friendship.

"I promise to see you as much as I can. With Samuel arriving home, I'll be busy with him and my father down at the mill. But, first chance, I promise we'll go riding or sailing or whatever you want to do." A wry smile curved his lips. "You know, Em, it's about time the two of us grew up."

She kept her eyes downcast and contemplated his words. She was not ready to share Evan with his brother again. She and Samuel had been at odds her entire life. He was jealous of his little brother's affection for her, and Evan could not see it. Emma, however, saw it all too clearly.

Her shoulders sagged with a deep sigh that voiced her confusion. The summer stretched out before her, and now the time spent with Evan would be limited, at best. She clamped her lips shut and busied herself with the mare.

Evan continued with maintained patience. "I've really got to be getting home. Samuel should be arriving in the next few hours." It was his turn to release a small sigh. He was getting nowhere with her. "Please, rethink the past. We're adults now, and I'm sure the three of us can get along."

He reached over and gave her stiff body a hug of goodbye, then gathered up his horse's trailing reins and swung back into the saddle. He looked down at her with a smile that touched his eyes and tried once more to placate her, this time with a little humor. It worked—usually.

"Now, be a good little girl and say farewell. Tell me how you'll be anxiously awaiting the return of my brother and me." He fought the grin that threatened to undo his stern and controlled expression.

No matter how she tried, Emma could not remain upset with him for very long and felt a tiny smile tug at the corners of her mouth. He always managed to cajole her out of a peevish mood. She loved him as childhood friends do and could not resist his teasing manner.

"Oh, go on with you, Evan! You're lucky I'm not strong enough to pull you off your horse." She shook a slender finger at him, and her own jaw stiffened in feigned sternness. "Just make sure you don't forget about me this summer!"

Evan laughed with relief. The old Emma was back. He blew a kiss in her direction and turned his horse toward the road. Waving goodbye, he kicked the animal into a gallop.

She watched him until he disappeared around a bend, then grabbed up the reins of her own horse to lead it through the doors of the stable. Her eyes searched for the stable hand as she entered the coolness of the straw-filled building.

"Hello? Jim? Are you in here?"

"Coming, Miss Emma!"

His voice rang out from the tack room to the left of the stalls and, a moment later, he came through the doorway. His freckled face beamed at the sight of her. Jim was sixteen years old, tall and gangly, and one of the best employees her father had ever hired.

"How was your ride, Miss?"

"Exhilarating! Papa couldn't have picked a better gift for my birthday. Bonnie flies like the wind and handles wonderfully!" She led the horse into a stall and reached up to remove the bridle.

"Yup, she sure is something," the stable hand replied dreamily as he followed her into the stall. He leaned against the gate, hooked an elbow across the top, and his appreciative gaze scanned Emma from head to toe, where she stood next to the mare. "You two make a perfect match, Miss. Why, her with her shining white coat and you with your flaming red hair, I..."

Jim's voice trailed off when he realized what he had just said, and his face reddened beneath his freckles as he straightened. He ran a nervous hand through his carrot-colored hair. "I mean, you being such a good horsewoman, and her being such a superb horse and all...what I mean—" He halted in mid-sentence, at a loss for words.

Emma chuckled at his fumbled attempt to flatter her and laid a gentle hand on his arm. "I know what you're trying to say, Jim, and thank you for the compliment."

The boy's face turned an even deeper shade of red.

"Jim, could you do me a favor?"

"Yes, ma'am!" he replied enthusiastically as, gratefully, she changed the subject.

"Would you finish up here with Bonnie? I'm running a little late. I'm sure my father is waiting supper for me."

"You go, Miss. I'll make sure Bonnie has everything she needs. Don't you worry about a thing. Hurry now, Miss!"

Emma left the coolness of the barn and, once again, Jim stared after her with admiration in his eyes, then he hurried to tend the horse.

* * *

Emma entered the dining room the following morning and found her father seated at the table, already enjoying his breakfast. The elderly gentleman met his daughter's glance with a grin on his lips, then laid the morning newspaper down next to his plate.

The fact that Emma looked so much like his late wife never ceased to amaze Edward Sanders. She had the same rich auburn-colored hair and green eyes that sparkled like shining emeralds. Emma was not as tall as his wife was, however, and took more after his side of the family. He, himself, was only five feet eight inches tall and, though he used to look his late wife squarely in the eye, Emma came up only to the top of his chin. His daughter often reminded him of a contented little kitten playing with a piece of string. She was always in a friendly mood, gracious to all, and in constant motion.

Edward loved his daughter's passion for life, her generous nature, and the level of intelligence she possessed—a quality that he insisted she develop at an early age. He even loved Emma's stubborn nature when it came to her insistence that she would never marry. She was determined to learn the shipping business from the ground up and would eventually take over its stewardship if ever the day came that her father decided to retire.

He used to think she would someday find someone and fall madly in love. All her girlish ideas of running the company would then slip away as she settled into a serious relationship. Lately, he was not quite so sure. Emma made a habit of stopping at the shipyard office every day—yet she very seldom accepted invitations from her various suitors.

Edward hoped that her feelings concerning wedded bliss did not result from years of watching her parents struggle to make their marriage work. They had each loved the other in their own way, but it was an arranged marriage and, although both he and Margaret had hoped to find passionate love, it never happened. Instead, they became contented partners in life.

After Emma was conceived, there was no longer a reason for the two of them to share a bed. Margaret Sanders never quite recuperated from Emma's birth, and Edward felt he should not force his husbandly rights on the sickly woman. So, instead, they became friends, found a harmony they could both live with, and tried to do right by their daughter. How they had created such a perfect creature was beyond him.

"Well, my dear! You are looking especially ravishing today!" Edward exclaimed when Emma whirled in a pirouette in front of him. As she spun to a halt, she leaned over and promptly planted a loud, smacking kiss on his cheek.

"Thank you, Papa!" Her responding smile deepened, and so did the matching set of dimples in her cheeks. She stepped back and held her hands out to her sides. "How do you like my new riding outfit? This style is all the latest rage."

"Latest rage for what?" Edward's brow dipped in disapproval. "You know you should be riding side saddle like all the other genteel ladies of society, and not racing astride like some hooligan being chased by the police—with a pair of pants on no less!"

Emma's laughter tinkled across the room as she seated herself at the table. "Oh, Papa, these are not pants! It's a split skirt for easier riding." She leaned forward with her elbows on the table and affected a sweet, angelic look. "Would you rather I rode through Central Park with my petticoats wrapped up around my waist for everyone to see, just so I could ride the way I want to ride?"

Edward almost snorted his morning coffee through his nose at the suggestion. "Good God, Emma, you are incorrigible! Fine. If you insist on riding like an Indian through Central Park, at least wear the new riding habit to cover yourself up." He sipped at his coffee a little more carefully. "Since you're probably fishing for a compliment, your new outfit matches your eyes perfectly."

His gaze was filled with such fatherly love that she felt compelled to rise from her chair, walk around the table, and kiss him on the cheek once again.

"I love you, Papa. Thank you for being so good to me."

"Yes, well, one of these days I'm going to marry you off and you can be some other poor oaf's problem." Edward pointed a finger in the air, never at a loss to bring up her unwed status. "And I'm going to make sure he's the kind of man that can't be swayed by your sweet-talking ways, like I am on a daily basis."

Her laughter filled the air again as she returned to her seat.

"By the way," Edward said while he finished the last of his breakfast, "I won't be at the shipyard today. I have a meeting with a man from Minnesota. I met his father once, years ago when he was just getting into the logging business out there. His son is now running the operation and searching for someone to ship his lumber to England." He nodded his head in approval and continued. "Quite smart of the young fellow. There's an untapped market in Europe and not many companies from America are willing to risk overseas shipping, what with all the pirating going on. If he does it right though, and I can talk him into the expense of sailing at least four ships together, I think he'll do quite well."

"Isn't that taking quite a risk?" Emma questioned. "Look at what he could lose if all four ships encounter bad seas and are lost."

"Look at what he could lose if one ship goes alone and is pirated," Edward replied. "With today's market being the way it is, I would..." He paused abruptly, then shook his head at his own foolishness. "Listen to me. You are my daughter! I should be talking to you about the handsome boy down the block or what you'll be wearing for some debutante's ball, instead of the European trade market and current business ventures."

"Oh, come now, Papa!" Emma waved her hand in his direction. "You know my brain would be wasted on endless prattle about dresses and boys."

The dip returned to Edward's brow, and Emma crossed her arms, leaned back into the chair, and decided to humor him in her own special way.

"All right, if it'll make you happy, we'll talk boys. I'll bet this 'boy' you will be meeting today from Minnesota hasn't worked a day in his life. His father was probably the key factor in this logging business of his, and he's just riding along on 'Daddy's' laurels. He's got so much of 'Daddy's' money that he's bored and has to figure out a new way to spend it."

"Shame on you, Emma, for judging someone before you've even met him! That's not like you at all. My correspondence with this gentleman shows him to be a smart businessman with a lot of potential to further his wealth."

Emma raised her hands in quiet deference. "Okay, okay. It's just that I don't think much of today's society of *men*. Most of them my age are too soft and too busy spending their fathers' money to ever really be a serious businessman." Leaning forward again, she proceeded to try and explain her feelings on the subject that continually rose between them.

"That's why I want to learn your business from the ground up. I want to run it the way you do—with a firm hand, but with fairness and with the idea that there's always room for expansion. I'm afraid you'll sell it to someone who won't take care of it properly. Just because I'm a woman shouldn't affect this matter at all."

Seeing where the conversation was going once again, Edward Sanders changed the subject without batting an eye. "So, what are your plans for today?"

Emma hid a smile and let him get away with it; she did not have the time this morning for even a good natured argument. "I'm going riding with Evan. It will probably be the last time for quite awhile. In fact, I can't believe he actually found time for me today."

"Why is that? I know how much you enjoy Evan's company and how often you two normally ride together."

"Samuel has finished his years at the academy and arrived home yesterday. I know he'll do his best to monopolize Evan's days."

Edward nodded. "Samuel's father did tell me that he was coming home for good. He mentioned how happy he was about it."

Emma nonchalantly buttered her toast. "I can't stomach Samuel, Papa, and I can't say as I've missed him at all in the last six years. He's such a bully. But, you know Evan. There isn't a mean bone in his body, and he feels he can't say 'no' to his brother after Samuel was gone for so long." Her lips pursed as she thought further on the subject. "Well, Evan can just spend time with him if he wants to, but he can do it without me. I've been pushed around by Samuel enough in my lifetime."

"I can't believe what I'm hearing come out of your mouth today, Emma! You're usually so fair minded, no matter who it is we're discussing. That's twice now this morning that I've listened to you shred someone's reputation without even knowing the true person."

"I'm sorry, Papa." Emma's response was conciliatory. "I guess I'm being selfish, because I'm going to have to share Evan this summer. He's my best friend, and I'm going to miss him."

"Well, honey, I'm going to give you the opportunity to make a more sound judgment of both men whom you have decided to dislike. On Saturday night, I'm holding a reception at the St. Nicholas in honor of our visiting guest from Minnesota. John and Miriam Fontaine will be among our guests, since they are suppliers of iron for the shipyard. Both Evan and Samuel have also been invited for the festivities."

Emma decided her father was right. She would let her feelings ride about both men in question—until she had reason to do otherwise. She could not resist one last comment, however; and her cheeks dimpled and bright green eyes lit with mischief as she contemplated a wager with her father.

"Let's make a deal, Papa. I'll wager your Minnesota friend is a pansy. I'll also wager that Samuel Fontaine is just as crude as he always was and we'll both find out Saturday night."

Edward rolled his eyes backwards. "Like I said," he replied with suppressed laughter shaking his shoulders. "You are incorrigible!" He stood and reached for his coat, where it was slung over the back of an empty chair. "And, by the way—you're on."

Chapter Three

Tyler stepped from the carriage at the front gate of Edward Sanders' home and his stomach did another quick flip. The bumpy, congested New York streets he had just traversed helped to contribute to a bad day that was rapidly getting worse. His mind flashed back to that morning, when a knock on the door to his suite woke him from a deep, untroubled sleep.

Tyler stumbled from the bed in wrinkled clothes, with his shirt hanging out of his pants. His bloodshot eyes were still blanketed with sleep. He staggered to the door and fumbled with the lock, then, finally prying the blasted thing open, poked his tousled head through the opening. A bellhop stared back at him with distaste written all over his tight-lipped, scrawny face. His expression made it obvious to Tyler that the young man was used to a higher class of patrons in the hotel. The Minnesota native looked like he had spent the night whoring and drinking.

"Yes, can I help you?" Tyler squinted through bleary eyes. The bellhop cleared his throat and, with a quick glance up and down, handed Tyler a sealed envelope. He pulled his hand back quickly, assuring that he did not make physical contact with the disheveled man in the doorway.

"This arrived at the front desk a little while ago for you...ah...sir."

Tyler reached for the envelope and quelled the urge to punch the ill-mannered bellhop in the mouth. The hotel employee ignored the other man's glare, however, and continued to stand stiff and expectant in the doorway. A haughty sniff came from the rude staff member next, and he raised his chin higher and peered at his "guest" through spotlessly clean spectacles.

Tyler shook the remaining cobwebs from his head, and it finally dawned on him that the bellhop waited for a gratuity. *Like hell, you arrogant little bastard,* he answered the other man's tolerant expression silently, then promptly slammed the door in the surprised man's face. Crossing back to the bed, he tossed the envelope onto the rumpled quilt and turned to the water closet.

He poured cool liquid from a fine porcelain pitcher into a bowl and cupped large hands to splash water across an unshaven face. Proof of his instant enjoyment came as an audible sigh. Tyler reached blindly for the towel that hung nearby, then his hands froze when the clean but unfamiliar smell reached his nostrils. He immediately thought of Mamie's towels—towels that always carried the fresh aroma that was Minnesota air—and a pang of longing pierced his chest. He dismissed the brief notion of just packing up and going home, then moved to sit on the bed, reached for the envelope, and tore open the flap.

The note was from Mr. Edward Sanders, welcoming him to New York. It stated that Sanders "hoped his journey had been quick and uneventful."

Tyler snorted at that. *Uneventful—yes; quick—no.* He could still feel the vibration of the bouncing train. He would rather ride a horse any day.

The letter continued with an invitation to lunch at one o'clock that very day; it seemed Mr. Sanders wanted to meet Tyler before sitting with the entire Board of Directors at five o'clock that evening. That way, he would find at least one familiar face at the meeting tonight. Sanders also wanted to discuss shipping plans, so as to be more informed of the extent of the lumberman's commitment.

"That crafty old dog," Tyler muttered. "He can't wait to see how much money he's going to make."

Turning his attention back to the paper, he read that Sanders would send a private coach to retrieve him in front of the hotel at twelve-thirty. It said nothing in the missive about where to send a refusal. Tyler's wide shoulders dropped with a heavy sigh, and he got up to ring the maid for some bath water.

Now, some hours later, Tyler stood in front of Edward Sanders' home. He surveyed the lush greenery that surrounded the front of the house and, as he opened the front gate, his keen mind noticed that not a single twig or dried leaf littered the flawlessly groomed lawn. The house, too, was anything but modest. Its whitewashed walls boasted red bricking around the outer foyer and windows, and a third story towered above the other equally lavish homes that lined the street.

"Well, at least I know the old man's business is thriving," Tyler muttered. "And it damned well better be, or Trevor and Cole can make the next trip."

Tyler stepped onto the portico and calmed his jangled nerves with three deep breaths. Before he could raise his hand to use the knocker, however, the door swung open and a neatly outfitted maid smiled up at him with a big toothy grin.

"Welcome, Mr. Wilkins. Mr. Sanders has been expecting you. If you'll follow me, sir, I'll show you to the library where he's waiting."

Tyler could not help but glance at his surroundings as he stepped into the cool foyer. The interior of the home was beautiful, but not ostentatious. It had a welcoming feel to it and, consequently, the warring emotions in his belly began to settle.

He followed the maid down the hall and entered a beautifully furnished library through huge mahogany doors. A man in his late fifties stood from behind a massive oak desk and stretched out a hand. His genuine, friendly smile put Tyler even more at ease.

"Ah, Mr. Wilkins. I'm Edward Sanders. It's so nice to finally meet you face to face."

"Hello, Mr. Sanders," Tyler replied as he accepted the warm handshake. "It's nice to finally meet you, too."

"Edward, call me Edward. I'm not one for formality." His sweeping arm indicated the two high-backed chairs that sat before the desk. "Sit down, please." The older gentleman's gaze shifted to the maid, who stood gawking at his guest. Edward chuckled and gained her attention.

"Angie, would you please get some coffee for Mr. Wilkins and myself?"

She bobbed her head in eager agreement.

"Thank you. I think we'll be eating informally here in the library. Would you arrange things for me?"

Tyler seated himself and waited patiently for his host to finish speaking, and for the maid to leave the room. "Excuse me, Edward, but, please, call me Tyler. I'm not much for standing on formality either."

Edward's responding grin showed his immediate pleasure. He had no doubt that he would enjoy the day with his guest immensely. The older man settled himself in the chair across from Tyler and began a conversation that would take them swiftly through the next two hours. By afternoon's end, they had developed a tenuous friendship born out of mutual respect and camaraderie.

Tyler settled back in his chair, confident in the fact that a business arrangement would be made before he left for Minnesota. He found himself actually looking forward to the next four weeks and was more than a little surprised to realize that he was excited about something again. It felt good.

Sara, I love you! I'm going to try to make it!

"So, Tyler..."

He was jolted back to the present by Edward's next question.

"...enough business for awhile. Tell me what northern Minnesota is like. Have you noticed any resemblance to New York's woodlands?"

Edward smiled inwardly as Tyler answered the inquiry. The man seated across from him was self assured, articulate, and intelligent. He was no *pansy*, as Emma called him earlier, riding on his father's laurels. This man worked hard to get where he was, and he exuded a natural penchant for business. In fact, if they did form a partnership, he would probably be working much harder.

Emma, he mused, *you just lost one of your wagers.*

Judging by the tittering going on out in the hall, Edward also concluded that Tyler Wilkins exuded a masculine eminence that had certainly not been missed by Angie, his maid, and the cleaning girl. There was something else about him though; something Edward could not quite put a finger on. There was a sadness that lingered just below the surface—a sadness that he hoped to someday discover the reason behind.

Edward took another sip of his coffee. "Well, Tyler, all I can say is that it appears your father built quite an empire out west."

"Yes, sir," Tyler replied confidently. "He was well respected in the business community. My father sincerely believed that the area's natural resources would make it a great state someday. I was only eight years old when Minnesota was admitted to the union, and I can still remember his pride. He deserved the accolades that were written about him."

"And you have managed to build upon his original foundation. One of the reasons I contacted Northern Pines Lumbering was because of its major growth over the last ten years. You and your brothers have done a fine job."

Tyler shrugged at Edward's comments. "My father taught us that hard work will eventually be rewarded if one sticks with it long enough."

A smile touched Edward's lips. Tyler's ego would not be inflated by compliments. He liked this young man more and more as the day passed.

He reached for a small box on the desk and offered Tyler one of the sweet-smelling cigars inside. "We've got some distance problems to work out."

Tyler's reply was instant. "With the prices of virgin oak, white pine, and tamarack being what they are, we would get a jump on the European market. My brother has the distance problem worked out neatly. I'm sure your Board of Directors will have no problem understanding how lucrative this partnership will actually be."

A slow smile crept across Edward's features as Tyler rose from the chair and moved to the open window, allowing the pungent smoke from his lit cigar to drift from the room. The elder man wanted to be around when Emma met this man—and he wanted to bask in the astonished expression on her face.

He did not have long to wait. The front door slammed and short, staccato steps neared the open door of the library.

"Papa?" a feminine voice inquired. "Papa?"

"I'm in the library, Emma!" her father answered. She burst through the door before he could rise from his chair to greet her.

"There you are! I had such a wonderful day today! I met up with Evan's cousin, Marion. You remember her." She barely paused between sentences as she crossed the length of the room, then stood on tiptoe to press a kiss to his cheek as he rounded the desk.

"She's the one from Boston. Remember? Well, she's in town to celebrate her engagement to a local man. Can you believe that? A *man* in New York City. Isn't that wonderful? Anyway, she invited me along to help her start shopping for a trousseau, and so away we went. We had lunch at one of the posh restaurants downtown and spent money like it was water!" Her hand fluttered across her chest as she continued.

"Oh, I met her fiancé, too, and he's quite handsome. Marion is absolutely ecstatic!" Without taking a breath, she rambled on while picking at the ends of her gloved fingers. She slid the costly leather from her hands. "Then we went riding in Central Park. The entire time, we talked about Samuel. Do you know she has been doing her best to dodge him? She doesn't care one bit for him, either." She tossed the gloves carelessly onto the shiny surface of her father's desk. "So, I'm quite sure that I won the wager. You know, the one from this morning? And, I bet I'll be right about our other wager, too!"

She crossed her arms in a pose meant to prove the point just a tad more. "So, tell me, how was the 'boy' from the backwoods of Minnesota? Was he a pansy, like I expected him to be? Come on, confess Papa. Was I right?" She leaned a slim hip on the edge of the oak desk. "Is he still trying to figure out how to use the indoor toilet at the hotel? Does he even know we even *have* indoor toilets in New York?" Her shoulders shook with glee upon coming up with such an ingenious assumption.

Edward cleared his throat uncomfortably, and it was then that Emma noticed the pained expression on his face.

"Papa, are you okay? You look sick."

Edward's eyes darted to the corner of the room, and then back to her. "Uh...Emma, I'd like you to meet my guest, Mr. Tyler Wilkins."

Emma turned slowly and, for the first time, realized that there was someone else in the room.

Tyler's first impression of Miss Emma Sanders changed from that of a petite whirling tornado dressed in green to that of a spoiled brat in a matter of seconds. Granted, she had a mop of the most beautiful auburn hair he had ever seen, and her riding habit clung alluringly to rounded lush curves, but the latter was probably due to the fact that she had never known a day's work in her life. She was obviously doted on by her father and accustomed to getting her own way. She rode about town on an expensive horse, spent money like it was 'water', and giggled at anything that walked by in a pair of pants. She was a prima donna to the core, who saw herself as better than anyone else, especially if that *anyone else* was from Minnesota.

"Oh, I'm sorry, Papa. I didn't realize you had company." She turned toward Tyler with a sheepish smile on her face. "Mr. Wilkins? I'm Emma Sanders, and I'm sorry about blabbering on like that."

Tyler stepped out of the late afternoon shadows, and a jolt of strange excitement coursed through Emma's body when she looked up at his rugged, finely-hewn features. The raw, male aura he exuded claimed her fast-dwindling composure, and she swallowed in an attempt to regain it. The effort proved useless, however, when he stopped only inches from her and reached for her hand. Slowly lifting it higher, he tilted his head and, never taking his gaze from hers, lightly kissed the back of her palm.

"I'm pleased to meet you, Miss Emma Sanders." His green eyes—so like her own—mesmerized her frazzled brain.

Emma snatched her hand away and hid it behind her back to hide its trembling. Clearing her throat, she struggled to make her voice sound normal.

"Are you from the area, Mr. Wilkins?" The words came out in something that closely resembled a squeak as Emma fought to pull her gaze from the dark curly hair that rested on the collar of his jacket.

Edward caught the devilish glint in Tyler's eyes and, once he realized his guest was not nearly as offended as he should be, began to enjoy the little show that unfolded before him.

"No, I'm sorry to say I'm not from your fair city. Since you seem to hold New Yorkers in such high esteem, I wish I could be among them." He took a step back and lowered his gaze to hers. "No, Miss Emma Sanders, I'm sorry to say I'm just in town on business." He paused for effect. "In town—from Minnesota."

If ever Emma had wanted anything in her life, it was that right at that very moment, a huge black hole would open under her feet and swallow her up. Instantly, her cheeks flamed with embarrassment.

"Mr. Wilkins, I'm terribly sorry. You see...this morning, my father and I...I mean—just me, well...my father had nothing to say about you except good things...please don't think he was a partner to my thinking..." Emma inhaled deeply in an attempt to seek some sort of composure. "What I'm trying to say is..."

Emma clamped her mouth shut when she realized he was enjoying her discomfort. He stood before her—so calm, so smug—and waited for an apology.

Why, the insufferable, arrogant bastard! Well, he can go to hell, because I am not going to apologize. In fact, I'll rot in hell before I apologize!

"Excuse me, Mr. Wilkins. I should never have interrupted your business meeting with my father. I'll leave the two of you alone now." She spun and exited the room in such haste that only a trace of perfume lingered.

Tyler winced and turned to his host. "I apologize for that, Edward. It wasn't right of me to purposely embarrass your daughter. It's just that I've never been called a *backwoods pansy* before and reacted without thinking."

Edward waved off his concern and burst out laughing. "No, no Tyler! It is I who should apologize for my daughter's behavior! I'm sorry to laugh, but that was the best dressing down I've seen in ages. Touché, my man!" He picked up the papers lying before him on the desk and chuckled aloud once more. "Now that you've had a chance to meet my beautiful, demented daughter, I think we should be leaving for our meeting with the Board."

Tyler followed the other man from the room with a shake of the head as he silently contemplated whether or not he should be angry with the little redheaded brat.

Chapter Four

Tyler dropped onto the bed at the hotel and, even though he was exhausted, his blood soared with excitement. The meeting with Edward's board members went well, and it had been a long time since he actually did something invigorating. His normal day consisted of rising from a troubled slumber to survive the following hours, only to get up the next morning and do the same thing.

Earlier that evening, Tyler was in complete control as Edward's associates fired one question after another at him. Before the evening was out, he had the entire group of men eating out of his hand. Tyler used his powers of persuasion carefully during the meeting and, after the first hour, concurred that he was thoroughly enjoying the whole affair.

He truly liked and respected Edward Sanders and hoped to strengthen the budding friendship between them. Throughout the entire evening though, and even during the late supper he and Edward partook of, he purposely kept the Emma Sanders episode at bay. Every time her father mentioned her name, he experienced a tightening in his chest that surprised him more than a little—a sensation that he purposely tucked away in the corner of his mind to be pondered later in the quiet of his room.

Now, lying on the bed and staring up into the half shadows, he envisioned her thick auburn hair, petite body, and those dark-lashed, green eyes so much like his own.

What was it about Emma that kept her constant image in his mind? It had to be the sheer loveliness of the woman. Tyler was sure he had never encountered anyone as exquisite as she, or as tiny and delicate. Even Sara, whom he always thought to be beautiful, did not possess such perfect physical features.

That beauty, though, did not parallel Emma's true nature. How could a man as courteous, hard working, and honest as Edward Sanders have such a callous and narrow minded daughter?

Toilet, indeed!

Her comments about the lowly country boy from Minnesota were uncalled for, to say the least. Or had he simply read too much into her remarks? He ran a hand through his dark hair in agitation. "Why should I care what she thinks of me anyway?" he muttered to the darkness.

Reflecting further on it, Tyler decided that loyalty and pride in his home had been offended, not himself personally. He lived where no police whistles blew constantly throughout the evenings. Minnesota nights were alive with noise, yes, but noise that came from nature's creations and did not seem out of place. The sounds of wolves howling to their mates was commonplace—or maybe the quiet pristine evening was broken by the lonely, haunting echo of a loon calling out across a moonlit lake.

If Emma Sanders could see those beautiful lakes and smell the pine-scented forests, she might think differently.

Minnesota was not a wasteland filled with illiterates, as the haughty New Yorker inferred. Opera houses could be found in the bigger cities, along with a fair amount of culture, and the families worked hard to carve out lives for themselves in a sometimes cruel environment. It was a land of raw beauty twenty-four hours a day; a place he was proud to call home.

So, what's the matter with me? His thoughts were not only absurd, but also contradictory. Did he want Emma Sanders to experience the Minnesota nights and all they had to offer? Did he need to confirm that he was not some backwoods buffoon? The mere notion baffled him; he did not think too highly of her character. In fact, he did not even *like* her. In short, Emma Sanders was beautiful—and he was a man. It was only natural that he should be attracted to her.

Why then, this overpowering need to prove myself to a spoiled, immature female?

Tyler clamped his eyes shut as the tendrils of shame crept forward to enclose his heart in a steely grip. Emma Sanders had been flitting around the corners of his mind all evening, when he should have been thinking of Janie and how she was handling his desertion.

He missed his daughter terribly. He missed the feel of her tiny body cuddled in his lap on a cold winter night. He missed the special smell that was just Janie, and he missed the feel of her tiny hand in his when they walked to the stable to see the animals. He even missed the quiet solitude that now surrounded her. She may be only a small child, but Janie was his lifeline. She was the reason he went on day after lonely day.

The mere thought of his daughter brought tears to Tyler's eyes, and he squeezed his lids to keep them at bay. *For a grown man*, he concluded, *I sure have been crying a lot lately.*

He rolled onto his side with an agitated groan and stared at the floral print on the wall. *Strange,* he thought as his eyes fluttered shut. *They're almost the same color as Emma's hair.* His lids flew open again. *Where in hell did that come from?*

Tyler muttered a curse beneath his breath as he flung himself onto his other hip and promptly and resolutely forced Emma Sanders from his thoughts. *Goodnight, Sara. Janie, I wish I was home to kiss you goodnight.*

As he drifted off though, images of thick auburn hair and sultry green eyes floated through his mind.

Emma tossed from side to side in the large, canopied bed as the day's events raced through her mind. She could not get Mr. Tyler Wilkins out of her mind and, every time she thought of him, her cheeks flamed anew. Her embarrassment was tempered only by the fact that she had found him to be as arrogant as they come.

She groaned with the realization that she would have to see him again Saturday night at the reception her father was holding in his honor. Short of drowning, there was nothing she could do to get out of going.

I'll just make certain I stay away from him the entire evening.

Emma willed herself to lay rigid under the coverlet and concentrated on falling asleep. Once she let go of her embarrassment, however, her curious mind wandered again, and she found herself speculating on how the excruciatingly tall Tyler Wilkins would look when decked out in his finest for the formal affair. She imagined wavy black hair and a tanned face, which sat above a starched white collar.

And those eyes! It was sinful that a man should possess such lashes as his—long, dark, thick lashes that fringed startlingly green eyes.

Her mind's eye traveled along broad shoulders next. There would be a black dinner jacket stretched tightly across their width, and long, lean legs—

She bolted upright in the bed.

"Stop it!" she hissed. *What is the matter with me? He probably couldn't participate in a decent conversation with polite society. He's already proven that he doesn't know the meaning of the word gentleman. No real gentleman would provoke me the way he did in front of Papa. No real gentleman would purposely embarrass me the way he did!*

Emma smacked her pillow with a closed fist, and then plopped back into its soft center.

Well, she thought, *I'm just going to ignore him through the entire reception. Maybe if he has a shred of decency, he'll leave me alone and pretend the embarrassing meeting between the two of us never happened.*

She would also do her best to avoid running into him for the rest of the week. She would stay away from her father's office at the shipyards and make herself scarce during any meetings they might have at their home.

And wait until I get a chance to talk to you, Papa, she mused angrily as she adjusted the pillow again. *You could have warned me there was someone else in the room. You enjoyed the entire humiliating episode, too! You just wait until you hear what I have to say!*

Emma rolled onto her back, brushed a wayward tear from her cheek, and squeezed her puffy eyelids shut, determined to fall asleep. Somewhere in the recesses of her mind though, she pictured dark curly hair and flashing green eyes that mocked her over the top of a trembling hand.

Edward rose from the breakfast table the following morning and prepared to leave for the office, but paused when Emma flounced haughtily into the dining room. She threw a swift glare in his direction, then ignored him as she moved to the buffet to fill her own breakfast plate. The serving spoon clattered loudly against the ceramic surface each time she scooped a portion onto the dish.

Edward raised an inquisitive eyebrow at her owlish behavior, not to mention her pale face and puffy eyes. "My, my...you look rather tired and out of sorts this morning."

Emma turned on slippered heel and walked stiffly to her seat, then set her plate down on the table with enough force to rattle the water glass sitting next to it.

"Thank you, Father, for the wonderful compliment. I shall carry it with me the entire day." The words were spoken in conjunction with another pointed glare.

"Oh, excuse me," he replied, "I didn't realize you were in a mood this morning." Edward sipped at his coffee indifferently as he resumed his seat and could not help but wonder what her problem was. Finally, her silence and his curiosity got the best of him. He stood hesitantly and rounded the table to drop a light kiss on the top of her head. "Okay kitten, let's start over. What's the matter, honey?"

"I'm sorry, Papa," she replied with a tired sigh. She would not look at him, however, and simply pushed the food around on her plate with a silver fork. "I didn't sleep well last night, and I guess I shouldn't be taking it out on you."

"That's all right. We all have nights like those." Edward rubbed her back lightly. "What kept you awake? Anything you need to talk about before I leave?"

"It's nothing. Well...yes it is." She laid the fork aside and looked up at him. "I'm a little perturbed with your behavior yesterday, and more than a little embarrassed about my meeting with Mr. Wilkins." Rising scorn etched her face. "It was as if the two of you enjoyed my discomfort."

Edward's mouth opened, but she halted his words with a lifted palm.

"And even if I *shouldn't* have said the things I did, I thought it was rather ungallant of Mr. Wilkins to back me into a corner the way he did—and rather rude of you to let him. I think he's arrogant and could use some lessons in gentility. As maybe *you* could, also."

"What do you mean? I think Tyler is quite upstanding. I'm rather impressed with him."

"Well, I'm not!" Emma pursed her lips together and tore angry eyes away from her father, then picked up her fork again and stabbed at the contents of her plate. "Fine. Just don't expect me to play hostess to him on Saturday night. I refuse to give him the time of day."

Edward rolled his eyes heavenward and sighed. "I'm sorry, honey. You never gave me a chance to warn you about his presence in the room yesterday, and you were rattling on so about your day that I didn't want to interrupt you. Then the next thing I knew, you had insulted him..." He gave her shoulders a quick squeeze. "Don't be angry with me. I'm sorry you were embarrassed."

Emma kept her features stern for as long as she could, but finally realized that her own words of yesterday afternoon could not be ignored. "You're lucky I can't stay annoyed with you."

Edward opened his mouth to speak again, but Emma charged on, wanting the last word.

"And even though I feel terrible, I still think I won the wager. Mr. Wilkins' actions proved him to be a backwoods oaf. Hopefully, we shan't meet up again, so be forewarned—I plan on keeping my distance next Saturday evening."

With that being said, Emma suddenly relented, much to Edward's surprise.

"Please, don't fret about my behavior this morning. You have enough to worry about at the shipyard. I'll try to get in a nap this afternoon and promise to be in a better mood when you come home."

She smiled up at him as he turned to leave the room, and Edward turned with a mischievous grin curving his own lips when he reached the arched doorway. "That would be a good idea, Em. We're having guests for dinner tonight, and I'm sure they would be surprised if you weren't in your usual congenial mood." He took another step from the room. "I left a note for Angie as to how many people will be attending. Would you please check the guest list for me and set up the seating arrangements? Angie has all the other details."

"Of course I will, Papa. Don't I always?"

Her genuine smile touched Edward's heart, yet he could not help but wonder how long it would remain as he listened to her next words.

"Now, before you leave, is there anything else you can think of that you would like me to do? Maybe this will be the one time you won't have to send a messenger with a last minute request." Her usual teasing banter was back.

"Oh, yes, there is one more thing," he replied over his shoulder as one more step took him even closer to the outer hall. "Make sure you seat Mr. Wilkins next to me. I want him to feel as comfortable as possible tonight."

With the plucky statement out of his mouth, Edward hurried into the hallway. He cringed, and then chuckled softly when the sound of breaking glass met his ears. He nearly bumped into Angie as she hurried around the corner with a concerned dip of the eyebrows.

"Better to avoid Emma this morning, Angie. You might get a plate broken over your head!" Edward jauntily plopped his top hat on his head, chuckled aloud at the maid's bulging eyes, and proceeded to leave for work.

Tyler entered the foyer of the Sanders home later that evening and the sound of boisterous voices filtered out to him from the library. Angie took the coat from his arms and started to lead him to the other guests.

"No need, ma'am. I can find my own way."

Angie grinned up at him, bobbed a small curtsey, and continued in the other direction with a dreamy look thrown over her shoulder and a toothy smile plastered across her face.

Tyler continued on toward the library door, but a movement from the stairs to his right drew his attention. He paused to glance upward and met with a vision in gold that glided down the flight of steps.

The sight of Emma Sanders small, yet shapely form snatched his breath away. Her long, flowing gown dropped from slim, satiny shoulders, collecting in a "V" across the tops of her creamy white breasts. Although only a modest amount of ample cleavage was exposed above the delicate fabric, it was enough to send a jolt through Tyler's body once again. The evening dress draped her slim hips, and then flared slightly to the tips of her gold slippers, which peeked from beneath the silken threads.

Emma saw Tyler at exactly the same moment he saw her. She hesitated for a split second at the top of the staircase, inhaled deeply to regain her composure, and continued down.

Papa, you are a dead man.

Emma forced a smile to curve her lips when she reached the bottom of the steps. *I can hardly ignore him when we're the only two people standing in the hall,* she decided.

"Hello, Mr. Wilkins." She felt heat flush her cheeks and tried valiantly to stop it, but to no avail. *Fine,* she mused silently. *I'll just ignore what happened at our first meeting, and hopefully, he will, too.* She took another deep breath, which caused his eyes to widen when her breasts rose slightly from beneath the golden threads. "It seems my father has decided to be the *host extraordinaire* while you're visiting New York. I hope he isn't taking up too much of your time?"

Tyler forced himself to drag his eyes from her flawless skin. "On the contrary, Miss Sanders. I am a lamb lost in this city of wolves and appreciate the friendship he has extended to me. And, please, call me Tyler. If your father has decided to be my mentor, I can't see the need for us to stand on formality."

Emma could do nothing but stare up into those smoldering green eyes. *Damn, but he is handsome!*

Thankfully, it appeared that he had decided to ignore the humiliating events of their first meeting also, and let bygones be bygones. Mentally shaking her head to clear it, she searched for something to say.

"Ah...if that's the way it is to be, then you may call me Emma. Miss Sanders makes me sound like a little schoolgirl."

His eyes sparkled when he smiled, and a sigh followed. "Ah, Emma, a schoolgirl you most definitely are not."

Her immediate discomfiture turned quickly to anger. *How dare he talk to me as if I'm one of the many prostitutes of the city?*

She straightened her shoulders, failing to realize that the movement made her breasts stand out even more impudently, then turned and took three steps toward the library door before remembering her manners. She stopped and cast him a quick, if withering glance over a creamy white shoulder.

"If you'll follow me, *Mr.* Wilkins, I'll show you to my father."

A smile played at the corners of Tyler's mouth. "Of course, I'd follow you anywhere!"

Emma slammed her teeth together and stomped on toward the library entrance without looking back. *To hell with him! He can follow me or stay behind! I couldn't care less if he winds up in the cellar!*

Tyler shook his head and, giving vent to a wry smile now, wondered what the hell had gotten into him. Only two days ago, he would never have dreamed of talking to a business associate's daughter as he just did.

Behave! he told himself sternly, but, forced to watch her perfectly shaped derriere, draped in gold and leading the way, he knew it would be a difficult task.

Emma tried valiantly for the next hour to ignore Tyler, but finally gave in to her own curiosity and covertly watched him from across the library as he visited with various board members. She was angry with him, true, but even so, was drawn to him in some inexplicable way.

She observed him swirl the amber liquor in his glass ever so slowly, and then throw his head back to laugh at something one of the men said to him. He was a head taller than any other man in the room, and his mere presence commanded attention from all those gathered.

Lost lamb, my eye! she spouted silently.

The men kept him in constant conversation from the moment he walked into the room and, for the last hour, Emma watched through seething eyes as the women whispered from behind delicate fans and ogled the guest of honor from every corner of the room.

Emma felt a headache start behind her eyes and wondered how she was going to make it through the evening with all the contradictory emotions that coursed through her body.

Thank goodness I had the presence of mind to seat him at the other end of the table for dinner!

Across the room, Tyler found it hard to concentrate on the flow of conversation around him. His eyes continually searched for Emma over the rim of his glass.

She's avoiding me.

That was fine though; it gave him a chance to secretly study the woman who had made his stomach roil from the moment he spotted her on the steps.

She visited with one of the elderly women attending the party and, though she tried to appear interested in the conversation, the constant—if discreet—fingers to temple motion indicated that she had a headache.

Thick auburn hair, piled high atop her head, shone in the bright gaslights that adorned the elegant library. When she moved, the golden gown shimmered and seemed to flow softly off her white shoulders like rippling water. Her face was flushed; whether from the champagne or the heat of the pressed bodies in the room, he could not tell. One thing though, he did know for sure; the overall effect was divine.

His attention swung back to the man who whispered a risqué story to him. He threw back his head and laughed, then admitted to himself how much he was enjoying the evening. It was a different sort of enjoyment from what he was used to. Lately, the only pleasure he derived from the sometimes endless days came when he held his young daughter in his arms while she fell asleep.

Now, he was reestablishing himself as a member of the business community; as an adult in the world of adults, and he was thrilled. He had retreated into his own little world for so long that he had not realized how much he actually missed.

He glanced up to see Edward walk toward him with a smile on his flushed face. The sound of a spoon clinking against his glass gained the attention of the small gathering. Immediately, the guests hushed to hear his words.

"I just have to say how happy I am to be forging this new partnership with Mr. Wilkins. It's been two very interesting days. His enthusiasm is contagious, and I'm looking forward to the next four weeks."

"I couldn't agree more with you, Mr. Sanders," Tyler acknowledged. "We've definitely got our work cut out for us."

Edward clasped his hands behind his back. "I hope you will all be able to attend Saturday night's reception. We've got quite a gala planned with many more guests from around the city. And, with that," he continued, "I have just been informed that dinner is to be served. So, if my beautiful daughter would be so kind as to let my guest from Minnesota escort her to the dining room, we can all retire there for our evening meal."

Emma longed to stomp on her father's foot, but he was not close enough. The crowd slowly parted in front of her, and she had no choice but to ignore her pounding head and force a wan smile to curve her lips again. Tyler moved across the room to offer his arm.

"Would you do me the honor, Miss Sanders?" He waited patiently as she graciously accepted his arm, and was amazed by the fact that she came up only to his shoulder. They proceeded to the dining room then, without a word, and finally arrived at the table, which was heavily laden with food. Tyler pulled out a high-backed chair and seated her in a very gentlemanly fashion, and Emma's good manners mandated that she thank him.

"Thank you, Mr. Wilkins. Enjoy your meal." She refused to look at him.

"You're welcome, Miss Sanders. I'm sure I will." With a nod of his head, he continued on to his seat at the opposite end of the table, near Edward.

The dinner lasted for two hours. Not once during the entire meal did Emma feel Tyler's gaze upon her. He sat an eternity away, by her own choosing, with her father on one side of him and an elderly matron on the other. The Minnesotan kept the conversation going throughout the entire meal. He laughed and chatted the evening away—and totally ignored his hostess.

Emma fumed at the other end of the table and failed miserably to keep her cleavage covered as best she could with a wine glass. The older gentleman who sat next to her had imbibed a little too much brandy during the evening and now openly ogled her chest. She felt his knee bump up against hers every so often and swore if she moved any closer to the edge of her chair, she would be on the floor at any moment.

Her headache now raged, and she did her best not to snap at the lecherous old goat beside her. Just when she felt she could take no more, her father stood to invite the gentlemen back to the library for a nightcap and a cigar.

Emma jumped up. "Ladies, why don't we retire to the parlor while the men end the evening with a drink." The invitation was issued through clenched teeth. "Angie has tea and coffee set up."

The women settled themselves in the parlor a few minutes later, amid sincere thanks for a delicious meal. The elderly matron, who sat next to Tyler during dinner, clapped to gain the women's attention.

"Ladies! I know how you all must be jealous of me! My, what a handsome fellow that Mr. Wilkins from Minnesota is! I haven't enjoyed a dinner companion such as the likes of him for some time. My goodness, if I were twenty years younger...Ohhh!" She waved a delicate fan in front of her face and rolled her eyes heavenward. The other women tittered along with her, which only caused more excitement concerning the handsome dark stranger who suddenly graced their presence.

Emma listened with an exasperated press of the lips as they expounded on the glorious traits of one Mr. Tyler Wilkins for the rest of the evening.

The night finally ended and the last of the guests took their leave. Emma closed the front door and heaved a tired sigh, then turned to lean back against the burnished wood. She closed her eyes against the tears that threatened to overflow, and another heavy sigh escaped into the quietness. It had been an awful evening. The muscles in her neck ached, and her head pounded ferociously.

One more comment from those old biddies about the wonderful Mr. Wilkins, and I would've thrown up right in front of them.

She pushed herself away from the door and kicked off her slippers. A sigh of sheer pleasure filtered through the still air this time with the feel of cool tile under her feet. She bent to gather up the slippers, then wiggled her toes, pushed her shoulders upright, and moved with slow, fatigued steps toward the bottom of the stairway. Her heart jumped erratically at the sound of his voice.

"You look as if you might not make it up the stairs."

Tyler stood in the hallway, his evening coat casually draped over a forearm and looking as fresh as if he had just awakened and was ready for some grand outing.

Emma's face flamed with her immediate, rising anger. He was the last person she wanted to encounter. She had listened to the ladies chatter about him throughout the evening, and enough was enough. Tyler had not given her the time of day since the sumptuous meal began, and had rudely ignored her when the men left for their cigars. And the other women thought he was such a gentleman.

Gentleman? Humph! I'll be damned if I'll sit and chitchat with him now.

She continued toward the staircase in a nonchalant manner and threw a caustic remark in his direction. "Oh, it's you. I thought you would have left by now."

"I waited so I could thank your father in private for the nice evening." He glanced down at her as she passed him and proceeded deliberately toward the steps.

"Well, I'm sure he was impressed with your thoughtfulness." Emma returned, refusing to even look over a white shoulder as she muttered the words. She started up the steps and could not resist one parting shot. "Good night, *Mr.* Wilkins. Don't let the door hit you in the backside on your way out."

You little snip, he ground out silently.

He watched her saunter up the steps to the second floor, then moved to open the front door. He turned again, just before he closed it, and threw one final comment in her direction.

"Oh, never fear, I'll watch so it doesn't, Miss Sanders. By the way, you should be more careful about whom you bend over in front of. I saw almost as much of your bosom as that lustful old man who sat beside you at dinner tonight."

He pulled the door closed behind him and, as the brass lock clicked into place, one of Emma's slippers bounced off the wooden surface and landed on the cool tile.

Chapter Five

Tyler stood in front of the mirror in his hotel room and adjusted his tie as he contemplated the coming evening. It was Saturday—the night of Edward's reception.

It had been a long week. The negotiations with Edward's Board members had been grueling, to say the least, and, when the daily meetings ended, someone in the group inevitably insisted that he dine with them. The meal always led to a late evening—something he was not accustomed to. If he were at home right now, he would be tucking Janie in and saying her prayers for her.

Tyler's shoulders sagged as the wave of homesickness hit him abruptly, and a deep sigh followed when he brushed it aside.

Life in New York was so unlike what he was used to back home. Most of the men he met were incapable of putting in even one full day of physical labor. An image of the family sawmill flashed in his brain, and he was forced to acknowledge the fact that he missed the smell of a newly cut tree and the sound of his crew laughing and discussing the day's work. Just about now, they were headed home for a hot meal and a well deserved night's sleep.

Tyler also missed his brothers' companionship. They would gather around the dining room table at the end of the day and enjoy a simple but hearty dinner while they made plans for the next day's work. This was also the time when his thoughts would turn to Sara—

Have I really not thought about her all week?

The guilt was instantaneous. "How could I just forget about her?" he chastised the reflection in the mirror. "Hell, I've still got three weeks here. A few more dinners, a few more parties, and will she be gone from my mind forever?"

Tyler's shoulders fell with a guilty sigh. "You shouldn't be here," he berated himself. "You should be home, sitting by Sara's gravesite and remembering all the good times."

I should be laying fresh wildflowers against her tombstone and quietly telling her about my day. He fought the lump that formed in his throat.

Somehow, Tyler felt closer to Sara when he visited the family cemetery. Granted, if anyone ever heard him talking to a stone and a mound of dirt, the person would think he had lost his mind. But sitting in the grass next to her final resting place was the only way he could find comfort, and he refused to give up that cherished bond.

"I'll be back, Sara," he told the man in the mirror. "In three more weeks, I can go home." A rueful grin touched his lips. "But, for right now, I'd better quit talking to myself or I'll be late for Edward's reception."

The reflection nodded its agreement, then Tyler turned and moved to pull his black dinner jacket from over the back of a nearby chair. He stuffed his muscular arms into the long sleeves, then reached for the door handle. He paused to glance around the room, though he was not quite sure what he sought. His tired eyes settled on the chandelier, and he stared at the numerous bits of shimmering crystal.

Pieces, he thought. *Pieces create a whole. Sara, I've got to keep trying.*

Emma stood before a gilded mirror and patted the finishing touches to her hair. She studied the soft, auburn curls that framed her face and reached for an emerald necklace and pair of matching earrings, which originally belonged to her mother. She clipped the earrings to her tiny lobes and closed the hasp on the necklace, then gently straightened the chain so the beautifully set emerald lay against the rise of her cleavage.

A quick glance at the clock told her that Evan would soon be knocking at the front door. During one of their now rare rides earlier that afternoon, he asked if he could escort her to the reception, and Emma agreed. She sank onto a nearby settee, and her mind shifted to their conversation as they leisurely walked their mounts through Central Park...

Emma teased him mercilessly about being quiet and secretive and, finally, he turned in the saddle to look at her. "Em, I've got something to tell you." He took a deep breath, then charged on. "I'm going to be leaving in two days."

"And where might you be going?" she asked in a light, bantering voice that displayed her immediate lack of concern.

Evan looked off into the distance and chose his words carefully. "Now that Samuel is home, he'll be able to help my father at the iron mill." He shifted in the saddle again and took another deep breath. "Let me back up a minute. You know I've never really had a genuine interest in the mill. My father has made it clear that he wants both Samuel and I to take over its operation when he's gone, but Samuel is the one who always talked about becoming the working manager. Now that he's back, I feel I can finally pursue my own dreams. He's been by my father's side since he returned and is doing a good job." He turned to look at her, and his eyes pleaded for her understanding. "Em, he's really changed since the academy."

Emma snorted in an unladylike manner with his last words.

"It's true!" Evan bristled. "Tonight when you see him, you'll know what I mean. I told you, he's been by my father's side constantly, going over the books and visiting the operation daily. Mother is so happy with the change in him. He's been considerate, kind, and genuinely happy to be back in the bosom of our family."

"Are we talking about the same person here? Samuel was one of the biggest bullies I've ever come across." Emma stated incredulously. "Don't you remember how he treated us?"

"Ah, Em, we were children when he left. I know at times he could be cruel and I often despaired that he would never change, but he's not like that anymore. You'll see tonight. In fact, I think you'll be quite surprised." His lips curved in another smile—one that begged for her to give his brother the benefit of the doubt. "Please, for my sake, try to get along with him and try to see him as the adult he is now, not the child that he was."

Emma shook her head. "I don't know if I can." She remembered all too well the times Samuel purposely tormented her when they were children—things that Evan did not know about. Even as a child, her friend looked for the good in everyone—including his malicious brother—and always held out hope that someday Samuel and Emma would mend fences. Apparently, he thought now was the time.

Emma did not. She refused to put forth the effort to "mend fences" where Samuel Fontaine was concerned. She had suffered the consequences of his cruel streak from the time she was very young and found it hard to believe that someone could simply change their personality—even in six years time.

Emma had been fortunate enough not to run into Samuel since his return, though she had managed to arrange several outings with Evan. Tonight, however, she would have to see the elder Fontaine brother again, and she was not looking forward to it.

"Emma, just give him a chance...for me," Evan interrupted her thoughts.

"Oh, all right!" She gave in. "I know if I don't agree, you'll hound me the rest of the day. Besides, right now I want to know where it is that you're going."

Evan took a third deep breath. "I'm leaving for Africa."

Emma's eyes widened in disbelief and she flashed him a quick look of surprise. "Africa? What on earth are you going there for?"

"I plan to leave in two days on a missionary ship. I've already discussed it with my parents. At first, they were upset, but Samuel helped me talk them into it. He'll be here to learn the business and, eventually, my father will hand over the reins to him. I, on the other hand, am finally free to do as I want." He reached out to squeeze her hand, and his eyes sparkled with enthusiasm. "Em, I'm so excited! I'm going to work at a mission and teach the local children Christianity. I'll also help treat their medical problems. We're even going to start a school!"

Emma searched the face of her dearest friend in the world and wondered what her days would be like without him. She had depended on his companionship her entire life. She had told him her deepest secrets and her wildest dreams. She had always been so sure that their lives would be entwined forever. Tears welled in her eyes at the thought of his imminent departure, and she leaned toward his mount and rested her hand on his arm.

"Are you quite sure about this, Evan? Isn't it rather sudden?"

"I've been thinking about this for the past two years," he replied. "Please understand, Em. Now that Samuel's home, it's finally my turn to do what I want with my life."

"But you've never said anything about this." Emma's gaze dropped to her lap as her hand again found the pommel on the saddle. "I guess I thought you and I would be...well...working together as...business partners until we were old and gray. Friends forever." A sad sigh escaped through her parted lips. "It's quite a lot to take in all at once."

It was Emma's turn to stare into the distance, and the only sound for a long moment was the creak of the saddle as it moved with the smooth rhythm of the horse beneath her. She swallowed the lump in her throat and, finally, met his eyes. "I guess that was rather selfish of me, wasn't it? I'll miss you with all my heart, but your happiness comes first. Promise you'll write long letters full of your days in Africa."

Evan grinned, reined his horse closer, and reached out his hand to hers. She grasped his fingers and gave them a quick squeeze while blinking the tears from her eyes.

"I promise to write every day." He brought her tiny hand to his mouth and gently kissed the smooth knuckles. "We'll always be friends, Em—forever..."

Emma clenched her eyes shut against a new rush of tears as she pushed herself up from the settee, picked up her evening shawl, and crossed to the door.

What will life be like after he's gone? she wondered again as she left the room, then her shoulders squared. *Well, at least he'll still be here to get me through tonight.*

The evening loomed before her like a thunderstorm on the horizon. Not only was she going to have to contend with Evan's insistence that she change her mind about his recalcitrant brother, but she would also have to see Tyler Wilkins again. She had managed quite adeptly to avoid being anywhere near him in the past week, but her reprieve would end tonight.

Try as she might, she could not sort out her feelings toward the arrogant Minnesotan. One minute he was the handsomest man on earth, and the next she was ready to scratch his rugged face bloody. Granted, they had been together only a few times, but each of those times he had gone out of his way to goad her. Consequently, she ended up either blubbering like an idiot in his presence, or acting like a shrew.

Emma caught her reflection in the gilded full length mirror at the top of the stairs and paused for a moment to study herself. *I wonder if he'll think I'm beautiful tonight?*

The gown was the same shade as her eyes. She had chosen it very carefully and, though she would never admit it—even to herself—she thought of him when she purchased it. The dress exposed a little more cleavage than she was accustomed to, but something made her throw caution to the wind. She wanted to look like a woman tonight.

For him?

Emma shook her head.

It's official. I'm losing my mind.

Tyler Wilkins *and* Samuel Fontaine were the last two men on earth she wanted to impress.

Well, I'll show them both that they have to treat me like a lady—or suffer the consequences.

Emma lifted her chin with new resolve and descended the steps to the foyer to greet her father and Evan. Her chin drooped again, however, when she overheard snatches of their conversation. They were talking about Evan's imminent departure.

The ornate ballroom was aglow with warm candlelight. The ten piece orchestra already provided soft music and most of the guests were in attendance. Emma's eyes roamed the crowd, searching for a familiar—yet decidedly disturbing—face. She did not see Tyler Wilkins anywhere in the close press of people.

"Are you okay?" Evan asked from where he stood beside her. "You look...tense."

"I'm fine, Evan," she said as she smiled up at him. "I'm just anxious about the evening being a success."

Her heart jumped a moment later, when Evan's parents called out a greeting. A tall man in his mid twenties stood beside them. His blond hair was neatly combed to the side and a groomed mustache curled over his top lip. The man stared quite openly at her and recognition dawned in both his and Emma's eyes at the same instant.

"Samuel Fontaine," she muttered.

An initial stab of fear pricked Emma's chest as she stared at him, then she took a deep breath and forced it aside.

Stop being so foolish, her mind chastised. *We're all adults now. He can't hurt you anymore.*

She clung to the fact that, even though Evan was sometimes naive when it came to his brother, six years had gone by since she last saw Samuel. Hopefully, the younger Fontaine brother would be right in the new assessment of his sibling.

The two groups met in the middle of the room. Emma looked up at Evan, read the plea in his eyes, and forced a bright smile.

"Well, well, well!" Samuel spouted enthusiastically. "Could this be little Emma all grown up?"

Her eyes darted to Evan again, and then to his parents, but it appeared that she was the only one in the small group to notice when Samuel's eyes discreetly surveyed her petite form from head to toe.

"Did you think I would stay the small child all these years, Samuel?" The reply was tinged with bravado.

"Well, I can certainly see that you didn't," he answered in a voice that deepened with his appreciation. His parents and Evan laughed, failing to notice the barbs that were already being thrown. They saw the meeting as a simple reunion of two childhood friends, who had not seen each other for many years. Emma's brittle smile mirrored the one plastered on Samuel's lips, however, and the hatred that jumped from one to the other was almost tangible.

Mrs. Fontaine rested her eyes on Emma. "My, but you do look lovely this evening, my dear."

"Thank you, Mrs. Fontaine. That's nice of you to say." Emma did her best to ignore Samuel's leering gaze as Miriam Fontaine slipped an arm through her eldest son's.

"Samuel's father and I are so happy to have him home. I have to admit it's been hard to share him since he arrived from the Academy. That's why you haven't seen him about the city. But I'm sure, Emma, that I can manage to give him up for a short while tonight so the two of you can catch up." She looked up at her son with a happy smile, and Samuel patted her hand gently.

"It would be delightful to talk with you later, Emma," Samuel's voice dripped with sweetness. "I hope you'll save a dance or two for me."

Emma could not suppress the cringe that was visible only to herself, and the promise in Samuel's eyes made his next thoughts only too clear.

I can't wait to feel that lush body of yours pressed to mine.

"If you can't get on her dance card, Samuel," Evan chimed in, "I promise to give up all my dances—except one."

The other members of the group laughed again, not realizing Evan's obvious attempt to convince his older brother and his best friend to put the past behind them. Emma's strained smile prevented a response, however, and she could only nod her head. Her heart jumped again when Samuel reached for her hand and lightly dropped a kiss on the back of her palm.

"I will eagerly await my turn, Emma."

She felt the bile rise in her throat and had all she could do to not make a scene by snatching her fingers away when he surreptitiously flicked his tongue over her silky skin.

"If you will excuse me," she managed as she slowly withdrew her hand from his, "there are still some things that I need to attend to."

Emma practically flew past the tables stacked with special delights prepared by the evening's chefs. She slowed her flight, smiled and chatted with people along the way, and displayed an unperturbed look of calm that belied her unsettled state and a racing mind.

I can't believe they all think he's changed! Samuel is still trouble, and I'm still the only one who realizes it!

Tyler watched her closely from across the room. He witnessed the entire interlude and stiffened almost imperceptibly when he observed the blond man take in Emma's womanly curves rather coarsely. It mattered little that he had done the same thing himself when she first entered the room on her escort's arm. What disturbed him most though, was how she just continued to smile at the ingrate.

What the hell...?

She let the stranger grasp her hand after a few words and laughs were exchanged. The blond man then kissed the back of her palm and made no effort to hide the fact that he looked right down the front of her gown—and again, Emma just continued to smile.

Christ, is she encouraging such behavior? Maybe Miss Emma Sanders of New York isn't the nubile little virgin I thought her to be. Hell, she's just a damned good actress!

The shame that had crept into his bones over the remarks he made to her that night in the foyer receded quickly, and a scornful smile curved his lips. *It doesn't take much to bring the worst out in her. I'll just make sure I get a chance to settle the score later this evening.*

A sudden scowl replaced the smile. *What in hell has gotten into me? I don't normally act this way!* His shoulders lifted in a matter of fact shrug. *Hell, she deserves it, and Lord knows she's made me say and do things I've never done before since coming to New York.*

Tyler continued to watch discreetly when Emma walked away from the intimate group of friends. The slim line of her back was presented to his wandering eyes, and the mere sight caused Tyler's blood to quicken. He ran a shaky hand through his dark, curly hair. *Christ—you'd think I was in rut! But, then again, it's been a long time since I enjoyed something so simple as watching a woman move.* His eyebrows raised in sudden understanding. *That's it! It's because I've been without a woman for so long—that's why I can't get her out of my mind.*

The music halted, and Edward Sanders stepped up to the podium to be better heard by the crowd.

"I'd like to thank all of you once again. As you know, the purpose of this reception is to introduce Mr. Tyler Wilkins to those of you in the business community who have yet to meet him. I'm sure you all have managed to figure out that the tall, dark-haired man being monopolized by my Board Members is none other than the man from Minnesota."

The crowd searched for Tyler and witnessed him nod his head toward Edward. Emma spotted him at the same time and, again, a rush of heat suffused her cheeks. The group applauded, and then Edward raised his hands for silence.

"Now, I'm sure you all would enjoy it if I just stood here all night and gave speeches—" more than one guest guffawed at his attempt at humor "—but let's begin the dancing. In fact, I'd like to start the evening by inviting my lovely daughter to join me on the floor." His searching eyes finally spied Emma in the crowd. "Emma, come dance with me!"

The crowd applauded again and moved aside as Emma crossed the floor to her father with the sound of a whimsical waltz in her ears. Edward gathered her into his arms, and other couples slowly joined the father and daughter. The evening was officially underway.

When the music ended, Edward spotted Tyler thanking an elderly woman for graciously accepting his offer to dance.

"Come, Emma! Let us save Tyler before another old society dowager drags him out on the floor!"

"But Papa—" Her father grabbed her by the hand and dragged her toward Tyler before she could object further.

"We came to save you, young man!" Edward chortled.

Tyler chuckled in return. "Thank you, Edward, but there's no need. I plan to dance with every woman in attendance this evening out of gratitude for the nice party."

"Well, I know Emma would rather dance with the dashing guest of honor than an old man like me."

"That's not true!" she sputtered. "I love dancing with you." *How am I going to get out of this?*

"You young folks enjoy yourself." Edward handed his daughter over to the tall man from Minnesota. "I feel the need for a glass of champagne. Get your dance in now, Tyler. All the young bucks will have her dance card filled shortly!" Edward saluted his guest, kissed Emma on the cheek, and disappeared into the crowd.

The music started once more, and Emma could do nothing but stare up at the man before her. *I may as well enjoy the dance. I've had worse partners—I think.*

Tyler found himself perplexed by the small grin that tugged at the corners of her lips. "What, may I ask, is so funny?"

"Oh, nothing," she replied with an airy quality to her voice.

He studied her quietly for a moment, then bent at the waist in a gallant bow. "May I have the pleasure of this dance, Miss Sanders, or do the other young '*bucks*' get you first?"

Emma was tempted to slap his sun-darkened cheek at the taunt. "I'm sure my father would be upset if I didn't dance with you. After all, you *are* the guest of honor." She stood stiffly in front of him and waited for Tyler to make the next move. She was not about to encourage him further.

Okay, you little twit. This dance is for your father's benefit. Tyler took her hand in his and gently placed his other palm on the small of her back. Slowly, he moved them around the floor.

His hand was firm and warm against her satin-covered skin and, without provocation, an indefinable emotion hit Emma with the force of a summer storm. Heat radiated from the spot on her back where he touched her, and her breath suddenly came in disjointed rasps.

She forced down both sensations and allowed herself to be amazed at his dancing expertise. For such a large man, Tyler moved gracefully and she relaxed against him. Neither spoke as they moved in unison, allowing the soft, floating strains of the waltz to propel them into a world where the other dancers ceased to exist.

Even Tyler fell prey to the moment. He pulled her closer, and the sudden contact with his hard, firm chest weakened Emma's knees.

I can't believe this! He infuriates me one moment and churns my insides the next!

Never in her twenty-two years had a man affected her like this. She had not known him long enough to make any sound judgments, and yet she was acting like some smitten schoolgirl, all aflutter with his mere touch.

Do I even want to know more of him? She asked silently as they glided around the floor. *Yes, I do. Well...maybe I do.*

Her eyes fluttered shut.

Tyler felt her chest rise and fall against him in a contented sigh and cursed silently. He had done nothing but think of her all week and now, to actually hold her in his arms made his blood boil. The feel of her soft breasts as they brushed his chest, the curve of her tiny waist beneath his hand, and the light scent of her perfume, all combined to affect him in ways he had not experienced in a long time.

Don't forget, he chided himself. *She's not what she portrays herself to be!*

He could not get past the sensations that ran through his body, however. It felt so good just to hold her. She was so delicate, so beautiful, and he could feel the envious stares of the other men in the room. *Eat your hearts out, gentlemen—she's dancing with me!*

He gently whirled her to the subtle beat, and Emma's breasts brushed his chest again. It shocked his senses to realize that, at that very moment, he wanted nothing more than to whisk her into his arms, carry her from the ballroom, and relieve the building tension in his body on the first bed he came across.

Christ, it's been so long!

He had not even thought about having sex in two years, yet now, as he held Emma in his arms, every carnal urge that had been buried for months emerged.

The guilt settled on his shoulders like a leaden weight. *What in the hell is happening here?* He had the sudden desire to flee to his room and wallow in thoughts of his beloved Sara—but Emma's allure was overpowering.

He gripped his emotions in a fierce hold, fought against the ones that led him farther from his dead wife, and finally won the battle that raged in his brain. His tortured mind demanded that he remember Sara and, when the music ended, so did his dance with Emma.

Tyler stepped back and glared down at her through guilt-ridden, disgust filled eyes.

Emma blinked and gradually became aware that the airy strains of the waltz no longer filtered through the room. Her mind had gone blank. Her body had moved to the gentle rhythm of the music of its own accord, and she had basked in the feel of his strong arms around her. She tipped her head back to thank him and recoiled from the contemptuous expression that marred his rugged features.

"Thank you for the dance," he muttered abruptly, then turned on booted heel and walked away.

Emma stood alone and bewildered. *What did I do?* Her confusion quickly turned to rage, however, and she trembled with the extent of her anger. *How dare he leave me standing in the middle of the room!*

A quick glance around the ballroom further fueled her ire. The women whispered behind their fans, furtively watching her next move.

Emma raised her chin a notch and, desperately needing some fresh air, walked with as much aplomb as she could muster toward the open doors that led to the balcony.

She crossed to the edge of the gallery and grasped the railing tightly in an attempt to stop the shaking of her hands. Her thoughts tumbled one over another in her mind.

What happened? One minute, she was being held in the arms of a tall, dark stranger who made her insides jump crazily and, the next, he scorned her as if *she* had done something wrong!

Emma took a deep, steadying breath and swiped a tear from her cheek with the back of a hand. The night was just beginning and already she yearned for the solitude of her room. It was not fair that he should upset her so!

Finally, the warm night air gently embraced her, and her churning thoughts calmed. She lingered though, to gaze out over the moonlit gardens in the hotel plaza.

Her brow dipped suddenly in confusion. What was it about Tyler Wilkins that stirred her emotions so? Most of her waking thoughts had centered around him since the disastrous afternoon they met. He had awakened something in her—something that she had never experienced before. She was not like most of the girls she knew; immature females who were all agog over the opposite sex. In fact, up until this week, she had never given men much thought. Now, however, all these strange emotions ran through her, and she did not know what they meant.

A soft sigh escaped her as she contemplated all the strange feelings. *I'll just have to figure it out some other time.*

She turned from the railing, intending to go back inside, and almost collided with Samuel Fontaine. The same, brittle smile was in place on his lips.

"I saw you leave the ballroom and thought this might be a good time for us to '*catch up*' as my mother put it." His fingers brushed the length of his mustache as his eyes wandered the length of her body again, and a quickening of fear stabbed at Emma's insides for the second time that evening.

"I'm sorry, Samuel, but I've been gone from the party far too long already and should be getting back. Maybe some other time." She attempted to skirt him, but he reached out to clutch her wrist tightly.

"Why don't you just stay a while and talk, Em? Or are you afraid to be out on a dark veranda with a man?"

His sneer catapulted her back in time. Samuel was still the bully, and he still liked to hurt her. She tried to shake her arm free, but his firm grasp only tightened.

"Let go of my arm, Samuel."

"I don't think so, Em. At least not yet."

Emma raised her chin in defiance and tried once again to rid herself of the uneasiness that spread through the pit of her stomach like an incoming tide. "To answer your question, yes, I might be afraid to be on a dark veranda with a man—if there were a *man* present, that is," she said with more bravado than she felt.

"You're still the snotty little bitch, aren't you Emma?" he gritted.

"Let me go! I'm no longer the little girl you used to torment. Grow up!" She yanked her arm hard enough to be free of his grasp this time and rubbed the soft skin on her wrist that was already turning red. "Go pick on someone else, Samuel. I'm an adult woman now, not a child, and I won't put up with the likes of you."

She moved to step around him and re-enter the ballroom, but found herself thrown up against the wall with enough force to rattle her teeth. Her heart slammed against her ribs, and she struggled to take a breath.

"Listen, you little red-haired bitch! No one talks to me like that and gets away with it—especially the likes of you. You haven't changed one bit. If you think you can look down your nose at me, *you are wrong*." He punctuated the last three words with small shakes of her body.

"You haven't changed a bit either!" she tossed back at him. "And if you don't release me this minute, I'll scream. What will your parents think about their prodigal son then?"

"Oh, so you think you'll scream, huh? Well, my dear Emma, you might find that a little difficult!"

His mouth plummeted to capture hers, and he ground his lips against her tightly closed ones cruelly, sadistically.

Emma shrieked her outrage against his mouth as she struggled to free herself from his steely hold. The anger quickly turned to panic though, when he changed position and the hard stucco wall of the building bit into the soft flesh of her back. Samuel held her prisoner with one arm now, as his free hand moved to her breasts.

Emma attempted to twist her head away from his punishing lips, but his strength was far too much for her. He ravaged her mouth for what seemed an eternity and his hands continued to paw the rest of her body until she went limp with defeat.

The kiss stopped as abruptly as it began. Samuel reached up to cover her trembling mouth with his hand and glared into her wide, frightened eyes while Emma gasped for air through the slits in his fingers. Her visible fear lit a spark of excitement in his eyes.

"I'll say one thing, Emma, you were right. You *are* definitely the woman you claim to be, and I've been yearning to prove it since the moment I saw you." She jerked when his hand moved to her breast again. He squeezed the soft mound mercilessly with his last words of warning. "I'm going to let you go back inside now, and you better not breathe a word of this to anyone. This is *nothing*—" he crushed her breast slightly harder between his fingers, and she yelped in pain "—compared to what I'll do to you if you even think of opening that beautiful mouth of yours. You can be assured no one would believe you anyway."

She bucked against his hold again and her eyes burned with hatred.

"Let's see," he mused. "What do I need for insurance? Ah, I know." His lips curved in a cruel grin. "Strange accidents can happen to people in foreign countries. You remember that if you care at all for my pansy ass brother. I'm not above hurting him." He removed his hand from her mouth and his knuckles moved to gently brush her cheek. "You remember, don't you, Emma?"

"You are a pig!" she spat, knowing from experience that he was only too capable of carrying out his threat. "And, so help me God, if anything ever happens to Evan—anywhere, anytime—I'll expose you somehow. Now, let...me...go!"

Samuel released her with a caustic chuckle, then watched as she hurried to the door. She paused to cast one last murderous glare over her shoulder while she took a moment to smooth her gown with shaking hands.

My God, she thought, *he hasn't changed at all—and he's even more dangerous now than he ever dreamed of being as a child.*

"Remember, Emma, I'll be right behind you. Better for you to keep your mouth shut." The quiet words held an ominous tone.

Emma took a deep, cleansing breath, pasted a wide, counterfeit smile on her lips, stepped into the ballroom and nearly bumped into Tyler. He conversed with a young couple just inside the balcony doors—a couple who had waylaid him when he was on his way to the veranda to apologize to Emma for leaving her alone in the middle of the dance floor.

"Oh Emma," the young lady said. "You must come and congratulate Priscilla Stanaway. She just announced that she's to have a baby! Isn't it thrilling?"

The excited other woman grabbed her hand and pulled her from the doorway, but not before Emma saw disgust spring from Tyler Wilkins' seething, emerald eyes.

Chapter Six

Tyler glared at the brandy in his glass with a steely gaze, and a foul curse left his lips as he tossed the amber liquid into the cold ashes of the fireplace. *I can't believe she had the nerve to saunter back into the ballroom with that drunken smile on her face.*

He savagely jerked open the buttons on his shirt, then dropped into an overstuffed chair, rested his weary head on the back of it, and went over the evening in his mind once again...

He was appalled at Emma's state of dishevelment when she re-entered the ballroom from the veranda. Two bright spots of color stained her cheeks, the beautifully coiffed tresses were slightly askew, and her smile was much too forced to be genuine. It did not take long for him to put two and two together when a blond man entered on her heels—the same blond man who's eyes boldly raked Emma's body earlier in the evening. He paused for a just a moment inside the balcony doors, straightened his jacket with an irritating nonchalance, then extended a steady hand toward Tyler.

"You must be Tyler Wilkins, the guest of honor," he smiled. "I'm Samuel Fontaine—a friend of the Sanders family. My father owns the mill that supplies the iron for Edward's company. I'm pleased to say that we'll be seeing much more of each other in the next three weeks. It's nice to finally meet you."

Tyler could do nothing but return the handshake—however warily—and attempt to ignore the other man's smug grin as he nodded in Emma's direction.

"I saw you dancing with Edward's daughter earlier. Quite the little bit of fluff, isn't she?" Samuel leaned closer and added, for Tyler's ears alone. "And a damn good kisser, if I do say so myself!" He threw another leer in Emma's general direction as she exited the ballroom. "My, but it was good to get—" he paused for effect "—reacquainted with her."

Tyler withdrew his hand slowly and lifted a skeptical eyebrow. Samuel chuckled and clapped a hand on the other man's shoulder.

"Allow me to give you a little piece of advice, friend." He leaned close again. "She comes across as a sweet, innocent little thing, but in truth, she's quite the man-eater. She'll gobble you up in one bite, so watch yourself." His laughter became downright vulgar. "Not that such a thing would be *all* bad!"

Samuel sauntered off then, leaving Tyler's jaw to harden with an uncustomary rage...

So, who exactly was I angry with? Her or him? Tyler ran a hand through his thick hair and closed his eyes. *Damned if I know.*

The rest of the night had dragged on for an eternity. He danced until his feet hurt, smiled until the curve of his lips more closely resembled a pained grimace and answered questions until he was tempted to strangle the inquirer. In short, he pretended to have a grand old time when, all the while, he watched for Emma to reappear. Strangely, he found himself both frustrated and happy when she did not. *Why in hell did I care anyway?*

Tyler stood, tossed his shirt on the expensive carpeting that covered the floor of the rented room, then paced between the bed and the fireplace as he attempted to sort out his feelings.

One moment I want to make love to her and, the next, I want to shake her for being so damned fickle. Christ! His shoulders raised then lowered with a mystified sigh. *Was she really out on that veranda allowing herself to be kissed and pawed and God knows what else?*

Edward mentioned at one point that his daughter was twenty-two years old. Evidently, she planned to remain single, but did that mean that she had already experienced the delights that a man's touch could offer?

Probably—and why does that bother me so? A week ago, I didn't even know she existed, and now I can't get her out of my mind!

Two years! He started pacing again. *It's been two goddamn years, and I haven't thought of another woman besides Sara. But now—now I'm walking around like a lovesick pup! Damn it!* He threw his head back and stared at the ceiling. *Is it just her I want or would any woman do?*

His fists balled in self-deprecating anger. *Well, my friend, you'll just have to go without, because I don't think it would be very prudent of you to bed your new business partner's daughter.*

Mentally shaking himself, Tyler finished undressing and dropped onto the bed's surface. He rubbed his eyes with the heels of his hands, then forced himself to put thoughts of Emma Sanders from his mind. His determination lasted all of five seconds.

Damn, but it felt good to hold her when we were dancing. She was aroused, too. I know it. I could've easily hauled her out of there and had my way with her...

Just the thought of making love to Emma caused his belly to constrict.

"God, I need to go home. Once I get away from here, I'll stop thinking about her."

He closed his eyes again and tried to ignore the quiet voice in his head that mocked him.

But is that possible?

Emma lay curled into a tight ball on the canopied bed. Hours had passed since her dreadful encounter with Samuel, and yet still she felt nauseous.

She managed to escape the reception early, pleading a fearsome headache and, upon arriving home, ordered hot water for a bath. She scrubbed her skin until it was raw, but could not wash away the bruises on her upper arms, where Samuel's cruel fingers bit into her flesh. Her lips were still tender from his crude kisses too, and Emma vowed to speak with Evan the next day. The discoloration on her arms should be enough to convince him of the abuse she suffered at the hands of his brother.

Now, as she lay in the darkness though, she knew she would say nothing. Samuel was evil enough to make good his threat if she spoke out against his character. Evan would pay—maybe with his life.

But how could he hurt him when Evan will be an ocean away? Do I dare chance it?

No. Evan would be unsuspecting prey for anyone determined to do him harm—even his own brother. *I'll just stay clear of Samuel until I can figure out what to do.*

Emma suppressed a shudder, then firmly turned her thoughts to the dance she shared with the guest of honor—and all the conflicting emotions that came with it.

Tyler Wilkins, what are you doing to me? And what did I do to make you treat me so horribly? Emma shook her head. Why did she come up against a brick wall every time she encountered the man from Minnesota?

She tossed her agitation aside, rose from the bed, and crossed to the open window. Emma stared out at the quiet night, and the warm air whispered across her skin and helped to relax her tangled thoughts.

What is it about him that draws me like a moth to a flame? And why, even with as angry as he makes me sometimes, does Tyler not frighten me like Samuel? She could still feel Samuel's groping hands on her body, and the mere thought made Emma's stomach turn again.

Being held by Tyler was totally different.

Emma closed her eyes and relived their dance. The feel of his strong arms about her; the clean male scent that emanated from every pore; his gracefulness as he whirled her effortlessly around the floor... Her heart quickened.

I wonder what it would be like to be kissed by him; to be held gently— without that awful scowl on his face. He made me feel safe tonight...until Samuel.

A small sigh escaped her as she realized that, for the first time in her life, her thoughts were those of a woman. She was twenty-two years old and attracted to a man for the first time. She was still not quite sure what it was about the Minnesotan that turned her knees to jelly, but she was not willing to just toss it away. With a determined straightening of the shoulders, she turned and padded softly back to the bed.

Tomorrow, she would seek him out. She would see just what that *something* might be. He aroused a curiosity in her, if nothing else, and Emma felt compelled to find out more about the man behind the aloof exterior that was one Tyler Wilkins.

The next day found Tyler in the hotel dining room. The food tasted like sawdust in his mouth, and the restlessness he awakened with that morning was still a constant companion. It was Sunday. There would be no business negotiations and a long, boring day stretched out in front of him.

Edward had invited him for Sunday dinner, but claiming that he had some paperwork to catch up on, Tyler declined. The truth of the matter was that he needed some quiet time. He had wrestled with his emotions all week due to Emma's unnerving presence and, after last evening's fiasco, he had no desire to see her again.

Now, however, he was not so sure he had made the right decision. Even a few hours of sparring with the uppity Miss Sanders would be preferable to an entire afternoon and evening spent alone.

He mentally checked off a list of New York City attractions as he chewed a piece of steak. There were museums to visit—although he was not much up for that task—or various historical buildings to tour...

He shook his head. The thought of spending another day cooped up inside four walls, no matter where they were, did not appeal to him in the least. Maybe he should rent a horse and visit the famous Central Park.

Yes—I'll do that!

The decision made, he attacked his food with vigor as he reveled in the thought of spending an entire afternoon in the warm, fresh New York air.

Tyler's hand froze mid-way to his coffee cup a few minutes later when he looked up from an almost empty plate. Emma Sanders stood across the room, her green eyes doing a delightful dance as they searched the crowded room.

What in the hell is she doing here?

The thought froze as abruptly as his hand when his own gaze scanned the blue taffeta dress that hugged her petite body in all the right places. A matching hat was perched jauntily atop her auburn curls, completing the effect.

Emma spotted him at the same moment, and her step momentarily faltered. The resolve to speak with him did not seem like such a good idea anymore. But, she was determined to see this thing through and, lifting her chin, continued forward with an aplomb she did not feel.

Tyler set his napkin aside and rose from his seat when she approached the table. He cleared his throat uncomfortably. "Hello...Emma," he greeted her rather hesitantly. "It's quite a surprise running into you here."

"Hello, Tyler." Her responding smile was just as apprehensive. "I hope I'm not interrupting your meal."

"Oh, no, I...was just finishing up, as you can see." He indicated his near-empty plate. "Please, sit down, or are you meeting friends?"

She fidgeted with her purse strings for a moment before looking up to meet his questioning gaze. A lump formed in her throat. *How can he be even more handsome in simple street clothes than he was last night in formal attire?* She took a deep breath to calm the erratic beat of her heart and answered his question.

"No, I'm not meeting anyone. In fact, I came expressly to see you." His eyes clouded with a guarded expression, and she rushed on. "Could you give me a few minutes of your time?"

Tyler's eyes continued to hold a decided wariness as he moved around the table to pull out a chair for her. She sat down, and he stared in total confusion at the back of her head for a moment before resuming his own seat.

"Is there something I can do for you? Your father is fine, I hope."

"Oh, yes, he's quite well." Emma took another deep breath and continued. "I came of my own accord to discuss last night—"

A dark brow rose at her statement. "Last night?"

"Yes. I...ah...wanted to apologize if I did something to offend you. I have thought and thought about it and am at a loss as to what I might have done. I know a look of reproach when I see it, Tyler." She met his gaze directly. "Did I do something I'm unaware of?"

Other than turning me into a horny old bull, and then carrying on a ribald flirtation with a man out on the veranda, no, he answered silently. Aloud, however, he spoke carefully and with the utmost politeness. "I'm sorry for my behavior, Emma. It wasn't you. It was me—for reasons I prefer not to discuss at this time."

She smiled with visible relief, and the twinkle in her eye and sudden softening of her porcelain features rammed him in the chest, momentarily robbing him of breath.

"Well, if you're telling me the truth, then I shall rest much easier tonight."

The tension of the evening before melted away, and they conversed for the next fifteen minutes about the weather and daily happenings around New York. Tyler was impressed with her knowledge of the city. It did not take long for him to realize that she was highly intelligent, and he was forced to reverse his original impression of a 'Daddy's little rich girl', who played her days away without a care in the world or an ounce of sense in her head. He still wondered, however, if she was as virginal as she appeared.

The light in Emma's gaze reverted to its former hesitancy a few minutes later, when the conversation faltered. "So, what are your plans for the day? Papa said you declined his dinner invitation because of some work you must catch up on. Am I keeping you from something?"

Tyler decided a little white lie was in order. "I couldn't keep my mind on business, so I've decided to lease a horse and see a little of this fair city of yours."

Never one to wallow in propriety, Emma leaned forward, rested her elbows on the table and gave vent to a sudden, wild idea. "I'd like to make it up to you for my uncomplimentary remarks at our first meeting."

Her cheeks colored to a becoming shade of scarlet with just thinking about that horrible day, and Tyler's stomach did a flip at the sight of her blush.

"If you wouldn't think it too forward of me," she continued in a rush, "please allow me to show you around the city this afternoon. I have an afternoon stretching out ahead of me, and New York is always better when seen through the eyes of a local resident. I'm also quite an accomplished horseback rider, so we could enjoy that, as well."

The look of genuine surprise on Tyler's face, followed by an emotion she could not quite read, were enough to make Emma backtrack quickly. "I'm sorry, Tyler. I didn't mean to put you on the spot. If you can't, it's quite understandable. The invitation *is* rather last minute—"

Tyler stared at her with a mixture of pleasure and disbelief, and it suddenly came to him that there was nothing he would rather do than spend the afternoon with her. There was something about her; something that caught his interest from the first moment they met; something that demanded he find out what kind of person she really was.

He held up a hand to silence her. "Oh, no! I'm honored that you asked me, Emma." He stood, tossed some bills on the table, then moved to stand behind her chair. "Shall we go then?"

Another blush—a happy one this time—flushed Emma's cheeks as she rose. She took a step away from the table, then paused when she felt Tyler's hand on the small of her back. Her heart knocked against her breastbone as she glanced up at him, and his responding smile served only to heighten the beat. He guided her through the maze of patron-filled tables then, and from the restaurant.

The afternoon passed quickly—much too quickly for both Tyler and Emma. After the initial awkwardness disappeared, they found that they had much in common. Both enjoyed discussing their individual state histories, spending time outdoors, and pitting their intelligence against others when it came to business acumen.

Emma also proved to be the perfect tour guide, having lived in New York her entire life, and Tyler had to smile more than once when her expression grew animated while telling him little tales about the city's history. It became obvious that she wanted him to appreciate New York as much as she did.

They rode through Central Park, and he could not hide his amazement that a city as big and populated as New York could boast a place such as this. The wide open, tree lined space brought the ranch to mind and, again, he felt a pang of homesickness.

"You should see Minnesota, Emma. It's a lot like this, but extends for miles and miles."

"Isn't it rather lonely though, when your nearest neighbor could be miles away?"

Tyler chuckled. "You have to understand that my home state is a very new, very virgin territory. People are just discovering what a wonderful place it is to live. At present, it's still wild and untamed and, yes, neighbors are few and far between. I live in the northern part of Minnesota, and the natural resources have barely been tapped." A regretful smile curved his lips. "But I suppose our secret will be out before too long."

"What makes you say that?"

"There've been rumors that entrepreneurs from the east will be buying up land rich in the natural ores used to make steel. Underground mining will soon follow. It's still a long trip inland from the Atlantic coast, but I imagine there might come a day when people will be shoulder to shoulder—sort of like here in New York." He glanced sidelong at her, where she sat on a beautiful white mare next to him, and smiled gently. "I hope it doesn't happen too soon, though. I'm rather selfish about my space."

His face softened as he spoke and Emma realized that this was a man who would never be comfortable living in a city such as New York. The entire afternoon, Tyler had compared her home to his own and, in his eyes, New York always came up short of his expectations. He needed the wide open spaces of Minnesota. A city such as this would slowly suffocate him.

A pang of regret jabbed at Emma's heart as she glanced surreptitiously at the man beside her. He would leave in only a few short weeks for the home he loved and, strangely, she was not at all happy with the idea. *I think I'm going to miss you, Mr. Tyler Wilkins.*

He had coaxed near hysterical laughter from her several times during the course of the afternoon with his sometimes ribald tales about growing up in Minnesota. He and his brothers shared countless escapades, from the many nights they spent sleeping under the open sky to the day when he was twelve years old and stuffed the school's stove pipe with cheese and straw, thus earning him and his brothers a free day to slide the snow-covered hills behind his home.

Emma's favorite story though, concerned his little sister, Carrie. Tyler, Cole, and Trevor convinced the little girl that if she entered the smokehouse, she would turn into a piece of ham and be served for dinner. Thus, for an entire summer, every time a platter of pork was placed on the table, Carrie was certain it was one of the hired help.

"You know, Emma," Tyler explained as he wiped a tear of laughter from his eye, "what we did to Carrie that summer might sound mean, but I guarantee you that if anyone touched a hair on her head, they dealt with three irate brothers."

Emma had no doubt that he spoke the truth. If nothing else, his stories that afternoon proved his love of family. *I think I was wrong about you, Tyler. I just wish I had more time...*

"Can I make a suggestion, Emma?"

Tyler's question brought her back to the present with a jolt.

"Of course."

"Could we visit Castle Garden? A lot of my workers came through there when they arrived in the states, and I'd like to see it."

Tyler knew from past conversations with his hired help that Castle Garden was the receiving station for immigration, located at the Battery in lower Manhattan. All immigrants entering the United States had to pass through its gate in order to be legally allowed into the country.

"Are some of your workers immigrants, Tyler?"

"Almost all of them," he returned. "They're hardworking people, doing their best to carve out a life here in America. Some of the men are single, but those who are married are working to have their families join them. It's a tough life, but my brothers and I do our best to help them meet their goals. We pay a fair wage and provide housing and meals when needed."

Emma was amazed at his kindness, or rather at the kindness of his family.

"Well, I can guarantee that's not something you would see here among the factory workers. I tend to think most of them are quite underpaid."

He lifted his shoulders in a shrug. "It's a different life out west. Without our crew, my brothers and I couldn't operate the mill. We expect the men to work as hard as we do—and most comply, because they've worked for other companies that didn't treat them as fairly. And, the harder they work, the quicker they'll get their families here."

Emma looked at the man beside her with a new respect. He was generous and fair—something unheard of among the New York City immigrant employers—and, as they proceeded to Castle Garden, she was certain his workers thanked their Maker everyday for guiding them to the wilds of Minnesota.

They entered the austere front grounds of the process center a few minutes later by way of a circular cobblestone driveway that led to the front entrance of the red granite building. The pair reined their horses to the right and paused before a side platform, where they would be out of the way of the quickly growing crowd.

Tyler pushed the wide brimmed hat back on his head, leaned back in the saddle and watched intently as a ship unloaded its cargo of foreign speaking men and women. The immigrants reached the landing stage at the shore's edge, and were then herded as one up a corridor and into the interior of the building. Their boxes and baggage were taken from them and removed to the luggage warehouses for examination.

Tyler watched in thin lipped silence as an Immigration Commissioner ripped a filthy rag doll from the arms of a blonde-headed little girl. Her pleas and accompanying tears were to no avail. The toy was tossed carelessly onto a pile of crates and baggage that awaited inspection.

Tyler's brittle green eyes continued down the line to another foreign family, who were in the midst of dealing with their three sick children. The boy and his two younger sisters vomited uncontrollably onto the wooden planking, and their parents could do nothing but watch through sunken eyes that attested to their extreme exhaustion as they patted each child haphazardly on the back.

Finally, Tyler could stand the site no longer. He dismounted, then lifted Emma from the back of the mare and, taking her elbow, guided her through the doors and into the station. They watched quietly as individuals were processed through the terminal. Tyler was humbled by the thought of his own men arriving alone in a strange country, unable to speak the language, wondering where their next meal would come from, and missing their families.

I know what it's like to miss someone...

They left the building without a word a few minutes later and strolled down to the dock. Another old frigate, anchored in the harbor, waited its turn to deposit a second load of immigrants.

"You know, Emma, for the first time, I think I really understand the awful conditions my men were forced to abide just to make it to the New World. It must be devastating to be packed like cattle into the hull of an old ship, not to mention being deprived of decent food and even safe drinking water. The men told me they were allowed to go topside for fresh air only at certain times of the day."

Emma shook her head sadly. "I guess you can't help but respect them for all the hardships they had to endure."

"That's for sure, and you can bet I'm gonna see that we do more for our own workers when I get home."

Emma and Tyler strolled in silence back to where the horses were tethered. Their lives were settled. They had roofs over their heads, plenty of food in their bellies, and those who loved them close by. The immigrants though, had no idea what lay in store for them and could only do their best to create a new life in a strange and unfriendly world.

They mounted the horses again and plodded down pedestrian and carriage-filled streets. He shook his head and glanced down at the beautiful woman who rode beside him.

"All right, Miss Tour Guide, how many people actually live in this city?"

She smiled with her newfound understanding of his disapproval. "Would you believe over one million?"

"You've got to be joshing!" The sheer numbers boggled his mind.

"Uh-uh. New York's populace has doubled from five hundred thousand to over one million just in the last thirty years."

"How can all these people live together in such close proximity?"

Emma laughed. "I guess if you've never experienced anything different, it doesn't bother you."

"I guess," he returned, though his tone was far from convincing and, more than ever, he longed for his home. His wide shoulders lifted in a shrug when his gaze turned back to her. "Someday, you and your father will have to come visit *my* home. The wide open spaces and friendly people will get under your skin. I guarantee it."

She looked at him with an almost challenging arch of the eyebrows. "Is that an invitation, Mr. Wilkins?"

Twin sets of green eyes locked, and they both wondered if it was.

Chapter Seven

The next two weeks passed all too quickly for Tyler. He rose early each morning, ready to greet the day with more enthusiasm than he had possessed in a long time. He did not know if his sudden lust for life was due to the fact that he had finally decided to put his wife's death behind him—or if it was due to a beautiful, red-haired woman named Emma Sanders. Maybe it was a combination of both. Whatever it was, he relished the change.

He had seen Emma often during the past two weeks, but the meeting that repeatedly entered his mind happened two days after their afternoon tour of the city. Emma entered her father's office, looking bereft and at a loss.

"Good morning, Emma." Tyler stood upon her entrance, then paused to glance at Edward when he noticed the tears in the young woman's eyes.

Edward rose too, and rounded the desk to stand before his daughter. "What's the matter?"

"I've just come from seeing Evan off." Her gaze shifted to Tyler. "You remember Evan, don't you?"

He nodded.

"He left on a passenger liner for Africa this morning and will be gone for quite a long time. I know it's foolish to act this way, but Evan is my best friend and has been from the time we were children." She swiped at her moist eyes. "I don't know what I'm going to do without him."

A sympathetic smile curved Edward's lips as he crossed to give her a hug, then he directed his comments to Tyler. "This little gal and her friend, Evan, used to get in more scrapes than two small pups on the loose in a china shop. Why, I remember one time when they decided to play pirate and chose one of the ships docked for repairs here at the factory as their vessel. Well, the ship had already been patched up and was about to leave port." Edward watched Emma's face flush slightly with his words, and he chuckled as he looked at Tyler again. "You can well imagine the captain's surprise when he discovered that he had two small children on board—and that one of them was *my* daughter. He lost an entire day's worth of travel, because he had to turn around and bring them back home."

Tyler's appreciative laughter filled the room. "And here I thought I had astounded Emma a few days ago with tales about my brothers and me!"

"No, you definitely bested me, Tyler." Her eyes turned to her father, and she addressed her next comments to the older man with a raised chin. "At least *I* didn't slink around a house of ill repute and peek in windows, like Tyler and his brothers did."

Edward warmed up to the more animated look on his daughter's face. "No, you didn't—but if I remember correctly, you and Evan once stole some sailors' clothing from the beach while they were swimming next to their docked ship."

Emma's blush deepened to a color near scarlet when she caught Tyler's raised eyebrows, and then another loud guffaw escaped his lips. "It wasn't my idea!" she spouted. "It was Evan's!"

"Don't believe that for a second, Tyler." Edward tried to keep his own laughter in check. "I saw the two of them run by my office window—both with an armload of pants and shirts in tow. By the time I got outside to see what was going on, Emma had dropped the clothes and stood on the dock, whistling and waving her arms to gain the sailors' attention." His eyes bored into his daughter, but the twinkle in them softened his bogus anger. "She didn't think the prank was so amusing anymore though, when the two sailors leapt onto the dock and tore after them— buck naked I might add—to retrieve their clothes. Those two lit out like the devil himself was chasing them!"

Emma wiped tears of laughter from her face as she gazed sidelong at the chuckling Tyler. "Stop it, Papa. I can't take anymore! What is Tyler going to think of me?"

"That there's more to the sweet and innocent Emma Sanders than she's willing to let on," he answered softly. The laughter left his eyes in an instant when they met hers, and they darkened with an emotion that Emma had become all too familiar with in the past two weeks.

Heat suffused her cheeks again, but she refused to lower her gaze. Her own eyes glittered with boldness. "You haven't begun to discover my deep, dark secrets, Tyler."

He stood and swept an arm before himself in a bow of supplication. "I fold, Madam, under the weight of your superior childhood feats—and I look forward to hearing more."

The light banter helped Emma to forget the pain of Evan's leave taking earlier that morning, and also erased Samuel's image, where he stood on the dock next to his parents, with hatred etched into his face. His mere presence had put her on edge, and she managed to stay as far from him as was physically possible during the departure.

The companionship she found in her father's office though, was a balm for her frazzled nerves. She would often arrive unannounced and, shortly, would be as engrossed as Tyler and Edward in the plans to refurbish the four ships that would carry Minnesota lumber to Europe. More space would be needed in the vessel hulls, and blueprints were spread out on every table in the room.

Edward watched quietly as his daughter and Tyler put their heads together. It would be difficult, but not impossible, to devise a way to move the interior iron crossbeams and create additional space, yet not jeopardize the integrity of the vessel.

I find it refreshing that, contrary to many of my other clients, he actually takes Emma seriously, Edward mused. *Why, he's even willing to bow to her years of experience in the fundamentals of shipbuilding.*

Edward smiled inwardly. *You have no idea, Emma, how proud I am of you. Here you sit, my daughter, a little girl who is now a beautiful woman with one helluva head on her shoulders—a woman who has no idea that she is falling in love with this man from Minnesota.*

Edward continued to watch as Emma leaned over one of the blueprints and showed Tyler exactly how the ship's galley could be moved to provide extra storage space. He did not miss the look of awe in Tyler's eyes either, when he responded that she was right.

So, Mr. Wilkins, what about you? You clearly look enamored with my Emma, but there's still something I can't put a finger on. Why do you always manage to quietly back away from a conversation when it becomes too personal? You don't act like a man ready to strike up a relationship with a woman on a permanent basis. Yet your face gives you away every time you look at her...

Edward was not above trying his hand at matchmaking, but somehow he felt that Emma and Tyler would not take kindly to his intervention. He longed to see his daughter settled with a husband and family, and a safe and secure future, instead of whiling away her days as a spinster and businesswoman. Up to this point, however, she had never even shown an interest in a man.

But maybe the right man just didn't come along until now.

Tyler stormed into Edward's office a week later, a terse look emblazoned on his face.

"You're here early," the elder man said as he glanced up from the paperwork that cluttered his desk. "And, by the look of it, you're upset about something. Anything I can do?"

"I'd like to visit the Fontaine mill, Edward. They're the only ones supplying iron for the ships' crossbeams, correct?"

"Yes. Is that a problem?"

Tyler sat in one of the chairs before the desk and rested his forearms on his knees. "I have all the faith in the world in you, Edward. I believe you conduct your business honestly and that your ships are built to exact specifications, but I heard something last night about Fontaine Ironworks that I want to check out personally."

Edward leaned back in his chair. "Go on."

"I was talking to some men about the pros and cons of using wooden beams versus iron beams in a ship's hull. As the evening progressed, they started to tell me about some of the practices being used in area mills. One of those practices regarded the substitution of cheaper alloying elements in the initial mixture. Another questionable practice comes into play during the cooling process. Instead of allowing a long, slow cooling period for the beams, some mills are quenching them rapidly. This saves additional cost when it comes to heating fuel, since the fires have to be gradually cooled along with the beams."

He sat back and his unflinching gaze met Edward's. "The gentlemen I spoke with insinuated that Fontaine Ironworks may be using some of these questionable practices."

Edward sat forward again and folded his hands on the desk. "Just what are you getting at?"

"This method of cooling sets up internal strains in the metal, Edward. Internal strains I can't afford to deal with." He lifted his shoulders in a shrug. "What happens if the ships run into rough seas and the beams start to snap under the strain? According to your daughter, the crossbeams are a fundamental part of a ship's overall integrity. Then, add the weight of all that lumber, and what happens? We have four ships sitting at the bottom of the ocean. As I said before, we cannot afford to lose the ship's integral strength before we're even at sea."

"Tyler, let me assure you that I have done a lot of business with John Fontaine over the years. Never once has he done anything covert behind my back in the name of 'saving money.'"

"I don't think it's *John's* business ethics we're talking about here. The men I talked to said that Fontaine Ironworks just started employing these shoddy business practices within the last couple of weeks—after John literally handed over management of the mill to his oldest son, Samuel. It appears that this man's character leaves something to be desired. The men I talked to don't think John has any idea of what's happening. It was also implied that Samuel Fontaine has a bit of a gambling problem, so therein lies a probable reason as to why the sudden cheaper methods in milling. I just wonder how he's managing to make it all look good in his father's eyes, and on paper, if that's what's actually happening."

Tyler ran a hand through his dark hair and heaved himself out of the chair. He crossed to the window and, pursing his lips, turned back to Edward. "If this turns out to be true, I'm afraid I'll have to withdraw from our partnership. It's a decision I feel I have to make for the good of my brothers and myself. Europe was just another way for us to expand the business, but we aren't willing to risk the lives of a ship's crew—or our investment—to do it."

Edward stood, closed the ledger in front of him, and raised his hands up in a plea. "Let's not jump to any conclusions before we know the facts, Tyler. We'll go find John right now and discuss the problem with him. We may find that there's nothing to worry about." Tyler nodded his head in acquiescence. As they left the office and entered the churning throng of pedestrians on the street, his thoughts turned again to Samuel Fontaine. If the information he received the previous night was true; if the man was capable of employing shoddy business practices just to save money, then he could not understand Emma's attraction to him. According to the men he met with last evening, Samuel Fontaine was a simpering, gutless 'daddy's boy,' who had never done a decent day's work in his life. He lived off his parents' money, and now it appeared as though he was stealing it, too, from right under their noses.

Damn, Emma, aren't you a better judge of character than that?

Yet, on the night of the reception in Tyler's honor, she allowed Samuel to openly ogle her and, later, spent time on the veranda with him, apparently enjoying his advances once again.

That doesn't bode well for you, Emma, or the company you keep.

Tyler had done his best not to think of that little episode since the night it happened—or about the fact that Samuel and Emma both disappeared after they returned to the ballroom from the veranda. Were they together then, too?

Hell, she's her own free agent, he told himself sternly. *I have no hold on her. And, besides, I'll be gone in a week and will probably never see her again.*

The idea left him with a decided lump in the pit of his stomach.

Tyler and Edward waited in the main office of Fontaine Ironworks when Samuel sauntered in through the open doorway. Dislike for the man roiled in the pit of Tyler's stomach once again, though he had little evidence to base the reaction on. He had always been one to trust his gut instinct, however, and his gut told him that this man was not to be trusted. *And it has nothing to do with any relationship he might have with Emma,* he told himself firmly.

"Well, Mr. Sanders, Mr. Wilkins," Samuel said as he nodded to each of them, "I was informed that you were here to see my father on business. I hope you won't mind discussing the matter with me, since I'm the operating manager at this time. Please, come into my office." He strutted like a peacock through an adjoining door and Tyler and Edward were left to follow as he took a seat behind a big oak desk. "My father and my lovely mother left yesterday for a four month tour of Europe. It's a holiday well deserved for both of them. My brother is on his way to discover the adventures of Africa, leaving me in charge of the mill." He smiled. "Of course, I'll eventually be taking over complete management of the company anyway, so my father wasn't concerned about leaving me with the reins now."

Tyler caught Edward's eye and the message in the older man's gaze was clear. *Let's just see what this is all about before jumping to any conclusions.*

Edward cleared his throat and leaned back in his chair before he directed himself to Samuel. "I'm surprised your father left the country without informing me when he was well aware of my venture with Mr. Wilkins. He did mention an upcoming trip to Europe a while back, but I didn't think he would be leaving so soon."

Samuel laughed lightly. "I almost hate to admit this, but I was supposed to notify you. Everything happened so fast. There were only a few ships leaving for Europe and, in order to secure tickets, my father had to make a quick decision. He felt I could handle any last minute details concerning your project. Unfortunately, I've been so busy running the mill that I guess it slipped my mind to let you know he was gone. A minor infraction, if I do say so myself." He fiddled with the papers on his desk and arranged the ledger books in front of him into a neat stack. "Now, what can I do for you gentlemen today?"

Tyler settled back in his chair, perfectly content to let Edward handle the situation. The older man continued.

"It came to our attention recently that some of the iron working mills in the area have changed their production procedures, perhaps to save expenditures. If that's the case with Fontaine Ironworks, then I think we deserve an explanation. Mr. Wilkins is concerned, and so am I, that the changes may result in a weaker product. Since *you* are the operating manager now, hopefully you can allay our fear."

Samuel's brow furrowed in a show of consternation, but it was gone as quickly as it appeared.

You look like you just got caught with your hand in the candy jar, Tyler mused silently.

A nervous chuckle escaped Samuel's throat, then he regained control and smiled succinctly at both men. "Gentlemen, I hope you're not insinuating that Fontaine Ironworks would sink so low as to follow in the footsteps of some of our competitors and sell a lesser quality product. I have also heard rumors of late about such unsavory practices, but I can assure you it's not happening here." He leaned forward, rested his forearms on the desk, and looked Edward squarely in the eye.

"Mr. Sanders, my father has been doing business with you for years and has always provided you with the best product possible. I plan on continuing in his stead. Once again, I assure you that such unsavory practices would not be tolerated in this plant. Now," he stood, "I hope this issue is resolved and that I've set both your minds at ease." His gaze moved to Tyler, and the look in his eye dared the other man to challenge him further. When the man from Minnesota said nothing, Samuel continued. "If there's anything else I can do for you, please let me know. I realize that there's a lot at stake here, and I want to assure you that I would do nothing to jeopardize the partnership on our end."

He moved around the desk and extended a hand to Tyler, signaling that the meeting was at an end.

The other man ignored the parting gesture and remained in his seat. *Kiss my ass, Fontaine.*

"Mr. Fontaine, if you wouldn't mind, Edward and I would like a tour of your operation. Now, if possible. Since the three of us will be entering into what could be a very lucrative partnership, I'm sure you wouldn't mind giving us a little more of your time." Tyler's tone held nothing but politeness, but his eyes dared the other man to say no.

Samuel knew he was trapped—and by his own words, no less. Had he not just stated that he would do nothing to jeopardize their business relationship? *You cunning bastard,* he thought. *You intentionally backed me into a corner, didn't you?*

The smile that creased Samuel's face revealed nothing of his inner turmoil. "Well, then, gentleman, shall we take a tour?"

The three men entered the main mill through the front entrance and encountered a heat so fierce that its force slammed them in the face. They were also met with the stench of sweaty, unwashed bodies.

Tyler's eyes adjusted to the darkness, and he was appalled at the sight that met his gaze. The workers were stripped to the waist in deference to the intense heat, and their glistening bodies packed into a large, unvented room. They stood over slabs of hot metal and hammered them into various shapes, mindless of the nearby kilns that shot out flames and ashes and nearly licked the skin from their arms. The few men who bothered to look up upon their entrance displayed no emotion and quickly returned to their duties.

A large man in his early forties, with the stamp of his Irish forefathers marked on his rugged features, stepped up to the platform on which they stood. Sweat ran from his body in rivulets. "Mr. Fontaine! I didn't realize you'd be back today. Are there new orders?"

This man must be the foreman, Tyler mused, *of this godforsaken job from hell.*

"Step back, O'Malley!" Samuel snapped. "Can't you see I have guests viewing the plant? Your unwashed stench is making our eyes water!"

Samuel pulled a handkerchief from his pocket and made an issue of shaking it open and placing it over his nose. The huge man ran a shaky hand through the curly orange hair that was plastered to his scalp and stepped back and away quickly. His head dropped in embarrassment, but not before Tyler saw the look of contempt that burned in his eyes.

Tyler shifted uncomfortably as beads of perspiration became rivers and trailed down his own back under the jacket. *How in hell can Fontaine expect these men to work in such harsh conditions?*

"Mr. O'Malley, is it?" Tyler took a step toward the other man. "Save your concern for where it's warranted. Any man working in this kind of heat would be hard pressed to smell like he just stepped out of a bath." He smiled. "In fact, I'm sure I don't smell much better myself right now."

Tyler swung to face Samuel and the words of reproach tumbled from his mouth. "The conditions in this building are appalling, Mr. Fontaine. How do you expect to get a good day's work out of these men when they're treated like animals? I'm of a mind to tell you to go to hell, but it would do little good, because I feel like I'm standing in the middle of it already!"

Samuel's jaw hardened murderously as he returned Tyler's glare, then turned to stone when he saw the small smile on O'Malley's face. "How I run my mill *and* how I interact with my workforce is none of your concern, Mr. Wilkins," he railed. "You're here to purchase the product I sell and the conditions under which that product is produced shouldn't concern you!" He wiped the sweat from the back of his neck with the handkerchief, and his next words came out through clenched teeth as he attempted to control his temper. "I'm sorry to sound so adamant on that point, but that's the way of it."

"And I'm sorry to have to disagree, Mr. Fontaine—"

"Look," Samuel rudely interrupted, "granted, this is not an ideal place to work, but the men are paid well for the sacrifices they make. All *you* should be concerned about, *Mr.* Wilkins, is that you receive a high quality product from their labors, and you will."

The Irish foreman's head came up with a jerk and he stared through wide, incredulous eyes at his employer. Samuel's responding glare was enough to make the man quickly drop his gaze again.

"I think it's time to end this tour," Samuel gritted. His eyes bored into the foreman again, and he could not resist getting in one more reprimand before he left the building. "You, O'Malley, get back to work! You've wasted enough of my time and money standing around! Make certain the current order is filled before you or any of the others even think of leaving for the day—even if it means working through the night! If the job isn't completed when I show up tomorrow morning, not a one of you will be paid."

He turned back to Tyler and reveled in the scathing expression that etched his opponent's features. "Since I'm sure you wouldn't want these men working in such *deplorable* conditions any longer than is necessary, I suggest that we end the tour so they can get back to work." His chin came up another notch. "I have other business to attend to. I'm sure you'll be able to find your way out."

He turned on his heal and left Edward and Tyler standing just inside the door before he completely lost control.

Edward looked at Tyler with a slow shake of the head. "I think we better go back to my office and discuss this further, Tyler. I have a sinking feeling that you might have assessed the situation correctly."

Tyler started to follow the other man from the building, but paused to look over his shoulder. His searching eyes settled on O'Malley, and he tipped his head in a respectful nod.

The foreman straightened his back in a show of pride and returned the gesture, then gave the man from Minnesota a quick, two fingered salute. He returned to work then, but his thoughts stayed with the man who now exited the mill.

It would be a fine thing, to be sure, to work for the likes of one Mr. Wilkins.

Samuel charged through the door to his father's office and slammed it with such force that the adjoining wall shook with the impact. He crossed to a large cabinet and threw open the heavy doors, unmindful of the dent it created when it banged the antique desk. He filled a snifter half full of cognac, tossed it down with one swallow and reached for the bottle again. Samuel refilled the glass a second time and stomped to the window that overlooked the plant yard. The blond man stiffened when he saw Edward and Tyler talking to a man on the loading ramp.

I need this partnership. Shit, I shouldn't have lost my temper! He would have to stay alert when it came to dealing with the likes of Tyler Wilkins. The man had proven himself to be a worthy adversary in the world of business. *That smart ass bastard was after me before he ever reached the office.*

Samuel slowly sipped the cognac as he watched the tall, dark-haired man.

How in hell did he get wind of what's going on? His jaw hardened. *Well, if Wilkins thinks I'm going to let him walk in here and ruin everything I've worked for, he's wrong!*

Everything was finally falling into place, including his simpering brother's trip to Africa. Hell, Evan had jumped at the chance to give Samuel complete control of the mill so he could pursue his own life. *Besides, I needed that little fop out of the way.*

After achieving that end so easily, Samuel wasted no time in talking his father into a European holiday—a move that put him in charge of the family business.

Upon returning home from the Academy, it did not take him long to figure a way to siphon money from the company. In fact, he had covered it up so well that his father was totally ignorant of the theft.

An errant smile touched Samuel's lips as he remembered the many things he learned at the academy that were not taught in class—including the art of error proof embezzlement.

A thoughtful frown furrowed Samuel's brow as he sipped the drink. *Cold, hard cash. That's what I need to resolve those gambling debts, and dear old Papa is only too willing to help—he just doesn't know it.* A few changes at the mill, along with a few well placed threats to keep certain workers quiet, and he had furthered the advantage for himself.

I need that cash to keep the wolves at bay, though. His hand shook with the thought.

"Christ, I've already banked on the credit this new venture with Wilkins and Sanders will bring." The words were muttered quietly, but echoed in his head. "I just need time to sort out the details. If Wilkins backs out now, I could lose everything."

His gaze returned to the window and he watched as Edward and Tyler climbed into a waiting coach. *I'll get you, you son of a bitch. If all the walls come crashing down before I get things resolved, I'll get you!*

He turned and set the glass down on the desk, then pulled a watch from his breast pocket. He smiled. There was still time to pay a visit to a certain little brunette at one of the local brothels. The whore was fast becoming his favorite—because she feared him.

It's amazing what she can do with her mouth after a few slaps and money on the bed stand. He chuckled out loud and felt himself harden at the thought. True, he would rather the mouth belonged to a certain red-haired wench, but for now the scrawny brunette would have to do.

Your day is coming though, Emma. Mark my words—and won't I have a fine time with you then?

Dougan O'Malley did not give Tyler another thought until two nights later, when the Minnesotan appeared on his front stoop. A few questions on the street and some well placed currency was all it took for Tyler to find out where the Fontaine Ironworks foreman lived.

"Good evening, Mr. O'Malley. I hope you remember me. I toured the mill the other day."

Remember him? How could he forget how this man took a stand for him and his fellow workers before an abusive employer?

"Would it be all right if I step in for a moment? I won't take up too much of your time."

Dougan O'Malley's weathered brow wrinkled in confusion upon the request, but he hurriedly ushered Tyler inside. His wife stood by the table and chewed her lower lip in concern.

Tyler's gaze scanned the cozy, immaculate kitchen and came to the conclusion that his earlier estimation of O'Malley was true. He was a hard worker, both in and out of the mill. It was a shame that such a man was forced to work for the likes of Samuel Fontaine.

"Uh...let me introduce my wife, Katherine, Mr. Wilkins," O'Malley stuttered as he pulled out a chair for his guest. "And please, the name's Dougan. If the neighbors heard a gentleman like you calling me '*Mr.*' O'Malley, they'd laugh themselves right into their graves!"

Tyler chuckled before he tipped his head in a respectful nod toward Dougan's pretty wife. "Nice to meet you, ma'am. I hope you don't mind my stopping by at such a late hour, but I have a matter of importance to discuss with your husband."

She gave a little bob of her head and a tentative smile curved her lips. "Please sit down, Mr. Wilkins. I'll be about perking some fresh coffee while you menfolk tend to your business."

* * *

Dougan, Katherine, and their late night guest still sat at the kitchen table two hours later. It took a little persuasion on Tyler's part in the beginning, but the foreman finally confirmed that Samuel Fontaine's business ethics were not up to his father's standards.

"I can't believe Samuel thinks he can get away with this!" Tyler exclaimed.

"Methods to decrease the cost of producing beams started almost as soon as he arrived. And that's not the only area where he's making changes." Dougan shook his curly head in despair. "My men be the salt of the earth, sir. Now he's got them working longer hours for the same money, and what they were making before was a mere pittance. None of 'em dare complain though, 'cause they need the job. The heat does take it's toll, though. There've been more than a few accidents."

It was Tyler's turn to shake his head and, combined with the new information he had received over the past two days, his concern only deepened. Since Samuel took over management of the mill, he had received credit against revenue sure to be generated by the coming partnership with Edward and himself.

"And you can be sure that money will go to pay his gambling debts," the formerly quiet Katherine O'Malley spouted. Her nose wrinkled in a distinct show of distaste before she continued. "And to pay for the services of any prostitute he can lay his hands on. And lay his hands on them he does, to be sure! The man has an evil streak, he does." She crossed her arms over her slim body. "Just this week, he battered another poor girl down the street who demanded payment for her services. Instead of money, he paid her with the back of his hand!" Her jaw set in stubborn determination. "And even though whores they may be, Mr. Wilkins, that don't give no man cushion to beat a woman. Gambling and whoring, that's the only thing that devil knows. If God were to show any justice at all, he would make Samuel Fontaine rot in hell someday."

Dougan blanched at her words. "Mind your mouth, woman," he mumbled as he glanced warily at Tyler, judging his reaction.

"It be God's truth, Dougan O'Malley, and you know it! Every morning, I watch you leave for that hell hole and I pray all day long that you'll return to me safe, instead of having one of the men show up at my door to tell me you've had an accident. The man can go to hell, like I say!"

Dougan reached across the table and took her hand in his. He smiled. "Katy, my girl, never would I not return to you. Have no fear on that account." He leaned closer. "Besides, who would you beller at to take off his boots, wash up, and hurry and sit down to eat the meal you've been preparing all day?" He rolled his eyes heavenward and released a heavy sigh. "I wait patiently all day for the whistle to blow just to hurry home to your abuse!"

"Oh, go on with you, you big, redheaded lump of a man!" She squeezed his hand and her love for him shone in her laughing eyes.

A bittersweet pang shot through Tyler as he sat and listened to them. He missed sharing his life with that one special person; a person who God created only for him. He missed the teasing banter, the day to day conversation and the intimacy shared by the couple before him.

Deciding that he had overstayed his welcome, Tyler stood to leave. "Well, it's getting late. Thank you for all the information, Dougan." He paused with his hand on the doorknob and turned back. "If you'll forgive my curiosity, just how much do you make working for the Fontaine's?"

The large man's eyes dropped to his dusty boots. "Two dollars a day," he muttered, obviously ashamed to admit the meager amount.

Tyler forced himself to contain his surprise and, on an impulse, reached into his breast pocket to pull out a money clip. He laid an amount on the table that was equal to three months' wages for the Irishman.

The O'Malleys' eyes widened in simultaneous expressions of surprise. Never in their lives had they seen that much money together in one pile. They had eked out an existence for the past twenty-two years and had come to terms with the fact they would never be rich.

"It would make me extremely happy if you two would take this money." Tyler drew their attention to him again. "With it, I'd like you to purchase two train tickets to Minnesota and any amenities you might need for the trip." His gaze shifted to the Irishman. "I'm offering you employment at my family's lumber company, Dougan. Believe me, we could use a talented pair of hands such as yours.

He turned to Dougan's wife next. "Katherine, we've had the same housekeeper for years. She's getting on in age, and I'd like to see her do less work and enjoy life more. Your responsibility would be to help her with the cooking and cleaning. She can be rather overbearing, but has a heart of gold. I'm sure with your forthrightness, the two of you would get along fine.

"I'll also provide a cabin for you to live in," he continued in a businesslike manner that he hoped would not offend the couple. "It will be rather rustic, but all our employee houses are sound and can stand up to any weather Minnesota has to offer. Tomorrow, I'll send a messenger with all the information you'll need to get to my home."

He fell silent then, and took in the astonished faces before him. The room was so quiet that he could hear the tick of a clock from somewhere else in the house. "If you can't see your way clear to accept my proposal, please feel free to keep the money as a thank you for all the information and for your hospitality tonight. The insight you gave me into Fontaine Ironworks will help to save a lot of money down the road. It's already helped me make a difficult decision."

The O'Malleys stared at him, then at the money, then back at each other, and then at Tyler again. A soundless chuckle shook his insides. *I bet it's the first time you've ever been rendered speechless, "Katy" O'Malley.*

"I don't expect an answer tonight," he concluded. "I'm sure you want to talk it over. It's a big decision." He reached for the doorknob again, but turned back one final time. "If you decide to accept my proposal, I'll plan on seeing you no later than the end of September. I'd like to see you settled in before the first snow."

He opened the door then, bade them both goodnight, and quietly closed it on his way out.

The sound of an ecstatic yelp met his ears a moment later, and he smiled. What he did not see, however, was Dougan O'Malley pull his wife into his arms and swing her crazily around the kitchen.

Chapter Eight

Emma drowned in emotions she could not sort out. It was Tyler's final night in the city and, whether it was fate or her father's ability to influence, he would be spending his last night at their home. Edward did not want his guest to deal with checking out of the hotel and, thus, chance missing the cab that would transfer him to the train station.

Emma mused over the events of the last week while she finished dressing for dinner. She and Tyler had spent most of the last few days together, since all business dealings with her father and the Fontaines' were put on hold. Her father, true to his old friend, would not take his business elsewhere until he had a chance to speak with John Fontaine personally—and that would not happen for another four months, when John returned from Europe. Tyler was only too happy with the decision; he needed to discuss the situation with his brothers.

Emma and Tyler spent the week visiting museums, riding, lunching, and even took in the current opera in town. She held her breath more than once when Tyler dropped her off at the door, thinking that he might attempt to kiss her goodnight, but he always retreated at the last moment.

And I want him to kiss me! I'm not ready to admit that it might be love, though. How can you love someone whom you've only known for a month?

Emma grabbed a pewter brush from the dressing table and took her frustration out on the long tresses curling down her back. *Why then, am I going to miss his so desperately? I want to know more of him. I want more carefree days to look at his handsome face and bask in his dark eyes.* She threw the brush back on the vanity and plopped down in front of the mirror to stare at the melancholy reflection. Grabbing a handful of hair, she wound the length around a shaking hand, swept it to the crown of her head, and jabbed pins into the silky thickness.

I don't even know how he feels about me. He watches me, I know, because I've seen him do it. And my touch affects him, just as his does me. Just a few days earlier, in fact, when she stumbled on the steps leading to the front porch, he caught her, and Emma was sure she felt his heart racing when she leaned against his firm chest. *I know my own heart was pumping crazily! But that detached look appeared in those eyes of his again, when I know he wanted to kiss me!*

Tonight, Tyler's last in New York, would be one of the worst evenings of her life, but Emma was determined to see it through with an air of aloofness. *If that's what he wants, then fine—I can do it. I'm happy that he can finally return home, since that's all he ever talks about. Let him go. I don't need him!* A single tear escaped her eye. *Why then, does my heart feel like it will break when he leaves?*

Tyler had never mentioned if he was married, or even if he had a sweetheart back home. His private life was a closed book and he never let anyone peer between the covers. Emma's father could not shed any light on the matter either. It was a subject that Tyler had taken pains to avoid.

Emma swiped at the tear, braced herself for the coming evening and, again, repeated her earlier thoughts aloud.

"If that's how he wants things to be, then I'll have to live with it." The softly spoken words held little conviction and, still not fully understanding her heavy heart, she proceeded downstairs.

"Son of a bitch!" Tyler sat on the bed in the guest room and tugged at his boots, then swore with impatience when one refused to slide over his heel easily. He stared at the ceiling. "Why in hell did I agree to stay here tonight?" he groaned.

He knew the answer, and it was a simple one. Edward refused to take no for an answer. Finally, Tyler capitulated and now his bags sat in the corner of the room, ready to be picked up in the morning. It was going to be a long night—one final night of fighting to keep his hands off of Emma—and, with her in such close proximity, it was going to be a difficult task.

More than once that week, he had wanted more than anything to pull her into his arms and kiss her. *To hell with every other man she might have been with, and to hell with Edward and any business relationship!* He wanted Emma, physically and emotionally, and the thought of leaving her behind settled in the pit of his stomach like a leaden weight.

So what is it, my man—love or lust? He snorted at himself. *Probably the latter, but it doesn't matter. She does things to my insides that I haven't experienced in a long time.*

His weary shoulders sagged. *I just have to hold out for one more night...*

The evening proceeded miserably for both Emma and Tyler. Edward had the cook prepare a sumptuous meal, and neither of them did it justice. She picked at her food, trying to maintain control over her emotions, and Tyler filled his cup with brandy more times than he could count. Conversation was about the mundane. It was only when the subject turned to his home in Minnesota that Tyler showed any interest in the discussion.

The topic now turned to sport fishing, and Emma was forced to grit her teeth with frustration. She wanted just one private moment with Tyler; one moment in which to say goodbye. When Edward filled their glasses with brandy again, however, she eyed the gray-haired man scornfully.

I'm sick of you, Papa, and your attempt to monopolize Tyler in conversation. And I'm sick of you, Tyler, for looking so forward to leaving, when all the while I ache for you to stay.

Little did she know that Tyler was all too aware of the fact that she reached up to rub her furrowed brow at the beginning of the meal. He longed to go to her, to rub the tender spot himself but, instead, he poured more brandy into his glass.

She was also unaware of the fact that he watched her when she cut a small bite of pheasant, put it in her mouth, and chewed it slowly. The simple movement was erotic as hell, and he refilled his glass.

When she leaned forward to reach for the plate of bread, he was sure her breasts would spill from the top of her dress. Or did he hope they would? Regardless, that little maneuver almost sent him toppling over the edge of restraint and deserved two more glasses of brandy.

She's ignoring me, he decided. *Probably for the best. I can't afford to give myself away at this late date.*

Emma stared surreptitiously at Tyler over the rim of her own glass as he laughed at yet another of Edward's drunken jokes. *Well, it's pretty obvious that my father holds his interest better than I do.* She straightened her shoulders in determination. *Remember, you can live with it.*

Tyler's bleary gaze wandered from the empty brandy bottle that Edward had just slammed down on the table to his host's ruddy colored cheeks. *Looks like the old man has had plenty.*

"Well, young man," Edward's voice was garbled. "It looks like we need to find another bottle—"

I've had about enough of this! Emma bolted from her chair and nearly sent her wine glass flying across the table. Both men gazed at her through liquid eyes, as if she had just materialized in the room.

"Well, I see the two of you are enjoying yourselves immensely, so I think I'll retire for the evening." Her gaze shifted to Tyler.

Please ask me to stay, she pleaded silently.

He rose unsteadily from his chair. "Thank you, Emma, for the tours of your beloved New York. They certainly helped me get through the days."

Please don't go, his heart answered back.

Edward, too, stood on wobbly legs and weaved a crooked course around the table. He snatched his daughter to him in a bear hug and gave her a loud, smacking kiss on the cheek.

"G'night, kitten." He turned a lopsided grin toward Tyler, and then looked back at Emma. *Funny,* he thought, *its taking time for my eyes to catch up with my head.* "I think we'll have one more to cap off the evening, eh ol' boy?"

"Sounds good to me, sir," Tyler replied with a slight dip of his head and a rather sickly smile on his face.

Emma swallowed back the lump that formed in her throat and forced a bright smile to curve her lips before reaching out a hand toward their guest. Instead of the impersonal farewell gesture that she planned, however, Tyler encircled her fingers with a warm, gentle hand and brought the back of her palm to his mouth. The familiar smell of her perfume floated to his nostrils and he steeled himself for the final goodbye.

I can do this.

He kissed her hand gently and his eyes searched hers. Were those tears sparkling in the emerald depths or was it the candle's glow shining back at him? *Wishful thinking on my part*, he speculated.

"It's been a pleasure meeting you, Emma Sanders. I wish you well with your future." He lifted his head again. "If I'm ever back in this fair city of yours, I'll be sure to look you up and renew our acquaintance."

Emma blinked back the forbidden wetness. *Just say goodbye and get out of this room!*

"Well...goodbye then, Tyler. I hope you have a safe trip home."

He swallowed convulsively. *Stay where you are. Don't touch her again or you'll be lost!* "Goodbye to you, Emma, and thank you for the nice sentiment."

She turned and walked from the room with measured steps, but, upon reaching the staircase, Emma slapped a hand over her mouth, stifled a sob, and raced up the stairs. Her tears flowed freely by the time she slammed the bedroom door behind her. She fell across the bed and wept into her pillow, releasing the anguish born of Tyler Wilkins' imminent leavetaking.

Emma rolled onto her back awhile later and stared at the ceiling. Tyler's face floated before her mind's eye and the full force of her feelings hit her squarely.

I'm in love with him—it's as simple as that. How would she survive without him? Why had she not recognized her emotions for what they were? *Why didn't I tell him?*

"Because you were afraid he'd throw your feelings back in your face." She spoke to the darkness. *And what if he doesn't return my feelings?* Or, even scarier yet...*what if he does?*

Rising from the bed, Emma trudged across the room to the small table that held the pitcher and basin. She poured water into the bowl, dipped a washcloth, and allowed the cool liquid to soothe her swollen eyelids.

She wanted to die.

She loved him, and it took his leaving to finally make her realize it. Emma drew a deep ragged breath, stripped the clothes from her body and donned a silken nightgown before returning to her damp pillow. When sleep finally came, it was filled with dreams of a tall, dark-haired man from the wilds of Minnesota.

Tyler fumbled drunkenly with the doorknob to his own room, after helping Edward to his. The twosome had zigzagged a path through unknown hallways and, finally finding the correct passage, Tyler pointed the older man in the general direction of his chambers.

"Helluva note when you can't find your own room," he chuckled.

The duo moved to the library after Emma's hasty exit. They finished the last of the brandy, and the 'final nightcap' of the evening turned into a full bottle of wine.

They guffawed loudly and told drunken, ribald stories, and all the while visions of Emma flitted on the edges of Tyler's hazy mind.

Just a few more hours and I'll be away from her, he thought to himself, and then laughed aloud, pretending to be amused by one of Edward's more humorous stories.

The casual observer would never have guessed that the calm, confident— and very drunk—Tyler Wilkins was falling apart. *Emma...where did you come from? Why did you have to turn my world upside-down? I have a family and a daughter and a home. I can't stay here. I can't wait to see if there is something between us. I'm not sure of anything right now, except that I want to hold you in my arms...*

Tyler closed the bedroom door and cursed the darkness that surrounded him. His hand fumbled along the edge of a dresser, almost knocking over the hurricane lamp before he found the wooden matches, struck one, and lit the lantern. He stared at the burning stick in his fingers, mesmerized by the glow, until it burned his fingertips. Muttering another curse, he tossed it onto a tray and turned to squint into the dimly lit room.

Who the hell changed the furniture around during dinner?

Emma awoke to the sounds of someone fumbling with her bedroom door. She sat up slowly, her mind still groggy with sleep—until a shadowy figure entered her room. She threw back the covers with a squeal of fright and poised herself with one knee on the bed and the other foot touching the floor. She held her breath when a male voice mumbled curses—a voice that was not her father's.

A match flared, and she was able to make out the figure of a large man—a man who, when the hurricane lamp cast its glow across the floor, she recognized as Tyler Wilkins.

"Tyler!" she exclaimed over the beat of her pounding heart. "What on earth are you doing in my room?"

"Emma?" he slurred as he took a few unsteady steps toward her. He squinted into the shadowed far corner of the bedchamber, where the huge canopied bed loomed in the semi-darkness. "I...I don't know. I must have entered the wrong room."

Son of a bitch, he chastised himself and tried not to stumble.

"Well, that's easy enough to believe when you drank enough to drown a horse," she threw at him.

"Madam, I think you may be right." A crooked smile reached his eyes, and Emma's, as he moved even closer. Tyler leaned forward, then swayed slightly with his effort to peer more closely at her. A vision in sheer chiffon met his blurred gaze—a vision with auburn tresses draped over barely concealed, creamy white breasts. He stared with mouth agape and said nothing.

Her green eyes sparked as she glared back at him. "I think you had better leave."

He stood frozen to the spot, and his appreciative gaze continued to boldly scan her sumptuous form. "Emma?" He wavered again. "Do you know what a fetching sight you are in that nightgown?"

The breath caught in her throat and her voice came out in a raspy whisper. "Tyler, you better leave before somebody hears you."

He moved another step closer and gazed down into her wide, questioning, incredibly beautiful eyes. *To hell with it*, his mind screamed. *To hell with everything!* His features softened and the equally hoarse voice that left his lips was not his own. "Ask me to stay. Please, Emma. I want you in my arms. I want to kiss you and never let you go."

Emma scrambled backward across the bed, ignoring the chilling thrill that raced down her spine. "You have to get out of here—now!"

No! her mind screamed. *You want this as much as he does!*

But this was no boy playing a game, her sensible side argued. He was a man ready to make love to a woman, and Emma doubted that she was woman enough to satisfy him. The feelings were still too new. She loved him dearly. She knew that now...*But does he love me?*

"I *said* get out of here, Tyler!"

He closed his eyes, pursed his lips, and stood quietly before her. When he looked at her again a moment later, the movement was accompanied by a heartfelt sigh of defeat. Tyler reached out though, to gently brush her satiny cheek with his fingertips.

"Such a beautiful face," he whispered. "Dear, sweet Emma. I'd love to stay, but know I must leave."

He turned on unsteady legs and started for the door. *Don't look back*, he told himself. *Just look forward.*

Emma watched his retreating form as it neared the door, and her heart splintered into a thousand pieces. *Isn't this what I wanted earlier? Didn't I want him to kiss me, to hold me?* The thoughts raced through her mind. *No! He wants more! He wants...*

She clamped her eyes shut against the conflicting emotions that constricted her chest. *It doesn't matter! He wants me, and if it's only for this one night, I don't care! I can't let him leave without at least once feeling his arms around me and his kiss on my lips.*

"Tyler!" The word exploded in the quiet room before she had a chance to pull it back.

He stopped abruptly, his hand on the doorknob, and did not dare to look back. *Ask me to stay, Emma. You have to ask—*

He would not, *could* not ask again, only to be turned away. He closed his eyes, and an eternity passed before he heard her voice again. It came from directly behind him this time, in the form of a whisper.

"Tyler...please don't go...I want you to stay."

He kept his eyes closed for a moment longer, willing the effects of the alcohol to leave his brain. *I must've heard her wrong.* Time stood still as he waited for her voice once again.

"Tyler, please, turn around. Stay with me. I need you."

He swung slowly to face her, and his eyes locked with hers. His heart pounded madly against his ribcage. "Are you sure? Once I've got you in my arms, Emma, I won't let you go."

She stepped closer and stared up into the burning gaze before her, then, slowly, her arms encircled his neck. She pulled his face down to hers and, going on instinct alone now, raised on tiptoe to fit her body intimately to his. Her answer was a whisper across his lips. "Please, don't go."

A muffled groan left Tyler's throat just before his mouth devoured hers and his hands gripped Emma's firm backside. He pulled her against his hard body. "I need you, Emma," he rasped against her silken mouth. "I've needed you for so long."

All inhibitions fled, and Emma's body became awash with desire. She pushed the shirt back from his shoulders, and all the while their mouths shared the glorious kisses they had both been denied for too long. She needed to feel his naked skin beneath her palms. She needed his heat against her. She needed him.

Tyler massaged her tight buttocks as he coaxed her mouth open once again. He explored the moist depths within and reveled in the sweet taste as her tongue meshed with his, and then darted away. The telltale smell of brandy reached her nostrils, and it only excited her more.

His hands left her body for only as long as it took to shrug off his shirt and unbutton his pants. The first garment found the floor, and Emma's exploring fingers delighted in the feel of his warm, lightly furred skin. Her frantic, clutching hands kneaded the taut flesh of his shoulders and back, and her mouth dropped butterfly kisses on his chest. The light spattering of hair beneath her worshipping mouth formed a sumptuous trail down to the open waistband of his pants, and then disappeared inside. She had never seen a half naked man, but knew instinctively that he was as fine as they come. Tyler's body was as hard as steel and excruciatingly long of limb. Slim, feminine hands traveled the length of his muscled arms and full, moist lips followed with tantalizing half-bites, half-kisses.

Tyler groaned. He needed to see her, to feel her silky body against his. His mouth moved quickly to the hollow beneath her ear, and Emma's head lolled to allow him easier access. His eager hands found the straps of her gown, and he slid them slowly over her shoulders, following the same path with light, feathery kisses. He tugged at the front of the satiny gown, revealing her succulent breasts, and then dropped to one knee to reverently kiss one of the pink tipped mounds. The gossamer material slipped to the floor as his mouth moved to the other breast.

He wanted her, and he knew that she wanted him. It had been so long since he experienced the sensation that throbbed in his loins, and he could wait no longer. Tyler stood again, swept Emma into his arms, kissed her long and hard and, with two long strides, placed her gently on the bed. He removed his pants with anxious, shaking hands and kicked them away.

Emma stared up at him through shuttered, passion-filled eyes. His body was perfection at its finest and, shuddering at the sight of his boldness, she pushed the initial fear aside. She needed him next to her, and a tremulous smile played about her parted lips as she reached out to beckon him nearer.

Tyler dropped onto the bed and gathered Emma tenderly to his side. They did not speak. There was no need; they communed as only man and woman can— with their hands, their eyes, their mouths and their bodies. They had fought their attraction to one another for the last four weeks and, now, with the moment of joining so close at hand—a moment neither thought would ever be—words were insignificant.

Emma did not know if he loved her and, at that point, she did not care. She needed him as she needed air to breathe. His hands moved over her body with an exquisite slowness and, wherever his palms touched, a trail of heat was left behind. Soon, her entire body was aflame and she yearned for something she could not quite comprehend.

Tyler existed in both heaven and hell at the same moment. It had been too long since his body experienced carnal relief, and the woman in his arms was hot with excitement due to his touch and his touch alone. He could not maintain control much longer, and yet he knew what the consequences would be if he did not.

He was past caring. His hand left her breast and traveled lower, over the smooth silkiness of her stomach, then slipped between velvet thighs. She froze for a quick, surprised instant, then strained against his hand. He stroked her warm, moist center until she thrashed with passion, and then she grasped at him for something more. Emma urged him on with eager lips and clutching hands until he could no longer stave off the surging emotions.

Rolling her beneath him, he poised himself on strong arms and stared into the green eyes that so mirrored his own. His lips searched for hers and, as his tongue delved into her mouth, he entered her with the passion of a man totally fixated on the woman beneath him. Her muffled scream reverberated in his mouth, but he was beyond knowing if the cry was one of pleasure or of pain. He continued the slow, rhythmic movements and was rewarded by the tightening of her muscles around him and the sensual rise and fall of her body.

Emma entered a world of skin against skin and tongue against tongue. The initial pain of his entry faded away, only to be replaced by a delicious sensation that grew by leaps and bounds within her. Instinct demanded that she increase the power of her own thrusts, to rise and meet his body, and she waited—waited for something she had never experienced before.

She held her breath. The flicker of heat that suffused the core of her being intensified into a flame, and Emma groaned as an excruciatingly intense inferno engulfed her entire body. Her breath came in gasps, mingled with small cries of ecstasy and then, slowly, the flame went out and she returned to a bed and a room and a man.

Tyler heard her groans, and then her cries of fulfillment somewhere in the recesses of his mind. It was the turning point for him; the moment when all reason was lost. He stroked harder, seeking his own release now, and finally spilled his seed into her depths and cried out his own rapturous fulfillment.

Like a feather dipping in the soft breeze, they floated back to reality. Tyler rolled carefully from her sweat slicked body and gathered Emma's silky form into his strong arms. With her head nestled against his shoulder, his breathing finally slowed to a regular rhythm, and hers followed suit. They lay quietly, their bodies and their fingers entwined in the aftermath of the storm they had created. Neither knew what to say, so they spoke of nothing. They simply held each other until sleep carried them into a world of blissful contentment that only lovers can share.

Chapter Nine

Emma drifted toward wakefulness slowly, and the sound of chirping birds filtering through an open window brought a lazy smile to her lips. Silken arms stretched languidly across the soft pillow as she pondered the feeling of contentment that threaded its way through her body—and then the events of the night before sifted into her fuzzy brain.

Green eyes widened and she sat up abruptly, then grabbed for the sheet to cover her exposed breasts. Emma's heart beat wildly as she collected her thoughts.

Did last night really happen? A heated flush reddened her smooth features when her gaze settled on the nightgown that lay in a heap on the floor across the room. The telltale ache between her thighs also served to confirm the question in her mind.

Falling back into the pillow, Emma stared at the ceiling, her face a deep shade of scarlet when she remembered the things Tyler did to her body—and how her body had asked for more. He awoke her sometime during the night with light kisses and hot, searching hands that moved with a seductive slowness across her stomach. He took her hand in his then, and guided it to him, showing her the gentle rhythm that resulted in him growing hard again under her touch. He rolled onto his back, taking her with him and, when neither could contain their need any longer, he let her lead the way to another glorious communing...

Emma's stomach muscles clenched with desire—desire for Tyler—and slender fingers covered her mouth in amazement. *My God, I love him*. When it happened, she did not know, but love him she did. She relished the emotion that now floated through her body with a happy sigh.

Emma glanced sidelong at the indented spot on the pillow next to hers—

the spot where his head rested during the late night hours. Rolling onto his side of the bed, she drew the headrest to her and breathed in his lingering scent. *He was here,* she smiled softly, *and he actually did all those things to me.*

The memory of his demanding mouth pressed against her lips and his gentle calloused hands sliding across her body brought another soft sigh, accompanied by a rush of liquid desire.

Emma stretched out on her back again and her gaze strayed to the window, flitted past the clock on the armoire, and then quickly returned to the brass timepiece. It was a few minutes past eight—the time Tyler planned to leave.

No! Where is he? Emma leapt from the bed and grabbed her robe. "Damn!" she muttered as she struggled to get her arm into the sleeve.

Please, Tyler, please be here! He can't be gone—her frightened mind insisted—*not after last night!* She ran to the door, threw it open with a bang, and raced down the hall to the guest bedroom.

The door was open to the chamber he should have slept in, but did not. Emma skidded to a stop in the center of the room. Her chest heaved, more from panic than the exertion of the dash from her bedroom to his. Frantic green eyes darted from the made-up bed, to the empty bureau top, to the vacant corner where he had placed his bags when she showed him to the room the day before. Her throat constricted with dread and she whirled to face the door again.

He's gone! But it can't be—not after last night!

Emma rushed to the open window, then stiffened when she saw Tyler standing on the cobblestone street below, shaking hands with her father.

Look up! her mind screamed. *Don't go away without even telling me goodbye!*

Tyler climbed into the waiting carriage, and Emma pressed white knuckles to her mouth to keep herself from calling out his name. He never looked back.

Tears slid down her cheeks as the buggy lurched forward and carried him away, then she turned, slid to the floor, and sobbed into her hands.

Edward ascended the staircase a few minutes later to check on his daughter. Emma was usually up and about by this time of the morning, and he was surprised when she did not come downstairs to see Tyler off. *I would have thought something might spark between those two.* He shook his graying head.

He headed down the hall toward Emma's room, but paused as he passed the guest quarters. A muffled sob met his ears and, when he glanced into the other room, the sight that met his gaze made his blood run cold.

His daughter sat on the floor, her arms wrapped around her robe-covered knees and her face buried in the soft fabric. Emma's shoulders shook with silent, heart wrenching sobs. Edward moved quickly to kneel before her and reached out tentatively to touch her shoulder.

"Emma? Honey? What are you doing in here? What's wrong?" When she just continued to weep, he asked again, more gently this time. "Emma, please, tell me what's wrong. You're frightening me."

The breath caught in his throat when she slowly lifted her head and looked up at him through swollen, tear-saturated eyes. Emma's chin quivered and a new batch of tears streamed down her face.

"Papa—" she whispered in a hoarse voice and choked back another sob "—he left...and he never even said goodbye."

"Oh, Emma," he returned as he pulled her closer. She wrapped her arms around her father's middle and rested her head wearily against his chest. Edward cradled his daughter in his strong embrace and absorbed the shuddering sobs that racked her slender body.

"Honey, I'm so sorry." Edward murmured as he gently rocked her back and forth. "I didn't know. I didn't understand how you felt."

He continued to hold her for a long while, until the weeping subsided, then leaned back to gently cup her face in his hands. His understanding gaze searched her grief-stricken eyes. "So, you love him then?"

The crestfallen look on her face provided the answer. Emma stared back at him and quivering lips worked to form words. "Yes...yes, Papa, I do—but now he's gone, so it doesn't matter." She wiped her face with the back of a trembling hand.

"Honey, why didn't you tell him?" he asked softly.

"I...I couldn't. I didn't know how much...not until I saw him climb into the carriage and leave. Now it's too late." Her head lolled in abject misery and she turned lifeless eyes upward. "I'll never see him again, will I?"

"Come, Emma." He helped her to her feet and, settling her under his arm, led her back to her room.

Edward eased his daughter down onto the bed, tucked the blankets around her, and then retrieved a wet cloth from the washstand. He sat quietly while she wiped the tears from her face, and his heart ached with his own inability to ease her pain.

"Emma, I wish there was something I could do for you." He brushed a kiss across her brow. "I love you, honey."

Her smooth features sagged with exhaustion as she leaned back into the pillow with a grief-stricken sigh.

"There's nothing you can do. He's gone, and I'll never know if he loved me or not. It doesn't matter. It's too late."

She closed her eyes and rolled onto her side to face the wall. An awkward silence followed and, finally, Edward stood and gently brushed the tear-dampened hair from her cheek and dropped another kiss on her forehead.

"You rest, kitten. We'll talk later. Remember how much I love you."

Edward crossed the room to the door, but paused to gaze over his shoulder. Emma had curled into a fetal position, as if the pose would ward off further pain. His heart broke as he closed the door quietly behind him.

Tyler stared out a grimy window and watched the scenery fly by as the train took him further from New York and closer to Minnesota. *I should be excited. I'm going home.* But the image of an angelic, sleeping visage in the early hours of the morning would haunt him for a lifetime.

I never should have taken her, he berated himself. But the alcohol and his overwhelming need to hold her had taken all of his restraint. He was lost when she asked him to stay.

Tyler leaned his head against the back of the seat, closed his eyes, and pictured Emma as he had last seen her...

She was tucked into the crook of his arm, her back against his chest, and her elfin, yet supple body unconsciously seeking his for warmth. She smelled sweet and feminine, and her thick auburn hair spilled across the pillow. One breast peeked out from beneath the sheet and, unable to resist, he cupped the firm mound in his hand. His hand slid to her trim waist then, and he pulled her against him, relishing the feel of her luscious backside as she snuggled even closer to him. A soft, contented sigh escaped her lips when he nuzzled her neck and inhaled the clean, perfumed fragrance of her hair.

I never want to forget the smell of her hair. A wayward hand traveled lightly across a smooth, rounded hip, and her lips parted slightly with his touch. He yearned to passionately kiss her mouth once more, but feared waking her. *How can I leave?* He clamped his eyes shut against the pain that seared his heart. *I have no choice. I can't stay. Janie is waiting—I have a life back home.*

He stared vacantly into the half-darkened room and came to the conclusion that it would be impossible to act the mere acquaintance in front of her father now.

I could never do that—I would never be able to say goodbye to her as if nothing happened. A heavy sigh escaped his lips. *It's best if I just leave...*

Quietly, so as not to awaken her, Tyler untangled his limbs from Emma's and slipped from beneath the covers. He stood beside the bed for a moment and looked down at her and could not help but wonder if he would ever see her again. *Would she even care? We never spoke of love.*

It would be better to just leave...

Now, as the train took him further away from her with every spin of the wheel, his thoughts turned to the long night of lovemaking. *She seemed to know how to please a man in bed.* She was uninhibited and had even urged him on. Emma was a wonderful partner in love.

Tyler tried to recall the exact moment when he entered her. What was her reaction? He remembered her muffled cry, but was it a cry of pain or pleasure? Had she been a virgin or not? Samuel Fontaine's words echoed in his brain—but was the man believable?

Damn! I had such a head full of liquor, I couldn't tell. A part of him hoped that he was her first lover, but Tyler seriously doubted that he was. She was simply too willing—and too knowledgeable. He would never know for sure now though, because he was leaving.

Earlier that morning, he had kissed her softly on the cheek and exited the room with a heavy heart. It could never be. They lived in two different worlds. His was back in the wilds of Minnesota with his family and his daughter. Emma's was in the hustle and bustle of New York.

Tyler closed his eyes again and slowly rubbed his stubbled face with his hands. *Why is the idea of going home not as appealing as it was four weeks ago?*

He could not look back. He needed to look forward.

The locomotive hissed and spit great billows of steam as it pulled into the Duluth, Minnesota train depot. Tyler reached for his bag, anxious to be off the rumbling, lurching mass of iron, and was up and moving toward the exit before the train came to a complete stop. His daughter, Janie, was on the other side of the door and he could hardly contain himself, knowing that shortly he would be able to hold her in his arms.

The conductor cast him an impatient glare as he reached to unlock the iron door, and Tyler threw him an equally scathing look in return. He had had enough of the bouncing train filled with June's humidity, of the obese woman next to him who told endless stories about her family, and of the cramped leather seats. He missed Janie and everyone else at the ranch, and just wanted to go home. The window on the door was black with soot, and his agitation rose when could not see any members of his family.

The door finally opened and Tyler was the first to step off the train. His tired eyes swept the length of the crowded platform. *Where are they? The damn train's not early—someone should be here.* Tyler shouldered his way through the milling throng and made his way inside the depot to see if any messages awaited him.

"Tyler! Over here!"

He spun at the sound of his brother Cole's voice. Janie ran toward him, with arms outstretched, and Tyler dropped to one knee just as she reached him. He clasped her small body to his, and cried out with the sheer joy of feeling her in his arms again.

"God, I missed you, Janie!" Her tiny face was buried in the crook of his neck as she clung to him tightly. The familiar scent of the little girl's soft, blonde locks reached his nose. *God, it's good to be home!*

He watched over the top of his daughter's head as his brother and sister worked their way through the crowd. Both Cole and Carrie wore huge smiles of welcome. He stood, with Janie still in his arms, and reached out to take his brother's hand in his.

"Cole, you are a sight for sore eyes!" Tyler's lips, too, curved in a huge grin as he accepted the firm handshake, and then moved to wrap his free arm around his sister's shoulders.

"Tyler, it's so good to have you back home!" Carrie squeezed his waist tightly in return and batted tears from her eyes. "We've all missed you terribly!" She glanced at Janie, then whispered for his ears only. "Especially one of us."

Cole stood back and took in his eldest brother's tall, lanky form. He had always been a man of few words, but it was obvious from the grin on his lips that he enjoyed seeing his niece in her father's arms again—where she belonged.

"It's good you're back, Ty," Cole murmured. "It hasn't been the same since you left for New York."

Janie finally loosened her hold on Tyler's neck, grinned up at her father, and then patted his shoulder to regain his attention. Tyler looked down at her beaming countenance and could not imagine any other place he would rather be.

Even in Emma Sanders' bed, his brain finished the thought.

"Honey, I sure missed you. Did you miss me?" He dropped another kiss on her soft cheek, and Janie's eyes were as big as saucers as she nodded her head 'yes.' Tyler set her down gently on the platform and dug into his bag. He pulled out a package wrapped in brown paper and handed it to his daughter. She reached for it with an even bigger smile and a twinkle of excitement in her blue gaze.

"Go ahead, honey, open it. It's from a big store in New York called *Woolworth's.* It just opened and is becoming famous all over the United States. Someday, you and I might go to New York and I'll take you there."

His daughter slowly pulled the string that held the package closed and unwrapped the parcel. Inside lay a soft, cuddly doll with a mop of red hair.

"Do you like it?" Tyler asked, hoping he had selected the proper gift. He received his answer in the form of an even larger grin and a vigorous nod. She wrapped her tiny arms around his neck once more in another fierce and loving hug.

Cole and Carrie watched the exchange in contented silence. It had been a long, sad month for Janie. She had existed with a total disinterest in every idea the family came up with to distract her from Tyler's absence and, as the days and weeks passed, her disposition only worsened—something Tyler need never know. He had needed the time away.

Tyler stood and gathered up one of his bags as Cole reached for the other. "Let's get out of here. I've had enough of train stations to last me a lifetime."

The cheerful group left the depot platform and headed for the carriage, and all the while Tyler rambled on about his trip. He was more animated than they had seen him in a long time.

Cole and Carrie's eyes met behind Tyler's back as he lifted Janie into the waiting buggy. Hopefully, his mood would last; it seemed that, at least for the time being, the old Tyler had returned. Only time would tell if the change would be permanent or not.

* * *

That evening, the entire family celebrated Tyler's return. Mamie outdid herself by preparing many of his favorite dishes and, when Tyler pushed himself away from the table, he groaned with pleasure and rubbed his full stomach.

"Mamie, not even the fanciest restaurant in New York can hold a candle to your cooking! I'm totally miserable."

Her round cheeks dimpled in a smile as she paused behind him to pat a brown hand lovingly on his shoulder.

"Tyla, it be a pleasure cookin' for you—and knowin' someone appreciates what I do 'round here. Why, your two brothers, they do nothin' but complain every time I put food on the suppa table. Yessiree!" She glanced at the grinning Cole and Trevor, and then winked at Tyler. He knew Mamie was fishing for another compliment and was sure his brothers would respond in kind.

Trevor jumped up, his face twisted in a comical display of outrage, and grabbed Mamie's bulk when she sashayed past him. "Mamie, I promise never to complain again! You're the best cook in northern Minnesota. Why, just feel right here. Look at what you're doing to my waistline!"

He grabbed her hand and held it against his flat stomach as the group around the table burst with laughter. Mamie smacked the middle Wilkins brother on the shoulder.

"Aw, go on with you! There ain't an ounce of fat on that body of yours and you knows it! You be tall and porkchop lean like them brothers of yours. You ain't foolin' no ones!"

Tyler watched the exchange and absorbed the sheer gaiety of the evening. He had missed them all terribly and, again, was thankful just to be home.

He pulled Janie from the chair next to him and onto his lap, then gave her a quick kiss on the cheek. *This is what's important—being with the ones you love. I've got to remember that always.*

Trevor seated himself again as Mamie poured after dinner coffee. With a raised eyebrow, he leaned back in his chair, met his eldest brother's gaze, and voiced the first question regarding Tyler's trip.

"Well, Ty, enough about the sawmill—let's hear about New York. Is it really as big as everyone says? What're your feelings on Edward Sanders? Cole and I didn't know if we should be reading between the lines of the telegrams you sent or not."

With the mention of Edward's name came a vision of Emma's red hair and sultry green eyes. He pushed the image aside with decided difficulty and brought his attention back to the conversation at hand.

"Edward Sanders is a wonderful man. Very forthright and honest. I liked him immediately. I think, eventually, we'll be able to forge some sort of business relationship. For the time being though, as I said earlier, the timing just wasn't right."

"I just can't understand why this Sanders won't go to some other mill for his iron," Trevor stated the easy solution to the problem. "Why is he so intent on buying exclusively from Fontaine Ironworks?"

"You have to understand what kind of man Edward Sanders is," Tyler replied. "He's been a close, personal friend of John Fontaine's for years. He's not the type to walk out on their business relationship without discussing the reason of his forfeiture to another company." He stifled a yawn and continued. "And, with John conveniently out of the country, Edward feels he must wait."

"Well, I guess you do have to admire the man's loyalty," his brother agreed, however grudgingly.

Tyler nodded. "There's a lot more involved here than a simple business arrangement, Trevor. It seems that John's oldest son, Samuel, might be embezzling from the company, and Edward feels obligated to protect his friend's interests until John returns from Europe. Samuel is the operating manager of the mill in his father's absence—something both Edward and I feel Samuel deliberately orchestrated in the first place. With his father out of the country, Samuel has free rein over the company funds and operating procedures."

"He must be quite an ass to do that to his own father," Trevor grumbled.

"You can say that again and, until Edward is able to get word to John about what's going on, I don't feel we should proceed any further. I respect Edward's business ethics and really don't want to go elsewhere for our shipping supplier. He's already put a lot of thought and hard work into the proposition and deserves some time to straighten this mess out." Tyler's shoulders lifted in a tired shrug. "In truth, I didn't want to make the decision on my own to go elsewhere."

Trevor eyed his brother with an admiring glance. Tyler had always been the cautious type and ever watchful over their best interests. Since their father's death, the eldest Wilkins son had taken it upon himself to oversee their financial future. Money accounts had been set up so each of them would be independently wealthy in their own right, even their little sister, Carrie. Now, the four of them worked together to increase both their individual and cumulative wealth via the family logging business.

The fact that they all lived together in the same, sprawling ranch house only strengthened their commitment to one another. They looked forward to spending the long evenings in each other's company.

Trevor could not help but smile when he remembered how surprised Tyler's late wife, Sara, was by their obvious family unity. When she married Tyler, the question of where the two of them would live never came up. Sara embraced them all as her extended family and, when Janie was born a year later, the family bond deepened even further.

Another bout of boisterous laughter from those seated at the table brought Trevor back to the present with a jolt.

"So," he continued his questioning, "what did you do for entertainment while in New York? Did you have a chance to enjoy a little of the nightlife?" His eyes twinkled into his brother's. "What about the women?"

The always observant Cole Wilkins noticed a sudden flash of remembrance—or was it longing—soften his eldest brother's rugged countenance for just a moment before it returned to normal.

"It seems the citizens of New York are hell bent on enjoying whatever the city has to offer—and into the wee hours of the night, as well." Tyler's responding smile turned rueful. "I've never been forced to make up so many excuses just to escape another evening out. Most of the men I met seemed to lead a life of leisure. I'm not saying they don't work, but their idea of hard labor is pushing pens around a desktop and checking the clock to see if it's time for lunch. It's definitely a different world than the one we live in."

"And what about the women?" Cole's repeat of Trevor's earlier question was prompted by the fleeting look he saw on his brother's face a moment earlier.

Tyler's eyes swung to his younger brother's and he paused to choose his words carefully before replying. "I really didn't meet many women while there. Most of the introductions were social. Edward's daughter, Emma, though, seemed to be pleasant enough. She reminded me of you, Carrie." He smiled at his sister. "She's very interested in the family shipping business and has notions of continuing in her father's stead when he's gone. You two are about the same age, I think. You'd get along well. In fact," he teased, "if we were to put the two of you together in the same room, you'd create a formidable force for anyone to deal with."

Tyler promptly changed the subject to New York City's historical sights then, but his evasiveness when it came to Edward Sanders' daughter did not go unnoticed by Cole. *So, big brother. Is there more to the story than you're willing to tell?*

"I forgot to mention that I offered jobs to one of the Fontaine mill workers and his wife," Tyler continued, interrupting Cole's train of thought. "They accepted immediately and can't wait to get out of New York. I hope to see them arrive sometime in September."

"What kind o' *job* offers?" Mamie, who had been standing near the kitchen door and listening quietly, questioned his statement immediately. Her voice was heavy with suspicion. "We always got room here for one more man, but what would his woman be doin'?"

"Helping around the house," Tyler replied matter-of-factly, but, inside, he cringed as he awaited her reply. He had not planned on Mamie discovering so quickly that there would be another woman entering her domain.

"I don't need no help."

"Mamie..."

"Said, I don't need no help."

Tyler counted to ten, took a deep breath and continued. "So, what was I supposed to do? Tell her husband to leave her in New York? Come on! These people were in dire straits. Dougan O'Malley makes little or nothing in wages. He's honest and hardworking. We need his type on the ranch."

"So he be needin' the job and maybe you needs him. But you got other men workin' in the loggin' camp who got wives, and none o' them is takin' over *my* house!"

Tyler sighed. "Come on, Mamie. I thought you could use the help. You work too hard. You'll like Katy...I told her about you, and she's most anxious to have you as her supervisor."

The pout on Mamie's face immediately lifted. "You mean I's gonna be her boss?"

"You're the only one around here who knows the complete workings of the household." He nudged Carrie's knee beneath the table, and his sister cast a discreet, yet knowing smile in his direction. "You'll love her, Mamie. Her house was spotless when I visited it. She also said that she couldn't imagine someone actually running a household as big as this single-handedly. She can't wait to meet you and learn all that you can teach her."

The praise worked. Mamie's chin came up in a show of pride, and her chest ballooned to match it. "Yas, I do have lots to teach her at that." She passed by Tyler's chair and patted him on the shoulder again. "Boy, you do me proud with your goodness. Iffn' that woman has a hard time, we'll just have to find a little patience with the poor thing."

The old negress turned away, and Carrie leaned over to whisper close to her brother's ear. "You're good. She never had a chance to put up a fight."

The conversation continued late into the evening, ranging from recent happenings at the lumber mill to family matters. Janie was sound asleep, nestled in her father's arms. A tiny, contented smile curved her lips.

"Well, it's getting pretty late," Tyler finally gave into his own fatigue. "I'd better get her to bed."

He stood carefully, so as not to awaken his daughter, then bid his brothers and sister goodnight and trudged up the staircase. He entered Janie's room, crossed to the bed, and tucked her gently under the covers. He stood quietly for a long time and studied her cherished features.

She looks so much like her mother. A heavy sigh lifted his chest. *My life is so different from the one I dreamed of.* He bent to drop one final kiss on Janie's forehead, then left the room and slowly closed the door behind him.

Tyler's legs were like leaden weights as he shuffled toward the master bedroom he once shared with Sara. The emptiness, the loneliness, surrounded him and he felt suffocated by its renewed presence. He had managed to stave off the feeling since returning home, but it crept into his being now and wrapped itself around his heart. He crossed to an overstuffed chair near the window, sank down into it, and rested the back of his head against the cushiony softness.

His gaze stared into nothingness. *I wonder what my homecoming would've been like if Sara were still alive?*

His eyes closed and his mind conjured up a vision of her face, flushed with the excitement at his return, then, later, provocative and filled with the promise of what was to come when they were alone within these four walls.

Tyler grasped at an invisible thread and held on until the burst of pain subsided. Being home, being back in this room after a month's time, was worse than he had ever imagined.

I can't go on like this.

Life dealt him an awful hand two years ago, but it was time to move on; time to steer himself in a more positive direction.

His thoughts slowly shifted to Emma and the weeks spent in New York. *Has she thought of me at all?*

"Of course she's thought of you, you idiot," he muttered into the darkness. "You got drunk, climbed into her bed, had a walloping good time, and then left without even saying goodbye!"

His thoughts tempered a bit, and he became more bemused than angry. Why had he felt so drawn to her? Why did he long for her as he had for no other woman since Sara's death?

He had almost made it through that final week without touching her, but that last night—the night she asked him to stay—his fledgling control was stretched to the breaking point. But could he really blame his high consumption of alcohol as the reason behind why he finally took her? Or, more realistically, had he simply suffered an unconscious need to hold a woman again—a woman who meant something to him—and finally move on with his life?

A woman who means something to me...

The thought came back to haunt him. What *did* Emma mean to him? *What the hell is it? Loneliness, lust...love...?* Tyler knew one thing for sure—those four weeks in New York with her were the happiest he had experienced since Sara's death.

Tyler's head spun with the questions that tumbled one over the other in his brain. Too exhausted to further battle his emotions at that point, he heaved himself out of the chair and trudged to the bed, leaving a trail of clothes in his wake. He dropped down onto the soft surface and, lying alone in the darkness, wondered if he would ever lose the sadness that followed him through his days.

Chapter 10

August 31, 1880
New York City

Emma entered her bedroom and crossed to the pink ceramic bowl that rested on the wash counter. She dipped a washrag into the cool water that filled the basin almost to the rim and dragged the cloth across her brow, and then down into the opening at the bodice of her cotton dress. A groan of pleasure escaped her throat at the small relief the dampened rag offered.

August was quickly waning and, hopefully, so would the string of dreadfully hot days. Emma looked forward to dusk, when she could retire to the terrace and bask in the cool night air as it flitted across her skin. The summer heat, combined with the depression she had not been able to shake since Tyler left, brought Emma to her wits end.

It's been nearly three months since he walked out of my life—and I still can't get the image of his face out of my mind.

Her slippered feet padded back across the Aubusson carpet, then she settled herself on the window seat and blinked back the seemingly endless flow of tears. *I wonder what the summer would've been like if we had shared it together? We could have spent countless summers with each other...we could have grown old together.* Now she would never have a chance to experience what a life with Tyler might have been like. He was gone from her life—but she would love him forever.

Emma reached for a small wooden bird that perched on the windowsill and studied the piece's intricate carving and elaborate workmanship. Tyler purchased it for her during his last week in New York, on one of the many days they had toured the city. They strolled through an open market, and she dragged him to a table of beautiful, handcrafted wooden items, each created by the gnarled hands of a wizened old Indian brave. The man's body was small and shriveled, yet he sat cross-legged on the ground with an aura of what he had once been still surrounding him. Emma sighed as she recalled the strange afternoon...

Tyler stood quietly, ever patient while Emma perused the objects on the table, as well as the ones spread out across the ground. His own interest was piqued, however, when his eye caught a small, wooden figurine that sat among others like it on a brightly colored blanket. Tyler looked at the old man wrapped in yet another colorful quilt and silently requested permission to examine the carving. The Indian nodded his approval and, before Tyler could say anything, spoke in broken English.

"It is the loon," he said, proud eyes never leaving the Minnesotan's.

"Yes, I know. There are many of these birds on the lakes near my home."

Emma watched quietly as Tyler's gentle, almost worshipful hands picked up the carved figure. He examined the intricate detail before his gaze returned to the Indian. "You've captured his spirit very well. It's beautiful."

The old man's lined and weathered features remained the same, but his eyes now held a light that had not been there before. "I once sang like the loon. I once flew free like my spirit friend." His gnarled fingers formed a fist and he gently held it to his breast. "I still carry him in my heart."

"It's a very honorable spirit you carry with you." Tyler's eyes rested on the small, broken man and a silent message passed between them. He glanced down at the figurine in his hand, and then back at the Indian's fiery gaze. "I'd like to carry this spirit back to my home with me, where it can be near the lakes and forests, where it belongs. May I buy it from you?"

The old Indian straightened, clasped his knees with steady hands, and closed his eyes. Emma and Tyler waited breathlessly for him to speak.

It was a full minute before the old warrior opened his eyes again. He surveyed his surroundings as if seeing them for the first time, then focused on Tyler's rugged features once more. "Take the loon, my friend. Take the spirit home. I will not accept payment if you will do this thing for me."

Tyler reached down to grasp the noble man's wrinkled hand, and rheumy black eyes locked with the younger man's green ones in a shared experience that excluded all others around them.

"The spirit will go home. I'll see to it in your honor."

Emma strained to hear Tyler's quiet words, but he placed his hand on her elbow and led her away before she could question him about the bizarre exchange. The old Indian watched them depart and his eyes clouded. He knew beyond a doubt that he, too, would soon be going home.

The couple had reached the corner of the marketplace before Emma was able to grab Tyler's arm and halt his determined march from the square.

"I can't believe he just gave that carving to you. What happened back there?"

"One second, Emma. I'll explain shortly." He grasped her elbow again and led her to where their coach and driver waited. Emma watched in amazement when Tyler handed the man a wad of bills. She was even more dumbfounded by the words that came out of his mouth.

"I want you to go to the middle of the marketplace and find an old Indian peddler, whose wares are spread on a brightly colored blanket." Tyler pulled the wooden loon from his pocket. "I want you to purchase another one of these carvings—and make sure you give him all the money."

The driver shrugged, took the money, and left to do as Tyler asked. Emma, on the other hand, placed her hands on slim hips and looked at the man beside her as if he had just lost his mind.

"What's going on, Tyler? That's far too much money for even two of those carvings."

He handed her up into the back of the coach and, once he was settled next to her, finally answered her question.

"I hope you can understand what I'm going to say. That old Indian back there was once a proud brave who lived freely on the land he loved. He cared for and protected his family until, most likely, the white man forced him from his home. Now, since there are no forests to hunt or streams to fish in, he sells his handmade wares in order to survive. He's alone, Emma, except for the spirit he carries within him."

"Spirit?" Her brow furrowed with her level of confusion.

"All Indian braves seek a 'spirit' when they reach manhood. They derive strength and direction from it throughout their lives, until the day they die. This Indian's spirit is the loon. It's a beautiful bird and hard to describe if you've never seen one or heard its cry." He paused for a moment as he struggled to find words that would help her understand. "Emma, that old man is dying, and I'm taking his spirit home, because he can't go there himself. Do you understand now?"

Emma eyes swam with tears as the full impact of his words finally sank in. She was quiet for a time before speaking her thoughts aloud.

"You live in such a completely different world than me, Tyler. What a wonderful thing to do for him! How did you know he wanted you to take his 'spirit' home? I think I understand what you're doing, but...how did you know?"

"I can't really explain it, Emma. It was just a feeling. I've come in contact with many of his people back home and, through the years, I've learned their customs. Most people think the Indians are savages, out to kill every white man, but it really isn't like that at all. They were just protecting their land and their homes from acquisition by the federal government. They never even had a chance to decide if they wanted to leave or not." A gentle smile touched his lips as he glanced down at the glittering green orbs before him. "Indians are a mystic people. How that old man got his message across to me so quickly, I'll never quite understand. But I do know that, in some unspoken way, he asked me to bring him home so he could rest in peace."

He rolled the intricately carved loon in his hands, contemplating the life of the old Indian—a life the proud and distinguished man would never know again. Finally, he placed the carving in the pocket of his shirt and sat quietly, leaving Emma to examine her own feelings.

The driver returned a short time later with another wooden loon and handed it to Tyler. He paused though, before climbing up onto the front seat. "Mr. Wilkins, it was the oddest thing. I just gotta tell ya. As I walked away from that old Indian, he called out to me. He said, '*Tell the keeper of my spirit to think of me when he hears the loon sing.*'" He scratched his balding head as he moved to scramble up onto the front of the coach. "Darndest thing I ever heard tell."

Tyler and Emma exchanged knowing glances. Tears glistened in her eyes again, but he simply smiled.

"See, Emma, you just have to believe."

"I've never experienced anything like that in my life. He knows you sent the driver to buy the other loon, doesn't he?"

"Oh, yes, he knows." He eyed her closely, and then reached for her hand. He placed the other loon in her tiny palm. "Here, this one is for you to keep. Consider it a thank you for bringing me here in the first place." He wrapped her slender fingers around the figurine. "Now you have a 'spirit' too, and, every time you look at it, you'll be reminded of that proud old man."

Emma did not think so. She knew that every time she looked at the carving of the loon, she would think of the kind, gentle man who had given it to her...

Now, weeks later, as she leaned her head against the glass pane above the window seat and studied the little wooden bird in her hands, she knew she had been right. The carving would always remind her of Tyler and, once again, a flood of tears ran down her cheeks.

A week later found Emma reluctantly dining at a posh new restaurant with her father. Edward had spent the better part of the afternoon coaxing her into accompanying him and, with her quiet and introspective mood, Edward wished mightily that he could catch a glimpse of her as she had once been. He was worried about her. Since Tyler's departure, Emma remained depressed, pale, and disinterested in everything around her. Tonight was the first time in weeks that she had even left the house.

Edward sat making small talk with his daughter when a business associate approached their table. He was both relieved and irritated at the same time. Emma needed a distraction at this point, true, and the man advancing toward them was sure to provide it. He was a known gossip, but Edward could not decide if he was in the mood for his "stories" or not. He plastered a fake smile on his lips and greeted the gentleman.

"Hello, Adam. It's nice to see you again."

"Edward, it's been awhile! Miss Sanders, you look beautiful as always." He took Emma's hand and kissed the back of her palm. She smiled politely before pulling her fingers back and tucking them securely into her lap.

"It's been quite a while since we last met up, Edward. I imagine things have slowed down a wee bit since the halt on that project with the fellow from Minnesota."

Emma's head jerked up at the reminder, and Edward gritted his teeth. The ingrate had no way of knowing, of course, that even Tyler's name had become taboo, but it did not make the situation any easier to handle.

"Well, Adam, I still have all my other customers to take care of." Edward was already regretting the man's presence. *You're just fishing for information to spread to the next table.*

"Speaking of your other customers, are you still doing business with the Fontaines? I heard just this morning that the mill is in quite a bit of financial trouble. Samuel has dug himself in pretty deep and, with his father out of the country, some vendors are stopping shipments due to lack of payment. Did you hear about that?"

Edward had heard murmurings in the past week about the very same thing, but was not about to add fuel to the fire.

"I'm sure it's all speculation," the businessman replied. "You know how people are. There isn't much going on in the city lately, so they make up something to get tongues wagging. And, with Samuel testing the 'manufacturing waters' for the first time, it gives everyone something to ruminate on." He hoped his comments would end the conversation and, apparently, Adam took the hint. It took him only a few moments more to say his goodbyes and move on to another party seated across the room.

"What was that all about?" Emma sat forward in her chair, showing interest in the conversation for the first time that evening. "Is it true? Is the Fontaine mill in trouble?"

"I'm really hoping it *is* just speculation, Em. For John's sake." Emma saw the doubt in his eyes. "But I don't think so. I've been trying to keep an eye on the situation, and it looks like the mill is headed for big trouble. There's nothing I can do for John at this point, though. It was his decision to put Samuel in charge." He ran a hand through his thinning gray hair and sighed. "Christ, I hope my letter reaches him soon."

The news broke three days later. Fontaine Ironworks had closed down, two hundred and fifty men lost their jobs, and Samuel Fontaine was nowhere to be found. Vendors filed liens at City Hall against any impending profit, in hope of receiving some sort of restitution. The story was splashed across every newspaper in the city.

Emma closed the morning paper, sick at heart for all the displaced workers who had families to feed, and hoping John Fontaine did not have all his money invested in that one venture. She could not help but wonder how long it would be before her father heard from John or Evan and, more importantly at this point, where Samuel had disappeared to?

I was right about him. I wish now that I had risked my reputation that night and exposed Samuel for what he truly is.

As it stood now, the Fontaines could lose everything.

Edward, with a steaming mug of coffee in his hands, entered the sitting room in search of his daughter. He spied the paper on the table before her and saw the concern in her green eyes.

"It's terrible, Papa. What do you think is going to happen now?"

"Hopefully John will get home soon and straighten out this mess. If Samuel reappears though, I'll be hard pressed not to physically harm him myself. I don't know what the hell he was thinking! Tyler was right about him, and so were you. I just wished I had listened to the both of you."

Emma stood and crossed to lay a comforting hand on his arm. "Papa, you are a wonderful friend to John. Don't blame yourself. Maybe things will work out when he comes home."

Edward pulled her into his arms and silently gave thanks for his own business acumen, then, still worried about his friend, he left for his office.

Emma dallied about the house that morning, catching up on her correspondence. By late afternoon though, the idleness was wearing on her and she stepped out onto the back veranda and looked in the direction of the stables.

I should walk down there and check on Bonnie.

It had been weeks since she had even taken an afternoon ride and now felt slightly guilty for putting her life on hold for so long. She knew Jim still exercised the big white mare, however, and she owed him a personal thank you for attending to her horse.

The smell of fresh hay reached Emma's nostrils as she entered the cool building. She strolled past the empty stalls and, not finding Jim anywhere, headed in the direction of the estate's small pasture. Emma passed the last stall, reveling in the smell of the clean animals and fresh straw. The overall coziness of the stables comforted her, and she continued on. Lost in thought in the quiet surroundings, she was taken completely by surprise when a strong arm grabbed her around the waist from behind. A sweaty hand clamped over her mouth, and pulled her into the empty box.

Emma's struggle against her unknown assailant increased, and she clawed at the suffocating hand that tightened even more over her lips. Any attempt to scream for help was useless, so she lifted a slippered foot and brought it back with ferocious intent. She hit her mark, and an angry oath hissed next to her ear. Still, her captor refused to loosen his grip. Her heart slammed in her chest and her mind screamed for Jim.

The attacker pulled Emma into the far corner of the stall before he whirled her around. A cruel hand still covered her mouth.

Emma's eyes widened in horrified shock when they settled on her attacker. *Samuel!*

Fear curled through her belly. *Stay calm!* she told herself firmly. He had already proven once what a warped man he was. *I've got to get away!*

"Hello, Emma. So nice to finally see you again," he sneered. "I was beginning to think you had given up riding forever. I've waited two days for you to come out of the house." He pressed her further into the corner in an attempt to halt her struggle, then leered down into her frightened eyes. "I was almost hoping you wouldn't come out today; I had a little visit planned to your room tonight."

The thought of him hiding out in the buildings on their estate, not to mention his planned encounter that evening, made Emma's stomach roil. *The man's insane!* She struggled to keep her body from trembling, but to no avail.

"Are you cold, Emma? My, and it's been so warm out, too. Hell, maybe we just need to warm you up a bit."

He slammed Emma down into the bed of soft straw, flung himself across her body and, clamping his hand over her mouth again, sneered into her pale face. "This is where you belong, Emma. Beneath a man. Were you under Wilkins like this?" He shoved his groin against her pelvis, and Emma shrieked into his hand. She shook her head.

"No? Well too bad for him, that arrogant bastard. He ruined me, Emma. Because of him, I lost everything. He pulled out of the deal when I needed him the most. Were you in on it, too?" She denied his assumption with a groan, which caused Samuel to press his hand even tighter over her mouth. "Don't lie to me, you bitch! I saw the two of you together. Did you go whining to him about the night of the reception, thinking he could be your knight in shining armor?" His eyes took on a devious, feral gleam. "He's not here now though, is he? And, since I can't bring him down, I've decided that you should pay the debt for the both of you. What have I got to lose anymore, Emma? I have no business—no friends. The two of you managed to take away everything I ever had."

Emma's eyes widened in disbelief. In his twisted mind, Samuel had managed to lay the blame on her and Tyler for all his own transgressions. Even more frightening, his warped sense of justice would allow him to make her pay.

His hand left her mouth and, in the split second it took for him to move his lips closer to hers, Emma gasped for air, turned her head away, and screamed. He smothered her terror with his own mouth, and his groping hands made his intent all too clear. She bucked beneath him and shrieked into his clamped hand again, then suddenly there was a muffled thud from above.

Samuel's body rolled away and, unbelievably, Emma saw Jim standing above them, a shovel raised and ready for a second blow if needed. Emma scrambled from beneath Samuel just as he rose to his knees. A shaky hand stifled the sobs that welled within her.

"Miss Emma, are you all right?" Jim's frightened eyes darted from the man whose back he had slammed with the shovel, to the mistress of the estate, then back again to the animal who now crouched in the straw. "You get away from here! Please, Miss Emma, go now!"

"Jim," she sobbed. "Come with me!"

Samuel rose slowly, his eyes never leaving the stable hand or the shovel. Emma's instincts told her to run for help, but her legs were frozen with fear.

The three of them stood face to face in the quiet of the barn, unsure of what to do next. Suddenly, Samuel sprang from the corner of the stable in Jim's direction. The younger man swung the shovel again, but Samuel was ready for it this time. He raised his arm, fending off the blow, then knocked the would-be weapon free of the other man's grasp. He grabbed the front of Jim's shirt and flung the stable hand against the side of the stall.

"You little bastard! I'll teach you." Samuel pummeled the boy's midsection while Emma frantically sought something to stop the abuse. Her gaze settled on the shovel, where it now lay in the straw and, racing to it, snatched up the implement and swung it ferociously at Samuel's back.

"Samuel!" she screamed. "Stop or you'll kill him!"

She kept up her attack, making contact with his body on every stroke, and, finally, Samuel dropped to his knees and his hands clasped his head. They both panted hard from the exertion and their hate-filled gazes locked as Jim's body crumpled to the straw-covered ground.

Samuel's eyes took on a sadistic, feral gleam again and he bounded to his feet with an animalistic growl—just as a horse thundered up the driveway toward the open door of the barn. A piercing scream left Emma's throat.

"This isn't over by any means, you slut. Someday you'll be totally alone, and then I'll make you pay." His battered body staggered in the direction of the back door and, a moment later, he was gone.

Emma dropped the shovel and hurried to kneel beside Jim's writhing body, where he still lay in the corner of the stall. She helped him to a sitting position just as her father ran through the front entrance of the barn.

"Emma! Where are you?" His voice rose with fear. "Emma!"

"Papa! Back here! Hurry!"

Edward bounded into the stall, then stopped short when he saw his daughter's disheveled state and the injured Jim in her arms.

"Papa! Thank God you came! Samuel was here and..." She choked back a sob. "He tried to...hurt both of us. He attacked me...Jim hit him with the shovel, and now he's hurt!"

"Miss Emma, I'm...fine," Jim mumbled. "When I saw that man and what he was doing to you...I grabbed the shovel." He looked into her eyes and pleaded for forgiveness. "Thank you for trying to stop him, Miss Emma, but I'm just sorry I didn't get here sooner—"

"Jim, you saved my life! It is I who should be thanking you!" She wiped the tears from her face and, with her father's assistance, helped Jim to stand.

"Are the both of you going to be all right?" Edward worried. He watched as the stable hand bent forward at the waist and inhaled deeply to fill his lungs. He shook his head. "I think you need to see a doctor, boy."

"I'm...fine, Mr. Sanders. It's Miss Emma I'm worried about." Edward's frantic gaze swept his daughter's trim form, then his eyes turned to stone when he saw the bits of straw in her tangled hair and the torn dress. His lips held an unspoken question, and Emma opened her mouth to reassure him, but the words became as hazy as the spots that formed in front of her eyes. Her world slowed as her father's arms reached out. His muffled words of alarm echoed in her ears, and his hands caught her just before everything went black.

"Emma, wake up. Come on now, young lady. Concentrate on opening your eyes."

Whose voice is that? her sluggish mind asked as she struggled to obey. It took a huge amount of effort just to lift one lid. *Where am I?*

Emma's vision cleared and she realized that she lay in her own bed and that the strange voice belonged to Dr. Benton, the man who had taken care of her since she was a little girl. He sat next to the bed and smiled down at her over the rim of his glasses.

"Well, young lady, it's nice of you to rejoin us! You had me wondering there for a while if you were ever going to wake up today."

She blinked, organized her thoughts, and prepared to ask him just what he was doing in her room. The words froze on her lips, however, when the events of the afternoon flooded her mind.

"What happened? Did I faint?" A quizzical frown furrowed her brow. "I did faint, didn't I?"

The old doctor reached over to pat her arm. "Yes, you did—and almost gave your father a heart attack in the process. How do you feel, young lady?"

"I'm fine, I guess, though slightly embarrassed for fainting. I don't think I've ever done that in my life." She grabbed at his arm and her eyes widened with sudden remembrance. "How is the young boy, Jim?"

"He's fine. He'll be rather sore for the next week, judging by the color of his bruises, but nothing is broken. He took quite a beating, Emma." He patted her hand again. "He explained to your father and me what happened. Now, I know this might be rather embarrassing for you, but the findings of my examination showed no...harm from Samuel's abuse. Is that true?"

Emma's face flushed hotly, and she knew it was a foolish reaction. This man was a doctor and had personally attended her throughout her entire life. She swallowed for composure before speaking.

"No, he didn't. But I know he would have if Jim hadn't come along when he did. Thank God it's over." She closed her eyes for a moment against a sudden bout of queasiness.

Dr. Benton stood and crossed to where the pitcher of water sat on top of the bureau. He poured a glass of the cool liquid and brought it back to her.

"Here, drink this." He handed the glass to Emma, sat in the chair next to the bed again, and leaned forward to rest his forearms on his knees. "Emma, as your doctor, I need to ask you something else of a personal nature." His questioning gaze held hers, and Emma sat up straighter, confused by his words and his actions.

"Emma...when was your last monthly time?" He kept his eyes on her face as he asked the question, and she shook her head in total bewilderment.

"What does that have to do with today's events?"

"I've been a doctor for many years, and you've been a patient of mine since you were a young girl." He reached for her hand, clasped it between his warm ones, and continued. "Emma, I'm quite sure you are in your first three months of pregnancy. That is probably the reason why you fainted today, combined, of course, with the traumatic events you experienced."

Her mind went blank as she stared into the gentle eyes of the man she had known her entire life.

Pregnant? How could that be?

And then, she knew.

Why didn't I see it?

She had been queasy in the mornings, and had even emptied her stomach a few times. She had also been overly emotional, terribly fatigued during July and August, and had missed her monthly flow twice—but attributed the symptoms to Tyler's leaving and the hot days of summer.

But, it's not because he left, and it's not because of the weather. It's because I'm pregnant—with Tyler's baby...

"Emma, you've been with a man, haven't you?" Dr. Benton pressed. "Please understand that I am not judging your morals. I'm just concerned with your overall health."

Her gaze strayed to the small wooden loon that sat on the windowsill. Thoughts of Tyler and the night they shared sifted through her mind, and the repercussions of their actions slammed into her chest. She was going to have his baby. *What will he think when he finds out?*

She looked at the kindly doctor again, with more resolve than she felt. "Yes, Dr. Benton, there is every possibility that I'm pregnant. I'm sure you're right."

"You need to discuss this with the baby's father before too much longer," the old doctor stated firmly, "and I think you should talk to your own father today. There are plans to be made."

"I will talk to Papa today. But, as far as the baby's father is concerned, he won't be told. He made it clear he doesn't want me, and I'd just as soon keep this to myself." The last few words were laced with pain and accompanied by a quivering chin.

Dr. Benton looked with affection at his patient of many years; a beautiful young woman who was clearly being torn apart by the rejection of a man she had given herself to freely. His shoulders fell with a heavy sigh. He had done his part. How Emma handled the situation was out of his hands.

He gathered up his medical bag and supplies, all the while explaining to Emma the need to set regular appointments to keep watch over the progression of her pregnancy. He reminded her once more to talk to her father. He would not forego his patient's right to privacy. The doctor slowly closed the door behind him as he left the room.

Emma left the bed and crossed to the window seat. Bewildered green eyes scanned the front yard of her home. The last time she saw Tyler, he had entered a coach that would take him out of her life forever and away from the memory of a beautiful night—the night when the baby she now carried was conceived.

Her eyes fluttered shut. *I wish this child had been conceived in love.*

Her hand dropped to her flat stomach, where the baby grew inside her at this very moment. *Pregnant! I never even gave it a thought after he left.*

Emma reached for the wooden loon and clutched it to her heart. *Would he even care?*

She knew it was a foolish question. Of course he would.

Tyler is a kind and gentle man, the type to take care of his responsibilities. His innate wholesome character would demand that he love this baby.

But can he love me?

She set the loon back on the sill with a heavy heart. The decision was in her hands. *I'm not going to tell him. I don't want to be in his life just because of some sense of responsibility he would feel toward me and the baby.* If she told him now, she would never know how he truly felt about her and she could not live with that. Emma decided that she could love the child and do well by it on her own.

She would be the talk of the city's gossipmongers—a single, pregnant woman, who refused to tell anyone who the father was. *It's my mistake—not the baby's. I'll get past the gossip.*

It was all she could do.

Emma stood, took a deep breath and crossed to her bedroom door. She was scared to death of what her father's reaction would be, but keeping the secret would do no good—for either of them. Emma swallowed down her own shock at her wanton actions of nearly three months ago and willed herself to continue downstairs to talk to Edward.

* * *

"What do you mean you're not going to tell him!" The words exploded from Edward's mouth as he paced back and forth between Emma and the fireplace. "That's one of the stupidest things I've ever heard! If Tyler is the father, then he should own up to his responsibilities!"

The discussion had been going on for the last twenty minutes and, up to this point, Edward had been surprisingly calm. He handled the news of his unwed daughter's pregnancy with grace and compassion. When he asked what her plans were, however, the dam burst.

Emma held her fingers to her temples, knowing that if she lost her patience now, she would never be able to sway him over to her way of thinking.

"Papa, please quit pacing and just sit down and listen to what I have to say."

Edward looked at her, opened his mouth once more, and then thought better of it. He dropped into the chair directly across from her and waited silently for her to speak.

"Papa, please understand how I feel. From the first time I met Tyler in this very room, something happened to me. I just didn't know what it was—that I had fallen in love with him—until the morning he left."

A vision of his brokenhearted daughter, as she wept in his arms on that long ago morning, flitted through Edward's mind, and he believed her beyond a doubt.

"I asked him to stay that last night, and I think the amount of alcohol the two of you consumed throughout dinner was probably the reason he accepted so readily."

Edward felt a stab of guilt pierce his heart for the part he had unwittingly played in his daughter's current situation. He opened his mouth to speak, but she held up her hand and continued.

"You have to understand that, even if I love him still, I don't think the feeling is reciprocated."

"And your mother and I—"

Emma was tempted to grit her teeth in frustration. *How am I going to explain this to him?* "I know you and Mama tried hard to have a normal life, and I know the two of you loved each other only as friends do. But don't you see? I can't have that kind of relationship with my husband. I want a deeper love than that—the kind of marriage I know is possible! Tyler never once alluded to the fact that he might truly care for me. If he is forced to accept me now as his wife, because of the baby, I will never know if he could have loved me for *me*. I will never know if he would have come back for me. I don't want him to feel just responsibility toward me, Papa. Can't you understand that?"

Her father's lack of interruption throughout her long explanation filled Emma with nothing short of amazement. Feeling more confident, she rose to look out the window. "You know that if Tyler were to find out about the baby, he would do what is right—because that's the type of man he is." She hesitated, took a deep breath, and plunged on. "I want to keep this from him. He left, Papa, without even looking back."

Edward sat in the chair, watching the straight line of her back. *God, you're my daughter, and I love you, but I must also do what's right for you, no matter how difficult.*

While Dr. Benton attended Emma earlier, Edward took the opportunity to talk with Jim about that afternoon's episode. When the boy spoke of Samuel's last threat to his daughter, Edward made a decision. Emma needed to be hidden some place out of harm's way until Samuel could be found. She was in real danger, and the thought made his stomach turn.

"Come here and sit down, Emma." She turned to her father with a pleading look in her eyes that tore at his heart. He reached out to take her hand in a gentle grip when she again sat next to him. "Honey, I do understand how you feel, but do you honestly think you're being fair to Tyler? He has a right to know that he's going to be a father."

She opened her mouth to object, but he squeezed her hand to silence her.

"No, let me have my turn to speak. I love you, and I respect your opinion. In fact, I would probably agree with you and just let it be done, but there are other factors to deal with here. Jim told me about Samuel's threat to you just before he escaped. Both you and I know we can't give him the chance to hurt you again. He *will* be back."

"And I can just stay here in the house and not go out alone. Surely, he will be caught soon and things will return to normal—or at least as normal as they can be until the baby is born."

"Emma, he hid here, at our home, for two days, and we didn't even know it! What if he were to get into the house when you're home alone? Are you willing to risk the baby's life and your own?" He squeezed her hand once more and, again, refused to give her a chance to speak. "Well, I'm not. You are too dear to me, and I refuse to give that madman another chance to hurt you. I'm sorry to go against your will, but, in the morning, I'm going to send Tyler a telegram, telling him of the pregnancy—and informing him that you'll be arriving in Minnesota within the week."

Emma was out of the chair and on her feet before the last words left Edward's mouth. Never had he seen such anger in her gaze before—anger directed at him.

"How dare you plan out my life for me?" Her green eyes glittered dangerously. "Do you think I want to be some sort of excess baggage Tyler accidentally left in New York? Do you think I want to show up on his doorstep, pregnant and looking like I need someone to care for me? 'Please take care of me, Mr. Wilkins. After all, you jumped in bed with me and had a smashing good time, so now it's time to pay up!'"

"Emma!" Edward was more shocked at her choice of words than at her outburst. He stood quickly. "This is for your own safety! Can't you see that? You need to be away from here as soon as possible. Tyler is your baby's father—so what better place to send you! Samuel will never find you if you move that far away. Being with Tyler is far safer than being in a hotel by yourself somewhere."

He reached out to clasp her arms in a gentle hold. "Honey, you mean the world to me and, though God knows I'll miss you terribly, the threat Samuel poses cannot be ignored." His hands dropped to his sides again. "I will be sending that telegram in the morning. If you feel you must stay angry with me, then so be it, but I will not let any more harm come to you, and that's the end of it."

Emma searched his familiar face—a face that held more lines now than it had an hour ago. She knew it would do no good to argue further, but she had to try.

"Papa, please don't do this to me." The tears rolled down her cheeks. "Please don't send me away—especially to Tyler."

"It's the only recourse I have, honey. I will not let the people in this city shred your reputation, and I will *not* allow Samuel another opportunity to harm you. And with Tyler being the baby's father, he needs to know."

Emma was blinded by tears as she whirled and ran from the room, leaving her father to feel like a traitor. He knew in his heart though, that he must stick to his decision. She and the baby must be protected from Samuel Fontaine, and he could not do it here in New York.

Edward crossed to the mahogany writing desk, pulled out his personal stationery, and took pen in hand. Sinking down into the swivel chair with a tired sigh, he stared at the white surface of the paper and devised the words he would send to Tyler. The telegraph office opened early in the morning, and he would be there when it was ready for business. He had to believe that Tyler would accept his proposition—especially with a baby on the way—and, if not, he would force the issue. Emma's safety remained uppermost in his mind and, hopefully, the love she held for Tyler would help carry them both through the storm that was sure to follow. Edward dipped the pen into the inkwell and sealed his daughter's fate.

Chapter Eleven

The black steed cantered past the house to the barn. Tyler sat atop its back with sagging shoulders that gave away his fatigue. He had spent many hours in the saddle that day, making a trip to the north end of the Wilkins' property. Normally, it was a trip to be made over the course of two days—a progress check of the skidding crews—but Tyler did his best, since arriving home a month ago, to never be gone overnight. His daughter hardly left his side his first week home from New York, and he despaired at ever getting back to a normal work schedule. He was infinitely thankful for the one event that changed her sudden clinging tendency.

He had been home for just over a week when he took Janie with him to the foreman's cabin to discuss a problem with one of the big saws at the mill. Most of the evening was spent in the cozy home around Tom and Mary Jenson's kitchen table. Janie sat on the chair next to him, always making sure some part of her little torso touched her father.

At some point in the evening, Tom's two young sons entered the cabin, each with a yellow, floppy-eared pup in their arms. Tyler noticed Janie's interest pique at the sight of the tiny dogs, but she still would not leave his side. It was not until one of the boys crossed to her, held out his charge, and offered it for her to pet that Janie was coaxed to move away from Tyler. Not long after, the little girl sat on the floor with the boys and played with the puppy.

Tyler concluded his business and prepared to leave. By that time, Janie sat quietly with the tired dog in her lap and slowly stroked the velvety ears with a contented smile. Tyler stooped down to her level and scratched the pup behind the ears.

"He's cute, isn't he, honey?"

Janie nodded her head in agreement.

"It's time we get a move on, though. Mamie's going to wonder why we're so late."

His daughter threw him a pleading look that said, *'Let's stay just a little longer.'*

Tom called one of his younger sons to him during the exchange between Tyler and his daughter. After a whispered conference, the young boy returned to Janie's side, hunkered down in front of her, and offered the pup to her for keeps. Blue eyes glowed with excitement and sought her father's for permission as the little girl hugged the tiny animal even closer to herself.

Tyler knew the battle was lost before it even began. Janie never asked for much. How could he resist giving her this one little bit of happiness? A rueful smile touched his lips.

"Having a pet to take care of is a big responsibility, Janie. It'll be up to you to make sure he's fed all the time, and your job to watch him until he's big enough to take care of himself. Do you think you can do that?"

Her blonde head bobbed yes, and the small round face glowed with pleasure.

Tyler smiled again. "Well then, I suppose this little fellow will be getting his first horse ride tonight. Up you both go now." He lifted the two of them into his arms while saying goodnight to the Jenson's, along with a hesitant thank you to all of them for the pup.

Thinking back on it now, Tyler realized that acquisition of the animal actually helped his work schedule return to normal. The month away from his daughter had been hard on her, but now Janie threw herself into the care of the puppy and had stopped clinging to him. Tyler was able to resume his usual timetable as far as the business was concerned without the accompanying guilt.

Reaching the entrance to the barn, he dismounted the massive black Arabian and thought longingly of a warm meal. *Christ, I'm tired—I should have let Cole go today.*

Earlier, his brother tried to talk him out of the one day trip or at least to allow him to ride along, but Tyler declined. He needed some time to himself, even though he knew he must return that evening; he would not put Janie through another night without him. His mind screamed to escape the confines of his daughter's need, and yet Tyler's love for her always pulled him back. He dealt with it by driving himself to the physical brink each day, so when he entered his own private hell at night, he would have the chance to sleep part of it away. Now, the long, hard, self-imposed workdays were evidenced in sunken cheeks and dark circles beneath his eyes. His family did their best to help him, but only Tyler could come to terms with his emotions. So far, he was still in the midst of his own battle.

He led the horse into the soft glow of the gas lantern, where it hung from a peg on the wall, and then entered an empty stall. From behind, he heard Clancey's voice coming from the tack room.

"Evenin', Tyler! Been waiting for you to show up. Didn't expect you for another couple of hours, though." The hired hand slung his elbows over the wooden gate.

"Hello, Clance. Things went smooth today, and I was able to head for home earlier than I thought."

The man looked at his boss, studied the weariness etched on his face, and made a quick decision. "Here, let me take care of that black beast for you. You go on up to the big house. I'm sure Mamie has a plate warmin' for you."

The stable hand poured oats into the feeder to draw the stallion's interest away from him. As good as he was around the ranch's riding stock, Clancey still gave the Arabian a wide berth. The horse was known to give warning bites and swift kicks when it came to anyone other than Tyler.

"You know, Clance, I think I'll take you up on that offer. It's been a long day. I'm hoping to see Janie before she falls asleep."

Tyler handed the stiff-bristled brush to the hired man and gave Storm one more pat on the neck. "You behave yourself, and maybe Clancey will give you an extra scoop of oats." The horse snorted when Tyler smacked him a second time on the rump.

"I stayed around, Ty, to let you know that the New York couple you offered jobs to showed up today. They're in the cabin you had ready, and I explained you'd be around in the mornin' to talk to them. Carrie and Mamie made sure they had some food supplies and got them settled in."

"Thanks, Clancey. I'm surprised they're here already. I didn't really expect them for another month. Good thing I listened to Carrie about getting the cabin ready."

"They seem like a nice enough couple. Both wanted to dig in right away, but neither one of the ladies would let them—insisted they just set up housekeeping on their own for now and talk with you in the morning."

"I'll do that." Tyler left the barn, and Clancey's laughter-filled voice followed after him.

"Hey, Tyler! You'd better go in duckin'! Mamie was madder than a wet hen earlier! Seems that pup of Janie's pulled her clean sheets off the line and dragged them through the mud. Also earned himself a good swat on the ass from the end of Mamie's broom! The little shit had the audacity to lift his leg and pee on the leg of her kitchen table!"

Tyler could hear his cackle halfway up to the house.

The scene he observed was not even close to what he imagined it would be when he opened the back door. Mamie sat at the kitchen table with her ever present basket of mending next to her. Janie scribbled on her chalkboard and the pup was lazily stretched out on his back in the basket placed by the stove. All four of his legs sprawled out in different directions and he was sound asleep. The mayhem of earlier seemed to have disappeared.

Janie leapt from her chair and ran to her father, only to be lifted through the air and clasped in a big bear hug. She promptly gave him a loud, smacking kiss on the cheek and Tyler chuckled at her actions.

"Janie, you have no idea how I needed that! So, how was your day today?"

He caught her telltale glance, which darted to Mamie and then to the pup, who woke with the small bit of commotion. Father and daughter watched as he sat up and yawned indifferently before padding clumsily over to them for a scratch behind the ears. Tyler accommodated him before speaking. "Heard tell someone got his little yellow butt in trouble today."

Janie's blue eyes widened along with another quick, darting glance in Mamie's direction. She then looked at Tyler with a tiny finger to her lips to shush him before Mamie heard. It was all to no avail. Mamie heaved her bulk from the chair and shook a brown finger at Tyler.

"Put that yellow beast outside before he pees in my kitchen agin! He be walkin' a thin line 'round me today! Tyla, don't know how much longer I can be puttin' up with the likes o' him. He be pee'in on my floors and dirtying up my laundry! Yessiree! Things be comin' to a head 'round here afore long!" She continued to mumble as she moved around the kitchen to ready Tyler's late dinner.

Tyler held back the small chuckle her words evoked. He knew Mamie was just blowing off steam at the day's events and, most likely, was not the least bit serious. The old woman just liked to be in control of any situation that had to do with her home. He whispered to Janie to let the pup out, and she did so before Mamie started to rant again.

Tyler sat at the table, ready to give the steaming food in front of him its due. He and Mamie made idle conversation about the O'Malleys and the day's events of moving them into the cabin on the far side of the property.

"Carrie took care o' everythin'. She shot orders to them brothers o' yours about gitten the O'Malleys belongin's inside." She chuckled and wiped at her eyes.

"I can just imagine Carrie—I know what she's like when she takes charge." Humor at what his brothers probably went through curled his lips upward.

"I don't think those O'Malley people ever had anyone waitin' on them in the whole of their lives. You could see that poor Missus wringin' her hands whiles Carrie told her to be sittin' back and enjoyin' her tea. And Carrie wouldn't take no for an answer! Yessiree! She had them two brothers of yours just a hoppin'! And Clancey, he insisted on takin' care of the hired trap and horse for the Mister O'Malley. I thought his eyes would pop plumb outa his head! We left both of 'em with smiles reachin' acrost from ear to ear, we did. Yessiree, we surely did!"

"I wish I could've been here to greet them on their first day." Tyler was sure though, that the O'Malleys were treated well by his family. He looked forward to visiting with them in the morning and could not wait to hear their account of their first day on the ranch.

Janie re-entered the kitchen, and Mamie started on the pup once more with a shake of a plump finger in the animal's direction.

"You go on and git back in that basket! There'll be no whizzin' no mores on my clean floor!" The pup knew what the shaking brown finger meant and made quick tracks to his bed, keeping a watchful eye on the old woman the entire time.

Tyler ate his meal and Janie scribbled on her chalkboard, doing the sums her father suggested. Observing her, Tyler made a mental note to speak to Carrie about bringing a tutor to the ranch. Up to this point, his sister took on the responsibility of instruction for his young daughter. With her disability, Tyler feared sending Janie to the small local school in the area.

"Have you come up with a name yet for the pup?"

Janie shook her head no.

"We really should start calling him something, honey. You've had him for several weeks now, and Mamie needs to know what to call him when she's smacking his butt with the broom!"

A snort erupted from the old black woman. "He don't be needin' no name for me to smack him when he's pee'in' on my floor!"

Janie listened to the exchange and suddenly grabbed the chalkboard in front of her. She scribbled quickly before handing it to Tyler. She pointed at the piece of slate, and then to the pup in the basket. Tyler glanced at her suggestion for a name and felt the laughter build inside him. Before long, he let it out along with a slap to his thigh. Mamie and Janie looked at each other in surprise. It had been a long time since they had heard that sound come from his lips.

"Look here, Mamie." Tyler was still chuckling as he pushed the board in her direction. "I think my daughter has come up with the perfect name for the...what do you call him, the *yellow beast*? She has cleverly given him the name of 'Whizzer'!" He chuckled once more, and a huge smile appeared on his daughter's face. She had actually made her father laugh! At that moment, he did not seem so sad, and it was all because of her.

Mamie concealed her delight at Tyler's laughter. "I think that daughter of yours be spendin' too much time with her uncles! She's startin' to sound like 'em now."

She softened her statement with a loving smile in Janie's direction and, a moment later, laughter again filled the cozy kitchen as they watched the newly dubbed 'Whizzer' sprawl across the floor. Trying to scratch behind his ear, he had missed his mark and plopped over sideways with a comical look of surprise.

"Come on, honey—show's over." Tyler said as he stood. "It's time for you to be tucked in."

Janie ran to Whizzer, kissed him on the nose, and crossed to Mamie to be wrapped in her comforting arms. She took her father's hand then, and they left the kitchen.

Mamie placed Tyler's dirty dishes on the counter to be washed. Whizzer eyed her every move, ready to skittle out of harm's way when the old woman offered him a small chunk of meat. She walked to the dog and bent over.

"Sit, you little heathen!" She watched as he quickly plopped his hind end on the ground, with his tail swishing a path back and forth across the floor. "This here is for you—for makin' my Tyla laugh again. And don't be thinkin' I'll ever be tellin' anyone I gives you treats! You be watchin' where you be liftin' that leg o' yours or you and me gonna knock heads! Yessiree! You be one sorry yellow dog then!"

She looked at the pup and shook her head at her own actions. After one last loving pat on the animal's head, Mamie extinguished the gas lamp on the table.

Tyler crossed the vast central room of the house early the next morning and his ears picked up the sound of voices coming from the kitchen. He was greeted by Dougan O'Malley's booming laugh when he pushed open the swinging door. The Irish couple sat at the kitchen table chuckling about something Mamie had just said.

Tyler glanced heavenward before taking his last step through the doorway. *Thank you for the help on this one!*

It seemed Mamie was readily going to accept Katy O'Malley into her domain—something she refused to do in the past. She had given so much to the family in all her years at the ranch. Now she could finally ease up a little.

"Well, I see you decided to take me up on my offer." He strolled across the kitchen to shake hands with Dougan, who jumped up from his seat at Tyler's entrance.

"Hello, Mr. Wilkins!" He pumped the bosses hand vigorously. "Katy and I are happy to be here. This country is beautiful, isn't it, Katy?"

His wife had also leapt from her chair when Tyler entered the room. She now gave a quick little curtsey, prompted by her husband's words. "Mr. Wilkins, the cabin you prepared for us is so lovely. We can't tell you enough how thankful we are for the jobs."

"Let me grab a cup of coffee and we'll get down to business. First, we need to familiarize you with the ranch."

Dougan and Katy exchanged wonder filled glances, still unable to believe the opportunity that had been presented to them. Their new employers were already treating them like part of the family, and the respect being accorded to them was something they had never before encountered.

The four sat at the kitchen table for more than an hour before Mamie left with Katy in tow for a tour of the house. The two women's jobs were outlined and easily agreed upon, and Katy O'Malley left with a happy glow on her face. She was anxious to start.

The men left for the stable shortly afterwards. Tyler brought up the subject of Fontaine Ironworks on their way across the yard.

"So, how did your leavetaking go over with Mr. Fontaine?"

Dougan shook his head, and a look of concern spread across his face. "Not well, I'm afraid. I went in the morning after you left my home. My first reaction was to never set foot in those four walls again, but I felt I owed it to my crew not to walk out on them overnight." It was the reaction Tyler expected from this man who took pride in any job he did.

"I asked for a meeting with Mr. Fontaine and was granted one that afternoon. I explained to him that I was offered another job, but was willing to work until he could find a replacement for me. Mr. Wilkins, I never had an ounce of respect for the man, but was willing to stay on a while longer to help him out. He fired me on the spot. That's why my wife and I got here sooner than originally planned."

Tyler placed a hand on the other man's shoulder as they walked on. "Better for you and better for me, Dougan. I'll expect you to work hard for what I pay you, but never will you be treated unfairly by anyone on this ranch. It's a policy we strictly adhere to. If you have any problems, please see me immediately, and they'll get resolved."

The big Irishman looked at his new employer. He believed Tyler would be true to his word. He and Katy had been treated wonderfully so far. Dougan stopped momentarily to fish an envelope from his front pocket. He held it out to Tyler.

"This is what's left of the money you gave us the last time I saw you. There are receipts enclosed for everything Katy and I purchased to get ourselves out here. We talked last night and feel we should give the rest back. If you think any of the purchases aren't warranted, please let me know and, between Katy and myself, we'll work them off."

Tyler glanced sidelong at the man, unable to believe how fortunate he was to have him in his employ. Dougan was honest and had great strength of character. He would be a good addition to the ranch.

"That money was given to you and Katy, Dougan, and I'll not accept its return. Put it away for something special. We made a gentleman's agreement that night; you've stuck to your end of the bargain and I plan on keeping with mine. Now, I want to hear no more about it. Agreed?"

"Thank you, sir. I promise you'll not be sorry for hiring me. I plan to work hard and treat this ranch like it was my own." He returned the envelope to his shirt pocket and continued on to the barn, listening intently while Tyler explained his duties as if the conversation about the money had never come up.

It was a sunny afternoon during the first week of September when Tyler slammed the door to his home office with as much force as he could muster. He tossed two pieces of paper onto the surface of the shiny oak desk, and then reached for the bottle of brandy sitting on the side cabinet. Pulling the cork from the neck of the bottle, he threw it angrily across the room before swallowing a long draught. He rammed the bottle back down onto the desktop, and dropped into the stuffed chair behind it. He sat for a long time and stared at nothing, numb to everything around him, then closed his eyes. A heavy sigh lifted his chest, and he leaned his dark head back against the soft cushion of the chair.

Emma was pregnant—and she had named him as the father. *It could damn well be possible, but I don't believe it for a minute.*

As hard as he tried, he could not forget their encounter that last night in New York. *Fool! The little wanton got herself in trouble, and now she says it's my fault.* Any feelings he might have entertained toward her were erased by sheer anger.

He leaned forward to take another swig from the bottle, then reached across the desk to drag the two telegrams a little closer. Leaning back in the chair again, he studied them with animosity etched across his rugged features. His shaking hand reached out again to pick up the one nearest him.

It stated that Fontaine Ironworks had closed down, and Edward implied it was for the reasons the two of them discussed before he left for Minnesota. The missive also stated that Samuel had dropped from sight, making threats before leaving.

I wonder what the hell that's all about? I suppose the bastard thinks it's my fault that the mill closed. Make all the threats you want, Fontaine—I'm half a country away from you.

He dropped the wrinkled paper and watched it flutter to the desktop, then turned his attention to the second telegram. Tyler took one more lazy pull of courage from the neck of the bottle and picked up the paper.

'Tyler—stop—Emma is with child—stop—informed in regards to your last night in New York—stop—I will send her to Minnesota because of threats—stop—'

"Probably all the damn gossip—little Miss Emma has been found out, and Daddy's going to save the day." His dark brows dropped again at the next words that leapt off the page.

I expect marriage immediately—stop—your responsibility—stop—dowry funds to be wired within the week—stop—further details to follow on Emma's September 10 arrival—stop—please respond—Edward Sanders.'

"A dowry? I don't want Edward's goddamn money or his daughter! What the hell? He expects me to marry her! No questions about who she's been with—just marry my daughter, or else!"

He rose from the chair to pace the room, all the while rubbing his hands through his thick, dark hair. *How in hell am I going to explain this to Trevor and Cole. How in hell can I stop this!*

He was not going to get the chance. Edward was putting Emma on a train in New York at this very moment, and he had made it very clear what he expected Tyler to do. *He expects me to marry her immediately without any further questions.* Apparently, he believed his daughter's assertion that only he, Tyler Wilkins, could be the father of her baby.

Emma would arrive in three days. Further details would be sent shortly as to the exact time she was expected in Duluth. He pictured her arrival—then he pictured his fingers around her neck.

Tyler was unusually quiet at the dinner table that night. Terse answers to the questions asked him were the only responses when he did speak. Trevor, Cole, and Carrie eyed him closely, trying to decide what was wrong. They were used to his quietness on some days, but Tyler had never been openly rude to any of them. Toward the meal's end, Trevor had had enough of his brother's behavior.

"All right, Ty. It seems you're having a problem with something, and I'm sure I speak for all of us. What the hell is going on? You've been slamming dishes and answering questions to the point of rudeness, and I feel you owe us all an explanation."

"Is that right?" Tyler tossed back as he banged his glass down with a glare. "Maybe it's none of your concern, and maybe how I *act* is none of your business."

Trevor bounded out of his chair, never taking his eyes from his brother's face, but before he could say anything, Tyler snapped at him again.

"Back off, Trevor. I'm warning you."

Carrie's gaze swung to her oldest brother, and her mouth dropped open in shock at his outburst. She leaned across the table and rested a gentle hand on his arm.

"Tyler, that's enough. Please don't be angry with Trevor. We all can see something is wrong. We just want to help you if we can. It's not like you to act this way."

Dark green eyes moved from his sister's face to the others seated at the table, who seemed to be holding their breath as they waited for his response. A muscle in Trevor's cheek ticked angrily, and Cole looked ready to leap to his feet if necessary.

Tyler breathed an apologetic sigh. "Trev...I'm sorry."

His brother slowly seated himself again. "What the hell's going on, Ty? Christ, I haven't felt like punching you in years. You never treat anyone like you have tonight."

Tyler sat back and inhaled deeply. A loud whoosh of air filled the room as he expelled it. "I suppose we should all talk about it, since you'll find out soon enough anyway." He got up from his chair and lifted Janie down from hers as the other three adults at the table exchanged worried glances again.

"Honey, you go in the kitchen and help Mamie. Daddy's going to have a short meeting in the library, then I'll come back and we'll read a story." He dropped a light kiss on her blonde head and sent her on her way. His gaze scanned those around the table and he invited them to follow him to the other room.

The small group seated themselves in the library behind closed doors and waited eagerly for Tyler to fill them in. Unsure of how to broach the subject of one Emma Sanders, Tyler decided to let them read Edward's two telegrams, and then take it from there. He handed the first to Trevor, who was closest, and saved the second until later.

Coward, he reprimanded himself, using the excuse—if only for himself— that he wanted them to read Edward's message about Fontaine Ironworks before giving them the other. Tyler waited quietly as his family read the words. All three looked confused; there was nothing in the message to warrant Tyler's earlier outburst.

"There doesn't seem to be anything so bad in this telegram, Ty," Cole spoke up. "So, Fontaine is putting part of the blame on you for the mill's closure.

Who cares? Probably Fontaine blowing a lot of smoke, if you ask me."

"There's a second telegram that came with this one. I guess I'll just let you three read that one, too, and then we can talk."

He pulled the second telegram from his pocket and felt like he was sealing his fate with the gesture. He handed it gingerly to Trevor, walked to the open window—and waited for a response.

The ticking of the grandfather clock was the only sound in the room, except for a crumpling noise as the telegram was handed from one person to another. Tyler felt three pairs of eyes bore into his back, gathered his courage, and turned to face them. When he did, all three found an interest somewhere else in the room.

Trevor squirmed in his chair, cleared his throat, then rubbed the palms of his hands on his thighs before reaching up to scratch the end of his nose. He cleared his throat again then, at a loss as what to do with himself.

Carrie was suddenly interested in a chipped fingernail.

Cole just sat calmly and waited for Tyler to speak. Finally, he decided to take the lead when it became apparent that his eldest brother was not going to offer any sort of explanation—at least not willingly. He casually stretched his long, lean legs out in front of him, glanced at his brother, inhaled deeply, and plunged in.

"Well, Ty, it seems you did more than just...negotiate...while you were in New York."

It was all Trevor could do to contain the snort that threatened to erupt from his throat. He immediately dropped his gaze to stare at the floor. *Christ—if he sees me laughing, he'll knock my head off!*

Carrie suddenly lost interest in her fingernail, covered her face with her hands, and pretended to rub her eyes. *I've got to hand it to Cole. He's not much for words, but when he speaks, he usually hits the nail on the head!* She cast a sidelong glance at Cole's face. He looked as innocent as a lamb.

Cole's twinkling eyes met his sister's, but the sight of her twitching lips was almost his undoing. A quick forced cough was the only thing that saved him from laughing outright.

Tyler looked askance until their reactions widened his eyes. "Oh, so you all think this is funny, do you? That man has already judged me to be the baby's father! He's closed the case and sentenced me to marry his daughter...or else!" His angry eyes swept the small group. "I can't see the humor at all! Emma is twenty-two years old. How the hell does he know if she's ever bedded anyone else?" His eyes scanned his sister's reddening face. "Excuse me for the crudeness, Carrie, but it's true."

Cole turned in the chair to face his sister. "Carrie, could you leave us alone? There are a few questions I'd like to ask Ty that are kind of personal, and I'm sure Trev needs to ask a few things, also."

Trevor waved his hand in the air. "Oh, you're doing just fine on your own, Cole!"

Carrie's mouth dropped open with surprise. "If you think the two of you are going to throw me out of here, well, just think again! I'm not a little girl anymore, and I can handle this conversation. Go ahead, Cole, ask away!" She settled herself firmly in the chair.

Cole shrugged his shoulders, looked at Trevor for confirmation to continue, and received an affirmative nod.

"Did you all forget that I'm in the room?"

Upon Tyler's stiff words, Cole leaned forward in the chair and addressed his older brother. "Well, Tyler," he scratched his ear. "It seems to me you should know whether this Emma had ever been with anyone before." He rolled his eyes heavenward for a brief second. "How can I put this delicately?"

Tyler could stand the dramatics no longer. "I don't know if she was a virgin or not! Is that what you're trying to ask?"

"Well...yeah, Ty." He sniffed before continuing. "How come you couldn't tell?"

"Because I was drunk!" Tyler roared and, with those words, Trevor was lost. He had controlled his laughter thus far, albeit with considerable difficulty, but knowing that his brother had rejoined the living with the rather sordid escapade in New York, the humor burst from his chest, and he slapped Cole on the back. Both his younger brother and sister were infected by his mirth and joined in Tyler's most embarrassing moment.

Tyler stared at the three of them as if they had all grown a second head. "Don't you understand how serious this situation is? Christ, I'm going to be forced to marry someone who claims I'm the father of her baby! That's not too goddamned funny!"

Trevor mopped his face and was the first of the siblings to regain composure. "Ty, whoever you decided to sleep with is your own business, but I'm sure I speak for all of us—she must be one heck of a lady. You've never been one to hop in bed with just anyone and, besides, she's Edward Sanders' daughter—the man who you've spoken so highly of. Surely his honesty and integrity must've rubbed off on his offspring at some point."

"But she's naming *me* as the father!" Tyler repeated what, in his opinion, was the most important point, and his appalled expression mirrored his stunned reaction to their response.

Trevor rose and moved to the liquor cabinet. He grabbed four glasses and a bottle of brandy. Returning to the group, he poured each one of them a stiff belt—each of them, except his sister. For her, he splashed only a small bit in the bottom of the glass. "Well," he smiled, "I think congratulations are in order."

Tyler's already incredulous expression now resembled astonishment. "What? Are you crazy, Trev? Don't you understand? I'm going to be forced to marry Emma Sanders and claim the baby as mine!"

Cole glanced at his older brother and, finally, sympathy set in. "What other recourse do you have? She'll be here in three days. I think, among the four of us, we can get a small wedding planned by then."

Tyler slammed his glass down onto the desk, and the other three cringed. "Why can't I make you see reason! The baby might not even be mine! For Christ's sake, she let Samuel Fontaine paw her the night of the reception and, worse yet, she enjoyed it! Why will none of you even consider that she might be a little tramp!"

"Ty—" Cole's voice was all together *too* reasonable.

"Fine!" Tyler pointed an angry finger at all of them. "You three plan the goddamn wedding and maybe, just maybe, I'll show up! And while you're at it, figure out a way to pick her up in Duluth because, in the morning, I'm heading for the logging camp." He turned to stomp from the room. Just before the door slammed, he flung one last caustic comment over his shoulder. "And I don't know when I'll be back!"

His siblings sat quietly as the last words echoed in their ears. They glanced warily at one another over the rims of their glasses until, finally, Carrie jumped from her chair. Sudden doubt marred her smooth features.

"Maybe he's right...maybe the baby isn't his. I've never seen him so angry."

Cole watched her pace before him and her words echoed in his head. "You could be right, Carrie, but I don't think so. Do you two remember the night he came home from New York? I sat and listened to him ramble on about the trip and was happy to see him finally showing some enthusiasm again, but there was something I couldn't quite put my finger on. Something that bothered me. Tyler was very evasive when we asked him about the women in the big city, and about Edward's daughter in particular. Now I know why. He was thinking of this Emma that night, and his guilt over what happened between the two of them was nipping at his heels."

"Well, she's got to have some redeeming qualities," Trevor interjected. "Tyler was still in pretty bad shape when he left for New York. He wouldn't be blindsided by just anyone. There had to be a strong attraction on his part for him to even consider—" Trevor's uneasy glance darted to his sister "—sleeping with someone. It's never been in his nature to have a quick roll in the hay, and then dump the woman. He had to feel something for her."

"You know what I think the problem is?" A grin tugged at the corners of Cole's lips. "I think our big brother is finally getting over Sara's death, and he's not dealing with it very well. Things are moving a little quicker than he would like, and the guilt is setting in. Hell, how would you feel, Trev, if you were a devout widower who was being forced to marry someone—even if that *someone* was a woman you were grudgingly attracted to?" He shook his head. "That has to be it—Tyler's finally found someone to love again, but he hasn't admitted his feelings yet—even to himself. He's pissed because he doesn't have time to explore other options, since there's a baby involved—and a quick wedding in the very near future."

"Tyler has always been a good judge of character. He would never take up with a woman who had loose morals, so I, for one, have to believe that he's the father of that baby." Carrie raised her chin a notch and crossed her arms. "Besides, it's out of our hands. The decision's been made already—she'll be here in three days, so we may as well get something planned. Are we agreed?"

Three sets of eyes met and, once again, Cole's response was as eloquent as ever.

"Hmmm...looks like I might have to oil up my shotgun for the wedding, though."

The three of them broke into near hysterical laughter again at their older brother's expense.

Chapter Twelve

Emma's contemplating eyes watched the miles slide by the train window on the last leg of her journey to Minnesota. Her father had stood his ground and informed Tyler of her pregnancy and, in no uncertain terms, told her to begin gathering what she needed, or he would pack for her. She did everything in her power to dissuade him from the deliberate course he set, but with no success. In the end, Emma had no choice but to prepare herself for the journey to her new home.

Saying goodbye to Edward at the train station and, not knowing when she would see him next, was dreadful. He held her close to hide his own tears and whispered how much he loved her.

"Em, please send me a telegram as soon as you arrive. I'll need to know you are settled in. And please, honey, don't be angry with me for making you go. I know in my heart it's the right thing to do."

She was sorry now that she had wasted the last three days wallowing in anger. She would miss the feel of his familiar chest against her cheek. "Papa, you know I love you." Her voice cracked with sadness. "It's just so hard to leave you. I'm sorry about being such a shrew these last few days. I think I'm still in shock at how my life has changed so quickly." She hugged him once more as the last call for boarding was announced.

She could still envision her father standing on the loading platform, his hat in his hands. The sadness in his eyes pierced her heart as effectively as a knife when the train pulled away from the station. Emma wiped at another tear.

Now, here she was, a few short hours away from seeing Tyler again. *Will he welcome me?* she wondered for the hundredth time.

Emma had spent the entire trip searching a soul that was filled with conflicting emotions, and her hand dropped to where their baby lay safely within her. *Will he ever find it in his heart to love me, or will he always think of me as the woman who forced him to marry against his will?* She could not imagine that he would accept her readily—not when the choice had been taken away from him.

Her gaze turned back to the sooty window, where the hills of Wisconsin rolled by, and realized how different the landscape was from her home state of New York. She had never been far from home and, now, could not help but be excited by all the new sights she was experiencing. Only when she thought of seeing Tyler again did that excitement turn to trepidation.

He sat motionless next to the blue water on a lake far north of his home, but thoughts of an unknown future raced through his mind. Soon he would be a married man again, and Tyler greeted the idea with more than a fair amount of anger. Reaching for a small round rock, he threw it forcefully across the water and watched the waves ripple outward from the point where the stone hit the surface.

He still found it hard to believe he was the father of Emma's baby. She had just seemed too experienced in bed for him to believe she was a virgin.

What sort of marriage can we build when it'll begin with a lie?

His first marriage was a wonderful union of two souls. He and Sara built that union on a solid foundation of love and trust and, still, they had a few rocky moments. His head dropped back against the tree behind him and his eyes slammed shut in frustration.

How can I have the same kind of relationship with Emma when we hardly know each other?

They came from two separate worlds and now they would be forced to raise a child together—a child that, for all intents and purposes, could be some other man's. And what about Janie and her feelings toward a new and unfamiliar mother? Was he just supposed to stand complacently by and watch their lives move in yet another direction he had not selected?

Tyler did not deny that Emma was a beautiful and intelligent woman—a woman any man would be proud to have by his side. What made him angry, however, was the fact that he would be forced into a marriage against his will.

A visit to Sara's gravesite the day before—a visit that should have provided some sort of comfort—succeeded only in agitating him like never before. He realized now that he went there to seek an answer to his dilemma, but the only revelation upon his departure was that, for the first time in two years, he walked away from her final resting place with less grief in his heart.

Why, Sara? Why do I suddenly miss you a little less?

His chest heaved in a sigh as he stood and stared down at the grave marker.

Is this marriage right for me, Sara? I still love you, but this situation has spiraled out of control. I made a mistake by giving into my needs that night, and now it seems I'm expected to make it right, even if the child isn't mine...

Tyler was so angry at his family's reaction to Emma's pregnancy that he had not even said goodbye to Janie before leaving her again. He still failed to see the humor of the situation—or the need to so haphazardly plan a private wedding for he and Emma, which is exactly what they were doing the morning he left. There was absolutely no concern on their part that he would be absent for her arrival. They simply continued to laugh and joke about seating arrangements as he stomped from the house.

Tyler tipped his face upward to bask in the warmth of the evening sun as he chewed thoughtfully on a sweet blade of grass. Counting out the days in his mind, he knew she would arrive tomorrow. *I can't believe she's coming here to be my wife. I thought I'd never see her again.*

The familiar sound of a loon singing to its mate met Tyler's ears, and he opened his eyes in search of the bird. His mother had called the bird's trill the song of love and life. A sudden image of the old Indian brave flashed through his brain. He had kept his promise and released the tiny wooden loon at a lake near the ranch. The Indian had called him the "keeper of the spirit."

Am I still the keeper, or is my job done? I hope the old man found his way home.

His thoughts shifted to the second figurine he presented to Emma. *Is she bringing her 'spirit' with her? Does the carved bird mean anything?*

His green eyes fluttered shut again. He closed his mind to the old man and Emma, content to simply listen to the forlorn calls of the loon and ignore the urge to return home.

Emma glanced at her reflection in a small, handheld mirror and sighed. She was pale and haggard looking from the long, overland trip to Minnesota, and she pinched her cheeks to regain some color before stepping off the train. Her stomach clenched at the thought of seeing Tyler again—and at the loathing that was sure to burn in his eyes.

Panic washed through her when not even one familiar face met her gaze. *Where is he? Surely he's here somewhere.*

Emma stood on the platform, her darting green eyes reflecting uncertainty as she inspected the nameless faces around her. Not one of them uttered her name and, a quarter of an hour later, she was left standing alone on the wooden planking.

"Miss, do you need assistance with your bags?" A young man stepped forward to gain her attention. "I can carry them inside for you, if you like."

"Yes, thank you. My party isn't here yet to meet me."

Emma followed the steward into the station and watched silently as he piled her trunks against the wall. Digging into her reticule, she pulled out a coin and pressed it into his hand before sitting on one of many hard benches that filled the large room. She sighed in relief. *This is so much better than being out in the sun.*

Emma ignored her parched throat and the insistent growling in her stomach and laid her weary head back against the wall as she waited for Tyler.

Two hours later, Emma still observed the comings and goings of travelers and station employees—and her fear grew by leaps and bounds. *I never should have let Papa get away with sending me here.*

The only response they received from Tyler was abrupt and told them nothing. *'I received your telegrams. Stop. Tyler Wilkins. Stop.'*

Emma blinked back the tears that threatened to burst forward at any moment. *I never should have come.*

The friendly clerk approached her for the third time to ask if she needed anything. She finally accepted a glass of water with trembling hands, hoping the cool liquid would help to control her flagging emotions. *Where is he? What should I do?*

The afternoon sun was now low in the western sky. Darkness would arrive soon. *What am I going to do?* she asked herself for the hundredth time. *I certainly can't spend the night here.*

She gathered her things and was about to rise from the wooden bench when two men and a woman burst through the doorway to the station. Their faces were etched with concern. They spied Emma, where she sat frightened and alone across the room, and a relieved smile broke across the unfamiliar young woman's features as she approached.

"Hello. Are you by any chance Emma Sanders?"

Emma swallowed back the threatening tears of relief. "Yes! Yes, I am!"

The other woman turned to see if her two male companions had followed, then glanced at Emma again.

"I'm *so* sorry we're late! I'm Caroline Wilkins, Tyler's sister." She waved in the direction of the two men behind her. "And these two scoundrels are my brothers. This is Trevor," she gestured in his direction, "and this is Cole."

Emma would have known Trevor Wilkins anywhere. He bore a striking resemblance to his brother—the man who was *supposed* to be standing before her. Both men possessed the same dark, swarthy good looks and bright green eyes. Caroline and Cole Wilkins carried some of the same features, but were lighter in hair color and possessed hazel-colored eyes. Tyler's brothers tipped their cowboy hats in a gallant show of politeness, and grins curved both sets of lips as their sister continued.

"The carriage threw a wheel on our way here, and there wasn't a way to get a message to you. We're so sorry that you had to wait and wonder if anyone was going to pick you up. I can't imagine what the last two hours have been like for you!" Her sincerity glowed in her round, hazel eyes.

Relief again washed over Emma's face and a hesitant smile lit her gaze. "I have to admit I was beginning to wonder what I should do. It was getting late, and I thought I might have to find a room for the night," she murmured as her gaze strayed to the station door.

Carrie immediately noticed the movement and shifted uncomfortably. *I wonder how she's going to take the news that he's not here.* She cleared her throat and charged on. "You're right, it is getting late, so we've decided to take rooms here in Duluth for the evening. You've had an awfully long day and probably haven't had dinner, have you?" A nervous giggle bubbled in her throat. "After the day we've had, I don't relish the idea of bouncing around in a carriage for another five hours, and I can imagine how *you* must feel. We live north of Duluth and, without the light of the moon tonight, it would be best to wait."

Silence descended on the group when Carrie finished her rambling speech. Finally, Emma spoke in a quiet voice.

"Is Tyler waiting outside?" She watched as three pairs of eyes met and held in an uneasy glance. Emma swallowed convulsively. *Something is going on and I don't think I want to know what it is.*

Trevor threw her another disarming grin as he picked up one of her bags. "There was a problem at one of the logging camps and Tyler's expertise was needed—so he sent the three of us in his stead." He closed one eye in a devilish wink. "Besides, you'll have a lot more fun with us. Tyler can be an old stick in the mud sometimes."

Emma's heart sank. *He's not here, and it's not because of any problem at the logging camp. He just doesn't want to see me.* She forced a wan smile to curve her lips.

Cole read the hurt in her eyes. *Tyler, you're a son of a bitch for not coming to meet her.*

Emma allowed herself to be led outside to the waiting carriage, and Carrie chuckled quietly to herself as Trevor and Cole tripped over each other in their attempts to help their future sister-in-law into the back seat.

"Watch your step, now! Here—sit right here." Trevor scrambled to take Emma's arm and patted the cushioned bench before her. She sat, and her wide eyed expression showed that she was a little flabbergasted by all the attention.

"I don't think you'll be comfortable there, Emma. Why don't you sit on this side," Cole insisted.

"I'm fine—"

Before the young woman had a chance to object further, Cole grabbed her elbow and whisked her to the opposite bench. "This way, you can look forward and have a better view of the town." He quickly settled her, ignoring his brother's hidden jab to his ribs.

Emma busied herself with adjusting her skewed bonnet, which now hung low over one eye from the forced flight across the length of the carriage. She missed the exchange between the Wilkins' men as Cole stepped to the ground and met his brother's offended gaze.

"She was fine where she was!" Trevor muttered across the expanse of the buggy.

"Just grab her bags—she would've got sick facing backwards. Use your head!" Cole jumped into the front seat and gripped the reins before his brother had a chance to get a hold on them.

Carrie was forgotten as her dubious gaze watched the men go in two different directions. She climbed into the carriage of her own accord, trying to hide the tiny smile that tugged at her lips. *I wonder what Tyler would think if he could see these two making such asses out of themselves.*

Carrie glanced at the woman across from her. She liked Emma already. The fact that she blushed with embarrassment at all the attention showed she was no prima donna, who expected to be waited on hand and foot—even in her present condition. Carrie had also noticed the orphaned look on Emma's face when she realized that Tyler was not a part of their group. *Poor thing,* Carrie mused. *Here she is, thrust into the midst of total strangers without so much as an ounce of support from Tyler.*

Trevor kept up a constant stream of conversation on the way to the inn, and his brother and sister added their own comments in an effort to lessen the pain of Tyler's absence. The laughter and jokes were always at their older sibling's expense, however, and, difficult as it was, Emma relaxed. These three virtual strangers already treated her like family—and she could only hope that Tyler would feel the same. A small tremble of apprehension accompanied the wish.

The group reached the hostelry a short time later. They entered the lobby through the front doors, and Carrie's hand held Cole back as Trevor and Emma proceeded to the check-in desk.

"Let's eat immediately. I'm a little worried about Emma. Did you notice how pale and quiet she is?"

"It's hard to miss," Cole replied as his gaze strayed to the now noticeable slump of Emma's shoulders, where she stood beside Trevor across the room. "That damned Tyler—"

"Well, we'll deal with him tomorrow. That poor woman has been on a train for three days and, right now, I just want to feed her and get her up to her room." Her words were silenced when Trevor turned to hail them to his side.

"My stomach is growling. How about the rest of you? Want to eat, and then call it a night?"

Emma stood quietly, but, inside, she fought a fierce battle to control the wave of dizziness that suddenly threatened to overcome her.

Carrie took in the ashen color of the other woman's complexion and the perspiration that beaded her brow, and grasped her arm. "Come, Emma. We'll be quick about supper and get you to your room."

Sitting in the unadorned, yet immaculate dining room, the small group conversed quietly. The Wilkins family let Emma's pregnancy go unmentioned for the time being and concentrated on telling her about the ranch. She, in turn, told them about her life in New York, and Trevor, Cole, and Carrie were all struck by her unassuming demeanor and obvious intelligence.

Cole was sure her face lit up every time she smiled. Trevor had already fallen in love with her dimpled cheeks. Carrie was simply pleased that her future sister-in-law looked physically better than she did an hour ago.

Emma listened to the flowing conversation around her and, finally, curiosity got the best of her when the name Janie came up once again.

"Excuse me, but I have to ask you a question. You're all talking as if I know this woman, Janie, but I don't. Does she live at the ranch?"

Emma held her breath. *Please don't let this woman be a special friend of Tyler's.*

The other three people at the table sat with fixed expressions of stunned disbelief on their faces. Apparently, Tyler had told her nothing about his personal life. Emma had no idea that he was once married or that he had a daughter. Trevor leaned forward, took a deep breath, and prepared to break the news.

"I can't believe Tyler didn't tell you about Janie."

Emma sat motionless and waited for the bad news. *Tyler has someone else in his life. He won't want me—and I can't blame him. I've simply walked into his world without being asked. How he must hate me!*

"Emma," Trevor's gentle voice brought her out of her self-destructive reverie, "Janie is Tyler's seven-year-old daughter."

Emma's face paled even further, to a color that resembled chalk, and Carrie reached out to squeeze her hand.

"His daughter?" she whispered. "He never said anything..."

Emma's voice trailed off, then suddenly she stared at Trevor, sure she had not heard him right. "Tyler has a daughter?" She shook her head, trying to ward of the confusion that threatened to engulf her. "I know this is going to sound foolish, but does he have a wife somewhere?"

She asked the question so softly that Cole had to lean forward to hear the words. He placed his hand on Emma's and answered for his brother.

"Tyler's wife, Sara, was killed in an accident two years ago. He never talks about it, so that's probably why he didn't mention it to you. Janie is the only child resulting from that union. Please, don't be angry with him for keeping something so personal from you."

Emma stared blankly into his beseeching eyes as the information sank in. *Tyler was married at one time, and his wife was killed. That accounts for the sad look I saw in his eyes from time to time. He also has a small child...*

The information was too much for her to take in after the last three stress-filled days. Exhaustion, along with Cole's words, helped to initiate a flow of tears that she feared would never stop. She bolted from her chair.

"Excuse me—I'll be ready to leave in the morning whenever you are." She fled the dining room and tore up the stairs to her room without another word.

Trevor, Cole, and Carrie stared at one another with a mixture of astonishment and guilt. Emma's sudden tears had caught them off guard, and they could not help but wonder what tomorrow would bring.

Emma lay in the unfamiliar bed, the covers pulled up tight around her neck. Sleep though, eluded her. "How could he not tell me that he's a widower and has a daughter?" she asked the quiet room. Her eyes widened in sudden horror. *And what on earth does his family think of me, traveling halfway across the United States, pregnant with their brother's child, and not knowing a single thing about his personal life?*

What was she going to do if neither Tyler nor his daughter accepted her? The three of them would be thrust into a family relationship, because of one fleeting moment of passion—but what if they did not want it? What if they did not want *her?*

Tyler had already proven his unwillingness to have her in his life with his refusal to meet her in Duluth. *I wasn't fooled for a moment with Trevor's lame excuse. He told me more than once in New York how capable his brothers were.*

Emma rolled onto her side and thoughts of Tyler flitted through her mind. She pictured his face; the drawn, sallow features at the times when he looked so sad. *He's still grieving for Sara.*

What was she going to have to contend with in the next few months? *If he still loves her, is there even a chance that he can love me?* Could the feelings she carried for him sustain her through this mess?

That old Indian man called Tyler the "keeper of the spirit." Does that mean he'll keep Sara with him always and never give the two of us a chance?

The questions kept coming late into the night and, as they raced through her mind, she cradled her stomach where their child lay. She would try her hardest to make this work, because of the baby. It deserved no less. She would love Tyler until he could fight it no longer, and then hopefully he would learn to love her back. She had so much to give him if only he could find it in his heart to accept it.

Settling the situation in her mind as best she could, Emma finally succumbed to exhaustion.

Trevor and Cole lounged in their room across the hall and discussed the incredible day. Emma was the main topic of conversation.

Cole sipped at the bottle of whiskey he shared with his brother, and thoughts of Tyler's impending marriage were foremost in his mind.

"I'll tell you what, Trev. I think she's one heck of a lady. If Tyler can't see it, then we're just going to have to step in."

Trevor shook his head slowly. "You know, Cole, you surprise the hell out of me sometimes. I've heard you talk more tonight than I have in the last month. Emma must've made one hell of an impression on you. You've been rattling on for over an hour now."

Cole assumed his favorite position—long legs stretched out before him and a lazy look in his hazel eyes.

"I watched her face, Trev. She's hurting, because of Tyler's pigheadedness. There's no damn reason for him not to have come to Duluth. He's the one who got her in this fix and, no matter what the situation, he should have his ass here." He took another swig from the bottle. "She loves him, you know."

"Oh, how in the hell can you tell that? They barely know each other, and *we* barely know her! They had some fun in New York and now they find themselves forced into a shotgun wedding, because there's nothing else to be done. Don't get me wrong. I think she's great and I think she's perfect for Tyler. But love? How do you figure that?" He eyed the whiskey bottle warily. "Are you going to drink that whole thing or are you planning on sharing it soon?"

Cole handed him the liquor and sat back with a smug grin. The youngest Wilkins brother had an uncanny knack for reading people's body language and the emotions that shown so blatantly on their faces; every expression on Emma's face tonight literally shouted out her feelings for Tyler. He had never been able to figure out though, why other people could not see what he did.

"Think about it, Trev. Have you ever known Tyler to casually hop in bed with someone? Something happened to him in the space of that one short month in

New York—and that *something* is called Miss Emma Sanders. Don't get me wrong. I'm happy for him, but I hope he doesn't screw it up. There's a lot of inner beauty that goes along with that little lady, and maybe she can end the self-imposed hell he's going through." A sudden smile curved his lips. "Carrie's already taken charge, you notice? Tyler doesn't have a gnat's chance in hell against her. If he doesn't do right by the lady from New York, I think our little sister will take his head right off his shoulders."

The two sat quietly for a while, passing the bottle between them, then suddenly a devilish look appeared in Trevor's eyes and Cole knew something was coming.

"Christ, she's beautiful, eh, Cole?" Trevor's words had a slightly garbled sound to them.

Cole's only response was a crooked grin, and he watched his brother take another pull from the bottle before Trevor pointed the glass container in his direction.

"I'll tell you what, brother of mine. It's no wonder Tyler fell for her charms. With a body like that, any guy would. Did you notice her figure?"

Cole shook his head, then waited a moment for the room to quit spinning. "How in the hell do you *not* notice? No wonder Tyler jumped in bed with her. Hell, I'm ready to jump in bed with her!"

Trevor grabbed the pillow on the bed and threw it at his brother's head. Cole ducked, causing him to slide from the chair and onto the floor. "I can't believe that just came out of your mouth! Besides, if anyone is going to be doing any jumping, it's gonna be me!"

The two brothers stared at each other in surprise at the sudden turn in the conversation, then they both burst into loud guffaws. Here they sat—trying to figure a way to get Tyler to acknowledge that he wanted a life with Emma and, at the same time, they discussed the option of bedding her.

Cole crawled across the floor to the fireplace, grabbed the mantle to pull himself up, then allowed himself a long and very vocal stretch before he fell across his own bed. He pulled the hat down low over his eyes with a soft chuckle.

"You know what, Cole?" Trevor mumbled from his side of the room. "I think you might be right about Emma. What woman in her right mind would travel halfway across the country to marry someone if she didn't care for him in some manner?"

He reached over the side of the bed and rummaged until his hand came in contact with the near-empty whiskey bottle. Bringing it to his lips, he finished off the small amount left inside and tossed it back onto the floor. A blurry picture of Emma entered Trevor's mind, and a slow, drunken smile curved his lips.

"Hey, Cole. If Tyler heard us talking about Emma like we were earlier, he'd knock both our fat asses on the floor." He received no response. "Cole? You awake over there?"

His answer came in the form of a loud, elongated snore from across the room.

Chapter Thirteen

The wagon ride to the ranch the following morning took Emma through some of the most beautiful country she had ever seen. The warm and sunny September day served only to excite her more, and the three Wilkins' practically burst with pride in their homeland.

The day proved to have a rather rocky start, however. Emma was embarrassed by her outburst the night before, and the Wilkins men were just as unnerved when they remembered their conversation in the hotel room. The tensions eased though, and a newfound camaraderie was established, which quickly grew into a cherished bond when Trevor, Cole, and Carrie regaled Emma with tales from their childhood.

As they bumped along the well worn dirt trail, Emma reflected on how different her childhood was compared to her three companions. Whereas she crawled into bed early each night in an elegant brick house, leaving her father to burn the midnight oil as he slaved over never-ending bookwork, these three most likely laughed and told jokes around the dining room table until the wee hours, sharing precious childhood secrets before retiring to their own rooms. Emma had never considered, until now, that being an only child had its downfalls. As she listened to the three Wilkins' siblings, however, she had her first inkling of what life could have been like with a brother or sister.

Emma continually pointed out the maple and birch trees, which gradually changed to the bright shades of autumn. She had never before seen anything quite like it—even in the state of New York—and her excitement grew by leaps and bounds. She fooled no one, however. The three Wilkins' knew that her enthusiasm had little to do with the scenery and *everything* to do with the fact that she would soon see Tyler again.

Emma's good humor infected the rest of her party. Green eyes sparkled as her pink cheeks dimpled in continuous smiles, and the two Wilkins men were completely enamored.

Carrie just shook her head. *They're so obvious,* she thought. *Good—she's going to need a few champions, especially if Tyler decides to keep hold of his animosity toward her.*

The carriage rounded a bend, and Emma's heart skipped a beat when Cole stopped the carriage on the top of a large hill.

"There it is, Emma," he murmured.

Her new home was nestled among some of the hugest pine trees Emma had ever seen. The sprawling log structure spread out in the form of an elongated "T", and a barn and numerous outbuildings filled in the landscape behind it. Emma had not known what to expect, and her new home far outweighed even her wildest dreams. The sheer beauty of the homestead took her breath away.

Her wide, worried eyes frantically searched for a sign of Tyler as the carriage bumped slowly down the hill, and her heart sent a silent message to wherever he was. *Give me a chance. It can work if you will only try!*

They entered the ranch proper through an immense log gate, and Emma's eyes still sought him. When the carriage drew to a halt in front of a massive porch, however, she was forced to hide her disappointment. He was not there to greet her. She clung to the slim hope that there really was a problem at the logging camp that demanded his attention—a problem that was more important than his future wife's arrival.

Emma's attention was drawn to an old Negro woman, who waddled out onto the front portico and wiped her hands on her gingham apron before sending a smile and a wave to the foursome.

"'Bout' time you be gittin' back! I was worryin' mysef sick there be no souls sittin' 'round my table tonight!" She lumbered down the steps one at a time, never ceasing her banter. "Cole! Trevor! You help them ladies offen that wagon! What's the matter with you boys, leavin' ladies to sit in the sun! Hop to it now. Yessiree!"

Both men leapt to the ground at her command. Trevor smiled as he lifted Emma down, and then bent to whisper conspiratorially in her ear. "I told you about Mamie, didn't I? Remember what I said. She's got a heart of gold and a lot of hot air to go with it!"

Emma allowed herself a muffled giggle as Trevor led her to the foot of the steps. Emma realized quickly that there was nothing wrong with the old black woman's hearing when a raucous laugh escaped Mamie's throat. She took a swing at the young man. "Pay no mind to that big mouth, young lady! Go on, Trevor, git! And makes sure you got a armful of Miss Em's belongins. Cole, you get offen your arse and help him!"

Cole and Trevor exchanged wide grins as Mamie shot out orders, and then the two men quickly unloaded Emma's bags from the back of the carriage. Tipping their hats to their future sister-in-law, they walked up the wooden sidewalk and into the house.

"Why, Carrie, this here lady be no bigger than a mite!" Mamie's glance swept Emma from head to toe as she rested her hands on her own ample hips. "Yessiree! We gonna take care of that! You come in the big house now, lil' lady, and we'll be gittin' you somethin' to eat and drink. I suppose those two lunkheads didn't even give you breakfast afore leavin' town, did they?"

Emma could not help but laugh at the other woman's colorful language as she ascended the stairs to the porch. "Miss Mamie, I have heard a lot about you. It's a pleasure to finally meet you in person. And yes, I was allowed to eat something before we left Duluth." She continued with a small smile. "Please, don't be too hard on Cole and Trevor. They've treated me wonderfully, and so has Carrie."

"Well, it be a good blessin' then, that they took to my promptin' when I told them two boneheads to be good to our new Miss Em! Figured Carrie be along to smack 'em upside the head if'n they go by the wayside." She folded Emma into her soft bosom and gave her a hearty squeeze. "Welcome, honey, to the Northern Pine Ranch. Now, let's be gettin' you inside and outta this sun so you can be restin' up after your long journey! Yessiree, it be a fine day in the makin'."

Mamie led her into the house then, and Emma offered up a little prayer of thanks that Tyler's family had accepted her so readily.

I only hope that Tyler will feel the same...

Tyler sat astride his black stallion, far atop a hill opposite the one the carriage traveled. The cowboy hat rode low on his forehead, hiding a heavy scowl as he watched the buggy pass through the gates that led to the ranch.

Emma was there, and he met the realization with mixed emotions.

Tyler spent four days at the logging camp, purposely avoiding her arrival. He had planned to make her sit around for an entire day and night, wondering if he would ever appear. Instead, without even knowing it, she had pulled one over on him. He was just riding in when he caught sight of the carriage coming over the hill. He reined Storm to a halt and eyed the returning group warily. *Dammit! They must've spent the night in Duluth!*

He watched through stony eyes as Mamie came out of the house, then his jaw hardened to match his gaze when Trevor effortlessly lifted Emma from the carriage and helped her up the front steps. He knew he was doomed when the old, black woman took Emma into her arms in a welcoming hug. *Shit! Mamie'll never get off my back now that she's decided this mess is going to work.*

His scowl deepened as he remembered the conversation he had with Mamie the morning he left for the camp. The old woman had already decided that 'Miss Em' was a wonderful person. She had to be, if she had fallen in love with him. He had lost his patience while informing her that love had nothing to do with it...

"Aw, go on, Tyla. Love gots everythin' to do with it! Why would a nice, upstandin' lady like Miss Em be takin' a chance and gitten hersef with chile if'n she didn't love you?"

"Mamie," he hissed through clenched teeth, "you have no idea if she's nice or not. And you certainly don't know if she's upstanding." Tyler paced before her with clenched fists. "I can't understand why you all refuse to see that there's a very good possibility the child isn't even mine. You don't even know her!"

"Don't have to," Mamie sniffed. "If'n you be with her, then she be nice. Tyla, I have faith in you, boy. No ways you be pickin' a piece o' fluff to be lovin' with. Yessiree! That be what I think. Now git! I gots a weddin' to get ready for."

The conversation had gone on for a good fifteen minutes, and Mamie would not budge. Tyler raised his hands, tempted to wrap them around her beefy neck. Her comment about the wedding though, was the final straw that snapped his patience.

"That's it! You all can think whatever you like, and you all can *plan* whatever you like! It doesn't seem to matter how I feel anyway. I'll be back when I'm damn good and ready!" He stormed out the back door and slammed it behind him.

Mamie smiled to herself. "Son, you be good and ready afor you know it. Yessiree..."

Now, he sat high on the bluff and watched until the entire group entered the house. "Why in the hell do *I* feel like the outsider!" he railed.

Tyler turned the big stallion away from the house with a jerk. *I'll be damned if I'll go in now. Let her wait until tonight and wonder where I am.*

Kicking Storm into a gallop, he headed north again.

Emma awoke with a long, luxurious stretch, and a glance at the clock on the mantel widened her eyes. It was late afternoon! Her cheeks flushed with immediate embarrassment. *How in the world could I have slept so long!*

She knew the answer. After Mamie fussed over her and fed her a late lunch, Emma was barely able to keep her eyes open. Carrie insisted that she rest, and rest she had. She sat on the edge of the bed with a groan, then, feeling a sudden burst of energy course through her veins, got up to unpack her belongings before going downstairs to join the rest of the family.

Emma surveyed her surroundings and, once again, was struck by the elegance of the Wilkins' home. The spacious log dwelling was divided into four separate wings, each housing a different necessity needed by the family. One of the wings contained the living room, library, and office, Carrie had told her; the second housed the kitchen and dining room and the last two parts of the "T" shaped structure housed the six bedrooms. The room she now stood in was as charming as anything she would find in New York, done up in colors of rose and green.

Her view faced west, as did Tyler's. Carrie had also explained that the master suite adjoined hers via a small hallway, with the water closet encompassing half of the area between the two rooms. At one time, the room she now occupied was used as a nursery. Janie had her own room now though, just down the hall, and the family remodeled this one as a spare room for visiting guests. Now it was hers, to do with as she liked.

I wonder if Carrie meant just for the present time, until the wedding, or for the duration of my marriage? Will I even get the chance to share Tyler's room? And what will his daughter think?

Janie. Tyler's daughter. Emma spied her for only a fleeting moment when they first entered the house. The little girl peeked at them from around a corner in the large foyer, then disappeared. Carrie and Mamie quickly assured Emma that everything would be fine. It would just take time for the child to become accustomed to the new arrangement.

She sighed now, as she put away her belongings in the various drawers, trying to make some sense of her hasty packing only a few short days ago. She opened one of the bags, then gently withdrew the wrapped wooden loon. She removed the tissue with careful hands, and could not help but wonder where Tyler was as she set the figurine on the chest of drawers. *Will he get 'accustomed' to the new arrangement, too?*

Her stomach jumped at the thought. Last night, she had vowed to make this marriage work, but suddenly she was not so sure she could make it happen. Emma brought her fingers to her temples and rubbed away a sudden ache.

He's deliberately avoiding me. Is it to make a point; to prove that he's not the least bit concerned that I'm here? Or does he really have some sort of pressing business?

Emma stifled a scream born of frustration.

She paused in her pacing to study the connecting door that led to his room. She chewed on her bottom lip for a moment in indecision, then moved to slowly turn the knob. Emma felt like a thief in the night as she passed through the small hallway and an alcove that hid a claw foot bathtub, then paused before the open doorway that led to the master suite.

His room took her breath away. It was spacious and airy and definitely masculine in design. An immense fireplace dominated the west wall, with windows flanking each side. A door stood to the left of one of the windows, and a quick peek revealed that it led to a small overhang on the exterior of the house. The oak furniture was polished to such a sheen that Emma could see her reflection in it. A huge four-poster bed sat against the north wall, with a beautiful hand-quilted bedspread covering the feather-tick mattress. Two massive overstuffed chairs sat in front of the fireplace atop an exquisitely braided rug. The room was cozy, and she could not help but feel that it welcomed her.

Emma was drawn to the bed, and her green eyes scanned the comfortable surface. *Will I ever share it with Tyler?* she wondered.

Lost in thought, she reached out to touch one of the tall posts, but pulled her hand back as if she had touched fire when a cold voice rumbled behind her.

"Find anything that interests you?" Tyler sauntered into the room, dropped a saddlebag on the floor, and never took his eyes from her face.

"Tyler!" Further words refused to come; the sight of him had rendered her speechless.

The worn cowboy hat, boots and cotton shirt and pants somehow made him even more ruggedly handsome than she remembered. His face was tanned to a copper color, which helped to define the dark lashes that shuttered his eyes, and his unshaven face gave him an almost roguish appearance. Emma's heart knocked in her chest, and her love for him soared through her veins.

He watched her from across the room with a totally nonchalant expression. Inside though, he struggled fiercely to control the emotions that raced through his body.

God, she's so beautiful!

The reason why she stood before him though, hit him squarely in the chest, and he forced all thoughts from his mind and all feeling from his heart. He would not make this easy for her.

Tyler ambled toward one of the overstuffed chairs in front of the fireplace, casually tossing his hat onto the bed as he passed it. He seated himself and, once again, his eyes never left her face—a face that held a myriad of emotions. *I will not give in!*

"So, how's our little mother feeling after her long journey? Sorry I wasn't here to greet you." He shrugged his broad shoulders. "I didn't think you would mind, since you're only here looking for a name for the baby."

Emma's heart lurched. She stood next to the bed, blinked back the threatening tears, and formed the next words in her mind before speaking them aloud.

"I want you to know I don't blame you for anything. I'm just as responsible for what happened as you are. I'm sorry if you don't want me here, but the decision was beyond my control. When my father found out about the...baby, he insisted on this marriage."

Tyler glared at her through suspicious eyes and said nothing. *Let her squirm.*

Emma took another deep breath, but her words came out in barely a whisper. "I had planned to raise the baby alone, Tyler, and not involve you. My father, however, felt differently. He didn't want it to be raised as a bastard and insisted I come to you. I can see now that it was a mistake. I thought maybe we could make this work, for the baby's sake, but I guess I was only fooling myself. If you'd like, after the wedding—and there will be a wedding, because my father was right that the child deserves a name—I'll leave."

Emma's heart sank to her toes as she spoke the words. Leaving was the last thing she wanted to do. *But how can I stay when he's making it so obvious that he'll never come to terms with being the baby's father? He doesn't want me—or this child—in his life.*

Tyler continued to watch her and, finally, he could hold his tongue no longer. "I want to know just one thing, Emma. Am I really the father, or are you just looking for a place to hide out when your pregnancy begins to show?"

She opened her mouth to respond, but his hand came up to silence her.

"I know it's possible that I could have sired the child, but I want you to be honest with me. Have you been with anyone else?"

His words slammed into her chest, and her eyes instantly glittered with anger. "How dare you even ask me that? Is that what you think, that I've been with other men and don't even know who the father is?" Emma's rage manifested itself in the tears that flowed freely down her cheeks. "A moment ago, I mentioned the word bastard in conjunction with the baby. Well, I was wrong! The only *bastard* in this room is you! You can think anything you like, Tyler! If you want to take the chance that this child isn't yours and throw us out, then so be it!"

Blinded by tears, Emma raced from the room and slammed the adjoining door behind her with as much force as she could muster. Tyler jumped up, ready to follow her, ready to continue the argument, but paused just short of the entrance to the adjoining suite. He tilted his aching head forward and rubbed his stubbled face with both hands. *What the hell was that all about?*

And then he knew. It was an act. It was *all* an act. His initial reaction to the sight of her standing in his room was that of immense joy—joy that lasted only a split second until her condition reared its ugly head and made him doubt her honesty. *Dammit, I won't be duped into claiming a child that's not mine!*

Tyler glared at the closed door before him, and his jaw hardened with determination. He had every right to go in there and demand the truth—the truth that he was *not* the father of her baby.

The decision was made. He shouldered his way through the connecting hallway and burst through the entrance to her suite. Emma spun when the door to her bedroom banged against the dresser.

"Get out of here!" she choked through the tears that still clogged her throat.

"Funny," he gritted through clenched teeth, "I was going to tell you the same thing!"

Emma's face paled to a sickly pallor and she stumbled back with the impact of his words. Tyler immediately regretted the caustic remark, but refused to allow the hesitancy to show on his face.

She sank into a nearby chair, wiped the tears from her face, and stared at him with sad, questioning eyes. She shook her head slowly. "What happened to you? You're not the same man I met in New York."

"What the hell am I supposed to think, Emma?" He plopped down on the bed opposite her. "I receive a telegram, out of the blue, that states you're pregnant with my child, and that in three day's time, you'll arrive for the wedding. Too many questions were left unanswered. Then you arrive on my doorstep—"

"You weren't even here to see me arrive!" As tired as she was, Emma could not resist tossing the remark back at him.

"What? Did you expect me to be waiting on bended knee?" His eyes glittered dangerously again. "Did you think I would welcome you with open arms?" He forced himself to lower his voice again and ran a hand through his dark hair in utter helplessness. "Tell me, Emma...tell me the truth."

The tears swam in her green eyes. "I already did!" She moved her gaze to a spot over his head and waited for him to leave the room.

He did not budge—and his expression became even more resolute.

Emma dropped her chin, inhaled deeply, and met his gaze. "Neither of us are on trial here, Tyler. This baby deserves to have two parents, who will love and cherish it, and that's the bottom line." The tears streamed down her face again. "You have to believe me when I say you are the father."

Should I tell him that I love him? No—I won't give him that weapon to use against me.

Doubt appeared as a shadow in his eyes—doubt that Emma interpreted as being directed at her. She rose and walked to the window, her stiff back turned to him.

"You need to make a decision, Tyler. I need to know if I should make plans to return to New York."

A moment later, the door clicked shut behind him.

* * *

Voices filtered out from the family room as Emma descended the steps. *Congratulations, Miss Sanders, for finding the nerve to leave your room. You are about to discover your future...*

Gathering all the reserve she could summon, Emma straightened her back and entered the room to find the entire family waiting patiently for her to join them—everyone including a clean-shaven Tyler. She paused in the doorway, unsure of the mood, and was saved when Carrie rose to greet her. Trevor and Cole followed suit. Tyler remained seated and calmly sipped a drink, his green eyes gauging her presence.

"Good evening, Emma," Carrie said. "I have to say, you look much more rested this evening. Come, sit down for a few minutes before we go in for dinner."

Emma felt Tyler's suspicious stare bore into her and swallowed the knot of nervousness that lodged in her throat. "I'm sorry if I kept you all waiting. I fear I slept longer than planned and the afternoon got away from me." *I wonder if he told them of our argument?*

Trevor hurried to show her to the sofa, his ever-present good nature shining through. "Don't fret for a minute, Emma! Tyler was just filling us in on his trip to the logging camp, and we didn't even notice the time."

After seating her, he returned to his chair and hoped like hell that someone would follow his lead and start talking. The tension in the room was thick enough to cut with a knife as the three younger Wilkins' waited to see what would happen next.

Carrie sent an encouraging smile in Emma's direction and decided to plunge in head first—anything to stave off the awful silence.

"Ah...Emma, a reverend from town will travel out here tomorrow to perform the ceremony. We know it must seem like you're in a whirlwind, but we all thought it best to be done with the marriage before your...condition begins to show."

It was the first time her pregnancy had been acknowledged aloud. Emma paled at the thought, but her heart sang loudly. *He's going to go through with it!*

She waited for Tyler to say something. When it became obvious that he would not, her tentative gaze met his cool one. "Does that meet with your approval, Tyler?" She searched his eyes for even a small sign of happiness. *Please, say something!*

He set his glass aside and never took his dark green eyes from hers. The others held their breath and awaited his words. "Well, Emma, it doesn't seem like either of us has much of a choice, now does it? If this is the course we're forced to take, then we may as well be finished with it as soon as possible." His answer sounded precise and practiced to everyone in the room.

Only Cole observed the grimace Emma tried so valiantly to hide, and his heart went out to not only her, but to his brother as well—*even if he is acting so asinine.* The two of them would have to come to terms with the situation in their own good time and, though none of them knew how long it would take, he could only hope for the best. He glanced at Carrie and tipped his head toward the dining room. She took his cue and stood.

"Maybe we should go in and eat. Mamie will have our hides soon if we don't do justice to the meal she's been preparing all day."

Trevor stood and offered his arm to Emma. *To hell with Tyler. If he doesn't have enough sense to treat her like a lady, then I'll show her that at least one of the Wilkins men has manners.*

Cole swung his gaze to his older brother. The murderous expression on Tyler's face showed that he was none too pleased. *Good, maybe this little show of jealousy on Tyler's part is a sign of better days to come.*

Tyler's daughter was not present at the dinner table, and Emma used the opportunity to speak to Tyler. Maybe this was one avenue of communication that would work between them.

"Is there a reason Janie isn't dining with us? I had hoped to get to know her this evening."

Tyler's eyes jumped to her at the mention of his daughter, and then he realized that Emma was not aware of Janie's aversion to speech. *It must be the only thing they haven't told her. Hell, according to Cole, they had no problem with telling her about Sara's accident.*

"Janie has decided not to come down tonight. She had a rather busy day, and I've already tucked her in. I'm sure you'll have plenty of time to get to know her later on."

Emma's eyes widened with his answer. *Does that mean he's not going to make me leave after the wedding?* She chanced a small, happy smile—in his direction. *Maybe there's a chance of making this marriage work after all.*

The entire Wilkins family, barring Tyler, showed themselves to be an entertaining lot. They laughed and teased one another throughout the meal, and Emma was drawn into the fun as the evening progressed. When the last bite of Mamie's homemade apple pie had been consumed, the group rose from the table.

"Emma, come sit in the family room for awhile," Carrie invited.

"I'm sorry to decline, Carrie, but I think the last few days have caught up with me again. I really need to sleep." *Not to mention that this tension between Tyler and me is grating on my nerves.* "Thank you all for the wonderful evening, but I think I'll retire immediately. I'll see you all in the morning."

She turned to leave, but was halted by his voice and his unexpected words.

"I'll show you upstairs, Emma." Tyler rose and joined her in the doorway. He stood stiffly beside her as Emma bid the others goodnight once more, then he followed his soon-to-be wife from the dining room.

Neither spoke until they arrived at her bedroom door. Emma was at a loss for words, so she simply offered a small nod of the head, hoping he would at least respond in kind. Tyler's gaze dropped to the floor and he took a deep breath, cleared his throat, then raised his chin again.

"There's something you should know about Janie." His eyes met hers and she read the hesitancy in his gaze. At that moment, Tyler seemed more like the man she met in New York—the man she fell in love with. "Cole told me he explained to you about...the accident two years ago. When it happened...after it happened, Janie changed. You won't be able to visit with her like you would another child. She hasn't spoken a word since Sara's death—not to me, not to anyone in this family. She's the most important thing in this world to me, Emma, and I won't allow her to be hurt by my actions of a few months ago. She's had enough pain in her short life without us adding more."

Emma stood quietly, watching the play of emotions on his tanned face. She had seen the same pain on Cole's face earlier, when he told her about Sara's death. It was obvious that the accident had affected them all, and that Janie was not the only one in this household who had suffered from the loss.

"I was rude to you this afternoon and, for that, I'm sorry," Tyler continued. "I want you to understand something, though. I still don't know if I should believe you when you say that I fathered your baby—for reasons of my own. But it seems fate has stepped into my life again and decreed another change of course. I will marry you, Emma, because there seems no way out for me. But it can only be a marriage of convenience. Right now, Janie needs me and nothing will come between me and my daughter." He took a step back. "Goodnight. I'll see you at the wedding."

He turned then, and Emma watched quietly until he disappeared down the steps and out of sight. The old grandfather clock in the foyer below ticked the minutes away, and still she stood in the hall—motionless.

It's all for nothing. The trip here, the wedding, our life together—all of this will be for nothing. He distrusts me and will never believe he's the father of this baby.

With a trembling chin, Emma entered the bedroom and closed the door silently behind her.

Chapter Fourteen

Emma opened her eyes to a feeling of dread. Today, her life would be joined with Tyler's. She met the idea with a fair amount of trepidation.

She listened closely for any sound from the room next to hers. When no footfalls met her alert ears, she pushed the blankets away, dropped her legs over the side of the bed, and stared out across the unfamiliar surroundings.

I don't know how many more nights I can take of this fretful tossing and turning. Emma dropped her face into her hands. *There are so many things to straighten out between the two of us—no...the three of us...* Emma's tousled head snapped upright. *Janie! I have no idea how she feels about all of this!*

Emma pushed her doubts aside and concentrated on what was most important right at that moment; she had to speak to the little girl. All this time, she had worried solely about herself and Tyler and had not even given a thought to how Janie felt about having a new mother—one that she did not even know.

Emma was instantly ashamed of her own selfishness. She had been wallowing in self-pity, and it was time for a change. Jumping from the bed, she grabbed her robe and left the safety of her room to search for Tyler's daughter.

Remembering Carrie's earlier explanation of the home's layout, Emma bustled down the hall. Janie's room was somewhere in the area she explored. Luckily, a peek through an open doorway a dozen feet down the corridor from her own room revealed a tiny, blonde girl, who sat on the floor playing with a yellow pup. Emma stood for a moment, studying the child, and her heart filled with an amazing realization. This little girl would be her stepdaughter by the end of the day.

The pup gave Emma away. His welcoming bark echoed in the large room, and Tyler's daughter spun to face the strange woman. Her blue eyes narrowed with wariness. A gentle smile curved Emma's lips as she crossed to seat herself tentatively on the floor. The pup jumped up to lick her face, and a startled giggle escaped her a moment later when the animal crawled into her lap.

"Oh, my goodness! This must mean he likes me!" Emma tussled with the exuberant pup until he calmed, then she turned a smile in Janie's direction. "Hello. My name is Emma, and you must be Janie. Is this your puppy?"

Tyler's daughter stared at her in wide eyed suspicion for a moment longer before committing to a small nod.

"I saw you yesterday, but I didn't have a chance to say 'hi'. Did anyone tell you I was coming?"

Again she received a small nod, and Emma's racing mind tried to think of something else to say. She glanced around the room and noticed that it was every child's dream. A worn wooden rocking horse stood in the corner next to a huge box of toys, and an intricately designed dollhouse topped off a small table built with a child in mind.

"You have a very nice room, Janie. My room looked kind of like this when I was your age." Emma rambled on, coming to the realization that it was hard to keep up a conversation with someone who could not answer back. "My Papa bought me a rocking horse once. If I remember correctly, his name was Rocker. Kind of a dumb name, wasn't it?"

Janie's tiny hand covered her mouth and hid a grin as she nodded her head.

Emma laughed. "Oh, I see you agree with me! Does your horse have a name?"

Janie looked at the toy horse, and then back to Emma with furrowed brows of indecision. Suddenly, the little girl stood and walked to the play table to retrieve a chalkboard and a broken piece of chalk. She hesitated for a moment before finally returning to Emma's side. She sat on the floor again and painstakingly scribbled something on the slate before handing it to the pretty lady to read. Strands of unruly blonde hair were pushed aside by chubby hands as the child waited for a response.

Emma studied the childish scrawl and deciphered the word. "Storm?"

The older woman glanced at the child, and then at the window with a questioning look. Janie leaned forward, pointed to the board, and then back to the rocking horse that sat beneath the window. Emma still did not understand. The child released a heavy, exaggerated sigh, took the slate from her new friend and labored once more with the broken piece of chalk. Finally, she held it up for Emma to see.

On the board she had written the words *'like my dad's horse.'*

"Oh, I get it now! Storm is the name of your daddy's horse, too?"

Janie nodded her head vigorously.

"Well, I think that's a very nice name. I used to have a white horse named Bonnie, and she ran as fast as the wind. Every night I would feed her a special treat, like a carrot or an apple."

The little girl sat with eyes wide and listened attentively to Emma's every word. *Thank goodness,* the older woman thought. *I've found something we both can relate to.*

"Janie," her voice was filled with hesitation, "do you think we could be friends? Friends often like the same things, and it seems we both like horses and puppies." She scratched Whizzer's ears as she spoke. "It would be fun if you could show me some of your special places outside. I've never been to Minnesota before. I'm afraid I might get lost if I go out exploring alone."

Janie's blue eyes moved to the pup, and Emma sat quietly, letting the child make up her own mind. Janie raised her eyes a moment later, allowing Emma to release the breath she did not even realize she was holding. A grin split the little girl's face, and she reached out her chubby little fingers to take Emma's slender hand in hers.

Emma's face glowed with her own responding smile. It was so important that she start out on the right foot with this little girl. She squeezed the small, dimpled fingers, and a pact was formed.

Tyler watched the exchange in silence from his vantage point in the hallway just outside the room. *Why can't I trust you like my daughter does?*

He backed away slowly, unwilling at this point to let them know that he had witnessed their tentative alliance of friendship.

Carrie assisted Emma with the final touches to her hair later that afternoon. In less than ten minutes, they would walk down the steps and Emma would pledge her life—and her love—to Tyler.

Her future sister-in-law handed over a small bouquet of freshly picked autumn wildflowers and took Emma's other hand in hers. "Come on, smile! This is your wedding day!"

The future bride's gaze dropped to the floor as she fought an almost overwhelming bout of sorrow. "It doesn't seem like it, Carrie. My father isn't here, and I'm quite sure my husband-to-be would rather put me on a train bound for New York than stand by my side in front of a reverend." She looked at Carrie through tears that threatened to overflow. "I don't know if I can do this. He doesn't want me!"

"Hush, now, Emma, that's not true. It's going to take time, but it will all work out. You just need to have a little faith." She hugged Emma tightly. "I'm so glad you're here. I feel we'll truly be sisters. I know we haven't known each other long, but in our case it doesn't matter. I felt a kindred spirit in you the first time we spoke."

"You and your family have been so wonderful to me. I just wish Tyler felt the same."

"Things will work out, Emma," she repeated. "Just give it some time." The two women shared one last hug, then Carrie urged her future sister-in-law through the doorway and down the stairs.

She stood next to him, her hands clammy and her normally pink skin ashen, as the reverend awaited her response.

"I do," Emma replied in a whisper.

Tyler's back was ramrod stiff as he listened to her answer, and a wave of *deja vu* washed over him. How many years had it been since he heard Sara say those same two words with such joy in her heart? He himself had experienced a giddiness on that long ago day that was as yet unmatched; a giddiness born of the fact that the woman next to him would be his partner, his friend and his lover for the rest of his life. He had loved her with all his heart and soul and, somewhere in time, it all went wrong.

Now, he repeated those same vows to a woman he hardly knew. *Sara, are you watching from some heavenly planet, wishing me well?* Or was she as confused as he, pondering why he would enter into such a sham of a marriage?

"—And, by the power vested in me by the state of Minnesota, I now pronounce you man and wife." The elderly reverend smiled at the pair before him. "Tyler, you may kiss your bride."

Emma turned to face her new husband, looked up through wide, uncertain eyes at his handsome features, and waited. Tyler bent to brush his lips against her cold ones and realized her hand was clammy in his. He looked deep into the emerald depths before him and could not hide his surprise at the anguish he saw there.

A resounding round of applause saved them both the agony of speech. They turned as one to look at the happy faces behind them. Other than the immediate family, only three additional people had been invited to the ceremony; an older couple and a handsome, blond man that Emma gauged to be about Trevor's age. She had not had the opportunity to meet them before the wedding, and now curiosity got the better of her as she wondered who they were.

Janie, dressed in a lacy yellow frock with matching ribbons in her hair, stood beside Carrie. The child's wrinkled brow made it obvious that she was totally confused by what had just transpired. The new bride smiled at her stepdaughter, and a wave of relief washed over her when the child answered with a grin of her own.

Tyler's brothers suddenly stood before her, and Trevor reached for Emma's cold hands.

"Emma, Tyler, congratulations to both of you!" His twinkling eyes met his older brother's wary ones. "My dear brother, Cole and I think we should both be afforded the chance to welcome our new sister-in-law to the family."

Tyler's eyes squinted even further with suspicion, and he spoke rather curtly. "So, go ahead, Trevor. *Say* what you need to *say*."

Trevor's grin quickly became a smirk. "Ah, Tyler, *saying* something just won't cut it. Welcome to the family, Emma." He pulled the surprised bride into his arms and gave her a hearty kiss on the lips. It was followed by a tight squeeze—and a leer directed at his younger brother. "Cole, isn't there something you'd like to *say* to the new bride, too?"

The glower on Tyler's face left Cole with the distinct impression that his eldest brother was ready to punch Trevor. He stepped up for his turn though, with obvious pleasure.

"Emma, I never was one for words." His mouth plummeted to capture his stunned sister-in-law's, but all the while he kept one eye on the red-faced man beside her. He ended the kiss with a loud smack, then quickly stepped back.

Tyler observed his brothers' antics through cool eyes, but, inside, his blood simmered. Carrie quickly stepped in, before they came to blows.

"Out of my way, you two!" She pushed Cole and Trevor aside and took Emma's hands in hers. "Congratulations, Emma! I'm so happy you're with us!" She turned to her brother. "And I couldn't be happier for you, Tyler!" She reached up to embrace him and whispered for his ears alone. "I love you, big brother. Everything will be fine, you'll see."

He stared back with a doubtful dip of the eyebrows.

Tyler's attention then turned to the family friends who attended the ceremony. He reached to grasp the hand of the blond man standing before him. "Hello, Steven. Thank you for coming." He tipped his head in the direction of the elderly couple, who had just joined them. "I would like you all to meet my wife, Emma. Emma, these good people are our nearest neighbors, Gregory and Laura Adams and their son, Steven."

Emma hid her nervousness with a forced smile and took Laura's hand. "It's so nice to meet all of you."

It seemed to Emma that another man had taken over Tyler's body—at least temporarily. The smile on his face produced the image of the typical proud and happy bridegroom, and the possessive hand on the small of her back only added to the charade.

"Gregory used to be the local doctor, Emma," Tyler continued. "Steven has taken over his practice now though, since his father's retirement. We're all grateful he decided to come back home and set up shop."

A soft chuckle escaped Steven's throat with Tyler's comment, then he turned his attention to the bride. "It's very nice to meet you, Emma. And the reason Tyler is so happy that I chose to set up my practice in the area stems from the fact that I grew up with him and his brothers. I know all the scrapes they get into, and one of us had to become a doctor to take care of the other three!"

Emma could not help but laugh, but before Tyler could retort, Mamie pushed her way through the small crowd as fast as her girth would allow. She dabbed at her eyes with a lace handkerchief.

"Tyla and Miss Em! I'm so happy I'm leakin' water all over ma' new dress! Come here, the both of you, and gives Mamie a hug!"

Chuckles resounded in the room as Mamie got her wish. She released the newlyweds a moment later, stuffed her white hanky into the pocket of her dress and addressed the small crowd. "Time to be celebratin' the nuptials, it is! We got a yard plumb full of lumberjacks and their families just awaitin' to congratulate the new Missus, and they be ready for some fun! Yessiree! Time to be movin' this party outside!" She turned with the expectation that one and all would automatically follow—and they did.

Janie, who had conspicuously turned up at her father's side during the introductions, slid her tiny hand into Tyler's and gave it a quick tug. He lifted the child into his strong arms before turning to the very quiet Emma.

"The masses await. Mamie will be hollering if we don't get outside soon."

He grasped her elbow with his free hand and, as a family, they ventured out onto the front porch.

Emma was taken aback by the large number of people who stood in the yard and by the thunderous applause that accompanied their appearance. A small group of men, equipped with fiddles, struck up Mendelssohn's *"Wedding March"* in their honor.

These people were employed by the Northern Pine Ranch, and Emma was overwhelmed at their unconditional acceptance of her. *I wonder if they know the real reason for the wedding?*

Forcing the thought from her mind, Emma raised her chin and gripped Tyler's arm, determined to enjoy the day if it killed her.

Trevor and Cole shouldered their way through the crowd and paused at the bottom of the steps. Each man held a glass of homemade beer in his hand. Trevor hailed the crowd to gain their attention and, as the clamor died down, he turned back to face Tyler and Emma with his glass raised. He placed a shiny boot on the bottom step as he prepared to begin his speech.

"I'd like to make a toast to the bride and groom! May they be happy and healthy for years to come and grow exceptionally old together!"

The crowd roared its approval. Trevor waved his hand for silence again, then shouted above the lessening din. "May they be prosperous their entire lives, and may they prove themselves forever young by begetting numerous children!" He waved his glass of beer in the couple's general direction. "Take a look at them, folks! That shouldn't be too tall an order for either of them, especially Tyler! Hell, he's been tellin' me and Cole for years that he's the *big* man around here!"

The crowd exploded with laughter and ribald comments abounded. It seemed that every man in attendance had ideas on just how to "beget" those children.

Emma blushed to a color near purple and Tyler threw his brother a malevolent look just before the younger Wilkins brothers raced up the steps, linked their hands together behind Emma, and swept her off her feet. The crowd hooted its approval as the two men carried her through the gathering and away from the house.

Emma giggled uproariously, her earlier sullenness vanishing with the sheer merriment of the day. "I beg you!" she screamed. "Please! Don't drop me!" She clung to their necks as the men chuckled and whisked her away.

The noise of the ensuing party was left behind when they rounded the corner of the barn. Cole and Trevor set their burden gently on an upturned barrel.

"Did you see the look on Tyler's face?" Cole laughed as he reached into a well concealed basket and pulled out a bottle of fine wine and three glasses.

Emma wiped the laughter-born tears from her face and shook a finger at her kidnappers while Cole proceeded to fill the crystal goblets. "You had this planned all along, didn't you?" Her answer came in the form of twin shrugs from her captors. "You two are cads for taking me away from my wedding celebration!"

A lopsided grin curved Cole's lips as he handed a glass to both Trevor and Emma. "We just thought we'd like to spend a private moment with you. We wanted you to know how happy we are to have you in our midst. Besides, the two of us decided years ago that it's great sport to get Tyler's goat!"

The trio clinked glasses, and the two men finished their drinks in one swallow. Emma sipped at hers thoughtfully and, a moment later, the gaiety left her green eyes.

"You two will never know how thankful I am that you accepted me so readily—especially when you consider the reason why I'm here in the first place." Her slender shoulders raised with a sigh. "I guess I can't blame Tyler for feeling the way he does about this whole thing. My father didn't give him a choice, and neither did I." Emma's gaze dropped to her lap, and she busied herself with brushing imaginary dirt from the front of her dress.

The younger Wilkins men exchanged worried glances, then Trevor spoke gently. "Don't worry yourself about the future, Emma." He reached out to take her hand in his and give it a reassuring squeeze. "Listen to me—I know my brother. There's no way you would be here if he didn't want you to be. He would've come up with some reason to keep you in New York, or he would've sent you packing the minute you arrived in Duluth. Time will work things out." He released her hand to pat her shoulder, albeit rather awkwardly. "Hell, look at what you've got to work with! Between Cole, Carrie, myself, and especially Mamie, he'll have to come around sooner or later!"

She responded with a shaky laugh. "You two are quite a pair, do you know that?" She pressed a kiss to each of their cheeks and, surprisingly, both men blushed. "Well, I think we should probably be returning soon, don't you?"

Cole retrieved the glass from Emma's hand and watched Trevor help her down from the barrel's surface. "Emma, excuse me if this is too personal, but I have to ask you something. In fact, I've wanted to ask you this since I first met you." His gentle gaze held her wary one for a long moment before he finally voiced the question. "How do you really feel about Tyler?"

The inquiry took Emma by surprise, but, as she glanced from one concerned face to the other, she knew she needed to be honest with them. She took both their hands in hers, and the two men observed the bittersweet smile that curved her lips.

"When I first met Tyler, I thought he was the most arrogant man I had ever met. But, as we spent more time together, he did something to my insides that no other man ever has. I couldn't get him out of my mind." Emma swallowed to regain her composure and struggled to find the right words. "The night before he left New York, we...ended up together—I'd rather not go into the details. The next morning, I watched from my bedroom window as he rode out of my life. I knew, then and there, that I'd fallen in love with him and hadn't even realized it." She looked up to meet her brother-in-law's understanding gaze. "And yes, Cole, I love him still, with all my heart and soul. I just wish I could tell him that but, until he's ready to accept me into his life completely, I have to keep that knowledge to myself."

"Emma—" Trevor rolled his eyes in exasperation, "—why don't you just tell him?"

"Because he wouldn't believe me. He'd just think they were empty words spoken to ensure that my baby has a name." She shook her head. "This is the way it must be, Trevor, at least for now. So, please, both of you, keep this conversation to yourselves. I just wanted to assure you both that I am not playing with your brother's emotions. I love him, and it will be up to me to discover if he can love me back."

Both men shook their heads slowly, and Cole shrugged his broad shoulders. "All right, Em, if that's the way you want it. We'll abide by your decision—but, just for the record, I, too, think you're making a mistake by not telling him." A mischievous grin lit his eyes a second later. "And don't be surprised if we give Cupid a helping hand once awhile."

Another squeal left her throat when her two handsome brothers-in-law swept her off her feet once more and carted her back to the celebration.

Trevor and Cole deposited the bride before her husband a few seconds later, then beat a hasty retreat in the direction of the beer table. Neither of them dared to glance back and check the expression on their brother's face. Emma, too, could not bring herself to meet his gaze and simply walked off to greet her guests.

Tyler's brow dipped in a frown as he watched her move gracefully amid the friendly crowd. She was in her element now—the perfect hostess—yet her face was decidedly flushed compared to its earlier pallor. His cool gaze strayed to his brothers, where they chuckled loudly and swilled more beer.

"I wish I knew what in the hell those two said to her," he muttered to no one in particular.

Tyler looked at Emma again and observed her take Janie's hand as yet another well-wisher offered congratulations. *Damn, but she does look beautiful in that white dress with the sun glinting off her hair. Ah, hell...*Tyler straightened his shoulders and started toward where Emma stood amid a group of merry lumberjacks. *I may as well play the proud bridegroom and glue myself to her side, instead of standing here grumbling by myself...*

The afternoon waned and dusk descended long before the lumberjacks and their families left for their own homes. The afternoon had been filled with music and dancing and enough food to feed the entire lot for a week.

Steven Adams and his parents sat in the large, open living room, enjoying one last nightcap with the Wilkins family before heading home themselves. Emma's mind wandered as she listened to the different conversations around her, and thoughts of the day floated through her mind.

Earlier, when the guests insisted that the newly wedded couple dance the first waltz, she held her breath as Tyler took her in his arms. Within his tender embrace, the more than one hundred onlookers ceased to exist and, as they slowly moved to the music, she recalled another dance and another time. The memory returned now, and she could not help but feel a sense of wonder at the strange turn her life had taken in just three short months.

Who would've ever thought, with the aftermath of our first dance in New York, that I would be here today and in his arms once more? He seemed to enjoy my company. In fact, he was very attentive all afternoon.

Now though, he sat on the opposite divan with Steven and discussed inconsequential happenings around the area. It was as if she was not even present in the room.

No one has said a word about where I'm to sleep now that we're married. Will I spend the night in his room or will he leave me to suffer another night in a cold and lonely bed—as he inferred last night?

Emma craved the opportunity to talk with him alone, to tell him of her dreams for their marriage, but did not want to appear eager in front of the neighbors. So, she sat patiently, playing the obedient wife, and waited for Tyler to make a move.

Emma pushed her uncertainties aside and used the opportunity to study the other personalities in the room.

Carrie sat beside her on the divan, opposite Tyler and Steven. Cole and Trevor flanked the first settee and teased their sister mercilessly about the rather tipsy young man who repeatedly asked her to dance earlier that evening.

Those two are like little boys, Emma mused. *They always find the bright side in every situation and, at the same time, manage quite adeptly to get themselves into trouble. Tonight though, they're content to just pick on their younger sister.*

She watched Carrie accept her drunken brothers' biting comments with good humor and yet, strangely, though Steven Adams was only too willing to add a comment of his own now and then, Carrie totally ignored him. *One would think, with the two families being such good friends, that she would at least acknowledge him at some point.*

Emma pushed that observation, too, from her mind. She was tired, and she was also imagining things.

Tyler watched his new wife surreptitiously from the corner of his eye. He had done everything possible to delay going upstairs and, in fact, had even gone so far as to invite Steven and his parents in for a nightcap.

I won't spend the night with her, he told himself firmly. *It doesn't matter that we're married now. I made myself perfectly clear last night when I told her it would be a marriage in name only, and I damn well plan to stick to my guns.*

Christ, we haven't even talked about the baby anymore. How can I take her to our marriage bed with the parentage of her child still hanging over our heads?

The moment of truth fast approached when their three guests stood, offered a few last words of congratulations, and left through the front entrance. Trevor and Cole, never ones to be discreet, winked at Tyler, and then headed for the stairs. Carrie, in turn, hugged both the bride and groom and whispered words of encouragement in their ears before retiring to her own room.

What must they all be thinking? Emma's cheeks blushed with renewed embarrassment. *How am I going to handle the next few minutes?*

Tyler poured himself another drink before he cast a hesitant glance in Emma's direction. "Would you care for a nightcap?"

"No, thank you," she declined. *Should I say something about our sleeping arrangements or not?* She decided on not. "Mamie did a wonderful job with the wedding."

"Yes, she did. She was determined to make it a nice day for everyone involved."

Say it...don't be afraid! "Tyler?" Emma eyed him closely, determined to begin the conversation that could make or break their future. *Say it!* "I have to ask you something." She swallowed convulsively, then her words came out in a rush. "Do you want me to stay or would you rather I begin plans to return to New York?" She held her breath as she awaited his answer, and her mind screamed a plea. *Please, give us a chance! Don't send me away!*

The minutes ticked by as he swirled the brandy in his glass, and the silence in the room resounded off the four walls.

What do I want? It seemed so clear yesterday, but now... He had watched her closely today—and he had watched his family. It was obvious that they already loved her. *Hell, even Janie walked around with a smile pasted on her face—the type of smile I haven't seen on her little features since Sara died.*

Thoughts of New York, of how he felt about Emma that last night, tugged at his mind. *And,* he mused as his gaze slipped to her again, *it doesn't help that she is so damned beautiful. It would be easy as hell to just carry her up the stairs to my bed.*

But did he believe her? Did he believe that she had been with no other men? Did he believe, unequivocally, that the baby was his?

No, I don't.

The evening of the reception in New York flashed through his brain. Emma, alone on the terrace with Samuel Fontaine, and then her disheveled condition when she returned to the ballroom after apparently enjoying his advances. It was a scene that would be forever imprinted in his mind. They also both disappeared after returning to the ballroom. Were they together then, too? Samuel said he was going to find her and finish what they started.

How many other men were there that I don't know about? Will I ever be sure that the baby is mine? A heavy sigh escaped Tyler's chest. There were just too many unresolved issues between them, and they could not be settled in the space of one evening.

Tyler rubbed his forehead with a shaky hand, then spoke quietly. "I don't know what to tell you, Emma, because I don't know how I feel right at this moment, and that's the way of it." He watched the glimmer of hope fade from her eyes. "Go to sleep. It's been a long day for you. I still have a few things to check on that might take me awhile." He stood, set his glass on the table, and glanced at her defeated expression one last time. "Goodnight. I'll see you in the morning."

He crossed the room and left without looking back.

Emma sat and stared at nothing for a long while. Tyler had thrown his decision at her feet, and the pain of his rejection flowed through her body as surely as the tears that rolled down her cheeks. *He'll never trust me...never want me completely in his life. He's the only man I've ever been with, and yet I have no way to prove it to him.*

Emma rose and shuffled up the stairs. She paused outside the door to Tyler's bedroom, and the pain of his dismissal deepened. She stifled a sob. *We should be in each other's arms right now, celebrating the beginning of our lives together and planning our future.*

Instead, she would sleep alone and ache for him to come to her in the dead of night.

Chapter Fifteen

Cole and Trevor stabled their horses late the next evening, after spending the day with one of the cutting crews. Their tired gazes were drawn to the barn's entrance when Carrie stomped through the open doors with a scowl etched on her face. She marched straight toward them.

"Shit," Trevor muttered to his brother. "She looks like she's carrying a head of steam."

Cole ducked behind his horse. "You handle this one—I'm too damned tired to explain why we're late."

"Hi, Carrie," Trevor jumped in before his owly-looking sister had a chance to say anything. "Don't nag at us for being late and missing supper. We had one helluva day and just want to get cleaned up, eat, and get some shut eye." He threw his saddle over the wooden gate and proceeded to fill the feed bin with hay.

She stared at them with arms crossed while her foot tapped a rapid beat on the straw-covered floor. "I've been waiting for the two of you all day! Did you by any chance run into Tyler on the trail?"

"No. Why, is there a problem?" Trevor turned with an armful of straw and met her gaze.

"Only that Tyler and Emma slept in separate rooms last night, and he took off this morning and hasn't returned yet. He left Mamie a note to tell the two of you he might not be back until tomorrow or the day after. Poor Emma was on the verge of tears all day. What are we going to do with him?"

Cole stepped from behind his horse and moved out of the stall. "How do you know they slept apart last night?"

"Because Mamie brought a breakfast tray up to Tyler's room, and he was alone. He almost snapped her head off, then told her he didn't need it, but to check on Emma in the *other room* to see if she was hungry. When she knocked on Emma's door, she didn't answer right away and, thinking she was asleep, Mamie opened it. The poor thing was still in her wedding dress, curled up in a chair, and the bed wasn't even mussed. She slept in that chair all night! Some wedding night, huh?"

The two brothers glanced at each other with a shared realization. Tyler had created an awful situation for himself—and for Emma.

"What in hell is wrong with him?" Trevor shook his head and tempered his words. "Look, all we can do is support both of them, I guess, and see what happens. Christ, with the mood Tyler's been in lately, if Cole or I say anything, he'll likely take a swing at us!"

"Well, Mamie is ready to start swinging at him! She mumbled all day about second chances and him not knowing what he's got. She's been slamming pans around in the kitchen like there's no tomorrow. Between Mamie's ranting and raving and Emma's tears, I couldn't take it anymore. I finally took Janie out riding just to get away for a while, and I left poor Katy alone with them."

Cole squeezed Carrie's arm as he walked by her. "You keep talking like that, and I'm gonna saddle up and head back north." He pushed his hat farther back on his head and sighed. "Let's just wait and see how this develops. Tyler will come to his senses eventually."

"Well, he'd better hurry before he makes Emma sick. She doesn't deserve this! She's got enough to worry about with keeping herself and the baby healthy!"

Trevor doused the light in the barn, and the three siblings walked back to the house.

"I wonder if things will ever return to normal around here." Cole's words echoed the thoughts of his family members. "As much as I've felt Tyler's pain the last couple years, I can't understand where he's coming from lately."

"I know." Carrie shrugged as she took his arm. "Emma's more than proven herself time and again. She's a wonderful person. If Tyler would only open his eyes and see what he could have, he might be truly happy again."

Trevor swung a jacketed arm over his sister's shoulders. "They've got to figure it out on their own, Carrie. Let's just give them time."

Tyler poked at the small campfire and added another piece of wood. As the flame flared, visions of Emma danced through his brain. He remembered her beautiful smile, and how it became wider and more frequent yesterday as the afternoon progressed—a smile that charmed just about everyone in her wake. He also remembered the pained expression on her face when he told her to go to bed alone—an expression that just about killed him.

It was not in his nature to be cruel to anyone, but then her comments last night surprised the hell out of him. *Because I agreed to the wedding, was she insinuating that we could forget everything up to this point and spend the night together? Christ, all I've done since she's been here is berate her. You'd think she'd be happy not to have to share the same bed with me.* He jammed another chunk of wood into the fire and watched the smoke carry the sparks upward. *So, why did she look so hurt when I told her to go up to bed without me?*

His chest tightened again with the memory and, to make matters worse, instead of staying home this morning and taking the opportunity to apologize, he rode out to fight his demons alone.

Tyler lay back and rested his head against the saddle, then gazed up into the night sky filled with thousands of stars. His throat clogged with emotion as he focused on one that sparkled brighter than the rest.

Is that you, Sara? I wanted so much for us—I wanted a long happy life with you and Janie—but fate stepped in and stole you from me. When I met Emma, the last thing on my mind was the thought of spending my life with another woman. Hell, it took me weeks just to get over my guilt for betraying you that last night in New York. A heavy sigh lifted his chest. *I know what you're thinking, Sara. It was foolish for me to try so vigorously to regain the life I had—a life that was so empty—but I never planned on there ever being anyone but you. I never planned on Emma moving into my heart.*

Tyler tucked his hands beneath his head and spoke to the ebony sky above him. "I'm sorry, Sara, but I don't want her to leave. I don't know what, if anything, is going to happen between us, but I do know that I need her to stay at the ranch if we're to ever straighten this mess out. I can't let her go."

And what about the baby? What if the child isn't mine? How am I supposed to handle that situation? I don't know if I can love another man's child as much as I love Janie.

"Janie means everything to me, Sara, and so does her happiness. She's accepted Emma unconditionally, and I don't want her hurt, simply because I can't figure out my own mind." He shook his head again and continued to stare at the twinkling star above him. "Is what I feel for Emma the beginnings of love? Can I love her the way I did you?"

Never once has Emma insinuated that she cares for me. All she said was that she refuses to raise the baby without a name. Hell, she called me a bastard that first night. Do you know how that felt, Sara? It felt like she stuck me in the gut with a knife, that's how it felt!

"We just need to find the right time to discuss everything rationally, I guess. I want to believe in her—it's the only way this marriage is going to work. Janie deserves some happiness and the chance to have a mother again." Sudden tears glistened in his eyes. "You can never come back, Sara, and, as hard as that realization is for me, I know in my heart that I need to let go of the past."

Are you trying to help me through this mess, Sara? His thoughtful gaze swept the sky above him one last time. *Did you send Emma to us, so we could be happy again?* The simple thought eased his mind considerably.

Tyler threw one more chunk of wood into the fire, reached for a blanket, and settled himself on the hard ground. "You could be sleeping in a soft bed," he muttered as he bunched his jacket into a makeshift pillow. He dropped his head, readjusted the coat when a button poked his ear, and then flopped onto his back. "You goddamn idiot—you could be in a warm bed with a soft woman next to you."

He tossed his thoughts away quickly. *No. I'm not laying a hand on her until I get this situation resolved in my mind—I need to trust her completely.*

He watched the bright star twinkle above him again and thought of Sara, and somehow he knew that she would not think he was forsaking her if he created a new life for himself. He hoped though, that she would understand the future course of events.

Emma stepped onto the front porch and hugged the woolen shawl tighter around her slim shoulders to ward off the chill of the night air—and her acute disappointment. The canter of horses' hooves in the yard earlier was due to Cole and Trevor's return—not Tyler's—and her spirits plummeted even lower with her husband's continued absence. Granted, they probably would not even have spoken to one another that evening, but just the knowledge that Tyler was home would have done wonders to raise her lagging spirits.

She waited for her brothers-in-law to settle themselves in for the night before quietly escaping the house to sit on the porch swing. Emma listened to the croak of distant frogs and the song of a nearby loon and pondered the life she had been thrown into.

Where are you, Tyler? Are you thinking about me?

She found it hard to believe that he could so callously omit her from his life—especially after what the two of them had endured in the last forty-eight hours.

A wolf howled in the darkness, and the lonely cry combined with the cool night air to raise goose bumps on her skin. The stars that twinkled overhead had a calming effect though, as she absorbed the beauty of the night.

This is what he told me about in New York—one of those beautiful Minnesota nights that he loves so dearly. Is he close enough to hear the wolf's mournful cry, too?

Emma rose from the wooden swing, stepped down off the porch and into the yard. Her gaze moved from one twinkling star to the next, but even the peaceful night could not ease her growing frustration. She called out to the darkness, unmindful of anyone who might overhear.

"I'll make you want me, Tyler! I know that you'll hold Sara's spirit close to you forever, because the life you shared with her can't simply be forgotten." Emma laid her hand on her chest, and her voice quieted to a punctuated whisper. "But I am flesh and blood, and I'm here! I won't let you throw away what we could have. I don't care if you never return my feelings! I'll love you forever, and that's the way of *that*, Mr. Wilkins."

She stood in the middle of the yard, her eyes closed and her face turned upward, and willed her whispered plea to reach him. The stillness of the moment engulfed her and tears started to roll down her cheeks—until the minute fluttering of butterfly wings quivered within her womb. Her eyes widened with wonder and, slowly, she brought a trembling hand to her stomach, the shawl forgotten as it slipped from her shoulders and drifted to the ground. She waited, breathless, and soon it came again—the barely discernable, feather-light touch deep within her.

Her child.

A gentle smile touched her lips. "Oh, yes, Tyler—someday, you'll want me."

* * *

The next morning, Emma was dressed and ready for the day by seven a.m. She felt filled with energy for the first time since arriving in Minnesota and, along with that energy came a new resolve. She would no longer press Tyler for a resolution to their problem, but neither would she permit him to walk away from her or their marriage. She was determined not to lose her temper again—as hard as it might be at times—but simply get him used to her presence in degrees. If her plan worked, he would come to accept her—eventually.

She opened the kitchen door, and then stopped dead when she saw the object of her thoughts sitting at the table. He conversed with his daughter, whose tiny chin rested on the palms of her hands atop bent elbows while she listened attentively.

Mamie crossed the kitchen with two plates full of pancakes and bacon. She set Tyler's dish before him with a bang, causing the contents to jump on the platter's surface.

Emma hid a smile. She knew the housekeeper's actions were a show of retaliation for his behavior of the last few days. When she spied Emma standing in the doorway, however, her mood changed dramatically. The old negress immediately ignored her "boss" and hustled the young bride to the table.

"You jes sit yoursef down and Mamie'll cook anythin' you wants for breakfast!" She pulled out a chair, laid her gnarled hands on Emma's shoulders and forced her to sit. "What be soundin' good to you this fine mornin', Miss Em? I gots ham, eggs, whatever your lil' heart desires. Yessiree!"

Tyler eyed the bowl of pancake batter on the counter and the bacon that lay on a tin plate atop the woodstove, and could not help but remember the words he had heard come out of Mamie's mouth countless times while he was growing up.

'I don't run no restaurant, where people can pick and choose their food. You swallow what I put in front of you, or you go hungry!'

Now, there she was, ready to go out back and kill a chicken, if that was what *'Miss Em'* wanted to eat.

Emma, well aware of Mamie's game—and still holding firm to her new resolve—thought it best not to start the day by antagonizing her new husband.

"Those pancakes look so tasty that I think I'll just have to try them for breakfast, Mamie."

Emma's eyes widened in horror when the old black woman whisked Tyler's plate from beneath his nose and set it before her.

"Here, Miss Em, you eat offen this here plate. It be spankin' hot and fresh as you'll ever get it. And Tyla, he can just be gentlemanlike enough to let his lady eat first."

Tyler sat with his fork held in midair—it would never cut into the pancakes, at least not that batch. Now, Mamie poked a finger at his shoulder, the other hand on her hip, and her stern expression dared him to disagree. "Ain't that right, boy? You gentlemanlike enough this mornin' to let your *wife* eat first?"

Emma lowered her eyes to the traveling plate of flapjacks in an effort to hide her amusement, and Tyler's gaze burned the top of her head. *How do I not laugh at Mamie's obvious performance?* She peeked up from under long eyelashes, and her eyes met the twinkling emerald ones before her. A hesitant smile curved her lips.

Satisfied, Mamie turned back to the stove and Tyler, in turn, rolled his eyes at Emma. He released his breath in a long sigh. "That's fine, Mamie. I can wait a few minutes longer." He reached for his coffee and waited patiently for another helping of buttermilk pancakes.

Sensing that her husband had set aside his intolerance of her, at least for the moment, Emma broke the impending silence.

"I wanted to ask if you have a horse that I might borrow. I wanted to go riding yesterday, but didn't feel I should just take one without your permission. You weren't here for me to ask...

There, I acknowledged his absence yesterday, but in a way that shouldn't anger him. "I promise I won't go too far until I know the lay of the land." Her steady gaze met his as she continued. "And I really do miss riding on a regular basis."

Tyler set his cup down and answered her in measured tones. "You are free to use any horse on this ranch, Emma. In fact, you can use *anything* you want, without my...permission. All I ask is that you stay on either the main roads or the well-used trails. It's very easy to get lost when the landmarks so closely resemble one another."

Her smile brightened with his answer and she attacked her pancakes with gusto. "Thank you, Tyler. I haven't ridden in a long time, and I can't wait to explore the ranch." She turned to Janie, who sat quietly listening to them. "Do you have a horse?"

The little girl nodded her head vigorously, and Emma swung her gaze back to her husband.

"Do you think Janie could ride along with me? I won't let the house out of my sight."

Tyler looked from one eager face to the other and made a quick decision. "You know, I have a quiet day today. How would you two like it if I tagged along? Then I could show you where to ride safely."

Emma's heart pounded wildly in her chest as she looked at the little girl again. *He actually wants to go with us!* "What do you think, Janie? I think it's a grand idea!"

The girl's head bobbed with enthusiasm.

Mamie placed a new breakfast plate on the table before Tyler. A huge smile now creased her dark face. "Well, that be one of the better ideas I seen planted around here in a long time. Yessiree! Tyla, you take Miss Em down to the barn and let her pick out a horse. Meantime, I be packin' a picnic lunch and, after Janie changes her clothes, I be sendin' her down with it. Yessiree! It be one fine day for a ride!"

Tyler's eyes followed the old black woman as she bustled around the kitchen, humming a happy tune. He shook his head slowly, then looked at Emma again and his smile melted her heart.

"Did you want to change clothes, too, before we leave? I'll wait here for you, and then we'll go down to the barn."

Emma gulped down the last of her pancakes and jumped up from the table. "I'll be right back!"

With Tyler in the lead, Emma and Janie turned off the main trail and moved slowly down a brush-covered slope. The hard-to-detect trail was steep, but not impossible for confident riders and surefooted animals. The trip down the path was worth the effort, and Emma gasped when she saw the clearing that stretched before them.

"Oh, Tyler, it's beautiful!" Her green eyes scanned the pond that lay before them—and the steady stream of water that fed the pool. It entered through a crevice in a huge rock, which rose twenty feet above them, then joined a ledge that extended past the waterline a good fifteen feet on either side of the small lake. Huge pine trees edged it, forming the remaining sides of the clearing.

"I thought you might like this place. Janie and I come here all the time."

Tyler dismounted Storm, then moved to lift Emma from the back of a gentle mare. Their gazes met for one heart stopping moment before her feet found the ground, and he quickly stuffed his hands into his pants pockets to hide their trembling.

The earth surrounding the pond was firm and level, and Emma had a strong desire to remove her shoes and bury her toes in the lush grass beneath her feet. She beat down the urge, however, and strolled across the clearing, only to pause again when she noticed numerous drawings that were etched on one portion of the rock wall. Moving closer, she recognized stick-drawn images of horses and various other animals. She ran a finger over the outline of one of the figures, then turned to her new husband with a questioning look.

"What is this place—and where did these drawings come from? They're like nothing I've ever seen before."

Tyler and Janie approached her, and he reached out to point to one of the drawings. He looked down at his daughter with a smile.

"Should we give Emma a history lesson?" She answered him with a small nod, and Tyler continued. "These pictures were drawn by the Indians who used to live in this area. See here?" His finger traced a pattern around the outline of one of the drawings. "This one signifies the hunt; a man on horseback with a quiver of arrows on his back. Here's the buffalo he's chasing." He moved his hand to the left. "Over here is a picture of an Indian couple and the teepee they live in. Here, you can see the outline of a child. If you look close, you can also see an etching of the sun. It's a little faded now from weathering, but the sun is shining down on the couple. It means that Mother Earth has been good to them."

Tyler watched her with concealed interest. *I hope she doesn't find the simple scribes on the rock to be childish.* "Look closely at the teepee, Emma. There's a picture of a wolf on it."

Emma leaned closer, in search of the object he spoke of. Finally, she was able to make out a wolf's head. "What does it mean?"

"The spirit of the wolf guards their home and guides the brave through his days."

Emma reached out and slowly brushed the image of the wolf with her fingertips. She turned to smile up into his eyes, remembering the old Indian they met in a New York market one warm afternoon so long ago. She hoped he remembered, too... "It's an honorable spirit, don't you think?" she murmured.

Tyler returned her smile, and their eyes locked for a moment with the shared memory. Her face literally glowed in the morning sun, and he had all he could do to bring his attention back to the present and the reason he brought them there in the first place.

Tyler ripped his gaze from his beautiful wife and looked down at his daughter. "Why don't you get the picnic basket, Janie, and we'll eat lunch."

The little girl turned and raced to her pony to free the container Mamie packed from where it was securely attached to the saddle.

Tyler busied himself with spreading out a blanket on the fragrant earth and, soon, the three were munching away at the lunch Mamie prepared for them. Emma picked at a cold chicken leg and glanced secretly at her husband. The change in him was nothing short of amazing. He was funny, attentive and, again, more like the man she met in New York—not like the stranger who greeted her so cruelly only a few days before. The sound of his voice brought her back from her reverie.

"You know, Emma, this is my favorite place in the world." Tyler leaned back on his elbows, and a lazy, contented smile curved his firm lips.

Her eyes scanned the cozy clearing again and rested on Janie's slight form, where she played by the water's edge. "I can understand why. It's so quiet and serene." She took another sip of Mamie's homemade wine. "Do you come here often?"

"My brothers and I used to camp here all the time when we were kids. We'd build a big fire and sleep under the stars. I guarantee you though, it wasn't all that serene when the three of us were here together. Trevor never shut his mouth."

A giggle escaped Emma's throat. "He does like to tell stories, doesn't he? He's quite the character."

"Hell, what you've heard come out of his mouth is nothing compared to when he was a boy. We had this hair-brained idea that we were going to breed horses when we grew up, and he could go on about it for hours."

"Tell me more." She tipped her head in his direction, and the simple movement caused the thick braid to fall from her shoulder and lay across an ample breast. The innocent display was enough to make Tyler's heart jump in his chest.

"It was always our dream to raise fine riding stock some day. We used to sit right here and draw pictures of foaling barns and riding paddocks in the sand."

"Why didn't you ever do it?"

He shrugged. "There just never seems to be enough time to make it happen. We still talk about it from time to time, but it would mean backing off from the lumbering business, and many of our men would be without jobs." He rolled onto his side and propped himself up on an elbow. "They're lumberjacks, Emma, not horse breeders. What would they do for a living?"

Emma was overwhelmed once again at the generosity of the Wilkins men. They had put a lifelong dream on hold for the sake of the families who worked so hard for them.

Tyler reached to pour himself another glass of wine as he reflected on his own words. "Maybe it'll happen someday. There'll come a time when there won't be enough timber to harvest, and we'll have to branch out into other areas. Conservation has always been high on our list, so we continually replant and replenish the forests, but it'll take years for those trees to reach cutting age. So, maybe in the meantime, Trevor, Cole, and I can finally achieve the thing we want most to do."

"I couldn't help noticing what beautiful stock you keep on the ranch." She glanced at her husband's horse. "Storm would make a wonderful sire."

"I agree, but we've already used him as stud to most of the mares on the ranch, so we'd have to bring in fresh brood mares with good sturdy lines. If we ever decide to look at this project seriously, it would mean taking time away from the ranch and the mill to do it right." His green eyes watched his daughter stack rocks next to the shoreline. *Could I leave her again for maybe weeks at a time?* "Maybe someday." He shrugged again. "I know one thing—it's been discussed a thousand times, mostly when we were young and right here in this very spot where we sit."

Emma listened to the cadence of his voice. She would never tire of it. His story captured her heart, and it was easy to imagine the three Wilkins men as young boys, dreaming of their future and making a pact to be together always.

Her gaze swept the clearing again—a place where dreams were made—and noticed for the first time an area where a campfire had burned recently. She brought it to his attention.

"It seems someone else has discovered your secret place—and in the last few days or so, no less."

Tyler, who was busy packing the basket for the ride home, finally glanced up at her. "It's my fire. I spent the night here recently."

He stood, casually brushed off his pants, and then crossed to Janie's pony to check the cinch and make sure it was safely secured for the trip back to the ranch.

Emma sat on the blanket and watched after him for a moment, then her eyes moved to the water and the ripples formed by rocks Janie threw into its center. *So, this is where he was last night—even though he won't admit it.* She glanced at the scribed pictures on the rock again. *I wonder if he heard the same wolf howl that I did. Does the fact that he brought me here today, to his special place, mean something?*

She decided not to question him further. This was a day she would always hold dear to her heart and she would not ruin the memory by bringing up the fact that he left her the morning after their wedding.

She stood, brushed off the back of her skirt, took Janie's hand in hers, and walked to the horses to return home.

Chapter Sixteen

The middle of October found Emma firmly ensconced within Tyler's home. She had been in residence for only a month, but already had become an intricate part of the ranch.

She also helped with the household chores, much to Mamie's contrary wishes. The old woman stated firmly that she received enough help from Carrie and the new woman, Katy O'Malley, and that Emma should not bother with such day to day tasks in her condition. Emma staunchly held her ground, however, and informed those around her that it was her home too; Mamie finally gave in and steered the easier tasks in the young woman's direction.

Emma was an avid pupil; the women of the ranch taught her how to can the vegetables they harvested and, when Carrie showed her how to milk a cow, they both ended up with tears of laughter streaming down their faces at Emma's inept attempts to fill her pail.

In New York, she had never had to participate in the actual management of the household and now found her days busy from morning to night. Janie taught her how to sneak eggs from the nest of a roosting chicken, and they spent hours together gathering the last of the harvest from the numerous vegetable gardens on the property. In the end, it was those first weeks in Minnesota that helped to form an unbreakable bond between the two females in Tyler's life.

The air turned cooler and colored leaves fell from the trees. Tyler spent most of his time now with Trevor and Cole at the logging camps. Winter would soon be upon them, and the brothers feverishly pushed the logging crews to complete the necessary harvest before the rivers clogged with ice. The area they lumbered in was too far away to skid the logs to the mill via the use of horses, and they would no longer be able to float the timber down the numerous tributaries that led to the mill once the weather turned.

The seasons changed and nights where the men returned home were few and far between—which only served to make Emma long for her husband more. Most times, they were able to send a message ahead of their arrival and Emma, Janie, and Carrie always prepared a special celebration in honor of their homecoming. Those evenings were always filled with laughter; Trevor never failed to regale them with stories about their days spent in the woods.

Emma's pregnancy was obvious to the casual observer now. Steven Adams came by the ranch often to check on her welfare and, consequently, doctor and patient struck up a comfortable friendship. On this day though, he also became her confidante when he surprised her with a personal question.

"Is there a reason why you and Tyler have separate bedrooms? I'm not trying to pry, but, as your doctor, I just want you to know it's perfectly safe to have intimate relations with your husband."

Emma cheeks colored to a bright, rosy hue as she sat quietly in the chair, pondering how to explain their situation. When she offered no information, Steven pulled up a chair and took her hands in his.

"You can talk to me, Emma. I'm not only your friend, I'm your doctor. Anything you say will be confidential."

He watched Emma's expression change from embarrassment to uncertainty and, finally, to determination.

"I suppose you don't know the full circumstances surrounding our marriage, do you?"

"What I know is that you and he met in New York. You became pregnant with his child, and then traveled here to marry him." He squeezed her hand gently. "Don't be embarrassed by the situation you find yourself in. Do you think you're the first decent woman to become pregnant out of wedlock?"

"I know, Steven, but there are so many other factors in our case." She patted her new friend's hand in thanks, and then rose to stand before the window. He sat patiently and waited for her to continue.

"Tyler and I have not occupied the same bed since the night we conceived this child. We spent that last night in New York together by a trick of fate. Tyler was pretty well intoxicated, entered my room by mistake, and I asked him to stay." She turned to seek his understanding gaze. "I want you to know that, Steven. I want you to know that this whole mess is just as much my fault as his."

"Go on, Emma. I'm trying hard to piece together your story, but I fear I don't know everything yet, do I?" She shook her head and a bittersweet smile curved her lips as she turned back to the window.

"Tyler doesn't believe the baby is his. He thinks I have been with other men and that I chose him, because he was my best prospect for a safe and secure future." She shrugged her slim shoulders. "At least that's the only theory I can come up with after trying to piece it together in my own mind. Apparently, he was too drunk to realize I was a virgin when he took me, and I can't seem to convince him of the fact. Because of that, he refuses to treat me as his wife and invite me to his bed."

Steven sat quietly and mused over her words. Her response reflected the current situation to a tee. "Emma, how does he treat you when the two of you are alone? From what I've seen, he's pleasant enough when we're all together."

She turned back from her study of the world beyond the window with a sigh. "The first few nights after I arrived were really rough. He was angry and felt cornered. My own behavior was none too ladylike, either." She shook her head and raised a rueful eyebrow. "I seem to recall telling him that he was more of a bastard than this baby could ever be. He left the morning after the wedding and didn't come back until the following day. Since then, we've been like strangers forced to live in the same house; amiable and polite, yet distant. It never goes beyond that." She crossed back to the chair next to Steven, sank down into it, and gazed at him with sad, defeated eyes.

"I know Tyler needs time to accept me as his wife, and I'm willing to wait as long as it takes. He's still grieving for Sara, and I would expect no less from a man who loved his wife as deeply as Tyler did. She's been gone only two years. I'm hoping though, that someday he will love and trust me as much as he did her."

The young doctor's thoughtful, understanding gaze moved over his patient's beautiful features with an invisible shake of the head. *You're a damned lucky man, Tyler, and you don't even know it.*

The thwack of axes biting into hardened tree bark, and the whine of double-handled saws echoed through the forest. Those sounds mingled with shouts of "timber!" from the lumberjacks and an occasional whinny from the horses to create an atmosphere of organized chaos. The logging crew was almost finished culling the last stand of timber, and the men could not work fast enough. Two more days would see them home again, with their families. No more timberline shacks. No more long days filled with hard labor. For most, it would mean home and hearth, and their wives beside them at night. For Tyler and Cole, it simply meant the end to another cutting season—a season that had grown agonizingly long.

"I'm glad I listened to Trevor and hired extra men to clear this stand of timber," the elder Wilkins brother commented as he and Cole oversaw the beehive of activity below. He continued as an image of Emma's smiling face flitted through his brain. "We wouldn't be near this close to finishing up if we hadn't. I'm ready to go home myself and just stay put for a while."

"I have to agree with you there. We should really see about keeping this last bunch of guys working, though. They've more than proven themselves in the last week." He turned to face his brother, and a sly smile lifted the corners of his mouth. "You know what, Ty? I, for one, am getting good and ready for some of Mamie's cooking, not to mention a nice, soft bed at night. Hell, I'm even more good and ready for someone soft to share that bed with!"

Tyler pretended not to hear his brother's last comment. Instead, he stretched his long arms above his head in a casual show of disinterest, then trudged back up to the top of the hill to watch the line of men who readied the trailer of logs that were to be sent down the embankment and into the river. His thoughts, however, gave him away—at least to himself.

He was ready to make peace with Emma. He had been at the camp for the past week, and his new wife continually invaded his dreams—both day and night. He visualized her naked in his bed, waiting for him with outstretched arms. His stomach tightened, along with a much more insistent part of his body.

He could no longer treat her like a permanent guest in his home—a guest who caused the constant agitation that plagued him whenever they were in the same room. When he could take her close proximity inside the house no longer, he urged Emma and Janie outdoors, where he could put a little distance between them.

The ruse also provided a means to observe his wife and daughter together. He could find no fault with Emma's attitude toward the little girl. She always made sure Janie's needs came before her own and, most importantly, the child adored her.

He shook his head at his own ignorance. The rest of his family, too, seemed entranced by her bright outlook in everything she did. Wherever Emma went, her good nature followed, and her admirers grew by leaps and bounds.

Tyler actually found humor in the fact that, if a decision were to be made that one of them had to leave the ranch, his family would pack his bags without a second thought.

He had gone over and over the situation in his mind and finally came to the realization that he wanted Emma in his life. *I don't care anymore if she's been with someone else,* he told himself firmly. *And I have to believe that the baby is mine.*

Tyler felt a weight lift from his shoulders with the decision. *Only two more days*, he mused, then he smiled. Two days that would seem like a lifetime now that he could not wait to go home to her. He would court her as she had never been courted before—until she was weak with desire.

Tyler walked down the hill toward the shore with a much lighter step, then paused when Trevor hollered to him from above. He turned, waved to let his brother know he was listening, and then Trevor shouted above the din.

"Get the men ready! We'll be sending the logs down in a minute. Whistle when you're set and we'll let 'em loose!" Tyler waved again in confirmation, and then continued down the trail next to the treeless skidway.

The earth shuddered a few minutes later and, nearly to the bottom of the steep incline now, Tyler whirled just in time to see the logs come crashing down the earthen ramp. His alert gaze swung back to the water's edge, where three men worked unawares, trying to break up a jam that had backed the logs up more than thirty feet from the shore. He waved his arms wildly and bellowed a warning as he raced toward the men, but to no avail. The rush of the river water was deafening, and the hired men were impervious to their employer's frantic calls.

Christ—if I can't get their attention, they'll be killed! Tyler jumped onto the first of the congested logs and his feet flew over their cut lengths in an effort to reach his men. *Why in hell did Trevor give the go-ahead to release the trailer?*

Tyler was within fifteen feet of the three loggers when one glanced up to see the gigantic timbers barreling toward them. He frantically motioned to the other two men. "Get the hell out of the way!" he yelled, and then leapt out of harm's way himself.

Tyler recklessly picked his way across the logjam as fast as his feet would carry him, then leapt to safety himself and turned to check the whereabouts of his men. The barreling timbers rolled down the hill less than six feet from him, and suddenly one log bounced off another and shot through the air. It clipped Tyler on the side of his head, and he pitched to the ground.

* * *

Tyler awoke in one of the logging shacks to a headache so fierce he could barely move his head.

"Jesus Christ, Tyler, you scared the hell out of us!" Trevor railed. He laid his hands on his brother's shoulders and held him down. "Don't sit up. Just stay where you are. The men are bringing a wagon around and we're going to get you home."

Trevor's face was the same pale shade as Cole's, and Tyler closed his eyes against the evidence of his brothers' concern. *What in the hell happened?* He struggled to remember the events leading up to the accident. Trevor was supposed to wait for his signal, giving him time to clear the area next to the shoreline.

He ignored the throbbing in his head, squinted into the light, and stared at his brother. "What the hell were you doing up there? You were supposed to wait for my whistle. I wasn't even to the bottom of the skidway yet! I could've been killed, along with three other men!"

Relief flooded Trevor's eyes. Tyler's memory seemed to be intact, but he still had a nasty, blood-oozing bump on the side of his head. They needed to get him home so Steve could take a look at it, and they needed to do it soon.

Trevor glanced up at Cole, who nodded for him to take the lead. "We were ready at the top of the ramp, Ty. When I saw you were still making your way to the bottom though, I went to talk to Cole and Jack. The next thing I knew, I heard the logs roll off the trailer. It was so damned noisy that we couldn't get your attention." His masculine features blanched once more at the thought of the possible outcome of the accident, and his voice lowered to a near whisper with the last. "One of the men saw somebody from the new group cut the main holding rope."

Tyler's fuzzy brain digested his brother's words. Someone had purposely tried to kill him and three others; his stomach churned at the thought. "Did you find out who it was? Where is he now?"

Trevor shook his head. "He's gone. With the logs rolling down the hill, everyone was just worried about getting your attention. Whoever slit the rope took off as soon as the logs started down the hill." He looked closely at his brother. "So, do you have any enemies we don't know about?"

He thought about the question for a moment before answering and, finally, his glassy eyes met his brother's concerned ones. "Well, apparently I must." Tyler winced. "Jesus, my head is pounding so hard that I can't even think."

At that moment, the foreman stuck his burly head through the open door. "The wagon's here, Trevor."

"Thanks, Jack," he replied, then looked at Tyler again. "Okay, let's take this nice and slow."

Cole and Trevor helped Tyler to sit upright. Immediate concern clouded their gazes when his eyes rolled back in his head and the gash on his forehead bled through the bandage.

They pulled him to a standing position and his body dipped in the direction of the floor, then everything went black.

Emma and Carrie hung laundry on the clotheslines behind the house, both of them laughing about something Mamie said earlier. Emma reached for another sheet and automatically handed one edge to her sister-in-law.

Carrie's eyebrow rose when she glanced across the length of white material and saw the happy sparkle in Emma's eyes. "You sure are enjoying the laundry today."

The other woman's smile widened as she threw her end of the sheet over the line.

Carrie placed her hands on her slender hips and met her sister-in-law's gaze. "Okay, you look like the cat who lapped the cream. What's going on?"

Emma's face flushed with excitement. "I'm just happy that the men will be home for good in a few days."

"You mean that *Tyler* will be home for good. You can't honestly tell me you're looking forward to having those other two idiot brothers of mine under foot."

The sound of Emma's laughter rang out in the brisk afternoon air. "Trevor and Cole are wonderful, Carrie, and you know it. You're right, though—I'm really looking forward to having Tyler around. Things may still be unresolved between us, but it will help my mood immensely to just see his face every day."

Emma and Carrie had just finished hanging the last of the towels when the door to the kitchen banged open and Katy waved her arms frantically to gain their attention. "Carrie! Emma! Come quick! A rider just came in! There's been an accident at the logging camp!"

Both women bolted for the house, then skidded to a stop just inside the kitchen door when they confronted a man with wood shavings stuck to his shirt. He nervously fingered the hat in his hands.

Carrie immediately took charge. "Who's hurt? What happened?"

The man looked from one woman to the other. "I'm sorry, Mrs. Wilkins— it's Tyler—"

Emma grabbed the chair next to her for support. "Please, tell me what happened!"

The man's eyes softened with compassion in light of her concern. "Ma'am, he took quite a blow to the head from a rolling log. It knocked him out for a time, and he's got a wicked cut on his head. Cole and Trevor are bringing him in. Cole told me to ride ahead and notify you they were coming. He says to send someone for Doc Adams, cuz he thinks Tyler needs stitches. Ma'am, if you'll give me a fresh horse, I'd be happy to start out for the doc now." He shuffled his feet nervously and waited for her answer.

Emma remained mute with fear, so Carrie spoke up. "Katy, show him down to the barn and ask Clancey to saddle a horse immediately." She looked at the lumberjack again, and a shaky smile curved her lips. "Thank you so much for your help. Hurry now, though—tell Doctor Adams to come immediately."

Katy left with the logger following in her wake. Carrie turned to Emma, and the sight of her pale face was enough to make her pull a chair away from the table. She forced the other woman down onto it. "Just take a deep breath, Em. The man said Tyler was fine, except for a cut on his head."

"But he said he was unconscious, Carrie...!"

"Yes—for a time. If you got hit in the head with a log, you'd be unconscious, too. I'm sure Tyler is fine." She spoke the words to allay her own fear, as well as Emma's.

"I'm so scared, Carrie! If something ever happened to Tyler, I don't know what I would do!"

"Well, you won't be doing anyone a favor if you make yourself sick." She patted Emma's trembling hand, and then gave her a quick hug. "Come on. We'll get out what medical supplies we have here, and then go out front to wait for them. It's going to be all right. I promise."

The two women stood on the front porch and scanned the horizon for any sign of a wagon. The better part of two hours passed before they spied the buckboard, as it lumbered down the hill. They hurried to the entrance gate and, when the wagon approached, Emma hopped into the back, with Trevor's help. She crawled to Tyler's side and touched a controlled hand to his shoulder.

"Tyler?" She whispered softly when he slowly opened his eyes. "You're home now. Steven will be here soon to take care of that head of yours."

The distraught woman of two hours ago was gone. Emma was now calm and in control, reacting to the situation with a composure she found somewhere in that space of time. Only she could feel the frantic thud of her heart against her ribs.

Tyler focused on his wife with some difficulty, and his head swam with the effort. "'Scuse me—" he mumbled "—if I don't talk much, Em. It's not you...my head hurts." His words were slurred, and she bit down on her lower lip in an effort to hold back the tears.

"Then don't say anything. You're alive, and that's what counts."

The wagon stopped in front of the house and Cole helped Emma down, then turned back to aid Trevor in getting Tyler out of the back. The two men sat him upright, then assisted him to a standing position. Tyler was forced to lean against the wooden side of the buckboard until his head and stomach stopped whirling. He hated having Emma see him like this—weak as a baby and dependant on someone else to help him walk—but the situation was out of his control. If his brothers let go of him, he would be face down in the dirt.

Steven raced into the yard astride his horse just as Cole and Trevor were helping Tyler up the stairway to the second floor. He leapt from the saddle, ran through the open doorway, and met them on the staircase.

Cole smiled a grateful welcome. "I think he's going to live, but he's got one helluva gash on the right side of his head. We figured we'd put him to bed. I don't think he'll be going anywhere for a while."

Steven looked up at Emma and Carrie's pale faces, where they stood at the top of the stairs. *They could both use a good, stiff drink,* he mused. "Carrie, do you have bandages laid out?"

"Of course I do! Do you think I've been sitting around here for the last two hours doing nothing? And it's a good thing I did, too. It took *you* long enough to get here."

Emma's gaze swung in Carrie's direction. *Where in the world did that come from? It's not like her to be rude to anybody.*

Emma did not dwell on her sister-in-law's attitude toward the good doctor. Cole and Trevor had finally reached the top of the staircase with their burden and now carried him into the master suite.

Emma ran ahead to pull back the covers on the bed, then the two men carefully laid Tyler on the white sheet. Steven unpacked his medical bag while Cole and Trevor began to undress their brother. No one noticed when Emma slipped quietly from the room and sank down onto a chair in the hallway. *I've got every right to be in the room—I should be helping them, but I can't.*

Emma had not seen Tyler naked since the night they made love in New York and was not sure he would want her to again now. So, instead, she fidgeted anxiously in the chair and listened closely to the muffled voices that came from the other side of the door. She could do nothing but wait to be summoned.

Emma counted the passing minutes with a sick feeling of dread roiling in the pit of her stomach. She clutched her hands in her lap to control their trembling. A sudden noise drew her attention and she glanced up to see Janie standing at the top of the stairs, with the pup at her side. The child's pale expression and rivers of tears tore at Emma's heart.

She opened her arms and the child ran to her. Janie clung to her neck in a silent plea for comfort. "Oh, Janie, I'm sorry I didn't come looking for you."

The girl's small shoulders shook with an almost tangible fear.

"Honey, don't cry. Your daddy is going to be just fine. I promise."

Janie shook her head 'no' against her stepmother's shoulder, and Emma held her at arms length in order to meet her gaze directly. "Yes, he will," she stated with more conviction than she felt. "As soon as your Uncle Cole and Uncle Trevor say it's okay, we'll go inside and you can see for yourself."

Emma pulled Janie onto her lap and held her tightly, willing away the child's certainty that she was about to lose her last remaining parent. She rocked the little girl slowly and waited for the quiet sobs to cease before pushing damp strands of blonde hair away from her wet cheeks.

"Listen to me, Janie. Your daddy isn't going to go away. We won't let him, because we love him too much. He's just got a bad cut on his head and Dr. Steve is stitching it up." She hugged her close once more. "You sit here with me and we'll wait together. How does that sound?"

Janie wiped her face with the back of a chubby hand and nestled her head against Emma's shoulder. As the woman gently stroked her soft blonde locks, she realized how much she had come to love Tyler and Sara's child.

* * *

Cole opened the door to Tyler's bedroom three-quarters of an hour later and stepped into the hall. Emma gently placed Janie on the carpeted floor and rose from the chair. Cole threw a quick smile in her direction before squatting to pat his niece's shoulder.

"Hi, Janie. I think your daddy needs a big hug from you. Make sure you don't forget when you see him, okay?"

A tremulous smile appeared on the child's face before she ran into her father's room.

Cole straightened. "Would you like to go in, Em?"

"How is he? Is he going to be all right?" Her voice broke, and Cole pulled her into his arms.

"He's going to be just fine, honey. Probably a little ornery for a while. I'm sure his head feels twice the size it should be."

She leaned back to look up into her brother-in-law's handsome face. "What happened? You all are usually so careful..."

"It was just a dumb accident, Emma," he responded with carefully chosen words. There was no need for her to know at this point that someone might be out to target Tyler's life. "I'm just thankful he's still alive, and that's all you should concern yourself with, too, at this point. Why don't you go in and see him?" He smiled. "Especially since it's easy to see that you'd rather be in there than talking to me in the hallway."

Emma entered the bedroom and met Trevor as he was leaving. He gave Emma's arm a quick squeeze. "He'll be fine. Go see for yourself."

He nodded toward the bed, where Steven placed the last of the blood-spattered clothes into a bag. Emma's stomach churned at the undeniable proof of Tyler's injury. The doctor grabbed the last of the rags and forced a stern look onto his face for his friend's benefit.

"I'm warning you, Tyler. You stay in that bed until at least tomorrow afternoon." The doctor cocked an eyebrow in Emma's direction and tried to lighten the gloomy mood in the room. "Make sure he doesn't escape and go bronco riding or some other crazy thing!" His statement produced a small, relieved laugh from Emma, and Tyler just grabbed his head.

"Get the hell out of here, Steve. Your rambling is making my head hurt worse." His expression sobered as he met his friend's gaze. "One more thing before you go—thanks, for everything. I'm serious."

Steve patted his buddy on the shoulder. "I know you're serious, Tyler, and you don't have to thank me. Besides," he added with a cheeky smile, "you probably won't be so grateful when you get my bill!"

"Go on, get out of here," Tyler chuckled softly. "I'll see you tomorrow."

Janie still stood only a few feet inside the door, and Tyler held a hand out in a silent invitation for the frightened little girl to climb up on the bed beside him. Emma whispered a thank you to Steven on his way out, then turned to help her stepdaughter up onto the feather tick. Once she was settled, Tyler tapped the bandage that was wrapped around his head. "Pretty nice, hey, Janie?" he quipped, trying to ease the fear he saw in her wide, blue eyes. "Uncle Trevor is mad that he didn't think to wrap his head up so he could get out of work."

A smile tugged at the corners of her mouth, and he took her small trembling chin in his hand. "Come on, let's see that smile you're hiding. Daddy is just fine, honey." Relief washed over him at the sight of her grin, and he pulled her close.

Emma saw the fatigue in her husband's eyes a short time later and reached out to pat Janie's hand. "Honey, why don't you go wash up for dinner. I'll be down shortly."

Janie bounded down from the bed and left the room, then Emma pulled a chair up to the bedside and sat down. Tyler shifted in search of a more comfortable position for his head and, seeing his struggle with the pillow, she stood again to lend some assistance.

"Here, let me help you with that." She reached across the span of the big bed. "Lean forward and I'll straighten the pillow."

The scent of his clean washed hair reached her nostrils as she adjusted the headrest behind him, and her stomach did a little flip. In turn, her perfumed fragrance caused his heart to beat a little harder. Their gazes locked.

I love you so much, her mind betrayed her, and she threw caution to the wind as she pressed her lips to his.

Her impulsiveness drew a raised eyebrow from Tyler, and he reached up to gently caress her silky cheek with his roughened fingers. The kiss deepened, and two hearts beat as one for a breathless and extremely fragile moment. The spell was broken when Tyler slowly pulled back to stare into the sultry green eyes above him.

"What was that for?" His words were barely a whisper.

"Because you're still alive. I was so scared, Tyler."

"You were?"

Her eyes widened slightly with disbelief. "Of course, I was." She sat back in the chair again, and her gaze dropped to her lap. "Tyler...we really need to talk."

"I know we do." He closed his eyes for a moment against the agonizing pounding in his head. "Please don't think I'm turning you away, Emma, but can we talk tomorrow? I can hardly keep my eyes open, and I ache all over. I know we need to talk, and I want to, but I can't give you the attention you deserve right now."

She stood and her dimples deepened in an understanding smile. He was willing to discuss the situation between them, and she could not ask for more. She squeezed his hand gently. "I'll stop by after supper and check on you. Maybe you'll feel like eating something." She bent to drop a kiss on his stubbled cheek and ignored the surprise in his eyes. "See you later."

Emma floated from the room with a song in her heart.

Later that evening, Emma balanced a tray with one hand and knocked on the entrance to Tyler's room with the other. Receiving no response, she slowly opened the door and her gaze fell on his peacefully sleeping countenance. He had rolled onto his stomach and the sheet had wrapped around his waist. The pit of her stomach clenched with desire at the sight of his broad, muscular, deeply-tanned back. *He must work outdoors without a shirt on,* she mused.

She crossed to the bed and, even though his body was relaxed in slumber, she could still see the subdued strength of his muscular body. She quelled the urge to run her fingers over the rippling sinews and placed the tray on the bedstand before she pulled the covers over him. "I love you," she whispered near his ear, then left for her own room, where she would spend another anxious night.

Tyler felt someone staring at him. He opened his eyes with a start and found Janie standing next to the bed, patiently waiting for him to waken. She held a tray in her tiny hands, which held toast and juice, and Tyler could not resist the urge to tease her.

"Well, hello there." A dark brow slanted over his left eye. "Are you the new maid Mamie hired?" His answer came in the form of a smile that creased Janie's face from ear to ear. She nodded. "Is that for me?" Again he received a quick smile and a nod. "Okay, but I'll only eat it if the maid shares it with me."

Tyler sat up with slow and measured movements, plumped the pillows behind him, and ignored the dull thud in his head. He took the tray from Janie's hands and waited while she scurried up next to him. Balancing the food on his lap, he proceeded to hand her one of the pieces of toasted bread and their makeshift "tea party" began.

Emma entered the room through the connecting doorway fifteen minutes later and was greeted by the sound of Tyler's deep laughter. Whizzer leapt through the air to catch the small piece of crust thrown to him from the bed.

"Well, this certainly doesn't look like a sickroom, now does it?"

He looked up at her with a welcoming smile. "Come on in, Emma, and join us! My beautiful daughter graciously brought me breakfast in bed. I think I'll have to jump in front of rolling logs more often if this is the sort of treatment I'll receive!"

"Don't even joke about that," she chastised as she moved to stand beside the bed. "You scared everyone half to death. If you want breakfast in bed every morning, I'll be happy to comply, and you don't have to get hit in the head with a log to get it!"

"I can't think of anything I'd like better." The suggestive words were accompanied by a dark, sensual spark in his eyes, and Emma's face blushed a deep red.

Tyler chuckled softly at her reaction—and at her meager attempt to find something to occupy her attention so she would not have to meet his gaze.

I have a feeling that life with her is going to be anything but boring. What in the hell was I thinking? It's high time I set aside my foolish ego and make this marriage work.

The realization that he wanted Emma in his life—and in his bed—manifested itself in the hardening of a certain part of Tyler's body; a response brought on by simple flirtation. *My God, how in the hell will my body react when I actually touch her!*

Tyler knew the answer only too well, and he also knew that she would flee the room in appalled outrage if she discovered his thoughts...or would she?

Emma's next words squelched any chance of finding out—at least for now.

"Why don't we go downstairs, Janie, and let your dad wash up. We can come back later."

"You'd better." Tyler's gaze held hers and, again, his hidden meaning was clear. They had much to discuss—not the least of which was whether or not she would share his bed that night.

Emma's cheeks flushed again, this time to a color near purple, as she took Janie's hand in hers and exited the room.

Chapter Seventeen

By noon of that same day, Emma was hard pressed not to snap at anyone foolish enough to get in her way. Tyler entertained one group of workers after another the entire morning and, though Emma knew she should be touched by the concern for their employer, it did not make her growing frustration any easier to bear. She wanted to talk with Tyler herself, with no interruptions, and plan the future she now knew he wanted as much as she.

She finally escorted the last of the visitors to the door, and then bounded up the stairs to his room before anyone else could intrude. Janie, with a fair amount of coaxing on Emma's part, finally agreed to ride with Carrie to a friend's house. They would not return to the ranch until just before dark. Mamie and Katie were busy in the smokehouse, and Trevor and Cole were off doing whatever it was they did during the day. She and Tyler had the house to themselves, finally, and Emma was not about to waste their time alone.

She knocked softly on his half-open door, then peeked around the corner. A smile curved her lips when she saw him sitting in one of the overstuffed chairs in front of the fireplace. He glanced up and motioned for her to join him.

"There isn't anybody else waiting in the wings is there?"

Emma shook her head as she seated herself in the chair next to his. "The house is finally cleared out and, for that, I'm grateful."

A moment of tense silence ensued as each waited for the other to speak first. Emma fidgeted in the chair, amazed that she could not think of one thing to say after waiting half the day for this moment. Tyler's expression was just as uneasy. He took a deep breath though, and started the conversation.

"Emma...I thought a lot about our situation during the last month I spent up in the woods."

"I know. I've also been agonizing over it, Tyler." She sat with her head tipped slightly downward and could not make herself meet his gaze.

"Let me back up a minute. I haven't asked you how you're feeling lately, with the baby and all, I mean. I can see you've changed your style of clothing slightly. I hope that means things are progressing well."

It was the first time they had talked in a civil manner about the child, and it did Emma's heart good when he asked the question.

"I'm feeling well. Steven says he's very happy with how things are going and expects the baby to be born sometime in March." She met his gaze finally and smiled. "I can feel it moving now."

It was Tyler's turn to drop his gaze to his lap. He was so out of touch on the subject of the child. The issue had not come up again since that first awful night after she arrived in Minnesota.

"Emma—" Tyler leaned forward in the chair and clasped his hands together "—do you think..."

"Hello!" Steven's voice echoed through the upper floor and, a second later, he poked his blond head through the open doorway of the bedroom. "There you are! Sorry I didn't get here sooner to check on you, Ty. I had an emergency and was tied up most of the morning." His glance swept Emma. "How you doing today, Em?

"I'm fine," she murmured through clenched teeth.

Steven was oblivious to the pained expression on her face as he turned to his patient. He set his medical bag on the table between the two chairs and rummaged through it for a stethoscope before he addressed Tyler again. "And how's the head today? Do you still have a headache?"

"I didn't until a moment ago," his friend muttered beneath his breath.

"I'm sorry, what did you say?" the doctor asked as he pulled the instrument from his bag and clipped it around his neck. "I missed that with all the rattling going on in my bag."

"Never mind," Tyler groaned.

"Okay," Steven replied slowly. "Come and lay back down on the bed then, Ty, so I can check you over."

Emma stood, and she and her husband shared a look of consternation at having to wait yet one more time to settle the matter at hand. "I'll leave you with Steven for now."

She started to leave the room then, but paused to turn back. "Steve, would you have a moment to speak with me before you leave?"

"Sure, what's up?"

"Oh, nothing. I'll wait for you on the front porch."

Tyler's quizzical eyes followed her slender form as she left the room.

The October sun warmed Emma's face as she sat and waited for Steven. She used the tip of her toe to move the wooden swing and mused about the fact that she was witnessing one of those rare days of Indian summer. Soon, they would have snow.

Tyler had informed her that winters in Minnesota were nothing like what she experienced in New York. Emma looked forward to the change of season with mixed feelings. The bitterly cold weather she could do without, but, if she could spend it being warmed in Tyler's arms, then it would be worth it.

Hurry, Steven! Be done! I need to speak with Tyler!

Steven finally strolled through the front door and onto the porch thirty minutes later. Spotting Emma on the swing, he crossed and dropped onto the wooden surface next to her.

"It sure is a nice day. Not many of these left before winter sets in. A warm October day is very rare in these parts." He paused and turned to look at her. "So, what was it you wanted to talk to me about?"

"How is Tyler doing? He's going to be fine, isn't he?"

"Yeah—be assured he'll come out of this completely unscathed. I left him in the library. He said he needed to get up for a while and wanted me to let you know that's where he'll be." Steven glanced in her direction. "I've come to know you pretty well, Em. What else is bothering you?"

"Tyler and I are finally going to settle this matter between us. In fact, we were talking about it when you came in."

Steven winced. "Ouch—I thought something was going on. I'm sorry my timing was so bad."

She waved her hand in dismissal. "No, that's quite all right. It wasn't until I saw you that I realized I needed to ask you something. I think most of the issues between us will be resolved today."

Emma stared straight ahead and finally found the courage to voice the question that sat on her lips. "I wanted to know if Tyler is well enough to..." Steven watched the blush spread across her smooth cheeks. She struggled to continue, but could not find the right words.

Steven could not suppress the chuckle that rose in his throat. He nudged her shoulder in a show of friendship. "If you're asking me what I think you are, then my answer is yes. Tyler will be ready for anything he decides he wants to do, barring another near miss with a rolling log. If you two can fix this thing, then I'm happy for the both of you and say go right ahead. Does that answer your question?"

She covered her burning cheeks with her hands. "I can't believe I asked you that—even if you are a doctor! I hope you don't think ill of me for asking you about something so personal."

"Come on, Em. Walk me to my horse." He grabbed her hand and pulled her up from the swing, and they left the porch. Steven released his grip on her hand and slung an arm over her shoulder. "I could never think ill of you, Emma. In fact, I think you're really good for Tyler. If, for some reason things don't happen tonight though, don't give up. I've known Tyler my whole life, and he's one helluva guy. It's just that Sara's death sent his world into a relentless spin. I've always respected him for his ethics and the love of his family and, trust me, you *will* be included in that select circle. You have to believe that." He squeezed her shoulder. "Quit worrying. Things will work themselves out."

They reached his horse then, and the young doctor untied the reins from the hitching post.

"Thank you, Steve, for everything. I'm truly lucky to have you for a friend. You've always been willing to listen with an understanding ear and have never been judgmental. That means so much. It was such a relief when I saw you coming up the stairs yesterday. I knew you'd take care of him. I love Tyler so much, and I don't know what I would've done if I'd lost him." She reached out to rest a hand on his forearm, and her eyes glistened with unshed tears. "Thank you for being his friend, too."

Steven wrapped his arms around her slender body and pulled her close. "Go find him, Em. Just go in there and tell him how much you care. You might be surprised by his response."

"What's that supposed to mean?"

"It means that I think he loves you, too. Good luck to you, hon, but I don't think you'll need it."

She stood on tiptoe to kiss him on the cheek, and a bright smile lit her eyes. "Thank you, from both of us!"

"Go in there now and be happy. I'll be back tomorrow to check his stitches." He mounted his horse and wheeled the animal around before waving goodbye.

Emma watched after him until he was out of sight, then turned back toward the house. Her future awaited her in the library, and nothing was going to come between them now.

Emma's heart took on an erratic beat as she hurried through the foyer. She stepped through the doorway to the library a moment later, and her voice floated across the room to where Tyler stood before the window.

"Hi. Would you like something to drink before we sit down? Mamie has some fresh squeezed juice in the kitchen." He did not turn at the sound of her voice. "Tyler? Did you hear me?"

She noticed his stiff back then, and her eyebrows dipped in concern as she crossed to stand beside him. She laid a gentle hand on his arm. "Tyler, is something wrong?"

He jerked his arm free of her touch, and his cold, uncaring eyes stared blankly through the windowpane and into the front yard. His square jaw was clenched with anger. "That was a touching scene I just witnessed." His voice was as brittle and unyielding as his gaze.

"I don't understand what you're talking about." Again, he did not respond, and she gripped his arm once more, tighter this time. "You're scaring me, Tyler. What is wrong?"

"I'll tell you what's wrong! I just stood here and watched you say a very *tender* goodbye to my best friend!" He turned to face her, and his hateful gaze caused her to recoil in shock. "I was ready to bare my soul to you, Emma; to work out a solution to our problems, so we could be happy! I've been up in those goddamn woods for the last month, fighting with myself, telling myself that I had to trust you; that I had to believe in your honesty!" The words tumbled from his mouth, and they became seething, caustic. "And how do you repay me? By carrying on with another man—a man who is *my* best friend! I saw you walk Steve to his horse, and I saw him put his arms around you! You not only hugged him back, but you *kissed* him! You could've at least had the decency to be a little more discreet, instead of flaunting your affair in broad daylight!"

He saw the shock in her eyes and the disbelief on her face. "Don't look at me like that, Emma. Your pleading and your lies won't do any good—not anymore." He turned then, and stalked toward the doorway.

"You're wrong, Tyler!" Her words stopped his exit from the room. "Steve has become a good friend, and I was simply thanking him for taking care of both of us! You can't honestly believe that we've been seeing each other?" She ran to his side and gripped his arm in a frantic hold. "Please, don't throw away what we could have, Tyler! I love you! I've loved you from the moment I met you!"

He whirled to face her again, and his eyes bored into her—eyes that were filled with the pain of betrayal. "How can you speak of love? You don't even know what it means! Your idea of love is letting some man maul you!" He grabbed her upper arms and pulled her to within inches of his face, and Emma could only close her eyes against the tears that threatened never to stop. His voice lowered to an ominous timber as he continued. "What happened that night on the veranda with Samuel Fontaine, Emma? Where did you go when you left the ballroom? Were you with him? Do you think what he did to you was an act of love? Well, believe me, it wasn't! Love is believing in someone, Emma! Love is *trusting* someone! Love is making a commitment to *one* person for the rest of your life, not passing your favors around freely, like you seem to do!"

"No! You've got it all wrong! Samuel attacked me that night on the veranda, because he has hated me his entire life! I didn't tell anyone, because he threatened to hurt Evan if I did. When I left the ballroom, I went home—alone! Please, Tyler, you have to believe me! I love you!"

He released her with a jerk and shook his head slowly. "I already told you, Emma. You don't know the meaning of the word. You proved that a few minutes ago. True love is what I once had with a beautiful, gentle, caring woman—a woman I would've gladly died for if I'd been given the chance. But fate took her away from me." His voice cracked with the forbidden tears that shone in his eyes. "I thought fate had handed me another chance, with you, but I was wrong." He paused before issuing the final ultimatum. "This marriage will never work. I want you to leave as soon as you can make the arrangements. I don't want you here anymore—and I refuse to raise Samuel Fontaine's baby."

Emma's tear-saturated eyes widened in horror. "Tyler, listen to me, please! This baby is not Samuel's! You are the only man I've ever been with! Don't make me leave—don't make a mistake you'll regret for the rest of your life! Please, give me a chance to explain!"

Tyler rubbed the back of his neck, trying to ease the throbbing tension, and then shook his head slowly again. "No more explanations. I'm done with your lies, Emma. I have to believe what I saw with my own eyes. I can't let you do this to me anymore."

Intense anger at his ignorance welled up inside of her, and Emma balled her hands into fists and pummeled his chest in a futile effort to let it out. Tyler flinched as he took the blows, but his icy gaze never softened as she screamed into his face.

"Do *what* to you? I have done *nothing,* except love you with all my heart! Well, I'll tell you something, you stupid, ignorant man! I won't give up, Tyler! I won't leave you! I won't throw away the first and *only* love of my life!"

Emma stumbled back, and her glittering eyes darted wildly around the room for an escape from the excruciating pain that seared her heart. The walls closed in and she ran past him, through the foyer, and out into the yard.

Emma raced to the barn. She needed to escape the house, to escape Tyler and his accusations.

Inside the barn, she grabbed a saddle, then dropped it twice on her way to the stabled horse that eyed her warily. She quickly threw a blanket over the mare's back and followed it with the saddle—and a sob. Sensing her agitation, the animal sidled away in fear.

"Stand still, you stupid beast!" She brushed a sleeved arm across her face to wipe away the blinding tears, threw a bridle over the mare's head, then tied the horse to the gate and fumbled with the girth strap. A sudden voice from behind was enough to nearly make her jump out of her skin.

"Miss Em? What're you doing?" Clancey's voice held an edge of uncertainty.

"I'm saddling this stupid horse! What does it look like I'm doing?" She swiped the tears from her face again and muttered a curse when she could not get the buckle to work. She refused to look at the hired hand.

"I can see something is wrong, Miss Em. Maybe you should calm down before getting on that animal."

She threw him a scathing glare over her shoulder as she led the chestnut mare past him and out of the stall. "Maybe you should attend to your own business, Clancey, and leave mine alone!"

Emma grabbed a whip that lay atop a hay bale, lifted her foot into the stirrup, and heaved herself up by the saddle horn. The hired hand reached up to grab at the bridle.

"Please, Miss Em, let's talk about what's wrong. If something were to happen to you out there, with you in such a state, Tyler'd have my head."

Sparks shot from the depths of her glittering green eyes. "Let go of the horse, Clancey, or I'll run you over. This is your only warning!"

Clancey tightened his grip on the bridle. "I can't let you go like this, Miss Em! I'm afraid for your safety!"

Emma raised her hand, brought the whip down hard on the mare's rump, and simultaneously dug her heels into the animal's ribs. It leapt forward, and Clancey lost his grip as Emma raced from the barn. Once she was clear of the doorway, she kicked the horse on to an even greater speed. Clancey ran after her and watched helplessly as she charged down the driveway, then reined the animal through the open log gate at the entrance to the ranch. Red hair whipped around her face as she left a cloud of dust in her wake.

A sinking feeling settled as a lump in the pit of Clancey's stomach. Emma was riding wildly and hell bent on going as fast as the horse could carry her. He shook his head, his fear allayed only by the fact that he knew she was an excellent rider. There was nothing he could do but wait for her return.

Tyler sat behind the large oak desk in the library, eyes closed and fingers massaging his throbbing temples. He could not find the simple strength to stand, let alone trudge up the steps to his second floor bedroom. He was emotionally exhausted and physically ill after the horrific argument with Emma and had been sitting for the better part of an hour going over it in his mind.

He had heard Emma ride out at a breakneck pace earlier. Even with as hurt and angry as he was, he had almost followed her. Her safety was still his responsibility, but it was quite obvious that she wanted to be alone—and away from him.

Tyler recalled his final ultimatum, and the mere thought of spending his days without her had his emotions in a turmoil.

You stupid fool!

He cursed himself and his bout with jealousy and could not control his actions as one angry swipe of his arm sent the contents of the desktop flying. He stared numbly at the broken glass on the floor and felt his throat close.

I'm going to be alone for the rest of my life...

Cole found his brother still sitting behind the desk in the library fifteen minutes later. Broken objects and strewn paper covered the floor. Tyler sat in the midst of the melee, his head slumped forward in the chair.

"Ty? I went to your room and you weren't there. What's going on here?" His worried hazel eyes observed the clutter, then they darkened with something akin to unbridled fear when he remembered his conversation with Clancey just a few minutes earlier. The stable hand rushed to inform him of Emma's state of mind and her wild ride out of the yard.

His brother's chin rose and he stared at the other man with dull eyes and a mindless shrug of the shoulders. "I'm still trying to figure that out myself."

Cole read the look of bewilderment on Tyler's face, and the furrow in his own brow deepened with his growing concern. "Clancey told me that Emma rode out of here in quite a state. Did the two of you have words?"

"Hmmph...'having words' is putting it mildly." Tyler's confused expression tempered to one that held a question. He rubbed a hand slowly through his thick, dark hair. "Cole, what do you think of Emma? Do you think she's trustworthy? Do you think I can trust her with Janie's happiness?"

"What the hell kind of question is that?" Cole took a step closer to the desk. "What happened here today to make you ask something as stupid as that?"

"We had one helluva row...and I told her to leave."

"You did *what?*" Cole kicked a nearby chair in a rare show of temper and sent it sliding across the floor. "Damn it, Ty, when are you going to open your eyes and see what's standing right in front of you!"

Tyler flew from behind the desk, and his arm shot out toward the window. His weak body swayed with the effort. "Yeah, well I *did* see what was standing right in front of me, and I saw it through *that* window! Steve came by to check on me earlier and ended up outside with *my* wife in his arms in a tender scene that turned my stomach!"

A flicker of doubt sparked in Cole's eyes. "What do you mean?"

"She *kissed* him, Cole! Right out there in the driveway, in broad daylight!"

"On the mouth?"

"No, on the cheek, but it doesn't matter. He also hugged her, and she hugged him back!"

The doubt slowly diminished as Cole continued his questioning. "What did Emma have to say about it?"

"She said she only kissed him out of gratefulness for helping both of us."

"And you didn't believe her," the younger Wilkins brother stated rather than asked.

"No, I didn't believe her, and neither should you!"

Cole moved to stand before his brother. "You know what? I'm going to tell you something about *your* wife. She loves you with a passion, Tyler, and if you'd take off your goddamn blinders, you'd see that you feel the same way!"

"I know exactly how I feel...!"

"Just shut up, Tyler!" Cole roared. "You asked my opinion, and you're damn well going to get it! I've seen the way you look at her, and I've read every damned emotion on your face! I've also seen how she looks at you! How in hell can you doubt her anymore? You weren't there to pick her up at the train station when she arrived from New York, but she let it go, hoping like hell you'd be here at the ranch waiting for her. But you weren't, because *you* decided to play the damned injured party here, because *you* felt cornered after jumping into bed with her! You took off after you married her and left her alone *again*, and she let that go, too. And, now what do you do? You come home from the camp periodically over the last month, throw her a few crumbs, and she's ready to get on her knees and beg for more, because she loves you! If you hadn't been so damned out of it when we hauled your ass home yesterday, you would have seen the sheer terror on her face! She was scared, Tyler! She was scared she was going to lose you! Why, I have no idea, because you've given her *nothing* to miss!" Cole took a step closer to his brother and met him eye to eye. "You know what you need, Tyler? You need your stupid ass kicked!"

Before Cole could continue with his tirade, Trevor barreled through the library door with an amazed look on his face.

"Jesus Christ! I could hear you yelling all the way outside, Cole!"

"Good! I hope the whole goddamn place heard what a stupid bastard Tyler is! Let the piss ant explain to you what he told Emma today. I'm getting the hell out of here!" Cole stormed through the open doorway without a backward glance, and the room reverberated a moment later with the slam of the front door.

Trevor took one look at Tyler's pale expression and moved to stand before him. "Sit down before you fall down, Ty. You're white as a sheet and bleeding through the bandage again."

Tyler moved behind the desk once more and dropped into the chair.

"So, what the hell's going on? Why is Cole so angry?" Trevor asked as he took a seat in one of the chairs facing his brother.

Tyler sat forward, propped his elbows on the desktop, and rested his head in his hands. "Because I might have made one of the biggest mistakes of my life. Emma and I had an argument, because I thought there was something going on between her and Steve. I told her to pack her things and leave." Trevor opened his mouth to bellow louder than his brother, but Tyler held up a hand in an appeal for quiet. "Don't even start. Cole already gave it to me with both barrels, and I know he was right."

"So, what're you gonna to do about it?" Trevor asked through clenched teeth as he struggled to control his own anger. "You know, we've all kept our mouths shut about this whole damn thing with you and Emma—our mistake. We know how Sara's death affected you, but I'm gonna go out on a limb and say something I should have said when Emma first arrived, whether you like it or not. You've been given a second chance at happiness here, Ty—a chance most people only dream about."

"I'm just beginning to realize that, Trevor."

"Then grab it, Tyler, and hold it close."

Trevor moved around the desk and rested a hip on the edge. He crossed his arms before his chest and looked his brother straight in the eye. "When Sara died, you and Janie weren't the only people in this house who lost something, Tyler. Cole, Carrie, and I also cried many times. Not only for you, but also with our own personal pain. She was part of our lives, too, and we mourned her death for a long time. But Emma has changed things. She brought sunshine back into this house— sunshine that's been missing since Sara left us. You can't let yourself feel guilty for loving again, Ty, and you know as well as I do that Sara would be the first one to kick you in the ass if you push Emma away."

Trevor watched the tears trickle down Tyler's face before he ducked his head to hide them from his brother. The younger man had all he could do to control his own emotions and swallowed the quickly formed lump in his throat. "You need to let go, Ty. You need to grab what life is offering you. You need to take Emma in your arms and love her for all you're worth."

A sob burst forth from somewhere deep inside Tyler, and Trevor wrapped his arms around him in brotherly love. The tears escaped his own eyes then, and the two grown men clung to one another; one needing comfort, the other giving it. Tyler felt the pain of the last two years rock him to the core.

"Sara was my life, Trevor!"

"I know, Tyler. I know. But Emma is here now, and she loves you more than you ever dreamed would be possible again. Don't let fate win again and take her away from you. Sara can never come back, and you have to accept that. You have to look to your heart. You need to admit to yourself that you can love again, and not let the guilt consume you. We can all see how you feel about Emma, and you have to let yourself see it, too. Look closely, Ty. Look deep within yourself, and you'll find the answer."

Trevor held his brother tightly, willing Tyler's anguish to be washed away, along with the pent-up tears. It was a long time later before one brother finally let go of the past and reached for a bright new future, and the other one gave silent encouragement for him to follow that path.

Tyler finally leaned back in the chair and wiped the wetness from his cheeks. Trevor, trying to lighten the mood, laid a hand on his brother's knee and smiled ruefully.

"A fine pair we are, hey, Tyler? Two big rough and tough cowboys, crying on each other's shoulders like babies. What would the ladies in town think?"

"Thanks, Trevor." He stood and patted his brother on the shoulder. "I think I'll go find Cole."

Trevor laughed, with a little more humor evident in his tone. "Good luck, but you better plan on doing all the talking. I think Cole's used up his words for the week!"

Tyler chuckled along with him and wiped again at the tears that had not dried. "Emma sure has had an effect on him, hasn't she?"

"She's had an effect on all of us." He lifted an eyebrow in question. "So, what are you going to do when you see her next?"

A weak grin preceded his words. "I'm going to start my new life—if she'll forgive me. And, if she does, I'm going to carry her up those stairs and not come down for a week."

"Good, and I'll run interference so no one bothers you!" Trevor rose from his own chair. "Now, go find that rattled brother of ours and make peace."

Trevor watched Tyler leave the room, and his smile faded into a look of concern. Would Emma forgive him? He sent a silent request to her wherever she was.

"Honey, you've gotta give him one more chance."

Chapter Eighteen

Emma ceased her relentless prodding of the horse's flanks and finally allowed the poor beast to slow its pace. The mare's sides heaved with exhaustion and froth bubbled from its mouth. Her anger had overridden better judgment, and Emma was ashamed of herself for treating an animal the way she had this one.

She reined the mare down a sloping trail and it plodded to a halt when she found herself at Tyler's special place—the same place he brought her and Janie after the wedding. Since then, they had visited the pond on numerous occasions, but, today, Emma unconsciously guided the mount toward the peaceful haven she could find nowhere else.

Horse and rider moved into the clearing and a small sigh left Emma's chest as she dismounted. Even in her distraught state, she could not ignore the beauty that surrounded her. Late autumn presented itself in the form of brittle, colored leaves, which lay scattered atop brown grass tinged with small traces of green. Snow would cover the landscape soon, and Emma could not help but wonder if she would be there to see it.

She strolled to the water's edge and seated herself on a log Tyler placed there for her and Janie during one of their many visits to the peaceful cove. The little girl loved going there as much as she did.

A sob caught in her throat. *How will I ever leave her and the others?* Trevor, and his ready and ever present smile; Cole, and his innate ability to read her emotions better than she could herself; and Carrie, who treated her like the sister she never had. She loved them all—Mamie, Janie, and most of all, Tyler. They were her family now, but, because of Tyler's distrust, she was in danger of losing them all.

Emma pushed herself up again and shuffled toward the rock wall to study the pictures that painted a story of an Indian family of long ago. Memories of the first time Tyler brought her there whispered around the edge of her brain, and she looked closely at the man and woman and the sun that shone down on them. She traced her finger along the bumpy edges of the teepee and realized with sudden clarity that the rough surface was much like her relationship with Tyler. *Will I ever be able to smooth it out? Will he even give me the chance?*

Her jaw hardened with determination. She would make him! They were connected now, both by the baby she carried and the love shared by all. A wry smile curved her lips as she thought about the direction her life had taken—a totally opposite turn from the path she thought it would follow. *But it's going in a direction I want with all my heart. I won't let him throw it away because he distrusts me!* Somehow, she would make him believe in her love and maybe, just maybe, he would be able to respond in kind. *Forever the optimist, that's what Papa always says...*

Emma leaned against the rock, closed her eyes, and pictured Tyler's square cut jaw, the black curly hair, and the green eyes she loved so much. She envisioned Janie and the rest of the family and knew she could never leave.

I will not give up on us, Tyler! She vowed to go back to the ranch and recruit his brothers' help, if needed. She would even send for Steven and allow the good doctor to beat some sense into his best friend's stubborn head. *If that's what it takes to make him see reason, then I'll do it.*

Tyler had said that he was ready to bare his soul, so, surely, he must feel something!

She turned with a lighter step and a steady resolve and walked back to the horse. She paused halfway across the small clearing, however, when a twig snapped on the trail. The hair rose on the back of her neck.

She watched the trail with wary eyes and, deciding she was overreacting, continued toward the horse. She froze a moment later when a man stepped through the thick foliage. Emma's heart skipped a beat as she stared into the face of the devil himself.

"Samuel!"

Samuel Fontaine leaned a shoulder casually against the tree beside him and crossed his feet at the ankles. He was almost unrecognizable in his disheveled state. His hair was long and greasy, and his body much leaner than the last time she saw him—when he attacked her in the stable. Filthy clothes hung limply from his body, and he glared at her through glassy eyes.

Emma paled and took a step back.

"Well, well, well. If it isn't the fine Miss Emma Sanders, lately of New York." His indifferent glance swept the clearing before his burning eyes again fell on her. "Fancy meeting you in a place so remote."

Emma's blood ran cold and, as he spoke, she mentally measured the distance between herself and the horse. Could she actually make it to the mare without him catching her?

She had no choice but to try. There was no doubt in her mind as to what would happen if he managed to get his hands on her. She took a slow, shallow breath and prepared herself for the coming leap onto the mare's back. She had to keep him talking though, and unaware of what she planned, if she wanted to have any chance at escape.

"What are you doing here, Samuel? How did you end up in Minnesota?"

The sneer on his lips widened into a leer as he watched her; his stance also became a bit more rigid than it was a few moments earlier. He noticed her chin rise slightly.

"Do I frighten you, Emma?" He chuckled. "I should, you know. Did you think that I'd let you and that upstart Wilkins get away with ruining my life? That I would forget everything you did and just let you go on your merry way?" He shifted his weight to the other leg. The movement made Emma flinch unwittingly. "I have to admit that finding you here with him surprised me though. Hell, when I was finished with him, I planned to go back to New York and make you pay for your part in my ruination." The leer appeared again. "Now, I won't have to."

"What do you mean when you were *finished* with him? He did nothing to you and neither did I! Anything that's happened to you, you did to yourself."

"Oh, I beg to differ with you, Emma. I lay the fault for my downfall directly on the two of you."

Emma's gaze strayed to the mare again. She had to keep him talking...

"Where have you been all this time? You dropped out of sight and no one knew of your whereabouts."

He took a few steps in her direction, and Emma knew she would have to act quickly if she was to escape him. Once more, she counted out the steps between her and the horse—and fought to control her trembling.

"I was making plans to come here—to get Tyler. It was so easy. I simply answered an ad for the extra crew your big man was looking for to log his stupid timber." A nonchalant shrug raised his bony shoulders. "I gave a false name and work history and was hired on the spot. I had so many chances to end his life up there in the woods, but every time the possibility arose, my plans were foiled. That is, until I sent the logs rolling in his direction yesterday." His jaw hardened. "But, of course, dumb luck was with him again. Now, I'll have to try again."

"*You're* the one who let the logs go?" Emma choked out.

He dipped at the waist in a gallant bow. "One and the same."

Emma's stomach rolled at the thought of this demented man laying in wait for Tyler—waiting for the perfect opportunity to kill him for something he had no hand in. She forced her attention back to Samuel when he spoke again.

"Tyler must pull a lot of weight around here. Wherever I went yesterday, people were talking about how he narrowly escaped death in a freak logging accident. They also talked about his poor Missus Emma and how terrified you must have been to almost lose your new *husband*!" His voice took on a deceptively soft note. "So, you married the bastard, did you?" When Emma failed to answer, he raised his voice to a shriek. "*Did you?*"

Emma jumped at the sound of his voice, but continued to hold her silence as, once more, she calculated the distance to the mare, how long it would take to mount the animal, and then get the horse moving.

"You know, you could have knocked me over with a feather when you tore past me on the road earlier. You never even noticed me. But then, of course, you never had time for me, did you Emma? So, I figured I may as well follow along and finish what your stable boy so rudely interrupted back in New York."

She could wait no longer. Samuel took another step in her direction, and Emma bolted to the waiting horse with a quickness that surprised even her tormentor. She saw a blur approach her from the side, increased her speed, and jumped at the exact moment she had planned. Her hands touched the saddle horn just as her left foot found the stirrup. Emma heaved herself up onto the horse's back, kicked it in the ribs and fumbled for the reins.

She could only find one!

Samuel held the other in his hand and frantically tried to subdue the circling animal just as Emma's free hand closed around the hilt of the riding whip. Raising it above her head, she brought it down on Samuel's shoulder with as much power as she could marshal. A strangled cry escaped his throat, but sheer insanity strengthened his hold.

Emma squeezed her knees together and fought to keep her seat atop the frightened horse. The usually calm mare now danced sideways as Samuel screamed into its face.

Emma was crazy with panic herself and repeatedly brought the whip down onto Samuel's head and arms. More than one blow ended up meeting the horse's neck and flanks, and the poor beast reared in objection at the brutal treatment. Samuel lost his hold on the bridle, and Emma slid sideways in the saddle. She clung desperately to the pommel, but Samuel grabbed hold of her leg and she felt herself slip with his last powerful yank. The mare bolted.

Emma's body collided with the ground, and her head hit next with a dull thud. Dazed and struggling for breath, she could do nothing but lay helpless on the hard earth. The mare paused in its frenzied flight a short distance away, and Samuel threw up his arms, screamed at the animal, and watched with a crazed gleam in his eye as it wheeled around and charged back up the path.

Emma rolled slowly onto her side and stared through terrified eyes as a wheezing Samuel bent at the waist and rested his hands on his knees. He glared at her from under lowered lids, then, finally, straightened and brought his hand to his cheek. The whip had laid open a wicked gash, and his fingers came away covered in blood.

"You bitch!" he screamed. "You've finally met with the day you will regret for the rest of your life! Do you hear me?"

Emma still gasped for air and fought valiantly to ward off the darkness that threatened to engulf her. Samuel staggered in her direction. Hatred etched itself deeply into his features and, totally out of control now, he kicked the toe of his dirty boot into her midsection. A lurid smile curled his lips with the accompanying rush of air from her lungs, and the moan that left her lips a split second later.

"Did you hear me, Emma? There's no one here to come to your rescue now!" He watched through glazed eyes as she crawled away from him, spurred on by pain and a burgeoning self-preservation instinct that insisted she escape the man who inflicted so much physical abuse.

Samuel threw his head back and laughed like the madman he was. Feeling the thrill of victory already, he kicked her down every time she regained her balance and tried to sit up. He toyed with her—and she was defenseless.

Emma curled into a ball and gritted her teeth against the cramping sensation that shot through her abdomen. Her hoarse plea was barely audible in the crisp afternoon air. "Please...Samuel, let me go. Don't do this...I'll give you money." She winced as another wave of pain rushed through her womb. "I'll give you anything you want! Please...don't kill me..."

"You still don't understand, do you? There's only one thing I want from you, Emma, and I've waited a long time for it. If you ask me, Tyler is a very selfish man, and I think it's about time he learned to share." His hands moved to the buttons at the front of his dirty, stained pants. "Besides, I like my women broken and pleading for mercy."

He grabbed her roughly by the arms and hauled her to her feet, then dragged her across the quiet clearing to the rock wall. He slammed her already bruised body against the hard surface and peered into her terrified eyes. "Do you like it standing up, Emma?"

Emma found it hard to concentrate on his words as a rush of warm liquid seeped from between her legs. The contractions came one on top of the other now, and her barely whispered words begged him to show even a hint of compassion.

"Don't do this. Please. I'm...pregnant...and—" She doubled over in his arms and groaned her agony.

Samuel snapped her limp body upright and his scathing gaze scanned her pale features. He shook her until her teeth rattled. "You're *what*? You let that son of a bitch get you pregnant!"His right hand balled into a fist and connected with her jaw, then the backhand caught her across the mouth. Emma spun free of his hold and landed in a heap on the ground. She felt his weight upon her only seconds later.

Samuel ripped open the front of her dress and tore at the underlying camisole, exposing her pregnancy-swollen breasts. His eager hands and mouth mauled her tender flesh, but Emma could not find the strength to scream. Another contraction gripped her a few moments later as he clutched at the skirt and shoved it up and out of his way.

Emma's weak attempts to stave him off brought little result. Black spots flickered before her eyes now, and the pain in her jaw rivaled the agony in her womb. She pleaded for her life in hoarse, choked sobs, but Samuel silenced her with yet another round of blows to her head and torso. Emma swallowed convulsively and tried not to choke on her own blood.

The undergarments left her body with a rending tear. Samuel paid little attention to the blood that poured from between her legs as he positioned himself above her, then plunged into her time and time again. Her feeble cries mingled with the song of a far off loon, and her tears merged with the blood on her face.

Samuel peered into the almost unrecognizable face beneath him, and the power that surged through his veins spurred him on. "Does he do this to you, Emma?" he panted. He grabbed her limp arms and trapped them above her head, never ceasing the rhythmic pumping motions that ripped her body apart. "Scream again, Emma! I want to hear you scream!"

One final, desperate sob escaped her lips as a horrific agony knifed its way through her lower abdomen. A vision of Tyler's smiling face floated through her spinning mind as she spiraled into a tunnel of darkness; falling, falling, until there was no more Samuel and no more pain.

Tyler found Cole mucking out stalls with a vengeance. He took a tentative step forward, then hooked his arms over the wooden gate and flinched when his brother viciously stabbed a fresh bale of hay with a pitchfork.

"I'd hate to be that bale of hay right now."

Cole spun, threw the other man a malevolent look over his shoulder, and then turned his attention back to the fodder that he scattered on the floor of the stall.

"Be goddamn glad you're not."

"Cole..."

The youngest Wilkins brother ceased his actions abruptly, turned on booted heel, and glared into Tyler's eyes. "What the hell's the matter with you—"

"Stop right there." Tyler raised a hand. "I came out here to tell you that you're right. I don't know what the hell got into me. Both you and Trevor made me realize that I've been an ass as far as Emma is concerned."

"Being rather easy on yourself, aren't you? Personally, I'd dub you a son of a bitch."

Tyler dropped his chin, then reached up a hand and ran it through his tousled hair, carefully avoiding the sutures near his temple. The gesture was enough to make Cole relent, if only slightly. He stabbed the pitchfork into the bale of hay again and leaned against the side of the stall. "You still gonna make her leave?"

"No..." Tyler's eyes rose to meet his brother's. "I couldn't let her go." He glanced around the barn. "I'd see her everywhere and be even more miserable. I just hope she accepts my apology and doesn't *want* to leave. I should never have accused her of the things I did."

"Well, I'm happy to see you finally realized that neither Emma or Steve would do anything to jeopardize your marriage. Steve is your best friend, Ty, and now he's Emma's friend, too. You should be happy they like and respect each other so much."

"I know, Cole. It's just that when I saw her hug him, and then kiss him goodbye, I got so insanely jealous I spoke before I thought about it."

"Emma treats everyone that way. If you spent more time around her, you'd know that."

Tyler grinned. "Well, you'll be happy to know that I plan on spending a *lot* more time with her. All I want right now is to find Emma and tell her how I feel— and to apologize for being such an ass. I'm going to make this work, Cole, if she'll only forgive me one more time."

Cole clasped his brother's shoulder with a tanned hand, his earlier anger forgotten. "She will, Ty. She loves you too much not to."

"How come I'm the only one who didn't know that?"

Cole laughed, his humor completely restored. "I wish we could blame it on that rap on the head you got, but that only happened yesterday! Come on. Let's go bug Mamie for something to eat. I promise, when Emma shows up, we'll all scatter so you two can be alone. I'm damn glad you finally came to your senses."

The two men left the barn, then paused when the sound of horse's hooves racing through the front gate caught their attention. The riderless mare, with reins trailing, veered past them, then came to a prancing halt in front of the barn's closed door. Cole ran to the frightened animal, with a weak Tyler following in his wake. Both men had their arms spread wide to corner the animal before it bolted. The mare reared and the two experienced horsemen saw the panic in her eyes. Cole spoke in a soft, soothing voice and inched his way closer to the quivering animal until he was able to grab the reins.

Clancey ran around the side of the barn and stopped dead in his tracks at the sight of the frightened mare. The horse's chest was sticky with blood, a result of the cuts on its neck and flanks.

Air whistled through Clancey's teeth. "Christ almighty! That's the mare Miss Emma rode out on!"

Tyler's face paled to a sickly pallor in an instant. "Clancey, saddle Storm for me and send someone for Steve. Emma might be hurt. I'm gonna go pack a few things, then I'm going to find her."

Cole grabbed his brother's arm as Tyler turned to make his unsteady way toward the house. "Let Trevor and I start out. How are you going to stay on top of a horse? You can barely walk across the yard."

"If you think for one minute that I'm staying behind, you're crazy. She's my wife, and she might be hurt. We've got to find her before it gets dark!"

Cole dropped his hand, knowing he did not have the time to argue. "All right. Let's get ready, then. Clancey, saddle all of our horses, and then get your ass to Steve's place and explain what happened."

Clancey grabbed Emma's mare and led it into the barn as the two brothers hurried to the house to spur everyone into action. The fear was evident in their tight expressions. Emma was a superb rider, but the bloody whip marks on the horse boded an ill wind, and they both tried to contain their quickly growing panic.

Ten minutes later, Tyler, Cole, and Trevor were mounting up just as Dougan O'Malley raced his horse through the log gate. He reined the animal in their direction. Dust billowed as the horse pranced to a stop before them, and Dougan's eyes immediately found Tyler.

"I need to talk to you about something. I was riding down from the camp and, a few miles back, I passed a man on the trail riding a beat-up Appaloosa. He was movin' like the devil himself was on his tail and headed north. Most people 'round here I know, but I didn't recognize this fellow until he passed right by me. I swear to you, Mr. Wilkins, it was Samuel Fontaine!"

Tyler nudged Storm closer to the Irishman. Concern coupled with fear to furrow his dark brows. "What in hell would he be doing in Minnesota? He dropped from sight in New York months ago."

"I know, sir, but I'm positive it was him. And I'm sure now he was the man I seen at the logging camp. He's been keepin' away from me, maybe because he thought I'd recognize him and tell you. When I went in for supper last week, he got up right away, kept his face hidden, and left the shack. I wasn't sure it was him then so I didn't say anything. On the road, I recognized that horse, though. In fact, I took a rock out of its hoof. The owner had the same greasy, long blond hair as the man on the road did. I got a good look at him this time, sir—it's Fontaine. I'd know that bastard anywhere. It's hard to forget the face of a devil!" Tyler looked sicker with Dougan's every word. "I wanted you to know, Mr. Wilkins, because you said Samuel blames you for him losin' the mill. I think he might be responsible for the strange happenings at the camp. It makes sense, don't it?"

There was no need to say the last statement aloud. It made perfect sense to the other three men—Samuel Fontaine cut the ropes the day of Tyler's accident. He was probably responsible for a few of the smaller incidents that had happened in the last week, also—incidents that never failed to jeopardize Tyler's safety.

"Stay here, Dougan, and watch the place until Clancey gets back with Steve." Tyler gathered Storm's reins as he shot out the orders. "Emma's horse came in without her, and we've got to start searching. Have Mamie give you a rifle in case Fontaine shows up. Get a buckboard ready; we might need to come and get it. Fire off a few rounds if she comes back." He wheeled the horse, gave it a swift kick and charged down the driveway. Cole and Trevor followed suit.

The three brothers methodically searched every path that led from the main road, looking for any sign of fresh hoof prints. When none were found, they moved onto the next path and began again.

Tyler was wound up as tight as a bowstring and blamed himself at every turn when they failed to find her. His head ached from the jarring ride, and he was sick to his stomach with worry.

Where is she?

He ran the conversation with Dougan over and over in his mind. *Samuel Fontaine! Emma tried to tell me that he attacked her that night in New York, and Edward stated in his telegram that she had to get away from the city because of a threat to herself and the baby—a threat from Fontaine?*

If Samuel had tried to kill him, what would stop him from harming Emma? If she had been hurt by his hand, he would hunt the bastard down and kill him with his bare hands. Once more, Tyler called out her name, and he heard his brothers do the same.

Another hour had passed since they left the ranch, and still there was no sign of her. The men met up again, and worry was etched deeply into all their faces. Dusk was near, and soon the sun would sink on the horizon. Consequently, the temperature would drop quickly. No one in their group knew if Emma even had a jacket with her to stave off the cold night air. And what if she was hurt? Not one of them voiced their thoughts aloud, but they all agreed that they needed to find her soon.

"Where in hell is she?" Tyler was beside himself with worry and guilt.

"We'll find her. She couldn't have gone that far." Trevor did his best to keep his brother calm. Fresh blood seeped through the bandage on his head again, and he grew more unsteady in the saddle with every passing moment. "You look like you're ready to fall off that horse, Ty. Why don't you head back, and Cole and I will keep looking. Maybe she's returned to the ranch—"

"Dougan would've fired shots. I don't care if you have to tie me to this damned horse—I'm staying out here. I'm the goddamn reason she left, for Christ's sake!" His words brooked no argument.

"All right." Cole nudged his horse closer. "Trevor, you ride with Ty and watch for any tracks leading off the road. I'll go north toward the camp. We've still got a little daylight left. When it gets dark—"

A wolf howled in the distance, and the hair rose on the back of Tyler's neck as he listened to the mournful cry. The sudden realization of where she was hit him hard in the gut.

He wheeled Storm about. "I know where she is!"

Tyler rode Storm at a breakneck pace all the way to the pond. He cursed himself for not thinking of it sooner. If Emma was riding as hard as Clancey said she was, it was not difficult to imagine that she could have gone that far out from the ranch.

Branches scratched his face when he turned Storm off the trail and headed down the steep slope. He pushed the horse to its limit, knowing in his heart that he would find her when he reached the clearing.

Emma! Please be alive!

The immense black horse crashed into the clearing, and Tyler leaped from the still moving animal and ran to her side. He dropped to his knees beside her, and one look at her tattered, near-naked body told him all he needed to know.

She lay on her back, arms outstretched above her head. Her face was covered by long red tresses, which were now matted with dirt and dried blood. The bodice of her dress was torn away from her body, the skirt hiked up, and she lay in a pool of blood. The inside of her thighs were stained with the color red.

"Emma! Jesus Christ, Emma, please don't be dead. Please, Emma!" Tyler reached for her battered body with trembling hands. He gathered her into his arms and tenderly swept the matted hair away from her face, all the while saying a silent prayer.

His jaw hardened murderously. The left side of his wife's face was severely swollen and bruised to a dark purple. Her lower lip was split at the corner and dried blood marked a trail down her neck. He pulled her closer, and rocked back and forth as tears slid down his cheeks.

"I love you, Em," he sobbed. "Don't leave me. Please, Emma, stay with me!" He felt her shallow breath on his neck and relief ran rampant through his body, but she remained limp and unresponsive to his pleas. "I'm sorry! This is my fault. I need you. Janie needs you. Please, stay with me. Emma, you've got to hear me."

Tyler continued to murmur repeated pleas in her ear and dropped countless kisses on her clammy forehead. He did not realize that Cole and Trevor had arrived in the clearing, too, until a hand gently touched his shoulder.

"Here's a blanket, Ty. Let's cover her up." Tyler's head jerked up, and he gazed at Trevor through pain-filled eyes. He let his brother gently cover Emma's bruised body with the blanket.

Tyler whispered hoarsely as his eyes moved back to her pale face. "He did this to her—Samuel Fontaine. I'll find him, I swear, and I'll kill him. I'll kill him slowly and make him suffer like she did. I swear it. I'll kill him..."

"And we'll help you. We'll help you find him." Cole placed a shaky hand on Tyler's shoulder. "But, for now, we need to get her back to the ranch. She needs attention."

Tyler looked up into his brother's eyes and nodded. "We've got to help her. I think she's losing the baby, Cole. He beat her, then raped her, and left her to die. I'll kill him when I find him."

"We'll get him Tyler, I promise." Cole spoke softly as he reached out to his brother's shocked senses. "But we *need* to go."

Tyler snapped out of his shock-induced reverie. He struggled to his feet with Cole and Trevor's help and, with Emma still in his arms, moved on a wavering path toward his horse. He carefully handed her to Cole as he mounted Storm, then reached down to take her back into his arms. He settled her on his lap, and then allowed his brothers to tuck the blanket around her motionless body.

Cole leapt onto his horse's back and raced up the path ahead of them. He had to ensure that Steven was waiting at the house. He kicked the horse into a breakneck run once he reached the main road, and then he prayed for Emma's life.

Please, God, don't let it happen to him again! Don't let it happen to any of us!
He repeated the prayer all the way to the ranch.

Tyler held Emma against his chest in a firm, yet gentle grip, never allowing Storm to surpass a slow, loping gait. Her body was icy cold, even wrapped in the blanket, yet still the warm blood seeped from her body. The fact that he was the reason she left the ranch in the first place sickened him. The attack was his fault and, with every plod of the horse's hooves, he berated himself—and pleaded with God for her life.

It was a quiet ride; both men carried fear in their hearts. Trevor, a rifle lying across his lap, closely watched the thick stand of pine trees along the trail. He would not give Samuel another chance. If Fontaine came back for Emma or Tyler, he would be ready. They had traveled a full mile before Tyler voiced his fears aloud.

"She can't die, Trevor. She's just lying here, and she won't wake up. If she dies, my life won't be worth living. I can't take it again, Trev. I...can't take that pain again. I love her too much."

"She's going to be all right. You have to believe that." Trevor hoped his reassuring words would prove true; when he first approached Tyler at the pond, he thought Emma was dead.

"I'm gonna kill him, Trevor," Tyler vowed again in a quiet, lifeless tone. "His life is worth nothing. No jury will ever get a chance to put him on trial, because I'm gonna kill him—quietly and slowly—and nobody will be the wiser."

The look on Trevor's face revealed his shock. Tyler was not a cold-blooded killer—but then, neither was he, and he agreed with him wholeheartedly. "I'll help kill Fontaine myself, Tyler—if the opportunity presents itself. Cole will have a hand in it, also."

The two weary travelers reached the bluff that overlooked the ranch house. Light spilled from every window, flooding the front yard. A rider galloped toward them and, when he yelled out, the voice identified him as Cole.

"Steve is here and ready with everything!" He reined his horse up alongside his eldest brother and studied his pale and drawn face. "Do you want me to take her, Ty? You look like you're ready to fall out of the saddle."

"I'll make it. She hasn't regained consciousness yet, Cole, and it scares the hell out of me." His listless gaze moved from Emma's ashen features to his brother.

"Did Carrie come home with Janie yet?"

"Yeah, they arrived just before dark. We've tried to keep Emma's condition from Janie, but I think she knows something's up, what with Steven being at the house and everyone on edge."

"Go back and make sure she's not there when I bring Emma in," Tyler's voice was close to a plea. "There's so goddamn much blood...I don't want her to see it again. Do you understand?"

"Carrie already had Katy take her back to their cabin. She's going to spend the night with her and Dougan."

All the Wilkins siblings shared Tyler's concern. Janie witnessed her mother's death, and they would do everything possible to keep the little girl from seeing Emma as she was now.

They reached the yard, where Steven, Carrie, and Mamie waited at the bottom of the steps. Mamie murmured to herself and dabbed at tear-stained brown cheeks. Carrie stood beside her, with an arm around the old woman's shoulders.

Tyler repositioned Emma's battered body in one arm, then held her carefully against his chest as he dismounted. Help was now at arm's length, and yet he was still reluctant to hand her over. Somewhere in the back of his ravaged mind, to let her go would mean losing control over whether she lived or died.

Tyler continued to hold his wife close against his own body when his feet hit the ground; his glittering eyes dared anyone to take her away from him. Steven understood the distraught man's dilemma and, without a word, moved to open the front door to the house.

"Come on, Ty. We need to get her upstairs."

Tyler was visibly staggering by the time he reached the top of the staircase. Instead of carrying Emma through the entrance to her bedroom, however, he walked past it, kicked at his own door and entered the master suite. He trudged across the carpeted floor, laid her gently on the big bed and dropped to its surface to take her limp hand in his.

"Emma, can you hear me? Please, honey, stay with me. Fight this. Janie and I need you. Emma? Can you hear me?" His heart lurched when she moved her head slightly on the pillow and moaned. "Emma, it's me, Tyler!"

She lay motionless again, her skin ominously pale beneath the bruises.

"Tyler?" Steven placed a hand on the frightened man's shoulder. "Let me help her now. I can't do anything with you sitting next to her."

The doctor's alert eyes had seen the unmistakable evidence of hemorrhaging and knew how critical it was to stop the flow of blood. Emma's life depended on it.

Tyler stood, slowly backed away from the bed, and turned pleading eyes to his friend. "Steve, you've gotta help her. You can't let her die!"

"I'll do everything I can, Ty."

Tyler's frightened eyes scanned Emma's broken body once more before he left the room.

Cole and Trevor waited in the hallway. They each grabbed one of Tyler's arms when he weaved precariously, then led him downstairs to the library. The shaken group met Carrie on her way up, arms piled high with linens. She leaned her head into Tyler's firm chest as he pulled her close.

"We have to pray she'll make it..." His voice cracked when Carrie pressed a kiss to his rough cheek.

"I've already been doing that for two hours, Tyler. We're not going to let anything happen to her. We'll pull her through this, I promise."

His eyes followed her up the stairs, then a wave of lightheadedness caused him to stumble back and into the stairway wall. Cole and Trevor grabbed hold of his shaking limbs and led him the rest of the way down the steps and into the library.

"Lay down before you fall down." Cole instructed, then watched as Tyler dropped heavily onto the leather sofa. He leaned forward and rested his throbbing head in his hands, but stayed in an upright position.

Trevor hunkered down before him. "Ty, why don't you lay back and rest that banged-up head of yours. I'll wake you immediately when Steve comes down."

"I can't, Trev." His tired, defeated gaze sought his brother's worried one. "What if something happens to her while I'm sleeping?"

Trevor patted his brother's knee with understanding and stood. "Okay, then we'll all just sit here and wait together. How does that sound?"

Tyler managed a slight nod of the head.

Cole moved to the liquor cabinet, poured each of them a stiff shot of bourbon, and passed the glasses around. Each man silently contemplated the horrific events of the day, and both Cole and Trevor knew that Tyler also dwelled on the fact that he lost his first wife just two and a half years earlier.

They waited and watched as the clock ticked on.

* * *

The hour grew late and Tyler was up pacing the room like a caged animal. Fear had now pushed him beyond the brink of his own injury.

"What the hell is going on up there? Why don't they come down and tell us something!" He marched on wobbly legs to the doorway and looked up the staircase for the hundredth time, then trudged back into the library. *I should just walk upstairs—but if no one's come down, that's got to mean she's still alive.*

Tyler's agitation brought him to the window. He closed his eyes, and his immediate reaction to the wolf's howl came to mind. It was simple gut instinct that urged him to the pond. Never in his worst nightmares did he think he would find her as he did—beaten, raped, and near death. Fontaine would pay dearly, whether Emma lived or died, and the revenge would be sweet.

Another hour passed. Tyler still leaned against the windowpane when Steven entered the library. His sleeves were rolled up around his forearms, and his face carried an unnatural pallor. Cole and Trevor bounded to their feet, but, before any of the occupants of the room could utter a word, the young doctor raised a hand for silence. He crossed to the now open liquor cabinet and poured himself a drink, tossing it down with one swallow. Steven sat on the edge of a nearby chair and took a deep breath before looking at Tyler.

"Is she alive?" The worried husband asked the question in a near whisper—and dreaded the answer.

"Yes, she's alive, Ty—just barely." The men watched Steven's struggle to find words. "I did the best I could for her. She miscarried, but at least the hemorrhaging has finally stopped." He reached up to rub his face with both hands, then continued. "I've got to be honest with you, Tyler. I've seen men twice her size take less of a beating and not make it. She doesn't have any broken bones though, which is a miracle in itself. He beat the hell out of her, and her entire body is bruised. The only thing any of us can do right now is pray—and see what happens in the next twenty-four hours."

Steven finally met Tyler's lifeless gaze. "I left a bottle of laudanum with Carrie. If she wakes up, see if you can get her to take some for the pain." The doctor stood. "You can go up and see her now, if you like. Mamie and Carrie are still with her—"

Tyler was out of the library before Steven finished speaking.

Tyler paused outside the open door to his room and inhaled deeply. Mamie and his sister were in the process of cleaning up bloodied rags, but it was not that gruesome sight that made his blood run cold.

Emma's dreadfully still body lay under the quilt in the massive bed, her pale face and slender arms covered with bruises.

I'll kill him, Tyler vowed, *with my bare hands if necessary.*

He passed the quiet Mamie and Carrie and lowered himself into a chair by the bed, then gently clasped Emma's cold hand in his and brought her fingers to his lips to seal the promise.

His sister came up behind him, wrapped her arms around his broad shoulders, and laid her face against his wavy hair. "She hasn't awakened yet. Maybe if you talk to her, your voice will bring her back to us." He felt the wetness of Carrie's tears slip from her cheeks and onto his neck. Tyler reached up, his eyes still on Emma, and squeezed his sister's hand. She tightened her hold momentarily, then kissed his whiskered cheek. "We'll let you sit with her for a while by yourself. Keep believing that she'll be fine—and make her believe it, too." Carrie patted his shoulder, and Mamie did the same before both women left the room, closing the door quietly behind them.

Tyler studied Emma's ashen face and listened to his own agonized whisper. "Will you be fine, Emma?" If she lived, the bruises would heal. But would her spirit be as resilient, or had Samuel taken something from her that she would never be able to recover? "Emma, can you hear me?" he whispered again. "I'll help you, I promise. I'll help you find your way back, if you'll only wake up."

Tyler received no response, but he refused to give up. He spoke to her of their future together, of all the things they would do and the places they would go—and he repeatedly told her how much he loved her. Still, she lay incognizant, lost in the healing sleep of a beaten soul.

Chapter Nineteen

Steven dropped back into the chair, settled himself against the soft cushion of the headrest, and stared blankly into the room. Cole and Trevor had not uttered a word since he entered the library and broke the news of Emma's precarious condition to Tyler. The two men now stared into their drinks, each lost within their own horrific thoughts.

"Christ," Steven said to no one in particular. "I can't believe she's still alive. That son of a bitch had to have been kicking her. She's one big bruise." His tired gaze swung in their direction. "I'm telling the two of you something right now—when you go looking for that bastard, you had better include me."

Cole sat quietly and contemplated Steven's words. He did not want anyone else to look for Fontaine. *I want him for myself.* He wanted to plan a slow, agonizing death befitting such an animal. Since Emma entered their lives, he had seen a change in the household—a step forward that was long overdue after the last agonizing years. He had come to love and respect her in a way that surprised even himself. Tyler and Janie would have a future again, and that opportunity was something Cole wanted desperately for them. He would avenge Emma if it took him the rest of his life.

Trevor rose from the small sofa and paced for a short time, then found himself standing before Steven. "What's your real prognosis, Steve? Were you just sugar coating it for Tyler's benefit? Can someone actually come out of a beating like that?"

Steven could not help but notice the frightened look in Trevor's eyes. "I don't know. It's a miracle that she's lived this long, but Emma's a fighter—let's just hope she has enough fight left in her to get through the night." He rose then, too.

"I've got to go outside and get a breath of fresh air. I'll be back in shortly, and then I'll check on her once more before I leave."

The doctor walked out onto the front porch, rested his forearms on the log railing, and studied the outline of trees against a moonlit horizon. Thoughts of Emma and Tyler and what they would endure over the next few weeks—that is if she lived to see tomorrow—bounced around in his brain. *She lost so damn much blood after miscarrying the baby. If she can just make it through the next few days, she'll have a fighting chance.*

"Do you think she'll make it?"

Steven spun to find Carrie perched on the porch swing, cloaked in a thick woolen shawl to ward off the chilly night air. He could not see her tears, but he knew they were there—he could hear them in her shaky voice.

"I didn't know you were out here." He hesitated. "Do you mind if I sit with you a moment?" She moved over slightly on the swing to make room for him, and Steven sank down onto the hard surface. "To answer your question, I don't know. But, if all the love being directed toward her can help, then she's got one helluva fighting chance."

"You were wonderful with her. Don't forget about your skill and what you did up there."

His gaze swung toward her in surprise. He and Carrie had been at odds since his return from medical school. Something had changed in their relationship during those years away, and he was never quite able to put a finger on the reason why.

Steven remembered her as a child, skulking around him and her brothers, always wanting to be part of their escapades. They had let her, because she was the Wilkins' brothers little sister. She never complained when they ganged up on her and had steadfastly stayed by their sides.

He also remembered how, wherever the young group went and whatever they did, she always materialized at his side. Her big hazel eyes watched his every move and, difficult as it was at times, he never discouraged her presence. Looking at her now, he realized that the little girl had turned into a beautiful woman somewhere in that space of time.

"Do you realize, Carrie, that this is the first time since I got home that you haven't tried to take my head off? Come to think of it, we worked together pretty well tonight. So, why the change of heart?" His brow knitted in a perplexed frown.

"In fact, what did I ever do to you in the first place?"

Carrie rose from the swing and stepped to the railing, then turned to lean back against the sturdy log banister and watch his handsome face in the dim light that filtered through the window.

Her mind returned to the day he left for St. Paul to attend medical school. Her child's heart broke that morning and, when he found her in the library, a young girl of eleven, she was crying out her frustration over the seventeen-year-old friend of her brother's who did not know she was alive. He crouched down before her that last day and asked her to wait for him, and she had promised that she would. It was a promise that Carrie never forgot. When Steven returned home for Sara's funeral, her heart thudded madly at the sight of him. He was a handsome man of twenty-six then, and she was still just Tyler's little sister—a little sister just turned nineteen, who was as much in love with him as the day he left. Now, two years later, he still could not see that she was a woman in her own right. She suspected that she was still Tyler's little sister, to be looked at as just another member of the Wilkins clan. Her pride would not allow her the luxury of fawning over him and, consequently, she was waspish at every turn.

How can I answer his question now, without giving myself away? She knew he saw other women, escorted them to various functions, and did not consider her in the same vein as he did them.

Carrie managed a mental shrug. Maybe she was wrong to hide her feelings from him. Maybe it was time to put all the years of anger and hurt aside and make him see her in a different light. Tonight they had worked side-by-side, Emma's life being their prime focus. She gained a new respect for him during those long hours—and her love grew tenfold.

Oh, what the hell, Carrie mused. *They say confession is good for the soul, and it certainly can't make matters any worse.* She took a deep breath and dove in with both feet.

"Do you remember the day you left for school?"

He shrugged. "How could I not? It was exciting to finally be on my way to college. But what does that day have to do with the way you've treated me since I got home?"

"Do you recall finding me in the library that day?" She watched his brow crease in thought.

He nodded slowly. "I remember finding you curled up on a chair—you were crying. I came looking for you because I wanted to say goodbye. That was a long time ago, Carrie, and I'm still confused as to what made you cry that day."

"You spent a lot of time at this house when we were younger. Heck, you've been a part of this family forever, just like Mamie. You and my brothers always included me in everything you did, even though I must have been a hindrance to all of you at times. You, though, were always patient with me. You were always kind and gentle when the other three teased me mercilessly." Carrie straightened and pulled the shawl tighter around her shoulders. "You've had your own life, separate from us, since you returned. You have your practice and your other...friends." A small, wry smile touched her lips. "I guess we all grew up, didn't we?"

"I'm still not following you, Carrie."

Her shoulders lifted in a sigh. "You told me that long ago day in the library that you wanted me to wait for you; that I was to hurry and grow up. Well, Steven, I did grow up, and I did wait for you, yet you haven't given me the time of day since you came home."

Steven sat on the swing—her words swirling in his mind, along with the implications they presented. He hardly remembered the conversation. *I probably said those words to ease a little girl's heart for the moment. What the hell does she mean now? That she took the words of a seventeen-year-old boy to heart and waited for his return all these years?*

Suddenly, Steven saw Carrie as a woman, not a child, and, much to his dismay, she crossed the porch to the front door.

"Goodnight, Steven. It's been a long, grueling day. I'm sorry for the way I've acted toward you." She entered the house then, and was gone.

He sat for a long moment, his mouth hanging open in slack-jawed amazement. In the short space of thirty seconds—the time it took her to speak the words—Carrie had become a different person in his mind. She was not a little girl anymore. She was a competent, full-grown woman, who had worked beside him tonight, trying just as hard as he to save the life of his patient—a patient who just happened to be his best friend's wife. She was not little Carrie anymore. She was now Caroline, and she had feelings for him—strong feelings.

"Who would've ever believed it?" Steven muttered and, rising from the swing, he let out a tired sigh and entered the house through the same door Carrie had only a moment before.

Hours into the night, after the rest of the family retired to their own rooms, Tyler still sat by her side. His tired eyes watched every small rise of her chest, fearing that each breath would be her last. Refusing to let her die alone, he heaved himself from the chair, climbed into the bed beside her, and gently pulled her bruised body close. Finally giving into exhaustion, his bloodshot eyes closed.

Emma floated across soft pillows of darkness. Her pain decreased with each step she took, and she could almost feel the bruises melting away. She was drawn to a distant brilliance—a light that beckoned her into the euphoria of its comforting center. And, as she neared the brightness, the warmth and peace engulfed her. A contented smile curved her lips. *What a wonderful place this is...*

Yet, there was something else, an equally strong force that pulled her back, but she did not want to return to that other world filled with so much agony.

A young, virile Indian brave stood at the outer edge of the light. A black-feathered band encircled his brow, and his strong, brown hand rested companionably on the head of a large, gray wolf that sat by his side.

"Emma," he spoke in a voice that was faintly recognizable, "you've come too soon."

"Am I not supposed to be here?" She gazed without fear into his vibrant dark eyes, then moved her emerald gaze to the soothing circle of light. Her smile widened. "I feel safer here than I ever have before." She glanced down at her silken arms, now absent of bruises, and held them before her. "I don't hurt anymore." Her eyes mirrored her confusion as she looked at him again. "Do you know how badly I hurt before I came here?"

"Yes, I do. I was with you then, too. But it is not yet time for you to come home, Emma. You have so much to accomplish. There are those who need you. You must return and help them find their way."

"But I'm at peace here. Nothing can hurt me now, and I'm not frightened anymore. Why must I go?"

Another figure materialized in the swirling mists of light—a blonde-haired woman sheathed in flowing white robes—and the muscular brave turned to face her. "Emma does not want to leave."

The specter's understanding smile reached Emma through the eddying fog. "Our friend is correct, Emma, when he says there are those who need you. You must return to them. It's not time for you to join us. The power that draws you away is the power of love, Emma, and it's stronger even than death. It's pulling you back as we speak." The woman reached out her arms, and Emma melted into her embrace. "Go to them, Emma. Take care of Tyler and Janie for me. It was meant to be."

The woman disappeared into the brilliance, and the Indian brave turned to follow, with the wolf at his side. He paused a moment later when another, softer male voice echoed through the mist. He glanced over his shoulder with a gentle smile.

"Listen. He calls for you. Be happy, Emma, and live your life to its fullest." He raised a hand in farewell. "We will meet again." The light dimmed and blackness surrounded her, and then there was nothing.

Emma's painful moans reached into Tyler's subconscious and his eyes flew open. Her bruised body writhed weakly beneath the quilt, her head lolled on the pillow, and her black and blue arms flailed blindly, pushing away an imaginary attacker. Tyler bounded from the bed and rounded the piece of furniture in an instant to sit beside her.

"It's all right, Emma," his tender voice soothed. "It's me, Tyler. Wake up now. You're safe, honey. You're home."

Her thrashing continued, and Tyler grasped her upper arms in a gentle hold and pulled her into his arms. A weak, strangled scream escaped her swollen lips.

"Emma, it's Tyler. Please, hear me! You're safe now, and I won't ever let him hurt you again. Open your eyes, honey."

His heart pounded in a rapid beat against his ribs until she calmed, and then he held her at arms length as she slowly opened her eyes and looked up into the worry-drawn face of the man before her.

Memories rushed in to assault her sluggish brain—Samuel, the beating, the rape, the contractions that ripped the baby from her womb...

Tears trickled down her swollen cheeks, and she turned her head from him in an all consuming shame.

Tyler tightened his grip on her arms ever so gently, and then spoke quietly, but firmly. "Look at me."

Her response came in the form of a quiet sob and a weak shake of the head.

"Emma...I'm here with you, and I'll keep you safe. I won't let anybody hurt you, ever again. You have to believe that."

Tyler was at a loss for words. *Should I say something about the baby...about the rape?*

Emma held her silence, so he simply pulled her close again and held her until he felt the weight of her head slump against his chest.

He carefully laid her back onto the pillow again, tucked the covers around her shoulders, and gently stroked her hair until he was assured that she slept and had not slipped into unconsciousness again. Moving to the chair, he watched quietly as her chest rose and fell with slow, even breaths. *I'll make it up to you, Emma. Somehow, I'll make you forget my angry words and Samuel Fontaine's abuse. I'll show you the way back, honey, if you'll only let me.*

Tyler leaned his head against the back of the chair and stared into the semi-darkness. Emma was his future, was Janie's future, and he would love her until the day he died.

Tyler awoke with a start when Mamie touched his shoulder, and then blinked the sleep from his eyes.

"Tyla, how come you be sleepin' in that chair all night long?" she whispered quietly so as not to disturb Emma. He did not bother to correct her, to tell her that he had moved from the bed to the chair only a few hours earlier, as she rambled on. "Come, son. Let's get you cleaned up and be inspectin' that head o' yours."

He hauled his stiff torso from the chair to sit on the edge of the bed and, paying no mind to Mamie, leaned over to check Emma's condition. He had slept fretfully during the past hours, waking often to see if she had moved. He could see now, by the way the bedcovers were still nestled around her shoulders that she had not wakened again. The swelling on her face was even more pronounced and the darkening bruises more noticeable in the light of day.

"Why in the hell did this have to happen to her, Mamie?" he asked, never taking his eyes from Emma's ashen face. "Where is the justice in this world? She wouldn't intentionally hurt anyone, and now look at her."

"That be a question, Tyla, that many ask in times like now. It's not somethin' that ever be figured out. Not by you, not by me, not by God, but we can conjecture why somethin' like this happens." Mamie wrapped her arms around him from behind, kissed the back of his head, and held him close. "When your mama died, God left four youngins—one, a brand-spankin' new life, without anyone to be lovin' 'em like only a mama can. Way I sees it, the only justice to be found by takin' her away is He gave me four souls to love—four beautiful souls that I probably would never bin' able to make on my own. I ain't been your true mama, boy, but I tried hard my whole life long."

Tyler turned and took her gnarled hands in his own. "Don't ever think you could have loved any of us more than you have."

"It makes my heart feel good cuz you be feelin' that way. See, Tyla? There be a silver linin' to everthin' that happens." Her head of gray curls nodded at Emma. "You love this girl, son?" He bobbed his head in admission. "Then be lookin' at the silver layin' in the bed. We're all gonna try our hardest to git her through this, then you can be showin' her the love you might not have found any other way. It be the devil's shame she went through what she did, but you and this little gal will be stronger for it happenin'. Do you understand what I'm sayin'?"

"I think I do. Mamie." A sad smile touched his lips. "You always find the good in even the worst situations. How can you continue to do that when life throws so many punches?"

"Because, Tyla, sometimes it can git so bad, that iffin you don't go lookin' for the sunshine, you'll jes always be in the dark." She kissed his unshaven cheek and squeezed his upper arm reassuringly. "Now, let's be lookin' at your cracked head and clean up that bandage. Carrie'll be comin' up shortly to sit with our Miss Em."

Tyler turned to gaze at Emma's broken body for a moment longer before leaving the room. He *would* help her find the sunshine again. *You're in there somewhere, Emma, and, I swear, I'll try my hardest to bring you back and make a life for us. I'll carry the load, honey. Just come back to me...*

Janie entered the house through the side door to the kitchen, hesitated a moment as she peeked around the corner and into the dining room, and then ran across the large living room toward the wide staircase that led to the upper floor. Something was wrong, and it had to do with Emma. She had slipped away from Katy's earlier that morning, unable to bear her own fear any longer. Her Uncle Cole looked so worried the night before when he raced into the yard on his big brown horse...

The little girl had strained to hear what was being said among the adults in the household, but then Cole pulled Carrie and Mamie into the kitchen. Nobody said anything to her yesterday about having to sleep at Katy's, yet suddenly Auntie Carrie packed her a bag.

Then Dr. Steve arrived, looking more scared than she had ever seen him. *Why did he come when he knew Daddy's head was fine, and why was Daddy looking for Emma last night?*

She heard Whizzer's telltale scratching at the front door and hurried back to let him in. Patting his head to keep him quiet, she scurried to the steps again and motioned for the dog to follow.

Janie reached the second floor and peered around the banister to see if she was alone. Seeing only an empty hallway, she tiptoed on to Emma's room and pushed open the door. The room was empty, and the bed was made. Her heart beat faster.

Where's Emma?

Whizzer sniffed at the closed door that led to her father's suite, and Janie hurried across the room. *Maybe Emma's in there or maybe daddy is. He can help me find her.* She grabbed at the dog's scruff, holding him back, and crept through the short connecting corridor. She pushed the other door open a crack and her curious eyes settled first on Carrie. The older woman sat in one of the overstuffed chairs, which had been drawn close to the bedside, and dabbed at her eyes with a handkerchief. *Why is Auntie Carrie crying?*

Janie pushed the door open a little more and her father's bed came into view. Emma lay under a quilt on the soft expanse, her face swollen and discolored. In between the bruises, her stepmother's face was as pale as the white pillow case her head rested on. Janie began to tremble with the height of her fear. *Mama looked like that when the horse ran over her...*

A vision of the horse racing toward her, and the feel of her mother's hand on her arm as she pushed her aside, assailed the child's frightened mind. Her mother's scream rent the air and, when the little girl looked again, the older woman lay on the dirt road with blood dripping from her open mouth. Her face was an ashen gray—the same color as Emma's was now.

The nightmarish memories rushed in at her and Janie heaved the connecting door open with a bang. Carrie jumped at the sound.

The little girl clawed at her clothing, trying to escape the exploding pain that closed her throat. *Emma's going away like my mama did!*

Janie stared at her stepmother through bulging, frightened eyes. Carrie approached quickly, with outstretched arms and tears still wet on her face, but Janie bolted around her and ran to the bed. A strange sound vibrated in her throat—a sound that turned into a strangled scream as the little girl draped herself across Emma's still form. She sobbed out her anguish, and repeated Emma's name over and over again.

Carrie stood dumbstruck upon hearing the forgotten timber of her niece's voice. More than two years had passed since Janie spoke, but now the child cried out her agony. She thought Emma was dead.

Emma fought the darkness that engulfed her. The sound of a child's weeping reached through the fog. Was the little one's undisguised anguish for her? Was she back in that special, soothing place she visited not long ago?

No. The pain was still there, and the peaceful bliss was not. There was no light now. Only a frightening darkness. Drawing on a reserve of strength, Emma opened her eyes and it took a moment for her to focus on the small, blonde head that rested on her chest. The child's tears dampened her nightdress. Slowly, she lifted a hand to stroke the little girl's silky soft hair.

"Janie?" she whispered in a hoarse voice.

Tyler's daughter jerked her head upright and bewildered eyes stared into her stepmother's face.

"Janie...why are you crying?" Emma tried hard to stop her world from spinning and concentrated on the realization that Janie had spoken her name aloud. "Did you say...my name, honey?"

Janie scrambled up to sit beside Emma, then reached out a trembling hand to gently touch the bruised face before her. "I thought you went away, like my mama did." The scratchy voice was foreign to Emma's ears, but she had never heard a more beautiful sound.

Emma ignored her own bruising pain, wrapped the little girl in her gentle embrace, and closed her heavy eyelids. A weak hand rubbed the child's back. "Honey, I'll never leave you. I just...fell off my horse and got hurt. I love you too much to leave. Don't be scared."

Janie's head lolled against Emma's neck. "I'm not scared anymore, Emma, and I love you, too."

"It's good to finally hear you say it." Emma managed the words, in spite of her bruised jaw and sapped strength. "Janie...can you tell your Daddy that, too? He needs to hear you say it."

The little girl sat up, pushed the strands of blonde hair away from her face, and leaned forward. Her eyes sparkled with excitement. "I can talk, Emma."

Emma fought the darkness that summoned her once more. "I can hear you. Will you come back and...talk to me again later? I'm really sleepy now."

Emma's eyes closed and her head moved slightly into the pillow.

Janie backed off the bed carefully and, as her tiny feet touched the floor, she turned to see her father standing in the middle of the room. Tears streamed down his face. He dropped to his knees and she ran into his outstretched arms, then he pulled her close.

"Daddy, don't cry. Emma is just sleeping now—she's going to be fine. Daddy?" Her eyes rounded in surprise. "I can talk!"

The raspy voice went straight to Tyler's heart and he hugged her more tightly.

He had heard the awful screaming from the kitchen and, thinking Emma had awakened again, bolted through the dining room and up the steps. When he entered the bedroom, his fear quickly turned to disbelief, and then to tears of happiness, and he was content to just stand beside Carrie and bask in the sound of his daughter's voice.

Carrie slipped past them to check on Emma. Realizing her sister-in-law was asleep again, she motioned for Tyler to take Janie from the room. He stood, with Janie in his arms, and carried her out into the hallway.

Mamie reached the top of the stairs at that moment, her face etched with concern. "Tyla, what's happenin'? My Gawd, how's Emma?" She panted from the exertion of climbing the steps at such a rapid pace.

"Emma's sleeping again, Mamie, but it wasn't her we heard. It was Janie." He tousled his daughter's hair with a trembling hand, and she hid her face in the folds of his shirt. Finally, she peeked up at everyone through wide eyes.

"Janie?" the old woman whispered her shock.

"You heard him right, Mamie." Carrie exited the bedroom and crossed to the negress. "I'll tell you all about it later, but I think Janie got so upset when she saw Emma that she just started to scream."

Mamie waddled over to her youngest charge and held out her hands. and Janie moved from her father's arms and into the negress' comforting embrace. She cuddled close to the old woman's ample bosom.

"Mamie...I can talk."

"Yes, you can, chile, and it be the most wonderful sound God ever be creatin' for us!" Deep brown eyes found Tyler's, and Mamie held out a hand to him. He clasped her fingers firmly. "See, Tyla? There be a silver linin' to everythin' that happens. Yessiree!"

That evening found Tyler stoking the fire in his bedroom. Emma had slept most of the day, yet still he did not leave her side. He straightened, set down the poker, and turned to find her awake and staring at him from across the room. Her eyes held nothing but a distant blankness as she watched him move to sit in the chair next to the bed.

"Would you like a drink of water?"

She nodded, however hesitantly, and Tyler reached for the pitcher, filled a glass, and handed it to his wife. She sipped slowly, her eyes downcast, then handed the half-empty container back to him. Tyler could not help but notice how careful she was not to let her fingers touch his. His heart reached out to her as he studied the bruised face before him.

"I'm going to go get Carrie, and she can help you get up for a minute. I'll be right back." Emma nodded again, and he left the room with measured steps.

As soon as the latch clicked shut, Tyler raced to Carrie's room and knocked loudly. His sister opened the door immediately.

"Emma's awake!" He ran a trembling hand through his dark hair. "Could you help her get up? I don't know what to do. She's been lying in that bed all day. Maybe she needs to...take care of some personal needs. See if you can get her to talk to you. She still hasn't said anything about what happened. I don't know if she even realizes she lost the baby. Steve said she was sleeping when he checked on her today, and they never had a chance to talk..."

"Tyler, slow down! Of course, I'll help her." Carrie was already moving down the hallway, with Tyler in her wake.

"I'll just wait out here until you're finished helping her."

Carrie's gaze swept her brother's disheveled appearance. He had not shaved since his own accident, and his eyes were bloodshot after the long, sleepless hours at Emma's bedside. She rested a hand on the doorknob to the master bedroom and paused. "Go throw some water on your face—you look terrible. Use Trevor or Cole's razor. I'll stay with Emma until you get back. And Tyler, if she doesn't ask about the baby, I'm not going to bring it up. I suspect she must know already."

Carrie entered the room to find Emma struggling to a standing position. She rushed to the battered woman's side, grasped her arm, and helped her to stand—then noticed her sister-in-law's overwhelming effort to hold back the tears.

"Oh, Emma, let me help you." Carrie fought to control her own emotions and lent her strength to assist Emma in crossing the room to the water closet. She left her alone.

Emma emerged from the small alcove a few minutes later, her skin a shade paler from the strain of being up and about. She walked back into the master bedroom, her eyes still downcast, but quickly raised an arm to halt Carrie's steps when the other woman moved to help her. Her lurching gait carried her back to the bed of her own accord.

The painful grimaces on Emma's face told Carrie that each step was sheer agony, but the physical evidence of her abuse was not what worried the other woman. The tight control of her emotions and the reserved expression on her sister-in-law's face were far more troublesome. Emma had locked herself away from all those who loved her, determined to bear her pain—and her shame—alone.

"Is there anything else I can do for you?"

Emma pulled the blanket up and eased her bruised body back onto the mattress. "No...I'm still rather tired after my visit with Janie earlier." A poignant smile touched her swollen lips. "Now that she's found her voice again, she has a lot to say. I'm happy for her."

"It's a miracle, Emma. I never thought we'd hear her speak again." Carrie sat down on the bed next to the sister-in-law she had come to love so dearly. "Would you like to talk? I really don't know what to say about what happened, but I'm willing to listen."

Carrie could almost see the shell encase Emma again. Her gaze fell to her lap and, when she spoke, her words were barely a whisper. "I can't. Not now. Not yet."

Carrie enveloped her in a gentle embrace, willing Emma to feel her love and concern. The woman remained stiff in her arms, however, and Carrie mentally cursed Samuel Fontaine for what he had done. She leaned back and nervously rubbed her hands together. "Well...I think Tyler is waiting outside, so I'll leave you now. I'll see you in the morning." She rose from the bed, took a step toward the door, then turned back. "On second thought, would you like me to stay here with you tonight?"

"That won't be necessary."

Carrie patted Emma's hand with gentle understanding, and then left the room quietly. Tyler leaned against the wall in the hallway. He had shaved the stubble from his face, but the haunted look in his eyes remained.

"She's still awake, but very unreachable. Be gentle with her. To be honest, I doubt that she'll talk about what happened. If you need me, don't hesitate to wake me up, okay?" She wrapped her arms around his middle and hugged him fiercely. "I love you, Ty. I'm so sorry."

He simply hugged her back, and then entered the bedroom. He cast a comforting smile in Emma's direction, then moved to check the fire again before he sat carefully on the edge of the bed. The facts of her brutal attack still remained unspoken between them. He knew she needed to talk about it if the healing process was to begin, but he also knew that she had to take the lead. He would be patient—for as long as it took.

"Steve left some laudanum for the pain. Would you like me to get you some?"

She shook her head, her eyes still downcast and studying her hands, which fidgeted nervously in her lap. "I don't want anything. I just want to sleep, if that's all right with you."

"That's fine, Emma. Sleep is the best thing for you right now."

She finally met his gaze, and her chin quivered with her effort not to cry. She was unsuccessful, however, and a lone tear escaped and traveled down her swollen cheek. When she spoke, her words were filled with anguish. "There is no more baby, is there?"

Tyler released a heavy sigh, hating himself for what he had to say next. He shook his head slightly and never took his eyes from hers. "No, Emma, there isn't."

He reached out to gather her into his comforting embrace, but she pulled the blankets up tighter around her shoulders and rolled away from his sorrowful gaze. Her reaction was unnerving, to say the least.

"Emma—"

"Goodnight." She dismissed him with just the one spoken word.

Tyler's hands froze in mid air, and he squeezed his lids shut. *I'll do this for us, Emma. I'll get you through this, I promise...* His eyes opened again as his shoulders sagged. "Good night, then. I'll come back and check on you..."

He left the room and closed the door silently behind him.

Emma caught the sob that rose in her throat before he heard it. She was in her own private hell now, and she would bear the suffering alone.

Chapter Twenty

A week passed, and still Emma refused to speak to anyone about the attack. She remained sullen and withdrawn, acting reasonably normal only when Janie visited her.

"I don't know what to do anymore," Tyler's voice was filled with desperation as he paced the library. His worried gaze moved from Steven, to his brothers, and then back to the doctor again. "She won't talk about it. She just sleeps, or sits and stares out the window. She's hardly eaten a thing." He stopped before his lifelong friend and spread his arms wide in supplication. "None of us can find a way to reach her. What should we do?"

"Be patient," Steven's eyes scanned all the faces in the room. "And that advice goes for all of you. Emma's sleeping so much because it's her body's way of healing itself. As for why she sits and stares out the window, I'm sure she's just trying to come to terms with all of this herself. Give her time—it's only been a week. When she's ready, she'll open up. Emma's one strong lady, but after what she's been through, you can't blame her for being distant. I don't mean to sound like I'm preaching, because I know she's received a lot of support from all of you, but you need to let her come around in her own good time."

He noticed the thin set of Tyler's lips and felt a pang of sympathy for the man, but there was nothing he could do for the family or Emma's emotional state— except find Samuel himself. "Tyler, have you heard anything on the whereabouts of Fontaine?"

The other man shook his head in disgust as he poured drinks at the sidebar. He passed them along to Steven and his brothers as he spoke. "I got another message from the private investigator a little while ago. It's as if that bastard has dropped off the face of the earth. Like I told you before, the trail has gone cold."

"I think Trevor and I should start looking for him." Cole sat calmly and sipped his drink. "We know this country like the back of our hands—your investigator doesn't."

"I agree." Trevor captured his older brother's gaze. "We might have more luck. Cole and I discussed it—we both want that bastard."

Tyler shook his head. "I need the two of you here. I've been giving this whole thing a lot of thought too, and planned to talk to you both. Now is just as good a time as any." He took a deep breath and dove into his proposal. "I want to back off from the mill indefinitely. I know it's a lot to ask, but, until Emma has completely recovered, I don't want to be far from the house. I can't do that if the two of you are gone."

"I can understand that, Ty." Cole stretched his legs out before him. "But what if Samuel's never found? I'd hate to see that son of a bitch walk away without paying."

Carrie entered the room, then paused to glance at the occupants. "I just checked on Emma. She's asleep, so I thought I'd work on the basket of mending I left in here earlier." Her gaze bored into her brothers. "You all look rather serious. What's going on?"

"Sit down, Carr," Tyler said as he moved to sink down into the chair next to Cole. "We were just trying to figure out how to go about running the business over the next few months."

"In regard to what?" She positioned herself on the sofa, across from Steven. She managed a quick glance in his direction, then looked away. His penetrating gaze made her nervous.

"In regard to the fact that I don't want to stray far from the house and Emma, which means that Trevor and Cole can't just up and leave to search for Fontaine. Somebody has to oversee the operation. Secondly," he continued in a no nonsense tone, "I don't want you, Emma, or any of the other women in this house to be alone. If I stay close to home, and to Emma, it will solve that problem, too."

"But, Tyler, you can't just forget about the business—" Carrie objected.

He held up a hand to silence her, then his eyes scanned the others in the room. "We know Samuel will do anything to get to Emma or myself.   He's more than proved it..." An image of his battered wife flashed in his brain. "I think he's crazy enough to come right here, to the ranch, despite what the investigator says."

Cole rose to fix himself another drink. "We've got a lot of good men around here, Tyler. Not a one of them would let Fontaine within a mile of the place."

"I know they wouldn't, but I don't trust any of them as much as I trust the two of you." Tyler's green eyes glittered with hatred. "I want Fontaine—and I think the only way we're going to get him is to sit tight and wait for him to come to us— even if it takes months. I'll still keep the Pinkerton agent on his trail, but for now, I want the two of you here."

"I think Tyler's right." Steven had quietly listened to the conversation, and now agreed with his friend. "I would hate to think of Fontaine getting into this house with the women—and none of you being around. Let the fox come back to the chicken coop—or at least let him give it a try." His gaze rested on Carrie, and the thought of what he might do to her, too, made him sick to his stomach.

"Okay, Ty. Agreed." Trevor set his empty glass on the table before him. "It's your call. Cole and I will figure out a rotating schedule at the sawmill, and we'll let Jack handle the logging crews. That way, there can be two of us here at all times."

Tyler nodded. "That's even better. We have to make sure that Samuel Fontaine never gets the chance to hurt anyone in this family again."

The October wind rattled the shutters as the group made plans for the immediate future. It was not long though, before Steven stood to leave.

"I guess I'd better head for home. It's getting late. As long as Emma's asleep, I won't bother her again tonight." He glanced at Carrie, who still sat on the sofa with Mamie's basket of mending on the floor next to her. She picked through it nonchalantly, as if his leavetaking was no great thing. "Carrie, could I speak with you privately for a moment?"

A flush immediately stained her satiny cheeks, and she ducked her head to hide from her brothers' view. Steven had arrived daily during the past week to check on Emma, and most nights he stayed for dinner. Having him constantly underfoot left her feeling like a schoolgirl in the throes of her first love. She had avoided him like the plague, however, since the night on the porch and had no desire now to be called to atonement for her confession—which she was sure was Steven's purpose in asking to speak to her alone. She was not about to make a scene in front of her brothers' though, and simply rose with a slight nod in his direction and quickly exited the room. Steven was close on her heels.

The other occupants of the room watched them leave, and Trevor's expression was a little nonplussed. "What's that about? Why would Steve need to talk to Carrie in private?"

"At least they're finally getting along," Tyler commented. "I've noticed Carrie has let up on her sarcasm when he's around. I've never figured out why she doesn't like him."

Cole stretched his arms over his head and chuckled aloud.

"What?" Trevor's voice was filled with confusion.

"It just never ceases to amaze me how some people can be so blind."

"What are you talking about, Cole?"

"Haven't you two figured out what Carrie's problem is yet? Where Steve is concerned, I mean."

"Like I just said," Tyler repeated, "I know exactly what her *problem* is. She's never cared much for him. Hell, can't you tell that by the way she snaps at him on a regular basis?" His dark brow raised in thought. "Although, like I said, she does seem to have backed off in the last week."

Cole simply shook his head in disbelief. "Man, you two are such total ingrates. She's in love with him, and always has been!"

The two older Wilkins brothers stared at him through eyes that mirrored their doubt, and Trevor snorted.

"Oh, come on, Cole. If *that's* how Carrie treats the guy she loves, I'd hate to see how she acts around someone she doesn't like!"

"Yeah, well a woman will resort to desperate measures when the guy is too dense to figure it out on his own."

"Carrie and *Steve*?" Trevor leaned forward, his interest piqued.

Tyler, too, could not quite stomach what his brother was telling them. "Cole, Carrie has never shown any interest in having boys around, and Steve is like a member of the family."

Cole smacked his forehead with the palm of his hand, rolled his eyes heavenward, and reached for his hat. "Carrie has never shown an interest in *boys*, as you so aptly put it, because she's always been interested in only one *man*. Wake up, you two! She's not a little girl anymore. Christ, Tyler, she's only a year younger than Emma and, sometime in the last week, Steve has changed his whole attitude toward her." He placed his worn hat on his head and adjusted it. "I'm gonna take one more walk around the place and make sure everything is secure."

Cole sauntered to the door and spoke over his shoulder. "And don't go out on the front porch. I think they're out there." He left his brothers with slack-jawed looks of disbelief on their faces.

Trevor's gaze swung to his remaining brother, and he scratched his head. "How does he do that?"

"We haven't had a chance to speak alone this week." Steven peered through the darkness at the woman standing before him.

Carrie's gaze dropped to her shoes as she struggled for an outward appearance of calm. A sudden shiver crawled up her back, and she did not know if it was due to the cold October wind that swirled around them or because she stood alone with Steven on the porch—but she was betting on the latter. She lifted her eyes to his again and watched him warily.

"The days have been hectic," she murmured as her eyes again found the planking beneath her feet. Then she sighed, frustrated with her own ineptness, and met his gaze squarely. "I'm sorry, Steven, if I put you on the spot last week. It was just a little girl's confession, from long ago. Don't take it to heart. Lord knows I haven't."

Instant anger flared inside Steven with her flippant remark. Being at the house all week, and in her presence, had forced him to look at her differently. She was not just Tyler's little sister anymore. She was the first thing he thought about when he rose in the morning, and the last thing he thought of at night. She had even invaded his dreams, as visions of her beautiful face floated through his subconscious. It took some doing, but he had finally acknowledged the fact that he wanted to explore her lips with his own mouth; he wanted to hold her woman's body close to his—and he wanted never to let her go. Now, she brushed him away like a pesky mosquito.

"So, just what the hell is that suppose to mean, Carrie? You told me that you waited for me, but, now, because I didn't know how you felt up until a week ago, it doesn't mean anything? I've spent the entire week unable to get you off my mind. I've watched you, I've thought about you, I've *dreamt* about you. You've got me, Carrie, and now you say you don't want me!"

"Oh, so that's how it is, huh? Just because *you* finally decided to notice me as a woman, I'm supposed to just fall into your arms and say, 'Fine, Steven. Whatever makes you happy?'" Carrie's eyes sparkled with a building fury that sprang out of nowhere, and she met him nose to nose. "Let's not forget the fact that *I* waited years for you to come home! Then, when you finally did, you were so busy fawning over other women that you *still* didn't know I was alive! And if you think the last few days have been easy for me, you're wrong! How do you think *I* felt all week after confessing my feelings? You've been in this house countless times, but not once did you seek me out. Not once did you even *try* to discuss it with me!"

"Christ, Carrie, your brothers have been with us constantly! Try looking at it from my point of view. How do you think it feels to know those three would throttle me if I tried to do anything *improper* with their little sister?"

"Hah! As if you're afraid of them!" Carrie rolled her eyes in a dramatic show of skepticism. "You'll have to come up with something better than that."

"That's not what I'm saying!" He balled his hands into fists in a futile effort to control his temper. "I just know how protective they are of you. They always have been! Hell, they'd probably kill me if they caught me kissing you in an unsisterly manner!"

Carrie snorted at his statement and tossed her head, sending her sandy-colored tresses flying. "Well, I don't think you have anything to worry about! I haven't seen any kissing going on around here! Have you, Steven? Hell, Tyler doesn't even have the guts to kiss his own wife! Now that I think about it, I don't think anything improper is *allowed* on the Wilkins ranch!" She peered around his shoulder. "Nope! I don't see anyone over there doing anything improper. Do you?"

"Goddammit, Carrie!" He yanked her into his arms, clamped his mouth over hers, and kissed her for all he was worth.

Carrie was so shocked that it took her a moment to realize what was happening. She had wondered for years what it would feel like to be kissed by him, and now she knew it was worth the wait. She wrapped her arms around his neck and pulled him closer.

The chill wind was forgotten, and the angry words lost in the blustery air. They clung to each other until their passion was spent and the kiss became just a playful touching of lips. Steven opened his eyes, and a lazy grin curved his mouth as he met her liquid, hazel gaze.

"Well, that shut you up."

Carrie's contented smile belied the excitement she found in his embrace, and her shaky hands spread across his chest to feel the beat of his heart—a beat that was as rapid as her own.

"Steven—"

"Shhh, Carrie. If you say one more word, I'll have to kiss you again," he whispered as his eyes danced over her face.

"Then I'm going to keep talking until—"

His mouth silenced hers once more, and he could not help but wonder how he had ever let the last two years go by without seeing her for the woman she was.

Tyler knocked softly on the door to his bedroom three days later and waited for Emma to invite him in. Her quiet voice came a moment later, and he entered the suite, his arms laden with a tablecloth, china plates, and silverware. She leaned against the window and gazed blankly through the frosty pane at the fresh blanket of white that lay across the landscape.

"You had a long nap today," he commented as he placed his load on a nearby table and moved to stoke the fire.

Her only response was a small shrug of the shoulders, then she presented her back to him.

Tyler stifled the sigh that rose in his chest. "Mamie said she would get a tray ready for the two of us tonight. I thought we could eat together. It must be getting lonesome for you up here." This time, Tyler was not even granted a shrug for his efforts. *I'm not giving up on you, Em. You'll not chase me away with your silence again.*

"What do you think of this weather? It's the first snowfall of the year."

Emma watched the snowflakes swirl outside the window and pulled the dressing gown more securely around her small body, realizing in some part of her mind that the movement did not hurt like it had a week ago. The first time she saw her face in the mirror, with its swollen purple marks, she was horribly shocked, but the tears would not come. Her body was slowly healing and the bruises lightening in color, but the pain in her heart would not recede.

Emma half listened as Tyler talked about inconsequential matters, and then moved about the room, doing equally inconsequential things. She knew that he waited for her to speak of Samuel's assault, but she had pushed the attack to the far corners of her mind, refusing to allow the pain to come full force.

The loss of the baby was something else they needed to discuss. The child was the one and only reason they were together—the one and only reason he had not callously ejected her from his home and his life. Her jaw clenched in an effort to prevent her chin from quivering.

How did he feel about her now, especially after what Samuel had done to her? *Does he consider me soiled goods?* His cruel words—words spoken that awful day in the library just before she lost the baby—came back to haunt her.

"Love is making a commitment to one person for the rest of your life, not passing your favors around freely, like you seem to do!"

The bottom line was that Tyler could not get past the idea that she was a wanton woman.

But he's been kind and attentive this past week, her gentler side argued, then her harsher side took over again. *Of course he has! He feels sorry for you! But he'll get over it once you're well. How could he possibly want you after what happened?*

"Emma?"

Realizing that he had spoken her name for the third time, she wiped a wayward tear from her cheek and turned to face him.

"I'm going to run down to the kitchen and see if supper's ready. I've got the table all set up in here." Tyler indicated the small table in the corner, which was now covered with a white cloth and held two place settings.

Emma gave his handiwork a cursory glance, then turned back to the window.

Tyler released another silent sigh. He was at such a loss when it came to her. Steven repeatedly told him to be patient, and he had been, but at times like this, he wanted to scream at her to just let him help—but he could not. He turned to open the door, but froze with his hand on the knob when Emma's strangled whisper reached his ears.

"I tried to get away..."

Tyler forced his heart to slow as he swung back to gaze at her stiff back. He held his breath as he waited for her to speak again.

"I tried to get away...but I couldn't..."

She continued to stare out the window, failing even to turn and see if he had left the room. Tyler crossed to stand behind her. He hesitated for a moment, and then placed gentle hands on her shoulders.

"I know, Em." Her body trembled beneath his fingers, and Tyler carefully pulled her back against his firm chest, slipped his arms around her waist, and rested his chin against her soft hair. He spoke quietly. "It wasn't your fault."

Emma squeezed her eyelids shut in an attempt to stifle the sob elicited by her husband's gentle touch.

"I managed to get on the horse and almost got away...but he pulled on my leg...and I lost my balance."

He could still feel the tremble of her body and pulled her even more protectively into his embrace, then tenderly kissed her satiny tresses. The sob burst forth and her body convulsed with the ache in her heart.

Tyler turned Emma in his arms, lifted her, and then crossed to one of the chairs in front of the fireplace. He murmured words to soothe her—words he would not even be able to recall later that evening—then seated himself and tucked her into his lap. He pulled a quilt around her for warmth as she wept against his chest.

"I knew...what he was going to do..."

"It's over, Em."

"When I fell off the horse...he kicked me in the stomach."

Tyler felt his own stomach constrict with her words and gathered her even closer within his embrace.

"I tried to crawl away...but he kicked me down."

"You don't have to tell me. It's over, Em. I know what happened. It wasn't you're fault."

She continued though, and left nothing out. Tyler felt the warmth of his own tears as she told the story between sobs of anguish.

Not once did he look into her face; Emma kept it hidden in the crook of his neck. She clung to him as her only lifeline in a world gone mad, needing to purge the experience from her mind while he kept her safe and secure in his arms and whispered that he would never let anyone hurt her again.

Tyler stroked her back in an effort to quell the trembling of her body and, finally, her head slumped against his chest as exhaustion overcame her grief.

Emma fell into a fretful sleep, and Tyler ached for her to regain what Samuel had taken from her. He tightened his arms around her and closed his eyes. He would not take the chance of waking her until she was ready to face the world again.

A creaking hinge caused him to glance up. Mamie stood in the doorway and watched them from across the room. Tears glistened in her eyes. Tyler tipped his head in a nod, and his lips curved in a bittersweet smile. The old negress backed from the room, closed the door again, and left them alone as the fire crackled and the snow fell against the window.

Chapter Twenty-One

The next month passed, and Emma finally left her room to rejoin the family. The bruises had completely faded and her body recovered from the miscarriage, but a quiet sadness surrounded her for all to see. She put up a good facade, working with Mamie and Carrie in the kitchen and playing with Janie outside in the snow, but she did not fool anyone—least of all Tyler. Emma's former spirit had disappeared, and the family despaired if she would ever be able to recapture it completely.

Tyler simply did his best to find the old Emma. They took long walks with Janie and Whizzer, laughing at the dog's antics as it bounded through the snow, and Emma seemed happier as the days passed. They spent close knit evenings before the warm fire in the library, playing game after game of chess, with Emma the victor more often than not. One night, she even got a little tipsy, along with the rest of the family, when they celebrated Trevor's twenty-eighth birthday.

Cole told Emma one night at dinner about Steven and Carrie's newfound love for each other, and she squealed with delight and hugged the happy couple. Overall though, the melancholy was still with her and nobody knew what to do.

Tyler now slept in Emma's bedroom at night and only entered his suite when he needed a change of clothes or some other personal item. He did not mention the less than ideal arrangement, however, until late one afternoon when he entered the master bedroom and found it bare of Emma's personal effects. The top of the dresser, where he used to push about her combs and brushes to get at his own toiletries, was now void of any article that belonged to her.

Tyler rushed to the oak armoire and threw open the heavy doors. Her clothes were gone. His chest tightened with rising panic. *Where in hell is she?*

He raced through the connecting hallway and into the adjoining room. His headlong flight caused the door to bang against the dresser and a startled Emma looked up from where she sat at a small desk, writing a letter.

"Tyler, you frightened me! Is something wrong?"

His shoulders sagged with relief as he moved to seat himself in a chair by the window. His searching eyes spied her brushes on the dresser and her jacket hanging from a peg on the backside of the hallway door.

"I went into the other room and noticed all your things were gone, and it just scared me for a minute." He met her hesitant gaze. "Why, Emma?"

She straightened the paper and pen in front of her with a shaky hand. She knew he would discover at some point that day that she had returned to her old room, but it just seemed less complicated that morning to make the move without informing him.

"It just didn't seem right that you couldn't sleep in your own bed—"

"So, you just moved everything back without even discussing it with me? There was no hurry, Emma."

Yes there was! We'll never share that room—not after what Samuel did to me—because you'll never want me! I just wanted the situation to be easier for you. She turned away, so he would not see the tears that shone in her eyes. *Please, Tyler, just let me stay here at the ranch. Let me see you every day. That's all I'll ever ask. Just don't send me back to New York!*

She took a deep breath, mentally straightened her shoulders and glued a nonchalant expression on her face as she turned again to face her husband.

"It wasn't a problem to move my things, Tyler. I didn't have much to do today and you're so busy—Katy was more than happy to help me."

She cringed inwardly with the lie. Tyler was not busy anymore. He was always just a step behind her this past month, gracious to a fault, and solicitous of her every need as she got continually stronger. This morning, however, when she discovered he would spend most of the day with Dougan, Emma quickly garnered Katy's aid before he returned. By taking the initiative and moving out of his room, her actions exonerated him from having to ask her to leave.

Not once had he mentioned the conversation they were to have the day of Samuel's attack...and not once had he ever mentioned the word love. As hard as it was, Emma finally understood that she would always be a wife in name only.

Tyler stared at her petite profile when she turned back to the desk and felt his world crumble. He had spent the last month waiting for her to be ready for him, physically and emotionally, yet now she had taken another step away with the simple act of moving from his room. *All I want to do is take you in my arms and say that I love you...*

But Steven had cautioned him to be patient with her and he would—no matter how long it took.

He could not imagine life without her anymore. His heart raced whenever she walked into a room, and he loved her more with each passing day. She almost died, but he pleaded with her to come back to him and she did.

I'm going to see this thing through to the end, Emma. I'll treat you gently and make you understand that all men aren't like Samuel.

Tyler watched her fidget nervously with the paper on the desk. *Christ, she looks like she's afraid that I'm going to demand she go back to the other room— and into my bed!* But, he would wait until she was ready and until fear no longer ruled her mind. Then and only then would he show her how much a man could love a woman.

"Well, then," Tyler stood and glanced around Emma's suite, "I'll just gather up my things and move them back to my room, if that's all right with you."

She could not watch him as he moved about the suite and held back the tears of rejection once more until, finally, he exited through the short hallway and closed the door quietly behind him. As it clicked shut, she dropped her face into her hands to stifle her sobs.

Tyler closed the door and leaned back against it. His eyelids drooped and he was only too aware of the heaviness that settled in his chest as he contemplated the long, cold winter nights ahead—nights he would spend in a lonely room.

* * *

"Hurry, Emma!" Janie stood outside her stepmother's bedroom door and knocked loudly.

"I'm coming! Is everyone waiting for me?"

"Yup! Uncle Cole has the sleigh all hooked up, and Uncle Trevor says he's going to come up here and throw you over his shoulder like a sack of potatoes if you don't hurry!"

Emma giggled at the picture Janie's words created in her mind, and then quickly grabbed her hat. She had no doubt her brother-in-law would do just that. She joined the little girl in the hall, and they hurried down the steps and out the front door.

Tyler stood next to the shaggy draft horses in the cold winter air. Plumbs of steam whistled from their snouts as the big animals stamped their feet, waiting to be off.

"It's about time, Emma!" he laughed. "Trevor was just on his way up!"

She threw a saucy smile in his general direction as he hurried to help her into the sleigh. "I couldn't find my hat!" A squeal of delight followed when Tyler scooped her into his arms, and then set her gently on the seat next to Carrie, who was already snuggled under a thick woolen blanket. Hot lightning shot through her veins with the simple touch.

Carrie pulled the blanket aside, waited for Emma to seat herself comfortably, and then tucked it across her sister-in-law's lap. "It's amazing how they can just toss us around, isn't it? The other day, Steve picked me up and threw me into a snow bank like I was a small child! Got him back though when he wasn't looking! I shoved snow down the back of his jacket!" She laughed like a woman in love.

"And I'm certain you're not telling me the whole story—like what happened when he caught you." The levity in her words belied the ache in her heart. If only she could have a relationship like that with Tyler...

Carrie's eyes twinkled merrily as she whispered for Emma's ear alone. "Just know that my brothers would not have been too happy with him!" Her infectious giggle caught Trevor's attention, and his curious expression caused her to cackle even louder.

Emma's attention was drawn from her giddy sister-in-law to her husband, when Tyler climbed up next to Trevor on the sleigh's driver seat. *I wonder how he's going to handle the sleeping arrangements when we get to Duluth?*

At the ranch, no one ever questioned the fact that they slept in different rooms. But in the city, and at a hotel, it could become awkward.

Her thoughts were forgotten when Trevor slapped the leather reins across the horses' backs. They were off then, with harness bells jingling merrily, bound for Steven's house, and then a Christmas shopping holiday that none of them would soon forget.

* * *

The group reached Duluth late that afternoon. Trevor drew the sleigh to a halt before The Clark House, and Emma sat in awe as she watched the bundled-up hotel patrons bustle up and down the full-length outside staircase in an attempt to escape the brisk Lake Superior winds. Her eyes danced with excitement when they fell on the ornate front doors, then moved to the white pilasters that lined the front porch. Each was decorated with red ribbons and cedar boughs in honor of the holiday season.

"Makes you feel kind of festive, doesn't it? Here, take my hand, and I'll help you out."

She dropped her gaze to Tyler's sparkling one, then reached for his hand and, before she knew it, she was in his arms again. Her feet touched the ground a moment later, and she grasped the first thing that came to mind when the thrill of his latest embrace faded away as quickly as the muscular arms around her. "The hotel is beautiful. I can't believe it takes up almost an entire block!"

"Wait until you see the inside. This building is only two years old and is as modern as they come."

He grasped her elbow and they followed the rest of the family up the staircase and through the front doors. Emma was awestruck again at the beauty of the marble floors and oak beams in the grand foyer. An expansive, white oak staircase, which was lined with mirrors, led to the upper floors. It was as fine a hotel as any that New York had to offer.

Tyler left her and crossed the shiny granite floor to join Trevor at the front counter and finalize the arrangements for their two day stay. The women stamped their booted feet in an attempt to warm them, more than ready for a warm fire and a place to rest before dinner. Tyler returned with three room keys and distributed them among the group.

"Okay, Trevor, you and Cole have a room and, Steve, I'll have you bunk in with me, so the ladies can have a suite all to themselves." He passed the keys out, handing one to Carrie, as if the fact that he and his wife would sleep in separate rooms was perfectly natural.

Emma's heart sank to the floor, but she kept the smile on her face for everyone to see. *If this is what he wants, then I can accept it in good grace.*

Tyler also forced a tired smile to curve his lips, for the benefit of the others, and Trevor muttered close to Cole's ear.

"I don't know how he does it. I applaud his ability though, to stay away from her."

"Yeah, you gotta give him credit. He's not gonna push her until she's ready." Cole shook his head at their inability to help the situation, then followed his family up the stairs.

That night the entire family, along with Steven, met at the top of the grand staircase. Tyler crooked an elbow, and Emma grasped it with a shy smile. He took a deep breath to calm his erratic heartbeat at the sight of her. Diamond eardrops hung to just above her bare shoulders, but Tyler was more interested in her evening gown's daring black velvet décolletage—and the sparkling jewel that rested in the satiny cleavage between her breasts. He swallowed. *Oh, to be that piece of jewelry.*

"You look beautiful. It's an honor to escort you to dinner, Mrs. Wilkins."

"Why, thank you, Mr. Wilkins. The short rest I had did wonders." She floated down the steps at his side and found herself looking forward to the evening with an excitement she had not felt in a long time.

They entered the large dining room as one, and Tyler hid a smile as every male head in the room turned in their direction. "Don't look now," he whispered to Emma, "but you and Carrie are causing quite a commotion among the other men in the room. I think they're actually jealous!"

A giggle bubbled in Emma's throat, and she could not help but respond in kind. "Hah! The women are the jealous ones. More than one is eyeing you four gorgeous men. Carrie and I won't stand a chance tonight."

"I think not, madam. I promise you my undivided attention for the entire evening." His husky words, spoken close to her ear, caused Emma's heart to skip a beat before he led her to their table.

The meal progressed and Emma found complete joy in the fact that Tyler was true to his word. She was not certain though, if the heat that suffused her cheeks was caused by her husband's cherished gaze or Trevor's ribald stories.

Tyler feasted more on Emma's candlelit face than he did the meal. He had never seen a more enchanting and beautiful woman. A soft smile played about her full lips throughout the entire dinner—even during the countless times she leaned over to cover Janie's ears, and then gently reprimanded Trevor for his choice of words.

Later, the table was cleared and the orchestra struck up the first waltz of the evening. Steven stood, bowed gallantly before Carrie, and asked her to join him on the floor. The happy couple excused themselves, holding hands as they left the table.

"Hey, Trevor," Cole grinned after his sister. "Can you finally tell that the two of them are in love, or are you still missing the fact?" He laughed heartily when Trevor leaned over to whisper what Emma was sure was yet another risqué comment, then the older of the two brothers stood and followed Steven's lead when he ceremoniously asked Janie to dance. The little girl could hardly contain her excitement when Trevor took her hand, tucked it under his arm, and led her out onto the floor.

Cole stood and bowed slightly to the two who remained seated at the table. "If you'll pardon me, I see a beautiful little blonde sitting across the way making eyes at me. I think I'll go introduce myself and see if she'd like me to impress her with one of my many talents."

"It wouldn't hurt to ask her to dance first, Cole!" Tyler called after him with a chuckle.

The other man turned to cast a smart salute in their direction, and then he was gone.

Emma had longed to be alone with Tyler all evening, but now that her wish had finally come true, she grappled for words. Her nervous gaze strayed to where Cole now talked with the "little blonde."

"Why is it that Cole and Trevor have never settled down? They both make such good prospects. One would think that women would be banging down the doors at the ranch to get to them."

Tyler smiled at her observation and shrugged his broad shoulders. "I guess they've always been so involved with running the ranch and the mill that they haven't had time for women. Don't worry about them though, Emma. I'm sure when they finally meet the right ones, there will be two women out there who won't stand a chance."

It was the only answer he could come up with and not disclose the fact that neither of his brothers were ready to make a life long commitment and chose to frequent a local brothel. The occasional "visits" filled a need—albeit a physical one only—but he was not one to judge. He had been lucky. He met Sara early on in his adult life and never felt a desire to visit such a place as he was certain his brothers would over next two evenings.

Tyler stood suddenly, and Emma jumped. "Let's dance, Emma. I think we both deserve a night of simple fun." He held out a hand and patiently waited for her to make up her mind.

Emma flushed with the invitation, but she was not about to give up the chance to be in his arms, even if it would only be for the length of one dance.

One dance led to another and, before long, the other members of the family ceased to exist. Emma held her breath each time Tyler took her in his arms, and she reveled in the fact that he pulled her a little closer each time a new waltz began.

Janie's eyes sparkled up at her Uncle Trevor. Carrie and Steve whispered to each other amid small giggles, and Cole managed to steal the petite blonde from the glare of her parent's watchful eyes, but Emma saw none of it. She was lost in a dream—a dream she hoped would never end.

Tyler simply basked in the realization that his wife seemed more like the Emma of old, and he could not help but secretly hope that she would be his soon— in the fullest sense of the word. He pulled her closer and pressed his cheek against her satiny tresses. *I want you so much, Emma.* He breathed in her perfumed scent and stifled the sigh that rose in his throat. *I'll bet you don't even realize that I've come close to kissing you at least a thousand times. Hell, I actually have to leave the house sometimes, because I'm afraid I'll give myself away.*

Why won't he give me a chance? Emma wondered with a fear-born desperation. *The family makes a point of leaving us alone and, though there have been hundreds of opportunities for him to kiss me, he always walks away.* Emma battled the sudden tears that stung her eyelids. *You know why! He will never want you as a man wants a woman. How could he, when you were used by another man?* She opened her eyes, looked up at Tyler, and saw his warm smile. She returned it shakily, then her head found his shoulder again and her reasonable side took over once more. *Yes, Emma, you were used. You did not give yourself to Samuel willingly, and somehow you have to make him see that.*

Emma tightened her arms around him, knowing that he would not callously push her away in public, and her jaw stiffened with a newfound determination. *I'm not going to let Samuel Fontaine rule my life any longer. I want a life with you, Tyler. I want to be your wife in every way. I'm not afraid anymore...*

The last song ended, and so did Emma's fantasy. Trevor sat at the table again, with Janie asleep in his arms, and Cole handed the "blonde" back to her parents. Steven and Carrie had already left the dance floor, to hurry upstairs and say goodnight in private. Tyler released Emma from his arms, however reluctantly, and returned to the table just in time to hear Cole address Trevor.

"Yes sir, Trev," Cole teased, as he eyed his sleeping niece. "You'll make a good nanny someday."

"Well, at least I'm not robbing the cradle. You'd better watch your back—that little blonde's father is scowling at you!"

Tyler lifted his sleeping daughter into his arms with a chuckle. "Thanks for making Janie's night memorable. We better get her upstairs."

The contented group ascended the circular stairway to the second floor as one.

Tyler left his brothers and sister in the hallway and entered the women's suite. Emma followed him in and closed the door quietly behind them as he carried Janie to one of the two double beds. He gently laid his daughter on the floral spread and kissed her soft cheek goodnight. Emma removed the little girl's shoes and tucked her beneath the covers and, all the while, Tyler longed for her to climb into the other bed with him.

Emma turned to face him, with tiny shoes in hand, and smiled. "I can't thank you enough for the wonderful evening," she murmured. "I don't ever remember dancing that much." She crossed her arms before her chest and the dimples in her cheeks deepened. "You are rather good, you know. I was the envy of every woman in the room. In fact, I saw more than one clasp her heart in despondency, because such a debonair gentleman failed to ask her to dance."

Tyler leaned a shoulder against the bedpost and a reckless grin curved his lips when he swept an arm in the direction of the floor. "Madam, these feet were for your use and your use alone tonight. Pity the old bags in the ballroom who are still searching for them."

"Tyler, shame on you!" A giggle burst from Emma's throat at his vain comment and, before she realized what she was doing, she leaned forward to give him a hug. "Thank you again for making this such a memorable night."

He slipped his arms around her slender waist and gazed into the sparkling green depths before him, then dropped a kiss on her cheek. "You are most heartily welcome, madam. I can't remember ever having such a pleasant evening either." *She doesn't seem to mind having my arms around her...maybe...*

He pulled her closer, lowered his mouth to hers, and Emma held her breath—until the door handle clicked. She jumped back and Tyler stifled a curse as Carrie entered the suite.

"Oh! There you are! I got so involved with those two idiot brothers of ours, Ty, that I lost track of time. Those two never know when to quit. Now, they say they're going to check out a poker game or two."

Tyler's shoulders sagged with the long sigh that escaped his lips. "I'll leave you two now. Make sure you lock the door behind me." He glanced at his wife, where she stood quietly in the middle of the room looking entirely too gorgeous. "Goodnight, Emma. I'll see you in the morning."

Tyler left the room with a decided nonchalance, as if it were perfectly normal to leave her with his sister, instead of hauling her back to his room for a night of passionate lovemaking.

Emma locked the door behind him and rested her forehead against the smooth surface. *If only Carrie hadn't come in when she did...*

Cole and Trevor sat at a table with three other men, chuckling over a lewd joke. Poker chips were stacked high on the green felt surface, and the air was filled with the scent of expensive cigars. A player piano trilled over the din of raucous voices.

The dealer paused before doling out another hand of cards when a pretty redhead slid a note across the table to Cole. He picked up the scrap of paper with a flourish and read the neatly scripted words. It was from Belle—the owner of the 'establishment'. He sent her a message earlier, informing her that he was in town, and then had waited patiently for her to respond. A wry smiled touched his lips.

Trevor saw his brother's grin and shook his head. "It's amazing..."

"What?" Cole glanced Trevor's way through eyes that were wide with innocence.

"You two play the same game every time we come here. Belle always let's you enjoy a few drinks, a few games of poker, and some time with the boys. I think she actually likes making you sit down here, eager as a lad awaiting her pleasures."

Cole was unflappable and tossed down the half-full glass of whiskey on the table before him. Trevor was not far off the mark. Sitting at the card table gave him time to think about the night ahead, and all the sensations Belle's experienced hands and mouth would awaken in his man's body. She had told him more than once that he would be a better lover if he had to wait—knowing she was just up the stairs and out of reach. *Maybe she's right,* he pondered. *I've been sitting here, only half concentrating on the game and waiting to be in her arms.*

Cole reached for his chips, took one more puff off the cigar clamped between his teeth, and then tamped it out in an ashtray. "Well, gentlemen, it's been a pleasure." Standing, he tucked the poker chips and some loose bills into the front pocket of his pants and cast a lazy glance at Trevor. A smug grin creased his twinkling eyes, and the dark brows did a little bounce. "Don't wait up, big brother. I got people to see and things to attend to and might not see you till morning."

Both the Wilkins men were a little tipsy and, as Cole sauntered toward the steps, Trevor snorted at his brother's cockiness. "Don't be so sure you'll be the last one back to the hotel, smartass!"

Cole simply pulled his black hat further down on his forehead, saluted, and slowly wound his way through the crowd. He nodded his head politely at every woman he passed, and Trevor watched as their heads turned. Each of them would have been more than happy to spend the night with the quiet cowboy.

Belle must be one helluva woman—he never asks for anyone else.

Belle was the Madam of the house. The first time Trevor and Cole visited her establishment, she took a shine to the younger of the two brothers and made it quite obvious to the other girls that he was "hands off." Trevor could not have cared less—the other ladies were just as enjoyable.

Trevor's eyes followed Cole to the top of the staircase. His brother rounded a corner at the same moment the hat was whisked from Trevor's head. He swiveled on the chair just as a voluptuous blonde plunked the Stetson down on her perfectly coifed tresses.

"Hello, cowboy. Care to buy a thirsty lady a drink?"

Trevor chuckled, pushed his chair back, and patted his knee. She dropped onto his lap and whispered in his ear. His chuckle grew into a full blown laugh as he suggested that, with the plans she had for him, he had better buy a bottle.

The pretty blonde toyed with the buttons on his shirt, then nuzzled his ear. Her whispered entreaties heated his entire body. Trevor helped her from his knee, patted her on the behind, and then followed her across the room and up the same set of stairs his brother had just climbed. Grabbing a bottle from the bartender as he passed the bar, Cole was the last thing on Trevor's mind as he watched the round, feminine bottom swing before him.

* * *

Cole knocked softly on the wooden surface before him, and a sultry voice invited him in. He pushed the door open and a low whistle escaped his lips when a vision in silk met his gaze. Belle stood in the center of the room, clad only in a filmy robe, the sash tied loosely around her shapely body. He stepped into the room, leaned casually against a fabric-covered wall, and failed to notice the equally appreciative smile that curved her sensual mouth. He looked incredibly delectable with his black cowboy hat tipped low, eyes half shuttered in the candlelight, and the lazy grin back in place.

"Hello, Cole. I was beginning to think you'd found some sweet, little virgin to while away your days with. I haven't seen you lately."

"No such luck, Belle. All the virgins I know are home tucked in their beds behind daddy's locked door."

"Too bad for them. How about you come over here and greet a *real* woman." Belle pulled open the sash on her robe; slowly, enticingly, revealing ample cleavage and other attributes. She reveled in the dark passion that jumped from Cole's eyes.

He inhaled deeply at the sight of her nude body beneath the silky material and, never taking his eyes from hers, ambled slowly across the room. He reached into his pocket and pulled out a one hundred dollar bill, then tossed it onto the dresser top on his way by. Standing before her, he reached up to caress her cheek, and then felt her tremble when he brushed his thumb across her full lips. He lowered his mouth. The gentle kiss ended quickly and Belle gazed up at him through passion-filled eyes.

"I missed you, Cole. Don't be such a stranger from now on."

Her fingers toyed with the buttons on his shirt as he tossed his hat on a chair. Cole held his breath as her hands pushed the material aside and kneaded the bare skin beneath. He shrugged the garment from his shoulders as her fingers moved to the buckle on his leather belt. She slid the trousers down and over his slender hips, and the cotton pants found the floor. Their gazes locked in anticipation and, a moment later, Cole reached inside her robe and pulled her naked body against his. His mouth found her neck as her hands slipped to his back, then traveled up and across his muscular shoulders.

Belle's husky voice reached his ears. "Don't make me wait any longer."

Cole moved his lips to her waiting mouth. The passionate kiss sent a chill racing up her spine, then she released her breath in a quick gasp when his calloused hands clutched her firm bottom. He lifted her in a quick fluid movement, and Belle wrapped her silken legs around his waist as he moved to the bed.

Cole's heart beat rapidly against his ribs with the familiar sensations she never failed to arouse. He lowered her onto the bed then, and entered her with one ferocious thrust, losing himself in the eager body that strained against his.

Their tongues danced and their bodies followed suit as she met each of his rhythmic movements, urging him on with breathless words that drove him to the brink of insanity. He pumped harder. A deep moan escaped Belle's throat a moment later, and the sound pushed Cole over the edge. He thrust deeply one last time and found an explosive release within her body once again.

Cole rolled off of her and onto his back, then pulled her on top of him. They clung tightly to one another as their breathing slowed. Belle's head lolled against his furred chest and she groaned with the sensuous feel of his hands as they moved across her shoulders, down to her firm buttocks, and back up again.

"Having sex with you is a heady experience, Belle." There was no coquettishness on her part. She wanted the raw sex as badly as he did and never begged for promises she knew he would not make. Belle sold sex for a living, but, regardless, Cole was her favorite. They both knew that there would never be anything more.

"Oh, Cole," she sighed as she snuggled closer. "How come you don't visit me more often? Just think; we could be doing this on a regular basis. Sex with you is always so much better than with anyone else."

He chuckled as he played with her long, flowing hair and contemplated her words. "I don't think I could afford you regularly! Before you know it, I'd be penniless and begging to have it for free, and you'd just slam the door in my face."

She raised herself up on her elbows and met his dark gaze, wishing this one time that circumstances could be different. She never had to fake a response with Cole like she did with her other clientele. His handsome face and lean, sexy body never failed to excite her, along with the gentle boyish charm that always surrounded him. She knew their visits would come to an end someday though, when an extremely lucky and much younger woman snagged him away from her. Until then, however, he was exclusively hers, and she would relish every moment.

"Do you remember the first time you and Trevor came here?" She laughed. "I was bound and determined to get you up to my room one way or another that night."

Cole chuckled as his thumb brushed an erect nipple. "How could I forget? I came in to play poker. I was a sweet, young virgin and you totally corrupted me before the night was over."

Belle cackled with glee and slapped him playfully on the arm. "That's bull, and you know it. Why do you think I warned my girls to stay away from you?"

"I don't know—tell me." His smile turned incorrigible. "It must be because I'm so good in bed."

"You're so damned handsome, Cole Wilkins, and you don't even know it." She shook her head. "Once I finally managed to coax you upstairs, I had one of the finest nights of sex I've ever had. There's no way I'm sharing that with my girls." The playfulness left her eyes. "Do you ever visit any of the other houses in town?"

"Nope. Why would I? You and I got a good thing going here, and I have no desire to be with anyone else."

She kissed him on the nose and rose from the bed. Completely at ease with her nudity, she walked to the liquor cabinet to retrieve two glasses and a bottle of cognac she kept on hand just for him. She was well aware of the fact that he watched her backside and was thankful she had managed to remain firm and trim— even though she was ten years his senior. Returning to the bed, she waited until he had positioned himself against a huge, fluffy pillow before she handed him the glass and slid under the covers.

"What's been going on up at the ranch? Word filtered down that your older brother got married again, and then he had some sort of accident. Care to fill me in?"

"Tyler went to New York early this spring on business and ended up finding himself in an...uncompromising position. He got the daughter of one of his business associates pregnant."

A loud, boisterous laugh escaped Belle's throat. She could not help but find humor in the fact that the "polite" girls of society had no idea how to keep themselves from getting in the family way.

"So, what's she like, Cole? From what you've told me about Tyler and his love for his first wife, it seems strange that he would even consider remarrying. It would be a rather awkward position to find himself in."

"Oh, believe me, it was. Trevor, Carrie, and I had a grand old time with it. Her father sent her out here though, lock, stock and barrel, and insisted that Tyler marry her immediately. There's a lot more to the story, but it would take me days to tell you about it."

She leaned over to kiss him, reveling in the taste of the fine liquor on his lips. "So, why don't you stay for *days*...and just tell me bits and pieces in between rounds?"

The course hair on his chest raked her sensitive breasts, and she could not help but elaborate on how wonderful it would be to find him in her bed every morning. The dip of his eyebrows though, told Belle that he was lost in thought, and she retreated, at least for the moment.

"All right, go ahead and finish what you want to say."

"Emma is one hell of a lady, Belle. She loves Tyler like there's no tomorrow, and she treats his daughter as if the girl were her own. She's the best thing that's happened to him in a long time."

"But...?" Belle sensed that there was more.

Cole sipped at his drink. "So much has happened since Emma first arrived. To make a long story short, some bastard from her past showed up at the logging camp and, not knowing who he was, the foreman hired him as part of a temporary crew. This guy felt that Tyler and Emma had a hand in him losing the family business in New York, and he tried to kill Tyler. The next day, Emma and Tyler had a bad falling out, and she tore off from the ranch on horseback. This man, Samuel Fontaine, must have seen her pass by on the road or something and followed her." He turned his head to meet her gaze directly. "Belle, he beat the hell out of her, raped her, and left her for dead. She miscarried the baby and is still recovering."

Belle listened in stunned disbelief. Her heart reached out to this woman, whom she did not even know. She sold sex for a living—but not once, ever, in her entire life, had someone forced it from her or treated her roughly. The stricken look on Cole's face—a look generated by his feelings for his brother's wife—left her feeling slightly jealous of this woman, who had gained the love of an entire family.

"So, why are you telling me all of this, Cole?"

"I want you to keep a look out for him. He's got a habit of frequenting places like this and beating up the woman he's with. By Tyler's recollection, he's just a bit shorter than me and, right now, he has long blond hair and is rather unkempt. One of the hands at the ranch saw him and said he was riding a broken-down Appaloosa. Just be careful, Belle, and tell your girls to be careful, too. If he happens to show up here, call the sheriff, and then get a message to me. I'd like to kill the bastard myself, and so would Tyler and Trevor."

"You must be right about this Emma," she observed quietly. "If the three of you are that bent on revenge, she must be something."

"She is, Belle. She sure is."

Belle took the glass from his hand then, and placed it alongside hers on the nightstand. She spread herself across the length of his body and smiled down into his upturned face.

"I think that's enough talk. Did you come here to talk about another woman, or did you come for the kind of fun that only I can provide?" She rubbed her body against his, then kissed him leisurely. A smile touched her lips when she felt him harden beneath her. "I want you to make love to me again. Make me forget, Cole, that you'll be leaving in the morning."

His hands were already traveling over her firm derriere and, flipping Belle onto her back, he kissed one pink tipped breast, and then the other. His hand moved to cover the velvety mound between her legs and Belle moaned as their passion rose again.

Chapter Twenty-Two

Tyler opened the door to his hotel room early the next morning and discovered his younger brothers stumbling down the hallway. Cole gripped Trevor under the arms and frantically tried to shush the crude ditty about a blonde with a round derriere that tumbled from his mouth.

Tyler could only shake his head and chuckle softly as he perused his brother's appearance. Trevor's shirt was buttoned unevenly beneath the open jacket, his hair was tousled and a lopsided, drunken smile curved his lips when he spotted his elder brother before him.

"Ty!" he slurred, then stumbled, and Cole almost lost his grip. "What a fine mornin' it is! I'll be ready for Christmas shoppin' in just a few short minutes."

"Sure you will," Tyler replied dryly. "I don't think you'll be ready for anything but a drunken sleep for the next few *hours*. The two of you smell like a cross between a whorehouse and a brewery."

Trevor's bloodshot eyes widened in mock horror as he swung his head and poked Cole in the arm. "Pssst! Cole..." He slammed an eye shut to better focus on his brother's face. "I think our secret is out."

Cole just rolled his eyes as Tyler's grin widened and concentrated on keeping his other brother upright while he dug in his pocket for the key to their room.

"Ty, help me get him in the room before Em or Carrie hear him, will you?"

Tyler stepped forward, gripped Trevor from the other side, and helped Cole to maneuver the drunken man through the doorway and to the bed. They dumped him unceremoniously on the chenille bedspread, and Cole tugged off his boots as Trevor mumbled incoherently and continued to chuckle to himself about the outstanding night he spent in the arms of an amorous woman. "Damn, but she was good! The things that blonde could do with her hands and mouth...!" He eyed his eldest brother through a liquid gaze. "You know, Ty, you should really try it with Emma! You two...should...be..."

The rest of the words were lost as his eyes fluttered shut and his breathing deepened.

"Don't mind him, Tyler," Cole intervened. "He's as drunk as a two-bit whore and doesn't realize what he's saying."

"Yeah, well, he's not so far off the mark now, is he, Cole?"

The younger brother read the frustration in Tyler's eyes, and shook his head sadly.

"It's not as if I don't desire my own wife. It's just that I don't know if she's ready yet. Emma has been to hell and back, and I don't want to scare her off."

"Man, you need to be nominated for sainthood or something! How much longer can you possibly wait?" He moved to clap a supportive hand on his brother's shoulder. "You have to push her a little bit, Ty. And, to be honest, I don't think she'd be *scared.* I've seen the way she looks at you. She cares a lot."

"Yeah, and I want her to continue to care. I want her to grow to care *more,* which means that I have to build her trust in me. I'm hoping my Christmas surprise will help to accomplish that." He sighed. "I guess we'll see."

A sudden loud snore from the bed drew Tyler's attention, and he cast a rueful glance over his shoulder, then looked back at Cole. "Are you coming with us this morning or do you also have a wild night to sleep off?"

"No, you can count me in. Give me some time to clean up and I'll meet you in the dining room." He stripped off his shirt as Tyler left the room and crossed the hall to knock on Emma and Carrie's door. It immediately swung open.

"Good morning!" A happy smile curved Emma's lips at the sight of him. "Come in and sit down a minute—we're just about ready." She opened the door wider and Tyler stepped into the room to receive an excited hug from his daughter. A few minutes later, the four met Steven in the hallway and proceeded downstairs to the dining room.

Cole arrived at the table just as the maître'd served breakfast. "Trevor isn't feeling too well this morning. He said he'd join us later."

Carrie eyed him suspiciously. "What time did you two get in last night?"

"Early," Cole answered matter-of-factly. *Early this morning.*

Tyler could not meet his eyes. To do so would guarantee a burst of laughter, which would surely give away the real reason why Trevor was absent from the group.

The morning was one of those fine winter days in Duluth when the sun shone brightly and the crispness in the air had taken its leave. Tyler and Emma fell behind the rest of the family as they strolled past shops decorated for the season. Heated kettles filled with steaming apple cider were placed along the boulevards and hawkers called out to the milling crowds in an attempt to get them to buy their wares. Emma's hand rested in the crook of her husband's arm and she grasped it tighter.

Tyler glanced down at his wife and chuckled. "You should see your face. You look as excited as Janie."

"I am!" Emma did a little skip next to him. "How can you not be? Everyone's got a smile on their face, the weather is warm, and I can't wait to go shopping. It's been a long time!"

"Well, I think we should start then. How about you, Carrie, and Cole go one way, and Steve and I will take Janie. We can meet in a few hours and switch partners." He neglected to mention the fact that, between his brother and the doctor, Emma would have at least one male escort at all times. Samuel Fontaine could not be forgotten.

"I think that's a good idea. Then I can buy Janie's gifts when she's not around." *And yours, too,* she added the last silently.

The two groups separated. Cole proved a good sport for the first couple of hours, carrying the women's numerous packages as he followed them from shop to shop. Finally though, he stopped them with a hearty laugh, and then a plea for mercy as he peered at Emma over the top of another wrapped box that she had just balanced on top of his load.

"Okay, girls, we have to come up with another plan. Let's find a reputable store, where we can trust the owner to deliver all these packages to the hotel. I'm turning into a pack mule and starting to hear snickers from the other men on the street!"

The ladies' arms were also full, so they ducked into an exclusive shop, bartered with the owner, and promised to purchase goods from his establishment if he would forward their packages to the hotel.

Emma strolled leisurely through the aisles of the quaint shop, pausing often to search the shelves—and fretting over the fact that she had yet to find anything for Tyler. Suddenly, her attention was drawn to a wide shelf that hung on the back wall, and her heart thudded in her chest as she focused her intent green eyes on a single item mixed in with the other gifts for sale.

An indescribable shiver ran up her spine as she stopped before the display and reached out a trembling gloved hand to grasp the beautifully carved image of an Indian. Turning it slowly in her palms, she examined it in wide eyed wonder. A bird sat perched on the brave's shoulder and a wolf crouched by his side. The near lifelike face stared back at her, and she was sure the eyes peered into her soul. There was something strangely familiar about the carving, but she could not quite place it... It was enough though, that the statue represented what she had found with Tyler. Hopefully, he would relate to the gift as she did now.

Emma stood rooted to the spot, seeking to discover the reason for her tumultuous emotions. She quickly removed her gloves and ran her fingers over the small statue almost reverently, amazed at the heat that coursed through her veins. She nearly jumped out of her skin when Cole spoke from behind her.

"Find something you like?"

"Cole! You startled me!"

"Where in the heck were you off to just now? I questioned you twice before you heard me."

Emma continued to stare at the Indian's face and missed her brother-in-law's last statement. "Isn't it beautiful? When Tyler and I were shopping in New York one day, we met an old Indian. This statue somehow reminds me of him, but there's something else about it, too..." She shook her head abruptly, ridding her mind of the eerie feeling that raised goose bumps on her arms. "I think I finally solved the problem of what I'm going to get Tyler. Do you think he'll like it?

Cole peered over the top of Emma's head to the figurine. "It's nice, but I think he'll like anything you give him, just because it came from you."

Emma ducked her head. *Is that really how he feels?* He was going to kiss her last night—just before Carrie burst into the room. She was sure of it. Was he finally ready to see that Samuel used her? Would he actually accept her as his wife now? She wanted her life back, and she sought to share that life with him. She wanted to be a mother to Janie, and she wanted to stay in Minnesota with the people she cared for so dearly.

Holding the carving close to her body, she turned and met Cole's gaze. "I wish I could feel as certain about that as you do." Before he could comment further, she walked around him and headed in the direction of the front counter, calling over her shoulder. "I think I'll have the shop owner wrap this for me before we leave."

Cole shook his head and followed. *Are the two of them ever going to see the light of day and admit to each other how they feel?* His jaw hardened with a sudden, renewed determination. *Okay. If something doesn't happen between the two of you soon, I'm gonna make damned sure that it does.*

He glanced at his pocket watch, then hurried the women along to meet Tyler and the others.

That night, Carrie and Emma sat on the sofa in their rented suite. The family had enjoyed a quiet dinner, then retired to their respective rooms after the long day of shopping. Janie was asleep and the two women visited quietly about the approaching holiday and how quickly the time had passed since Emma came to live with them.

"I can't believe it, Carrie. I had no clue any of you even existed a year ago, and never in my wildest dreams did I imagine I would spend this Christmas in Minnesota."

"I know how you feel. I was still pining away for Steven then, and being as rude as a rich old biddy because I felt so invisible whenever he was around. A lot has happened in both our lives this past year."

A flicker of pain crossed Emma's face just before she ducked her head, and Carrie was immediately apologetic. She reached for her sister-in-law's hand. "I'm sorry, Em. I didn't mean to be so insensitive. I wasn't thinking."

Emma squeezed her hand and forced a quick, wan smile. "It's okay, Carrie. We can't pretend that it never happened. I'm trying, but I don't think I'll ever forget the pain and the terror I felt that afternoon."

Carrie breathed a silent sigh of relief. It was the first time the two women had discussed the rape, which meant that Emma was starting to heal.

"Can I ask you something?" Her sister-in-law's question brought the other woman back to the present. "How was Tyler after...after what happened? I was in such a fog that first week that I don't remember much."

"What do you mean, *how was he*?"

Emma stood and paced the area between the sofa and the bed slowly, trying to form her next words. "Before I left the house that day and before we fought, Tyler told me he was ready to discuss our marriage." She looked at the other woman. "It's no secret that we still have separate rooms. I really thought things were going to be straightened out. But after the...after what Samuel did to me, Tyler has stayed at arm's length. He's been kind and attentive, yes, but he doesn't treat me like his wife...not in the way I would like him to." Her brows dipped slightly as she turned her back to Carrie again. "He had a rough two years after Sara's death, and then I barged into his life through no choice of his own. At one point though, I really thought he might finally be ready to accept me as his wife." Emma closed her eyes and her mind returned to that long ago day. "We had such a horrible argument before I left the ranch that day." She whirled suddenly and, facing her sister-in-law, blurted out the words. "How upset was he when he found me?"

Carrie rose from the sofa and took Emma's hands in hers. "You really love him, don't you?" She watched through sympathetic eyes as the other woman nodded her head sadly. "So, why don't you tell him?"

Emma shook her head adamantly and opened her mouth to object, but Carrie's hold on her hands tightened, silencing her outcry.

"Come sit down and listen to me." Carrie led her to the sofa again, and Emma waited for the younger woman's sage advice.

"What happened to you was awful, Emma. No woman should have to go through what you did, but you seem to be forgetting that you were the victim, *not* Tyler. You have to give him a little credit. Do you think he's so shallow that he'd think you aren't good enough for him anymore?"

Emma's eyes shone with tears. "How could he want me, Carrie? Samuel ruined whatever chance of happiness I could've had with Tyler!"

"That's not true! If you love my brother, and he's too dense to figure it out, then *make* him understand. Emma, I've never heard him speak in a way that would make me believe he doesn't want you because of what that evil man did! When Tyler brought you home that night, he was beside himself with guilt and fear. He stayed with you all night, trying to get you to wake up—pleading for you to wake up! He was terrified that you were going to leave him." She took Emma's hands in hers again and squeezed them tightly. "Be strong enough for the both of you, Emma. *Show* him what you could have together. Go to him and start the life you want so badly!" Carrie gathered her into her arms and hugged her fiercely, then leaned back. "When you think about it, what do you have to lose? Are you even a little bit happy right now?"

The tears escaped and rolled down her cheeks. "I'm miserable, Carrie. I watch you and Steven, and I'm actually jealous of how much the two of you love each other."

"And I had to practically beat it into his head before he finally noticed me as a woman. It worked for me, Emma, and there's no reason it can't work for you, too." She lifted her shoulders in a small shrug. "Like I said, what have you got to lose?"

Emma stood to wander the room again as she thought about Carrie's words. What if she was right and all Tyler needed was a little push in the right direction? She wanted desperately to be a real wife to him; to be loved totally with no barriers.

She turned to face her sister-in-law again. "Thank you, Carrie, for understanding what I'm going through. I'll think about doing what you've said, but it scares me."

"Don't let it, Emma. You're one of the strongest ladies I've ever met and, believe me, I know my brother. There's no reason for you to be afraid."

December twenty-third arrived cold and clear. The ranch house was decorated with the holiday theme and filled with the odor of delectable baked goods that Mamie turned out in pan after pan. The family was gathered in the open living room now, ready to rearrange furniture for the next day's events.

Emma struggled with a small, but heavy table and, seeing her dilemma, Tyler rushed to her side. "Here, let me help you with that."

"When are you getting the Christmas tree?" She watched her husband lift the heavy table and easily move it into the corner.

"You mean when are *all* of us going to get it?" He smiled at his wife, and she returned the gesture, albeit rather contritely. He shrugged. "Hey, it's always a big event around here. Tomorrow morning, we'll take a trek up the hill behind the house. There's a great stand of Norways up there to choose from. We'll get the tree decorated before the employee party." He shook his head with a chuckle. "Wait until you see the feast Mamie and the logger's wives put on. Eventually, one or two of the men will pull out a fiddle, and then the dancing will start."

"It sounds fun. Christmas in New York was always a quiet affair, with just Papa and myself." Her eyes filled with an instant sadness.

Tyler moved to stand before her and lifted her drooping chin with a forefinger. "I'm sorry your father couldn't make travel arrangements. I know you miss him."

Emma shrugged lightly to cover her gloom and the shiver that ran through her with his touch. "His last letter said he would get out here in the spring." *That is if I'm still here after I finally get the courage to talk to you...*

Emma turned, pretending to busy herself with a crate of decorations, and squeezed her eyes to keep the tears at bay.

Tyler's heart fell with her sudden quietness. A moment ago, her eyes had sparkled happily, then the mere mention of her father had ruined the moment.

Carrie interrupted his thoughts a second later. "Tyler, would you lift this crate onto the table? It's too heavy for me."

He did so, then left the women to dig through the box.

"Emma, come see all the decorations. We've all made something for the tree, or purchased a special ornament." Carrie reached into the box, pulled out a dainty oval frame, and turned her gaze to her sister-in-law. "This was my mother's. It's a picture of her and dad."

Emma took the delicate object with gentle hands and peered at the images inside. "You look like your mother, Carrie. The likeness is amazing."

"That's what everyone tells me. I wish I could have known her." She shrugged off a moment of melancholy, then looked at Emma again. "You know, you're going to have to come up with something for the tree. It's your first Christmas with us, and we need to commemorate your becoming a member of the family. Can you think of anything?"

"I wish I'd known about the tradition when we were in Duluth," she commented. "I'll give it some thought. Maybe Janie and I can go outside later and find a pinecone to decorate."

Tyler listened to their conversation from across the room, not surprised in the least that Emma would include his daughter in her search. His wife had a close bond with the little girl and involved her in everything she did. He knew, without a doubt, that she loved Janie completely and thanked God that the little girl felt the same.

He watched quietly as Emma laughed with Carrie, and how she

unconsciously reached to give Janie a hug when the little girl approached her. *My own need is just as great, Emma. I wonder if you realize just how important you've become to me.*

Trevor was right when he said that Emma brought sunshine back into the house; every day, when he looked at her, Tyler felt her presence warm his heart.

A twinge of guilt jabbed his insides when Janie and Emma fell back onto the braided rug and laughed at some shared secret.

So much time has been wasted because of my inflated ego and misplaced jealousy.

His mind flashed back to the day of Samuel's assault, when Emma pummeled her fists against his chest. She told him that afternoon in the library that he was an ignorant man and that she would never give up on the two of them. That was before she was abused, however, and before she miscarried the baby. How did she feel now? His heart sank at the mere thought that the day might come when she would ask to go back to her former home, because there was nothing to keep her in Minnesota.

I won't let that happen. You're mine, Emma, and I'll never let you walk away. That's it...no more running. We're going to have this out, and you're just going to have to trust that my feelings will carry us until you're ready to be mine in every sense of the word.

"Tyler! Are you going to pick up your end of the sofa or not?" Cole bent over the other end of the massive piece of furniture and stared at his brother in exasperation. He had watched the play of emotions on Tyler's face—emotions that gave away his love for Emma. Cole pitied the couple, but the two of them still drove him crazy. Any fool could see how they felt about each other, but, for some odd reason, Tyler and Emma refused to see it themselves.

"What?"

"I said, are you going to help me or not?" Cole straightened and shook his head. "I don't know why you don't just go over there and kiss her." He grinned. "I promise we won't look."

It was Tyler's turn to throw the exasperated look, and Cole chuckled. "Come on, pick up your end."

His brother still remained unmoving. "Do you think she has any idea about her present tomorrow?" he whispered. "Nobody has given it away, have they?"

"No. Since you made me haul her damned packages that day in Duluth, I had Trevor take care of the details concerning your *surprise*. He could handle that much—even with a hangover."

Tyler nodded his approval, then hefted his end of the couch with a decided grunt. The two men set down the sofa against the far wall.

"So..." he looked at his brother with a knowing smile. "I never had a chance to ask you. How's Belle?"

Surprisingly, Cole's face tinged scarlet. Belle was so much a part of his life, but in the same sense, separate. It was indeed a shame that she could never be a part of his family—no matter how much he might wish it. It amazed him that Emma and Tyler could not settle their differences, simply because of Tyler's misguided jealousy. Cole, on the other hand, found no problem in the fact that Belle had a different man in her bed every night.

"She's doing well. I told her what happened to Emma and asked her to keep a look out for Fontaine. She said she'd get a message to us if he shows up at her place."

"I can't believe that bastard just disappeared into thin air," Tyler said as he sank down onto the misplaced sofa. The hatred rose again as he listened to Janie's near hysterical giggles, where Emma tickled her mercilessly across the room. "I'll never give him the chance to hurt anybody in this family again, Cole. I swear to God, if he shows up, I'll kill him."

"Well, move over and wait your turn," the other man said as he plopped down beside his brother. "But, I guess we can't let ourselves worry about it. Every man on this ranch is watching for him. If he shows, we'll get him."

Tyler glanced up just as Emma and Janie grasped hands and hurried from the room amid a bevy of hushed whispers. A short while later, they returned to find everyone taking a break and Mamie serving sandwiches. Emma secreted an object in her palm and announced that she had come up with an idea for the tree.

Crossing to Tyler, she held out her hand with a shy smile. The carving of the loon he purchased for her on that long ago day in New York lay on her outstretched palm. A small length of ribbon now adorned the neck of the figurine, and a loop on the other end provided a means to hang her decoration from a tree limb.

"Would you mind if this was my donation to the tree? Everyone has something special...and this is special to me." She peeked at him from beneath long lashes to gauge his reaction.

He had seen the loon where it sat in a place of prominence on her dresser top, but the two never spoke of it. A warm smile flitted across his lips. "I think it's perfect, and you don't need my permission to put it on the tree. In fact, I'm happy that you want to share it with everyone else."

The other occupants of the room observed the exchange with interest, wondering what significance the small, wooden loon held for the two of them. At that moment, it was easy to see they had forgotten everyone else in the room.

A loud knock sounded on the front door, shattering the fragile moment, and a cold blast of air preceded Steven into the house. Carrie jumped up to greet him, and the rest of the afternoon was spent working on the preparations for the next day's events.

Emma tossed fretfully in her sleep, kicking unconsciously at the heavy comforter that pinned her to the flat surface. She could not run! Samuel gained ground and she knew, with certainty and fear in her heart, that he would catch her and her torture would begin again. She gasped for air and a blood-curdling scream left her throat as he grabbed her, threw her to the ground, and dropped heavily on top of her. He laughed wickedly.

"I'm going to kill you, you little bitch...after I'm done having some fun with you, that is."

"Please!" she sobbed, "not again—" The words froze in her throat when his fist blotted out the sun...

"Emma!

"Please!" she choked out a sob. "Don't hurt me again!" She struggled fiercely against the hands that grasped her arms in a gentle grip.

"Emma, it's Tyler! Wake up. You're having a nightmare!" He shook her gently in an effort to wake her. "You're safe. He can't hurt you now!"

Her frightened green eyes snapped open, beads of sweat dotted her brow, and her chest heaved with the effort to escape her tormenter. Finally, she focused on Tyler's concerned visage, stifled another sob, and threw herself into his arms.

"It's all right, Emma. You're safe. He's not going to hurt you again."

"He was here, Tyler!" She clung to him, her eyes wide with terror. "He's going to kill both of us!"

Tyler pulled her closer, rested his chin on the top of her head, and stroked the soft red tresses. "It was just a dream, honey. I promise you, I'll never let him get near us. Now, just take it easy, and I'll stay with you until you feel better."

He was not quite sure if his words had reached her frightened mind, so Tyler continued to hold her until the trembling stopped, amiss to let go even when he stood to add wood to the glowing embers in the fireplace.

Emma pulled the blanket up around her shoulders to ward off the chill in the air, and her gaze settled on his muscular back. She watched the glow from the flames flicker across her husband's bare skin when he hunkered down before the hearth to poke at the charred logs. Just having him in the room was enough to make her feel safe.

Tyler stood, wiped his soot-covered palms across his trousered thighs and crossed back to the bed.

"The fire should be good until morning," he said as he sat on the mattress beside her. "Are you okay now, or do you want me to sit with you a bit longer?"

"I'm sorry I woke you," she replied softly, the memory of the rape still fresh in her mind. "But I'm fine now." *Please don't leave me again.*

Tyler ran a shaky hand through his tousled hair. *Ask me to stay*, he pleaded silently.

She held her tongue though, so he bid her goodnight, crossed the room, and closed the door quietly behind him.

Tyler stood in the center of his room and his shoulders sagged. *Why in hell didn't I just climb in bed with her?* His conscious answered him back. *You know full well why you didn't. She's still frightened, and the nightmare proved it.* How would she react if she knew how badly he wanted her?

Cold tendrils of air crept through the room and touched the bare skin of his upper torso, and he trudged to his own fireplace to add wood to the dying flames. *Damn it! Why don't you just walk back in there and tell her how much you love her!*

Instead, he removed his pants, dropped them on the floor, and climbed back between the covers. His sad eyes followed the flickering shadows across the ceiling, then he clamped them shut against the vision of her terrified expression when he finally managed to wake her.

He placed his hands behind his head and opened his eyes again, knowing sleep would not come easily. Would Emma ever totally recover from her experience and accept him as a man? Would she ever trust him enough to know he would never hurt her? He rolled onto his side with a heavy sigh and stared into the fire across the room.

The telltale click of a door opening reached his ears a moment later, and Tyler bolted to a sitting position just in time to see his wife's slender figure step through the doorway. "Emma...are you all right?"

Even in the darkness, he could read the hesitation in her eyes as she took one slow step forward, and then another, until she stood next to the bed. His heart pounded against his ribs.

"Tyler—" she spoke softly "—I need to tell you something." She wrung her hands nervously, and then her gaze dropped to the floor.

It took exceptional strength for Tyler to wait patiently, especially when he wanted nothing more than to just pull her into his arms.

She finally lifted her chin and met his understanding gaze. "I know we came to be married through circumstances that were out of our control, and I understand why you didn't want me here. But I need to tell you...before you left New York...I had already fallen in love with you."

He opened his mouth to speak, and she stopped him with a raised hand.

"Please, let me say this!" She took a deep breath and continued. "I've come to love you more every day since I arrived at your home. But, after I...lost the baby...I realized we have nothing to bind us together, except a piece of paper saying we're wed." Tears welled in her eyes now, but Emma blinked them back, knowing she would seal her future one way or the other in the next few minutes. "I have also come to understand that you can probably never love me in return, because of what Samuel did, but can we at least try to have some sort of life together, for Janie's sake? I love her as if she were my own, Tyler, and I can't imagine leaving any of you. I can't imagine not seeing *you* every day." The tears flowed down her cheeks now. "I want to be with you forever. I want to be by your side at night. If you can't love me, that's all right, but, please, don't send me away."

The weight of the last two months lifted from Tyler's shoulders in an instant, and he reached out to gently pull her down next to him on the bed.

"I've been so foolish." His thumb tenderly stroked the tears from her cheeks. "I've known from the day I found you standing in this room that I could never let you go. You were right when you called me an ignorant man, Emma, and I hate myself because I've caused you so much pain. And, if you think I've stayed away from you because of what Samuel did, you're wrong. The only reason I've stayed at arm's length is because I wanted you to be able to trust me completely; to know that all men are not like him."

He watched her expression change from doubt, to awe and, finally, to happiness—and he saw the love that shone in the depths of her misty eyes. He wanted desperately to kiss her, to love her as she had never been loved before, but, instead, he continued, saying the things that had needed to be said for so long.

"When we argued that day in the library and I told you to leave, it was because of my own stupidity. For some reason, I decided to believe that you and Steve had an affair while I was up at the logging camp. I guess that was easier than admitting how much I loved you—and how unfaithful I was being to Sara because of that love. When your horse came in without you though, I was beside myself with fear. I didn't know where you were or what had happened, and nothing else mattered except finding you and never letting you leave me again."

"How did you find me?" she whispered. "The pond is so far from the ranch."

He pulled her into the circle of his arms and leaned back against the headboard, and his heart soared when she did not resist his embrace. Tyler remembered the feeling that surged through his body when the wolf howled.

"I can't explain it. Cole, Trevor, and I were at our wits end. We didn't know where else to look for you—and then I heard a wolf howl." He shrugged, and his eyes followed his shaky fingers as they traced a path over the smooth skin of her cheek. "I just knew." A vision of her face, as it looked like when he found her lying in a pool of her own blood, flitted through his mind and his hand trembled even more. "When I first found you, I thought you were dead. I wanted to die myself, Emma. I was so afraid of being alone again. Even more so, I was terrified that I'd never have the chance to tell you how much I'd come to love you—how Janie and I couldn't live without you in our lives." He pressed a kiss on the top of her head. "I also needed to tell you how much I grieved, too, over the loss of our baby."

Her eyes widened incredulously. "Our baby?"

He tipped her chin up until she met his teary eyes. "Yes—*our* baby. I'm so sorry that I questioned who sired the child. You have never given me reason to think anything else—yet I foolishly held onto that one fact to ease my own guilt over falling in love with you. Do you believe me, Emma?"

Tears saturated her cheeks now, and she could only place her palm over his warm hand and nod her head.

"I wasn't going to wait much longer before coming to you." His hand stroked the length of her silky arm, and then back up to the drawstring that held the nightgown together across her breasts. His fingers plucked at the lace tie as he spoke. "I was just trying to find the courage, but you beat me to the punch. All I've wanted, Emma, since the day I left New York, is to hold you in my arms."

She swallowed convulsively and barely breathed as he tugged at the silken string, then shivered when his warm knuckles burned her skin. He opened the bodice wider.

"All this time, you actually *wanted* me?" Her voice was filled with wonder.

"More than anything, Emma."

Her hand shook even more violently than his as she reached up to touch his stubbled cheek. "I'm here now, Tyler, and I don't ever want to be away from you again."

"I love you," he whispered before he lowered his mouth to hers. "Don't ever leave me, Emma. I couldn't bear it."

His lips moved to nuzzle the soft skin beneath her ear, and Emma pulled his face closer. His breath was hot against her breastbone as he pushed the nightgown back from her shoulder and dropped moist, feathery kisses along the satiny path.

Emma gasped with the desire that mounted rapidly within her, then groaned when he pulled the nightgown up and off her body and tossed it carelessly to the floor. He pulled her across the width of his body then, and she whispered his name as his calloused hands raked the silky skin of her back.

Unable to bear the sweet torture any longer, Emma sat back to drop kisses along the broad expanse of his furred chest, reveling in the clean male scent that tantalized her nostrils. Tyler groaned. He pushed her down into the pillows and stared into the face of the woman he had come to love so dearly. His fingers threaded their way through her thick, red hair, and he marveled at how soft the tresses were against his roughened fingers.

"We've wasted so much time, Emma, because of my foolish jealousy. It's been so long since I've believed in anything and, I swear, I'll spend the rest of my life showing you how sorry I am."

"No, Tyler," she whispered. "Spend the rest of your life *loving* me."

He dropped another soft kiss on the moist lips that were mere inches from his own. "Promise that we'll never be apart. Promise that you'll love me forever. I believe in you, Emma...I believe in *us*."

She reached up to gently cup his face in her palm, and her eyes glistened in the firelight with the solemn promise she spoke aloud.

"I'll never leave you, Tyler. You're my shelter in the night, and the love of my life. To be separated from you would be like severing a part of myself." A slender finger followed the curve of his lips. "I love you too much."

Tyler began his slow assault against her senses. His palm cupped a swollen breast, and Emma gasped when his mouth plundered its twin. She closed her eyes, reveling in his touch as the hand brushed a sensuous course over the velvety skin of her stomach. When he trailed gentle kisses along the same path, she prodded him on with soft, incoherent moans. She groaned louder as he tortured her navel with quick darting thrusts of his tongue, and all the while his hands elicited a scorching trail of heat from her hips to her knees and back again.

A small smile curved Tyler's lips as he moved sensuously across her stomach again, then lowered to taste the succulent skin of her inner thighs. She opened her legs wider, pleading for release from the uncontrollable passion that built by leaps and bounds within her. Emma begged for him to stop, and then implored him to continue. He brought her to the edge of a reeling precipice, then suddenly he stopped all movement and glided back up and over her luscious body to gaze at her face. He clasped her hands and held them gently over her head.

"Open your eyes, Em," he commanded softly. "I want you to look at me..."

"Tyler, please...don't make me wait!" She bucked slightly beneath him, pleading for an end to the sensuous torture that shook her to the very soul.

"No, Emma. You have to look at me first."

She opened her eyes and focused with some difficulty on his smoldering green gaze.

"I want you to see my face before we go any further. I'm the man who loves you, Emma. I'm the man who would never hurt you, because of that love. Do you understand?"

He waited. That moment and her answer would define their future, and he would not enter her body without her permission. It had to be her choice. He wanted Emma to remember how beautiful sex could be. He wanted her to remember that, with the two of them, the act was an extension of their love—not a vile act of power and violence. He wanted to erase the memory of Samuel's rape from her mind.

When she did not answer, he spoke softly again. "I want to be inside of you, Emma, but only if it's what *you* want." His thumb brushed the silky skin of her cheek. "Tell me what you want, Emma—tell me what you desire..."

His words reached out to her and the tears flowed freely down her face again, and onto the pillow. She pulled her hand from Tyler's gentle grip and tenderly touched his lips with shaky fingers. Her eyes met his, and her own widened with wonder. He loved her! He *really* loved her, and she knew beyond a doubt that he would be content to just hold her if that was what she wanted. That was why she had to give him more. She opened her mouth, and her words came out in the barest of whispers.

"How was I so fortunate to find you?" she murmured in a voice that was clogged with emotion. "Never in my life have I met anyone so kind and gentle. Never have I trusted anyone as I trust you now. Make me whole again, Tyler. Make me forget everything but you..."

Their gazes locked and slowly, languidly, he moved into her warm depths.

"I love you, Emma...never forget how much I love you..."

She watched the muscles ripple in his upper arms as he held his weight off of her and moved ever so gently in slow, rhythmic motions.

He, in turn, watched her eyes—eyes that became shuttered with the height of her passion. Her moist lips parted, and he lowered his head to run his tongue sensuously over the delectable expanse, then it darted into her mouth to taste her sweetness. The pressure of her warm folds around him almost drove him to the brink—but he would wait...wait until she found what had been forgotten for so long. He pulled back, almost exiting her, then slid into her deeply again, his movements always measured, always languorous, until—finally she lifted her hips to meet his. Her increased momentum was what he waited for. He wanted her to take the lead in their lovemaking; she *had* to take the lead. She had to have control over what they were doing. Never did he want her to think of Samuel again—not when she was making love with him.

Tyler responded to her urgent need by increasing the power and speed of his strokes. The small groans of pleasure that emitted from Emma's throat quickly grew to a rapturous cry of fulfillment, and she clung to him as she spiraled toward a crest she thought never to surpass again.

"Tyler!" she screamed as he plunged into her one final time and her name, too, burst from his lips in a strangled cry of release.

The thought of physically parting was more than either lover could bear, and he stayed inside her, nuzzling the soft skin of her neck between murmured words of love. Emma clung to him, reveling in the moment as she examined the never-ending tenderness of the man who filled her, body and soul. He had given her a precious gift—a gift that she would cherish for eternity.

"I love you, Em." His warm breath whispered across her neck, and she shivered with the extent of his adoration.

"I love you, Tyler, and I'll never tire of telling you so."

He rolled off of her and onto the mattress, then pulled her against him. They whispered late into the night about the wealth of mistaken ideas that had plagued their relationship over the past months. Emma also told Tyler of her life in New York and growing up with Samuel and Evan; and he spoke of his days with Sara, before the accident.

Emma reached up to caress her husband's stubbled cheek. "I hope you never stop loving Sara."

"How can you say that, Em?" He clasped her hand and pressed a kiss into the palm. "It was my love for Sara, and the grief I suffered due to her death, that caused you so much pain."

Her head lolled on his shoulder. "I could never be jealous of her, Tyler, and I would never seek to take away the beautiful memories of the life you shared with her. I respect your grief, and I always have. I don't want Janie to forget her real mother. Sara was a part of your life and, therefore, she's a part of mine. Is that idea so hard to comprehend?"

He pulled her closer and buried his face in the thickness of her hair. "Woman, you have about the biggest heart of anyone I've ever met. If I had been more like you, we wouldn't have had these awful months apart."

His hands moved over her body again and, just when Emma thought he would put a particularly passionate end to the foreplay, Tyler grabbed her and his experienced hands tickled her until she shrieked and laughed and begged for mercy.

"Stop! I can't take it any longer!" She threw her legs over the side of the bed in an attempt to escape, then her playful yelp followed his wicked chuckle as he pulled her back and on top of him with a very definite amorous intent. He rolled her beneath him and whispered all the things he would do to her before morning, and a contented Emma gave herself up to his demands.

Chapter Twenty-Three

Emma wiggled her soft bottom into the solid band of heat that arched against the back of her own body and, immediately, her husband's hand slid upward to cup her breast.

"I'll give you twenty minutes to stop that," his husky voice whispered next to her ear.

A quiet giggle bubbled in her throat and she squirmed even closer. His muffled groan reverberated in the room as he hardened against her.

"One would think you'd be tired after last night," she cooed. "After all, you are an old man of thirty years."

Her delighted squeal rent the air a moment later when his hand moved with lightning speed to pinch her derriere, then flipped her over to tickle her mercilessly. Emma began her struggle in earnest, tangling them in the blankets, then they both froze when a heavy knock sounded on the door. Emma blanched when she heard Trevor's voice come from the other side.

"Tyler! You up in there?"

"Pssst!" Tyler's voice hissed in her ear. "He doesn't know how accurate his question is, Em."

Her playful slap was accompanied by a frantic whisper. "Don't joke around! I have to get out of here before he comes in!" She jumped from the bed, intending to make a hasty exit into the next room, but realized too late that her leg was tangled in the blanket. Her frenzied attempts to free it succeeded only in worsening her ordeal, and her grinning husband was absolutely no help as his warming gaze devoured her naked body.

"Tyler! Get off the blanket! I'm stuck!" Emma yanked her leg free at the same moment she bent to retrieve her nightgown from the floor. Trevor's call reached them again.

"Tyler, you better make yourself decent. I'm comin' in!"

"The door's open," he yelled in return.

A loud squeak left Emma's throat as she dove back into the bed and under the covers. Her nightgown floated to its former place on the floor. The blanket found her chin just as her brother-in-law stuck his head through the opening between the door and the jamb.

"Hey, are you going to sleep—"

The words froze on his lips when he took in Emma's red face and the nightgown on the floor. A grinning Tyler sat up in the bed, propped a pillow against the headboard and leaned back, looking like the proverbial cat that had just swallowed the canary.

Trevor answered his brother's smile with a knowing grin of his own before he turned his gaze back to his blushing sister-in-law.

"Good morning, Em! And what a beautiful day it is!" He crossed to the fireplace, added some wood, and fanned the small flame created by the glowing embers. "I love Christmas Eve, don't you? Mamie always prepares a special breakfast, and then we're on our own until the troops arrive for the party." He cocked his head, picking up the sound of footsteps in the hallway. "Hey, Cole! If that's you, we're in here!"

Emma sank lower under the covers, and her blush deepened to a color near purple. *Okay, that's it. I want to die...I don't care if we're married.*

Trevor made a show of turning one of the overstuffed chairs toward the bed, then seated himself entirely too casually as he waited for his younger brother to enter the room.

I'm going to kill him... Emma tightened the blankets around her slender neck.

Cole strolled through the open doorway, his attention riveted to a button on his shirt. He secured the fastener and looked up—then managed quite adeptly to hide his surprise, but not the twinkle in his eye. He dropped his gaze to yet another button and spoke to no one in particular.

"You know what? I never have liked this shirt. The buttonholes are too small to get it hooked up properly." He raised a dark brow and glanced at the pair in bed again. "Mornin', Emma. When are we going for the Christmas tree, Ty?" He raised his arms high over his head in an exaggerated stretch. "Boy, it's a nice day outside! The sun is shining like crazy on my side of the house." He turned the other chair and seated himself next to Trevor, then stretched his legs out before him with the same Cheshire cat grin on his face as his eldest brother and sniffed loudly.

Emma wished for a hole to crawl into. Words refused to make their way through the embarrassment that clogged her throat, and she could only remain motionless under the covers, which were still pulled up to her chin. Cole and Trevor's nonchalance rankled her to no end. *How am I supposed to get up and get dressed, if they won't leave!* She peeked up at Tyler from beneath long lashes, and his obvious effort to hold back the silent laughter that shook his broad shoulders served only to incense her further.

"You know, Ty, I was thinking about something the other day," Trevor mused. "You've already made yourself scarce at the mill, but I think Cole and I should follow your lead. The crew knows the procedure and, now that we're not going to be doing any cutting for a while, it's time to just sit back and reap the benefits." His gaze slanted to the man beside him. "What do you think, Cole? Does that sound like a good idea to you?"

"Yup, sounds like a good idea to me, Trev," he returned, as he struggled valiantly *not* to look at the pair in the bed. "It would be nice to just hang around the house all the time, like our wayward elder brother. And, hell, he would have even *less* to do than he does now, if we were around, too. What do you think, Emma?" He leaned forward in the chair and rested his forearms on his knees. His face was the picture of innocence. "Would you like it if Tyler had even *less* to do during the day? Of course, then you would have to find *something* to keep him busy, or he would be constantly underfoot."

"Yeah!" Trevor chimed in. "You could get him *up* every morning and get his lazy ass out of bed."

Cole warmed to the teasing, and his eyes took on a decidedly devilish glint. "That's right, Em. You could *straighten him out* every morning when you wake up and every night before you go to sleep!"

Emma felt her husband's body shake with mirth beside her, and she reached over to pinch his naked thigh with vicious intent.

"Ouch!" He looked down at her red face and rubbed the tender spot on his leg. "What did you do that for?"

"You're just as bad as they are!" she hissed.

Tyler's gaze moved from his mortified wife to his grinning brothers, and he finally relented. "Okay, you two have had your fun. As you can clearly see, Emma and I finally figured out our differences. Now, get the hell out of here so she can get dressed." A mischievous sparkle lit his eyes just before he peeked under the covers. "Yup, she definitely needs to get dressed!"

Loud guffaws exploded across the room before his brothers stood, however reluctantly, and left the master suite. They closed the door quietly behind them.

Emma sat up, holding the blanket in place over her breasts, and a decidedly stern look hardened her delicate jaw. "And I repeat—you're just as bad as they are!"

Her creamy shoulders were open to his appreciative view now, and he leaned in to kiss the one closest to him. His hand moved to the blanket, and he tugged it down just before his dark head dipped and his eager lips nibbled at her now exposed breasts.

She closed her eyes with a sigh. "Tyler, we really should get up," she murmured.

"I already am, so why don't you join me?"

His mouth devoured hers, and he carried her to frenzied heights again quickly before someone else entered the room.

That afternoon, the family worked together on last minute preparations for that evening's party. Each of the Wilkins noticed the happy smile that turned up the corners of Emma's mouth at least a hundred times that day, and they could only guess that she dwelled on how her life had changed in the last twenty-four hours.

Earlier, after she and Tyler finally left the safe haven of their suite, the family bundled themselves against the cold and marched up the hill behind the house to find the perfect tree. The Norway Pine was erected in a place of honor in the living room and, as a last touch to the already beautiful decorations, Emma now placed her contribution on a branch halfway up the tree. Her husband approached from behind and wrapped his arms around her slim waist, and Emma sighed her happiness as she leaned into the security of his embrace.

"Do you ever think of that old Indian we met in New York?" she asked as her almost reverent gaze took in the small figurine that dangled before her.

He laid his cheek against her hair and looked at the wooden loon, where it now hung in a place of honor on the tree. "All the time. When I got home, I heard a loon singing and some part of me hoped it was the old man's spirit calling out to me. It means something totally new now, when I hear them sing."

She turned in his arms. "What did you do with the other carving?"

"I did what the old guy asked me to do. I released it on a nearby lake and let it float away. It may sound rather foolish, but I hope his spirit was riding on the back of that little carving, and that it took him home."

"It doesn't sound foolish at all, Tyler. I like to think that everything has happened as it should." She turned back to look at her own *spirit,* where it hung from the branch, and Tyler tightened his arms around her. "Every time I looked at that little loon, I thought of you. I thought it was the only part of you that I had left."

"I've made so many mistakes, Em, and I'm sorry for causing you so much pain." His soft breath stirred wisps of hair on the top of her head. "When I let the first carving float away, I had the strangest feeling that I would never be able to get *you* back." He turned her in his arms again and kissed her. "Mamie says everything happens for a reason. Maybe we had to go through all that we did in order to get to where we are now. One thing I know for certain, Emma; I love you more than life itself and, if I could, I would take away all your pain."

She wrapped her arms around his waist and rested her head against his chest. The steady beat of his heart had an unusual calming effect, and she blinked away tears of happiness. "For whatever reason, we're together now, and I'll thank God for that every day for the rest of my life."

Tyler left her a short time later to attend to some business outside and, seeing that she was without her protector, Cole and Trevor resumed their persistent teasing. Emma accepted their shenanigans with good humor, but Carrie had finally had enough. She chased her remaining brothers outside, threatening bodily harm if they did not behave themselves.

"You can't help but laugh at them, Carrie," Emma said as the front door slammed shut behind the two men. "You should have heard them this morning when they found me in Tyler's room!"

"I can just imagine!" She moved to give her sister-in-law a hug. "We're all so happy for you and Tyler."

"Thank you for listening to me when we were in Duluth—and for making me realize what I could have with him."

Carrie lifted her slender shoulders in a shrug. "We could all see how much you two cared for each other. You and Tyler just got lost for a while, that's all. I didn't do anything that those two meathead brothers of mine weren't thinking of doing." She reached out to give Emma's hands a squeeze. "But give yourself some credit, too. You were the one who finally had the courage to speak up." She released Emma's hands and wiped her own on the apron tied around her waist. "Okay, enough of that before we both end up crying. Let's go see what else Mamie needs."

Tyler and Janie entered the room before Emma had a chance to follow her sister-in-law. Her stomach jumped at the sight of him, and her green eyes sparkled brightly as she moved into the welcoming circle of his arms. She glanced down at her grinning stepdaughter and reached out a hand to ruffle her soft, blonde hair. "And what have you and your daddy been doing outside?"

"I can't tell. It's a surprise!"

"Oh, a surprise?" Emma cocked a suspicious eyebrow when she took in her husband's blasé expression. "And just who would that be for?"

"It's a surprise, Emma," he reiterated his daughter's statement, then a devilish grin curved his lips as he tipped his head to whisper for her ears alone. "But if you come upstairs with me, I just might be convinced to spill the beans."

Emma stepped back out of his embrace and shook her head. "You just don't quit, do you?" she laughed, making it obvious that she did not object to this new Tyler at all; the one who had bombarded her with amorous insinuations throughout the day.

"Nope, and don't ever expect me to." He dropped a kiss on her lips, then turned his attention to his daughter. "Janie, run in the kitchen and get Auntie Carrie and Mamie. I think we'll give Emma her surprise before everyone gets here for the party."

The little girl ran from the room, nearly bursting with excitement.

Emma eyed her husband warily. "What's going on? I can wait until tomorrow, like everyone else, to receive my gift."

"Well, my dear, you might be able to wait, but your present can't. Now, put on your wrap; we have to go outside."

Janie returned, with Mamie and Carrie in tow. All three had donned coats and boots and were ready to brave the elements.

"Well, it seems that everyone is in on my Christmas surprise." Emma could not help but wonder, with growing excitement, what her present might be.

Tyler grasped her hand and led her through the gaily decorated living room and into the foyer, then ducked behind her to place his warm hands over her eyes just as Janie opened the immense oak door that led to the porch.

"I can trust you back there, can't I?" she whispered between giggles before they stepped outside.

"I wouldn't if I were you," he whispered back. Before he could act on his words, however, Janie took Emma's hand and led her carefully through the open doorway.

The excitement around her became almost tangible. "Are you going to remove your hands, Tyler, or do I have to stand here and freeze along with everybody else?"

"What do you think, Janie? Should we let Emma see her surprise?"

Janie jumped from foot to foot, and a huge grin stretched from ear to ear. "Yes, Daddy! Don't make her wait any more!"

Tyler removed his hands as Emma felt the warmth of his whisper against her ear. "Merry Christmas, honey."

She opened her eyes, squinted into the bright sunlight that reflected off the snow, and finally focused on five of the most beautiful horses she had ever seen. The animals stood in a line at the bottom of the steps. Their powerful hooves stamped the cold ground and steam erupted from their noses with each annoyed snort while eyeing the humans gathered around them.

Emma spun to face her husband, and the excitement leapt from her eyes. "Is this my present?"

"Well...part of it."

"Are these horses really mine?" She whirled back to scan the animals before her. One of the mares was as white as the snow she stood in, and Emma could not help but voice her thoughts. "If I didn't know better, I'd say that one was the horse my father bought me for my twenty-second birthday. She looks exactly like Bonnie!"

"It is your horse, Emma!" Janie exclaimed, unable to contain her enthusiasm any longer.

Emma swung back to face Tyler. "But...what...why is she here?"

"Do you remember my telling you that Trevor, Cole, and I wanted to breed fine riding horses someday?"

"Yes, but what does that have to do with my gift?" Her eyes widened in sudden dawning, and a startled gasp escaped from her throat "Oh, Tyler! Are you really going to do it? Are these the horses you said you needed to start fresh?"

"Yes, they are. I remembered the beautiful mare you used to own and, knowing how much you missed her, I had her shipped out here. The other horses though, are Trevor and Cole's way of saying that they want you to be a part of this enterprise, too."

"We're really serious about this, Emma," Cole spoke first. "We figured that, with you constantly biting at our heels, the idea just might work. Tyler was the one who came up with the idea of shipping this fine piece of horseflesh out here from New York, though." He patted Bonnie's flank, and the mare tossed her head as if in agreement.

"We really want you to be a part of this, Em," Trevor added. "Will you accept our offer?"

"Now, how could I resist the three most handsome men in Minnesota? Thank you all!" She rushed down the steps to hug her brothers-in-law, then returned to throw her arms around her husband. "I really think we can make this partnership work, Tyler, and I'm so excited you finally decided to do it!"

He pressed a kiss to her lips, and then released her. "Well, I think you'd better go check out that horse of yours. It's been months since you've seen her."

Tyler's eyes glittered with sudden anticipation when Emma turned to walk down the steps. His voice floated on the breeze behind her. "Hey, mister, could you please bring the white mare closer?"

Emma noticed the man who held the lead attached to Bonnie's halter for the first time. He stood on the horse's left flank, and the animal blocked his view of the porch.

Emma's foot touched the bottom step just as the man stepped out from behind the mare. "Papa!" she cried. "Papa, it's you!" She flung herself into his waiting arms. "Oh, Papa! I can't believe you're here!"

"I've missed you so much, Em! How have you been, kitten?" He held her at arm's length and looked into her face, then saw her tears and struggled to control his own. "You're just as beautiful as you always were."

Tyler approached them and slapped his father-in-law on the shoulder. "Why don't we go inside, where you and Emma can have your reunion next to the fire."

Edward placed an arm around his daughter's shoulders and steered her toward the steps. She still wiped at tears of joy.

"I can't believe you're here to spend Christmas with us." She reached for Tyler's hand and gave it a loving squeeze. "I've never had a gift as special as this. Thank you so much for arranging it."

He dropped a kiss on her cheek as he fell in step beside his wife, then slipped an arm around her waist. "I just wanted you to be happy and, when your father decided to bring the horses out here himself, it was the icing on the cake."

The three of them entered the house, followed by Mamie, Janie, and Carrie, after introductions were made quickly in the cold afternoon air. The two younger Wilkins' brothers hung back though, then led the string of horses to the stable. Trevor nudged Cole as they entered the barn.

"Are you thinking what I'm thinking?"

"That depends. What are you thinking?"

"Well, that's a first!" Trevor chuckled as he led a small, brown roan into the first stall. "You usually know what's going on in somebody's head before they do."

Cole let the other four horses make their own way down the wide space between the stalls, then hooked his elbows on the gate behind him, leaned against it, and pushed his hat back on his head. A cocky grin creased his face. "Okay. You're thinking that Tyler is going to be one lucky cowboy tonight when he climbs into bed, because Emma is so damned excited about her father being here."

Trevor tossed a glove at his brother and shook his head in wonder. "Jeez, Cole, how do you do that?"

"When you first wired me about this idea of yours, Tyler, I thought you were a little touched in the head," Edward remarked from where he sat on the sofa across from Emma and his new son-in-law.

Janie sat next to the older man and stared up at him through wide eyes, still filled with awe at the idea that she had a grandfather like other children did. The two met each other in secret earlier that afternoon and, with the characteristic bluntness of a child, she asked him if he was her grandpa. Edward replied that he guessed he was, and the two formed an instant bond.

Tyler smiled to himself as he watched the two across from him, then was jolted back to reality with Edward's question. "It's something my brothers and I have always wanted to do. We're pretty much set financially because of the lumber business, and it seemed like the right time to try something new." He squeezed Emma's hand. "Trevor was the one who insisted that Emma be a part of the venture, too. With her love of horses and her head for business, she'll be one hell of an asset." He looked down at his wife and smiled. "I have to admit, Em, that I had a hidden agenda though, in bringing your mare out here. She'll be prime breeding stock." His gaze moved back to Edward. "I'm just glad your father decided to come along."

"So am I," she murmured softly.

"I'm relieved to see that you look so happy, Em. I was concerned for a time—" Edward reached across the space between them to take her hand in his. "I wish I could have been here when you lost the baby, honey. It must have been very difficult for you."

Tyler squeezed his wife's other hand in gentle support, but his mind betrayed his true feelings. *You have no idea, Edward...*

A telegram a few weeks earlier had broken the news of the miscarriage to Emma's father. Her wishes though, were that Edward not be made aware of Samuel Fontaine's involvement, and Tyler had abided by those wishes.

"It was hard, Papa," she murmured. "But there would've been nothing you could do, even if you were here." She batted back tears and quickly changed the subject—and Edward let her. "How did you ever manage time away from the shipyard? This is your busy time, what with refurbishing damaged vessels and new orders under contract for the spring."

Edward looked at his daughter, and she read the hesitation in his eyes. *What's the matter with you, Papa?*

Edward cleared his throat and shifted uncomfortably. "Well, Emma, since you brought it up, I guess this is as good a time as any to talk to you about the shipyard. I know you always wanted to take over the operation, but things have changed now. It's easy to see that you're deliriously happy in your new life and, believe me, the knowledge sets my mind at ease considerably." He took a deep breath, and his next words came out in a rush. "I sold the shipyard, honey. I've decided to retire."

"You sold the shipyard!" Her brow wrinkled in total confusion at the new turn of events. "You never said anything about it in your letters."

Tyler held his silence. This matter was between father and daughter. He remembered vividly though, Emma's interest in every aspect of her father's business.

Edward leaned forward again and clasped his hands together. "Honey, I'm not a young man anymore. My entire adult life has been devoted to running the yard and watching over our interests, just as I have always watched over you. Maybe, if I had spent more time at home, your mother and I could have had a stronger marriage. But, with the never-ending emergencies and meetings, I never seemed to have time for her."

Emma's bewilderment only increased with her father's sudden change of topic. "What does Mother have to do with this?"

Edward held her gaze, and his own became determined; almost passionate. "I've met someone, Emma and, though we haven't known each other long, we're planning to be married." His expression became a plea. "Please, give me your blessing, kitten. I haven't been this happy in years."

Tyler felt Emma's hand go limp in his as she stared at Edward through incredulous eyes. He squeezed her fingers again, this time in encouragement, hoping that Edward's trip would remain a happy one. He stood, finally, and lifted Janie into his arms.

"Come on, honey. Let's let Emma talk with your new grandpa alone for a while. We'll go check on some last minute details for the party." He bent to drop a kiss on Emma's cheek, then whispered in her ear. "Em, remember how happy we are now. Your father deserves the same." He left the room with Janie riding high atop his shoulders.

Emma watched them go and could not help but think about how important they had become to her. A year ago—no. Only eight short *months* ago, she did not even know they existed. Now, they were her whole life. Realizing how fast things could change, she turned to her father again, who still watched her through nervous eyes as he awaited a response.

"Can we start this conversation over, Papa? Let's see, we were at the point where I was surprised at the idea of you selling the shipyard, and then even more surprised when you announced that you were going to be married."

Edward was still unable to read her expression—until he watched two dimples deepen in her cheeks and her green eyes sparkle with amusement. Emma could not contain her laughter at his pained expression. She rose from the sofa and moved to seat herself next to him.

"You look like you're ready to be sick!" She took his large hand in her much smaller one. "I'm sorry about my initial reaction. I guess I was a little shocked at first. I mean, to think you would sell the shipyard—your life's work—and then find someone to marry after all these years." Her expression saddened. "You and Mama never had a deep, abiding love, did you?"

He patted their clasped hands with his free one. "It's not that we didn't try, Em. We just never found the spark, at least not the type of spark I think I'm seeing between you and Tyler. Don't get me wrong. Your mother was a wonderful person. I respected her and confided in her as I would a best friend. But a deep love? No, Emma, not anything like what I've found with Clarice."

"This Clarice, what is she like?"

"Honey, she makes me laugh, and I feel like I'm twenty years old again. But I'm not, and neither is she. That's why, at our ages, we decided to marry quickly and not wait through a proper time of engagement. Emma, I don't want to be alone anymore. I don't know how many years I have left and would prefer to live out my remaining life with Clarice. Can you understand that?"

Emma examined her father's lined features. If he had not been so adamant about her going to Minnesota to marry Tyler, they might both have missed out on the opportunity to find a devoted partner for life. How could she even consider withholding her blessing for him to seek what she had already found?

She squeezed his hand. "I'm happy for you, Papa. My days of wanting the shipping business are over. What I have here with Tyler and Janie could never be duplicated. I'm selfish enough though, to be happy you're here with me for Christmas, instead of back in New York with Clarice. Why didn't you bring her with you?"

"Because I needed to make sure you were settled and happy before I could make the final decision to marry her. I'm sure she's back in the city pacing her yard as we speak, waiting to hear from me. I told her I needed to see you before we could finalize anything."

"And how did she feel about that?"

"She loves me enough to understand why I needed to come here without her. In fact, she encouraged me to go."

Emma wrapped her arms around her father's bulk. "Papa, she sounds wonderful! You have my complete blessing—with one condition."

"And what would that be?" Edward smiled.

"That you bring her out her as soon as possible, so I can meet the woman who has made my father so happy!"

He sat back. "Done! Maybe we can plan a trip this spring, if all goes well."

The door cracked then, and Janie poked her little blonde head through the opening. "Emma? Daddy said to tell you and Grandpa that our guests are starting to arrive. Do you want to come and meet them?"

"We'll be right there, honey." She stood and pulled her father up with her. "Come on, *Grandpa*. It's time to see what a Minnesota Christmas is all about!"

Just as Tyler predicted, the party was barely an hour old when two men pulled out fiddles and another joined in with his harmonica, and the dancing began.

Emma remembered most of the women from her wedding day, and they treated her as one of their own. Momentarily putting aside the hard work they were all accustomed to on a daily basis, they were loud and boisterous and ready to enjoy the evening. The lumberjack's wives were decidedly different from the socialites she had been exposed to her entire life, but Emma respected their simple values and their love for their men—something she had seen very little of among the other group of women.

She watched her father, where he sat in a corner with Trevor, Cole, and four other men. They tipped their glasses of ale and laughed heartily, and she knew with certainty that they would carry around sore heads in the morning. Her brothers-in-law had made her father feel totally welcome, and she loved them even more for the hospitality accorded him.

Carrie and Steven did not miss a dance. They whirled about the floor, whispering secrets that only lovers could understand. When partners suddenly changed during a Virginia Reel, Emma ended up with Steven by her side. She laughed aloud when he asked Emma if she thought Carrie's brothers would miss them if he were to sneak his sweetheart away for a few stolen kisses on the porch. Emma winked and assured him that Trevor and Cole were too busy celebrating to notice anything other than the next bottle, and she would keep Tyler busy.

A short time later, she watched as the couple disappeared through the doorway. Tyler's gaze, and then his scowl, followed after them—until Emma pulled him into her arms.

The last of the guests left and, when the door closed behind them, the Wilkins reveled in the silence. Edward had already gone upstairs, and Cole and

Trevor said their goodnights as they, too, headed for bed.

Janie leaned heavily into Emma's skirt, and Tyler gathered her into his arms. He slipped his free arm around Emma's shoulders then, and the three of them headed to the little girl's room. They settled her under the covers, and Emma leaned down to kiss her flushed cheek. "Hurry and go to sleep now or Santa won't come!"

The little girl's eyes closed even before her father had the chance to give her a hug.

Tyler wrapped his arms around Emma's waist and pulled her back against him as they watched his daughter sleep. "As long as she needs that goodnight kiss, I hope you'll be here with me to do it. I need you with me always, Emma. You don't know how you've changed our lives."

Emma closed her eyes and released a heavy, contented sigh. "I'll always be here, Tyler. I love both of you."

He took her hand then, and led her to their room. Emma could not help but smile as she passed her old bedroom door and walked with him to the master suite. Tyler closed the door behind them, then his eyes widened in surprise when he saw the package that lay in the middle of the bed.

"What's this?"

"It's your Christmas gift. I wanted to give it to you in private."

"I can wait until—"

"Don't tell me you can wait until tomorrow! I seem to remember a certain man who couldn't wait to give his wife a gift earlier today."

He smiled as he sat on the bed. She watched intently as he untied the string and opened the cover on the box, then sat next to him as he folded back the tissue paper. The smile drained from his face when he stared at the contents. Reaching inside, he carefully lifted out the statue of the Indian. He slowly turned the figurine in his hands, examining it closely before meeting her gaze.

"It's beautiful," he spoke softly. "It's our Indian, isn't it?"

Emma let out her breath in a relieved "whoosh" and smiled. He understood. "Yes! When I saw him, I knew it was the perfect gift. When you gave me the carving of the loon in New York, you said that I then had a *spirit* to keep with me always." Emma reached out to touch the figurine with reverence. "When I saw this, I was strangely drawn to it. It was a feeling I couldn't quite grasp. Do you remember when that old Indian called you the *keeper of the spirit*?"

He nodded.

"Somehow, I think he was right. You've done so much for me, Tyler. You brought me back when I thought I would never be the same again, and you continued to love me, regardless of what happened."

Emma rested her head on her husband's shoulder and stared at the statue cradled in his hands. "I can't help but think that Indian is somehow a part of our lives, and also part of the reason we're together. Do you understand what I'm saying?"

He held the statue with one hand and slipped his free arm around her shoulders. "I feel it too, Em. When I first saw this, I, too, felt something unexplainable, deep inside." He stood to place the statue on the window ledge, returned to the bed, and pulled her into his arms. He nuzzled her neck. "We'll never know who the credit goes to for us being together. I'm just thankful that you're finally here with me."

He kissed her then, and Emma raised a hand to run her fingers through the soft black waves at his temple. "Merry Christmas, Tyler."

"Merry Christmas, Emma," he whispered before he pushed her back into the pillows.

Chapter Twenty-Four

Emma stood on the front porch and let the morning sun warm her face. Spring had arrived, and her first winter in Minnesota was coming to an end. She secretly smiled to herself as she remembered the other family members' desire to see the snow and cold leave.

Emma crossed to lean a slim shoulder against the wooden porch banister, scanned the few remaining piles of snow that dotted the shaded areas in the front yard, and thought of the nights she had spent warmed by her husband. *Hmmm...I wouldn't have minded another few months...*

Her stomach quivered as she recalled her and Tyler's most recent lovemaking session, earlier that morning. It never ceased to amaze her that their relationship only got better, and their love for one another, stronger. Never had she dreamed that she could be this happy...

Emma was still lost in thought when Tyler stepped out onto the porch.

"There you are! Sorry to keep you waiting."

She looked up at him, her eyes liquid with the memory of their shared passion just a few hours earlier.

Tyler stopped short at the almost sensual expression she turned in his direction. "If you keep looking at me like that, we'll never get anything done today."

"Have I told you how happy you've made me?"

"Only every day," he chuckled as he moved to sling an arm around her shoulder. "What brought that on?"

"I was just thinking about this morning—and how much I love you," she murmured as they walked down the steps and headed in the direction of the barn.

"And here I thought you were just excited about starting our new business, when all along it was me!"

She elbowed him in the ribs with a laugh. "I am excited about today!"

Three of the new mares were ready to be bred and, hopefully, the other two would see their time come within the next few weeks. This newest venture was all the Wilkins' had talked about that past winter. The preparations had been made, and now their dream was about to become reality.

The mill began operations a few weeks earlier minus the presence of the three Wilkins men, who had come up with an idea that would eventually work them out of the lumber business. Each of the men who worked for the company had been given an equal share of stock, and the employees hoped that they would be able to buy out the previous owners within the next year.

The three Wilkins men were like young boys in a candy store now that their lifelong dream had reached fruition, and Emma's involvement only sweetened the pot.

Tyler and Emma entered the barn just as Cole hooked a lead to one of the mares and led her through the open door behind them. Storm whinnied loudly and stamped his feet in another enclosed stall. Instinct told the huge stallion there were mares near—mares that were ready to be bred. He had been kept separate from the females until now, until they were sure the fillies were ready to accept him.

A group of hired hands congregated as Tyler led the prancing and snorting Storm into a small indoor paddock. The big stallion sniffed the air, and then pawed the ground with his eagerness. He would be allowed to mate once with each mare, then the process would be repeated on each consecutive day until the females refused to accept him.

Knowing what would happen next, Emma excused herself from the large group of men who surrounded the paddock and entered the tack room until the huge stallion had finished mating, then berated herself for the totally feminine reaction. She would have to overcome her modesty if she was to be a true partner in the business.

As she perched on a bale of hay, Emma contemplated yet another reason she had left the boisterous group of men. Their excited banter about how next spring would bring the birth of new foals had struck a melancholy chord deep in her soul. *I want my own baby!* She leaned back against the wooden slats behind her and closed her eyes. *I don't understand why I can't get pregnant. I thought for sure it would have happened by now. It's not fair. I paid my dues...and still I have to wonder if it will ever come to pass.*

Tyler found Emma sitting on a hay bale. He took one look at the sad dip of her brow and knew something was wrong.

"There you are," Tyler's words broke into her reverie. "You disappeared before I knew it. What's the matter?"

"I couldn't watch. I know it's foolish, but I just couldn't. If it was just you and I, it wouldn't have been so bad, but with all the ranch hands standing around and me being the only woman..."

"Come on, Em. There's something more than that—I saw it on your face."

She shrugged, dropped her gaze to the straw-covered floor, and chewed on her bottom lip. "When did you get so good at reading expressions?" She looked up and a tiny smile appeared on her lips. "I thought Cole was the only Wilkins man who possessed that talent."

Her husband crossed his arms before his muscular chest and stared at her with a raised brow of expectation. Knowing he would not give up, Emma sighed. "I'm just sitting here feeling sorry for myself. Everyone was so excited about the possibility of new foals next spring. What about me? I want a baby, Tyler, and it's just not happening."

He smiled his understanding before he pulled her up and into his arms. "I'm sorry that it hasn't happened yet, too, and you have to quit worrying about it or it never will. Our time will come." He tipped her chin until she met his eyes. "Who knows? By next spring you might be holding our son or daughter." He stepped back. "Now, do you want to go back to the paddock with me?"

Her eyes widened at his words. "No! And not because I'm pouting. I'm just not comfortable being the only woman."

"It's okay, Emma," he was quick to reassure her, "and don't feel that you have to be a part of everything. We can handle this aspect of the business if it makes you feel uncomfortable."

Her cheeks tinged red. "Do you think that would be okay for now? I promise to get used to it—eventually."

Tyler laughed outright, then slipped an arm around her shoulder and walked her back to the house. He dropped a quick peck on her lips before he turned and loped back to the barn.

Emma watched him until he rounded the corner of a storage shed, and then shook her head at her own foolishness. Maybe she would never conceive again, but she had Tyler and Janie, and the rest of the family. *I should count my blessings.*

Emma entered the house and headed for the office. She plopped down behind the desk and flipped open the ledger book to record the date and the names of horses that had been bred.

The mid-July sun baked the landscape and, just when Emma thought she could bear the heat and the doldrums no longer, Tyler invited her to join him on the long ride up to one of the logging camps. The brothers still made themselves available, albeit only once a month, if the new "owners" had any problems or questions when it came to running the complex operation.

Looking forward to the time she would spend alone with her husband, Emma stuffed a saddlebag with an extra pair of pants, a shirt and a few personal items. The men's trousers were Carrie's idea. The younger woman often wore them around the ranch and, once Emma tried a pair herself, she realized how comfortable they were compared to the riding habits she had worn all her life. Upon their next trip to Duluth, she had a totally appalled seamstress make her two pair.

A quick glance at the full length mirror next to the dresser was enough to pause Emma's quick movements about the room. She walked slowly toward her reflection and was a little taken aback by the woman who stared back at her. White cotton shirt sleeves were rolled up to the elbows, revealing slender, sun tanned arms. The garment was tucked into the tiny waistband of tight-fitting brown pants and, instead of the red hair being piled glamorously atop her head, it now hung loosely down to her waist and was pulled back by combs on either side of her head. Her face, too, was brown—a totally unacceptable malady in *proper* New York society—and made her green eyes stand out with even more clarity. There was something else though, she realized. Her complexion actually *glowed* with happiness.

Emma snatched her cowboy hat from atop the dresser and plopped it on her head just as Whizzer loped through the open doorway. She watched with a quizzical dip of the eyebrows as the dog jumped onto the bed, then smiled when he wagged his tail and let out a deep, resounding bark. "Well, Janie can't be too far behind you!"

Her stepdaughter bounded through the doorway a moment later, munching on a freshly baked cookie. "Hi, Emma! Daddy says you're going with him to the logging camp, and that I should tell you goodbye."

She scrambled up onto the bed, then swatted at the dog when he tried to steal the cookie from her hand. Whizzer's resulting whine was enough to persuade her to break off half of the treat and feed it to him with a giggle.

Emma smiled. "Don't let Mamie see you feeding him the products of her hard work."

Janie rolled over onto her stomach, popped the rest of the cookie into her mouth, and watched Emma close the saddlebag. "Mamie's full of hot air."

"Janie!" Emma struggled to control her laughter and maintain a stern expression. "That's not a nice thing to say!"

"But, it's true, Emma! Uncle Trevor said so! Mamie's always hollering about Whizzer being in her kitchen, and she chases him with her broom." At the sound of his name, the dog cocked his head to look at the little girl. "Then, when she thinks nobody can see, she gives him treats. She even saves him a plate of scraps and scratches him behind his ears."

Emma could hold back her laughter no longer. "Well then, I guess Trevor is right. Just don't let Mamie hear you say it." Emma paused to study her stepdaughter's adorable face. "Janie, it's all right with you that your dad and I are going to be gone overnight, isn't it?"

"Sure! Auntie Carrie's taking me to Steve's house. We're going to cook him a special lunch, because he's been working so hard lately." Her nose wrinkled suddenly with disdain. "Emma, do you think they kiss all the time, like you and Daddy?"

Emma snorted, ruffled Janie's hair, and reached for the bag. "You're sure full of the dickens today, aren't you. Come on, walk with me downstairs. And, if Auntie Carrie kisses Steve all the time, it's because she loves him as much as I love your daddy."

Janie jumped off the bed, and the yellow dog followed at her heels. She took her stepmother's hand. "You know what, Emma? I'm glad you came to live with us. Daddy is happy all the time, and I like having my best friend tuck me in at night."

As they walked down the steps hand in hand, Emma blinked back happy tears. "I'm glad I came here to live too, honey."

* * *

They had almost reached the logging camp when Tyler reined his horse to a halt beside Emma. "Take a look behind you, Em."

She swiveled in the saddle, and the view took her breath away. They sat high atop a ridge and, directly below, endless forests and sparkling lakes came alive in the afternoon sun. The panorama in the far northern reaches of Minnesota was like nothing she had ever seen, and never would she forget the majestic beauty.

"What do you think, Em? Isn't it a sight to behold?"

"It's beautiful!" She nudged her horse closer to his, her eyes still glued to the magnificent expanse.

Tyler watched her profile with an almost worshipful gaze. *Why didn't I bring her here long before this?*

"It looks so wild and untamed that I feel like I should almost be frightened," she murmured. "And yet, when I see all this unexpected splendor, it makes me realize what a surprise gift from God it really is." She reached out to capture his hand in hers, and they sat in silence for a time, mesmerized by the beauty that stretched out before them.

"I was so frightened when I first came here," she continued in a near whisper, her eyes still glued to the vista below. "But now I feel like this land has welcomed me. I feel a sense of belonging that I never felt in New York, maybe because I took my life for granted there. Here, in this country, a person has to work hard to carve out a life. And, if you do right by it, the land grants you the privilege of seeing another sunrise." She sighed and a small smile curved her lips. "It's such an immense feeling of accomplishment to crawl into bed at night knowing that you will be rewarded for a hard day's work." She finally looked at her husband. "You've lived here your entire life. Do you ever feel that way?"

"All the time. I remember trying to explain to you in New York what you just so eloquently described to me. This land *is* a gift to be cherished." He squeezed her hand. "I'm glad you feel the way you do."

Tyler studied her sun-darkened features and long, flowing hair, and it dawned on him how much she had changed since arriving in Minnesota on that warm September day so long ago. She had overcome almost insurmountable hurdles and had demonstrated more courage than most men. She had matured into a beautiful and confident woman in her own right and had made his life livable again. He would cherish her forever.

Emma and Tyler arrived at the camp an hour later. They ate dinner with the crew, and Emma was caught up in the pride necessary to make a success of such a booming lumber company. These men were not afraid of hard work, nor did they let the constant loneliness dampen their determination. They did ask her to give them time to write quick letters to their families, however, and Emma promised to hand deliver them when she returned home.

By the time she and Tyler mounted their horses, Emma's pack was full of scraps of folded paper. Each man had printed his wife's name on the outside. She secured her precious cargo, then turned and waved once more before she and Tyler rounded a bend in the trail and disappeared from view.

"How long until we stop for the night?" Emma asked a short time later. She had been surprised when Tyler told her they would sleep away from the logging camp that night and, both anxious and a little nervous, she was eager to try the new experience.

"Why?" His lips curved in a lurid smile. "Are you anxious to snuggle that gorgeous body of yours against mine under only a blanket of stars?"

She rolled her eyes at his nonsense, but her skin tingled with the promise. "I've never spent the night outdoors, Tyler, and, yes, I am excited."

"And here I thought your enthusiasm was due to the fact that we'll be totally alone tonight." His chest heaved in an exaggerated sigh. "Okay. I plan to erect a small tent about an hour down the trail, have a little something more to eat, and then...who knows?"

His smoldering gaze caused her stomach to do a quick flip and, without another word, they both kicked their horses into a faster gait.

Tyler built a fire, prepared a quick bite of venison, and then stretched out, with his back propped against a log. Emma leaned against his broad chest and stared into the flames as she sipped from the coffee cup they passed between them. They talked quietly about the ranch and the horses, about Steve and Carrie's upcoming wedding, and the possibility of a trip to New York to visit her father and Clarice. It was when they discussed how fast Janie was growing up that Tyler noticed Emma's sudden silence.

"What's wrong, Em?" He rubbed her shoulder with his free hand.

She sighed. "You know I love Janie like she was my own daughter, and I'm sure she loves me, too. No one could ever take her place in my heart. But...I can't quit thinking about the fact that I haven't conceived again." She leaned forward and wrapped her arms around her raised knees. "I got pregnant so easily the first time, and it just surprises me that it's taking so long now." Sudden tears shone in her eyes as she looked at him and voiced her fears. "Do you think that maybe...because of what Samuel did...I'll never be able to have children?"

Tyler leaned forward to pull her back into the circle of his arms. "Em, you've talked with Steve, and he told you that there was no physical reason why you couldn't have another baby, right?"

She nodded.

"Don't dwell on it then. When the time is right, it'll happen. And, if it doesn't, we'll deal with it then." He nuzzled her neck. "I love you, Emma, and that will never change, whether we have children together or not."

She turned in his arms and studied his handsome face. "But I *want* to have your children, Tyler. I want us to create a tiny being to love and protect..."

His kiss stopped her words and, gathering her into his arms, Tyler stood and carried her to the small tent. They shed their clothes in frantic haste and came together and, as they loved one another through the night, a wolf howled in the distance.

The end of August arrived and, with it, the completion of a new twenty-stall stable that was the first in a long line of projects. The massive dwelling would house the five mares Emma had been gifted with for Christmas and, hopefully, would boast some of the finest horseflesh in the country as the years went by.

Emma and her three partners sat at the dining room table, discussing yet another construction project when Trevor pushed aside his mug of coffee and pulled a stack of papers closer. "Has anyone given any more thought to what we're going to name this new business of ours? We really need to come up with something. It looks like we'll be out of the lumber business by the end of the year."

"How does Lakota Pines Riding Stock sound to all of you?" Emma leaned forward and waited for a response.

Trevor looked up from the numerous papers scattered before him. "That's a possibility, Em. How did you come up with that?"

"I've been doing some research into the State's history. Since the ranch is already called the Northern Pine, I thought it would be logical to combine the present name with the new one. We could have a sign out front with a wooden statue of an Indian standing under a big pine tree, with a horse next to him." She looked at Tyler and received a gentle smile when she continued, knowing he understood where the idea came from. "Lakota means 'allies' in the Sioux language. Now, that's what we all are, aren't we? Allies, who are working together to create something good for the future."

Emma's gaze moved from one rugged face to the next as they pondered her words. The importance of the Indian name went unspoken, but she hoped dearly that they would agree with her.

"What do you think, gentlemen? She might have something here." Tyler rested his forearms on the table as he, too, waited for a response. Cole and Trevor exchanged glances, then tipped their heads in unison and the name was written across a blank piece of paper.

Emma stood at the front of the church, holding a bouquet of autumn wildflowers. Her gaze never left Tyler, as he escorted his sister down the aisle and toward the altar. Carrie was resplendent in a gown of white satin and her face glowed with happiness. Her eyes rested on Steven, where he stood in a dark suit at the front of the church. The doctor asked Tyler for permission to marry his sister at the beginning of July, and now, at the end of September, their waiting had come to an end. Carrie had asked Emma to serve as the Matron of Honor, and Steven chose Trevor as his Best Man.

Emma smiled as she remembered her own wedding and could not help but wonder what kind of toast Trevor would make at the reception. She forced her attention back to the approaching couple then, as Tyler placed his sister's hand in the groom's much larger one.

Emma listened quietly as Carrie and Steven repeated their vows, promising to love and cherish one another for the rest of their lives. She also thought about how different their wedding was compared to her own. She and Tyler had been forced into a life together—a life she wanted, and he did not. She closed her eyes and thanked God for his change of heart.

A tear escaped and ran down Emma's cheek when the newly-married couple turned to face the congregation. She would miss having Carrie around on a day to day basis, but, as with the other well-wishers gathered for the nuptials, she wanted only happiness for the pair. The church was filled to capacity, and the beams shook with their congratulatory applause.

The reception was held at a large meetinghouse, built in the nearby town of Colby for just such an occasion. As they crossed the dusty street, Tyler put an arm around Emma's shoulders and teased her quietly about the tears that still dampened her cheeks. She poked him mercilessly with a pointed elbow.

"Come on, be nice," he wheezed. "Aren't you happy that they don't have to go through what we did?"

"That's exactly what I was thinking during the ceremony, and don't make fun of my tears. I'm going to miss her terribly!"

"They're not gonna be that far away, Em. We'll visit often, and they'll probably be out at the ranch more often than we want." He tightened his arm around her. "Now, if I could just marry off those two idiot brothers of mine, I'd have you all to myself."

Emma was not in the mood for his levity. "It's not going to be that easy, Tyler. Carrie is going to help Steven with his practice. She's going to be busier than she ever was."

"It'll be fine, Em, you'll see," Tyler struggled to keep from gritting his teeth with the words. *What's with her? It's not like her to be selfish.* He pushed the troublesome thoughts aside as they entered the large building and joined the rest of the guests.

The night passed quickly and, before long, Carrie and Steven were saying their goodbyes to the family. The newlyweds would return to Steven's house for the night and, in the morning, leave for Duluth on a long anticipated honeymoon. Steven's father had agreed to handle any medical emergencies in his absence. The two talked of nothing else but the lazy, uninterrupted days to do as they wanted.

Carrie hugged Emma goodbye, and both women sniffled.

"I'm so happy for you, Carrie. Have a wonderful time in Duluth—but I'm going to miss you terribly."

"I know, Emma. I feel the same way. We'll see each other all the time though, I promise." The bride's eyes shone with unshed tears. "I love him so much, Em. I can't believe all the years of waiting have finally ended."

"I heard that!" Steven approached, kissed his wife on the cheek, and squeezed her waist. "Are you ready to go, Carrie? I finally got permission from your brothers to leave."

Emma and Carrie broke into near hysterical giggles with his innocent remark. It was a well known fact that the Wilkins brothers scared the hell out of Steven, at least where Carrie was concerned. The four men had been best friends all their lives—but never before had Steven wanted to make love to their sister.

The couple waved from the doorway, and then disappeared. A short time later, Tyler escorted Emma and Janie to the waiting carriage, with Cole and Trevor in the driver's seat. The moon was full and bathed them in its glow as they returned to the ranch.

When they arrived home, Tyler helped Emma haul water upstairs to the small antechamber between the two connecting bedrooms. He watched her disrobe, then step into the soothing water. Reaching for a scented bar of soap, Tyler lathered her back, then smiled at her sigh of pleasure.

"It was a fun day, wasn't it?" He swirled the soap slowly across her skin, hoping the gentle touch would elicit the response he desired. It did.

"Mmmmm," she answered.

His brow creased with worry again. "Why are you so quiet then? Are you still upset because you won't have Carrie around to talk to now?"

"Nope. I'm just enjoying the feel of your hands on my back for as long as possible before I ask you to climb in here with me."

Tyler shed his clothes so fast that the frantic motions made Emma giggle. He stepped into the tub and sat down across from her, then pulled her close for a leisurely kiss. He reached for the soap again then, and lathered her breasts, and Emma leaned back with a huge sigh. Her eyes fluttered shut.

His hands continued their ministrations and, strangely, her breasts seemed heavier than usual. "Can I ask you something?"

Emma's head dipped in a small nod.

"You seem to be gaining a little weight. Is there a reason for that?"

"Mm Hmmm."

His hands froze. "And what would that reason be?"

Emma did not answer, but a tiny smile curved her lips. Frustrated, Tyler pulled her to within inches of his face. Her eyes opened, and his heart pounded a rapid beat against his ribs when he saw the sparkle in her beautiful green depths.

"I'm pregnant, Tyler, due sometime late next spring."

"Why didn't you tell me!" Her smile was contagious, and a wide grin creased his rugged features.

She shrugged her naked shoulders. "This was Carrie's day. I didn't want to spoil it by drawing all the attention to us." She leaned forward to give him a fierce hug. "Isn't it wonderful? We're finally going to have a baby!"

"Well, I guess that explains why you were so moody earlier. You were close to tears all day, and I couldn't imagine why you were so upset." His lips curved in a smile of admission. "In fact, I was even a little frustrated with you earlier, because I thought you were being selfish." He reached up to cup her face in both hands. "I was watching you tonight before you climbed into the tub and thought there was something different about you." He pressed a kiss to her lips. "I couldn't be happier, Em. How long have you known?"

"For a while now—well, I suspected it over a month ago. Steven confirmed that I was pregnant last week."

"Steve knew before me?"

"He's a doctor, Tyler. I didn't want to say anything until I knew for sure." She took his hand in hers. "Please don't be angry. I already told you that I didn't want to take attention away from Carrie and Steven. It was their time to shine." He still looked doubtful, and a contrite grin appeared on her face. "I was getting ready to tell you when you asked me."

"You were, huh?" the tone of his voice told Emma that he was weakening, and she decided to take advantage of his change of heart—quickly.

Her expression twisted into a playful scowl and suddenly she splashed water in his face, then watched him sputter and flick the wetness away. "And what was that comment about me gaining weight? You're lucky I told you at all after that!"

Tyler grabbed her hands, and the smiles left both their faces as their gazes locked.

"Em...a baby? I can't believe it finally happened." He kissed her gently, then stood and lifted her from the tub. Reaching for a towel, he first wiped her body dry, and then his own before he led her to the comfort of their bed.

Tyler held his wife against him in a tender embrace. His hand drifted down to her stomach, and she smiled as sleep claimed her for the night.

* * *

Tyler and Emma announced their news to the rest of the family at breakfast the following morning. Janie shot off her chair and ran to give Emma a fierce hug. "Oh, Emma! I'm finally going to have a brother or a sister! Can I help you take care of it after it's born?"

"You'd better, Janie. I've never had a baby before, so I'm going to need lots of help." Emma hugged her back, and a huge weight lifted from her shoulders. It appeared that Tyler's daughter would be very accepting of the new baby that would arrive in the spring. "In fact, I think you will be the best big sister any baby has ever had!"

It was a few minutes later before the other men in the family could find their voices—at least their *normal* voices. Cole and Trevor stood then, to shake Tyler's hand

"Congratulations, Ty," Trevor smiled. "This is some of the best news in a long time."

Cole approached Emma first, pulled her up from the chair, and wrapped her in a loving hug. "I'm so happy for you, honey, and for Tyler." He glanced at his brother, where he was still busy with Trevor. "I can see he's finally at peace."

Emma looked up at her brother-in-law and thanked God for the special bond that had always been there between the two of them. She loved Trevor and Carrie, but Cole held a very special place in her heart.

She, too, looked at her husband, where he now accepted Mamie's hug. "He is at peace, isn't he? We've all been through so much in the last year, but you've remained positive and have always supported us. I can't thank you enough for that."

He shrugged matter-of-factly. "I always knew you were perfect for him." He pressed a kiss to her cheek. "Congratulations, honey."

"Hey! What are you two whispering about over there?" Trevor rounded the table to take Emma's hands in his. "How long have you known? Man, wait till Carrie hears! She's going to be so excited! Do any of you realize how crazy next spring is going to be with a new baby and new foals all coming at the same time?"

Trevor enfolded her in a bear hug, and Emma looked over his shoulder to where Tyler stood, with Janie in his arms. He smiled at her, with pride etched on his face. This man had shared so much with her—his devotion, his passion, his family—and now a child had been created out of the love he gave to her so freely.

A sudden need to hold it all close, to guard her cherished life assaulted Emma with the force of a thunderstorm—even as a shiver of foreboding trickled down her spine.

Chapter Twenty-Five

An elegantly dressed man stepped through the front entrance of Belle's Place. The last vestiges of a wicked March wind followed him in, and he pushed the door shut with an arrogant kick of his heel. He peeled the costly leather gloves off finger by finger as his furtive gaze surveyed the large room. Fifty or more men played cards at more than a dozen tables, and piano music mingled with the acrid odor of cheap perfume and cigar smoke to assault his senses. Overall though, he had to admit that this house was a step above the others he had frequented in the last year.

Traversing the short stairway that entered the main room, he moved to the bar and ordered a whiskey. He sipped the drink casually as, again, his calculating gaze perused the crowd around him. A quiet chuckle followed when he flicked a piece of lint from the sleeve of his pricey woolen coat.

He had managed quite adeptly to overcome poverty in the last year, gambling and cheating his way back to the point where he did not have to worry where his next meal would come from. His face had lost its raw, sunken look and the hard edges were now filled in. He looked and felt the part of a gentleman again—a lifestyle that was his due. His money belt was full, his clothes were impeccable, and not a blond hair was out of place.

Samuel Fontaine had come back into his own. It had been a long, hard year-and-a-half, totally unnecessary in his own eyes, and he was back in Minnesota to tie up a few loose ends. If anything, the last months had made him even more determined to end the life of the one person who had caused him so much grief. He would not leave this God forsaken wilderness until he accomplished what he set out to do.

Samuel observed various high paid whores as they picked their next conquest, and then made their way up the staircase, only to disappear behind a closed door. *I might just have to sample one of them later. Lord knows they're a far cry from the ugly bitches I've been with lately.*

At the moment, however, he planned to play some cards and further his wealth. Grabbing his drink, Samuel swaggered over to a table and asked to be dealt in. A chair materialized out of nowhere and he sat down, casually throwing a wad of bills on the table before him.

The number of spectators grew around the table as the evening progressed—and the piles of chips grew higher in front of Samuel Fontaine. Word passed quickly that a major gambler was in the house, and that he was winning more often than not. It was uncanny how often the cards turned in his favor. The men in the crowd laughed and slapped each other on the back every time Samuel reached to drag the chips back to his growing pile. The onlookers also made side bets among themselves as to whether or not the high roller would take the next hand.

Belle watched him—and had been doing so for the last hour. The handsome stranger caught her gaze more than once over the top of his cards. She observed him with a practiced eye, trying to determine if he was cheating. If that proved to be the case, she would have the bouncers throw him out on his ear. Not once though, did she see evidence of sleight of hand.

He smiled openly in her direction now and, as he gathered his chips, she approached the table. "If you'd like, I could have one of my men cash those chips in for you."

Samuel stared at her through heavy lidded eyes and affected a grin meant to draw her into his web of deceit. "Under one condition—if you consent to join me at a quiet table and have a drink...or two."

Belle snapped her fingers and a young man appeared out of the crowd. She whispered close to his ear, and a basket materialized. She watched quietly as Samuel dropped his poker chips into the container and stood. He swept a hand before himself in a show of gallantry, then followed her to a table in the corner. They did not speak until the drinks and his cash had been delivered, and they were alone.

"I get the impression that you're the owner of this fine establishment. Would I be correct in that assumption?" Samuel never took his eyes from the voluptuous woman seated across the table.

Belle leaned back in her chair to study the handsome face before her—and the scar that ran from his cheekbone to the line of his square jaw.

"Yes, that's correct. You caused quite a commotion tonight with your adept card playing. I have to admit that I was certain you were cheating."

Samuel laughed with a flash of white teeth. "Ma'am, what kind of gambler would I be if I gave out all my secrets? No, I can assure you, I've just run into quite a streak of luck lately." His eyes held hers, and a smile curled his thin lips. "And, if I'm reading your signals right, that streak of luck might include you."

Belle leaned closer, rested her elbows on the table, and slowly sipped her drink as she eyed him thoughtfully over the top of the glass. "I don't even know your name, and I normally let my girls handle the *needs* of my customers. Although—" she ran a slender finger down the length of her glass "—with the amount of money you won, you might be able to afford me. That is, if I feel like it tonight."

Samuel's eyes hardened almost imperceptibly, but the smile remained in place. *I'll screw this enticing bitch if it's the last thing I ever do. They're all the same—they think they're worth so much.* "Well, if it's just a simple matter of knowing my name, then you can call me Sam. And, as far as affording you, you're right. The proof of that was seen earlier at the poker table."

Belle observed him as the bartender brought them another drink. *He's a fine specimen. It might be rather enjoyable to spend an hour or two with him.* She had not allowed another man to enter her suite since Cole Wilkins' most recent visit a month earlier and had to admit the urge to have a good time.

They sparred for a while longer, both knowing how the evening would end, but enjoying the game nonetheless.

Another round of drinks had passed the table before Belle stood and threw him an inviting glance. Samuel tossed some bills on the smooth surface and followed her up the stairs.

They entered Belle's room, and he watched through cool eyes as she sashayed to the small bar and poured them one more glass of whiskey. Samuel took the opportunity to reach behind him and turn the lock on the door. He coughed into his hand to hide the sound of the telltale click. He crossed to a chair then, and waited for her to hand him the drink. Belle returned to sit on his knee and held her glass up to meet his.

"To us," she said with a brief arch of her eyebrows.

His fiery gaze never left hers. "To us."

Samuel set the glass on the table next to him and pulled her close. His moist lips devoured Belle's mouth, and the kiss deepened as his free hand increased the pressure on the back of her head. She pushed him away a moment later with a nervous laugh.

"Whoa there, Sam. We've got all night!"

"I don't want to wait all night. You've been flirting with me for the past hour, and I'm ready for you now."

Belle's heart pounded in her chest. It was exciting to know she could still have that effect on a man.

"I want you to strip for me."

She stood and placed a hand on her hip, looked down at him with a flirtatious smile, and tossed her chin upward. "I know we've agreed on a price already, but it'll cost you more for the show."

Samuel's steely gaze never wavered as he dug in his breast pocket and flung some bills on the table next to him—an amount that was three times the sum they had agreed upon earlier.

"Take off your clothes, Belle. I'm all paid up."

He watched through flaming eyes as she slowly unbuttoned the front of her gown and slipped out of the sleeves, then loosened the waist and let the dress fall around her ankles. She stood before him in a short camisole now, and his eyebrows lifted in surprise when she raised a slender foot and placed it between his thighs. She proceeded to unsnap the garters attached to her silk stocking, then rolled the sock sensuously down her thigh and calf. Removing the silken hose, she repeated the same procedure with her other leg.

Samuel's breath came in small pants now, as Belle wiggled out of the camisole and stood naked before him. An inviting smile touched her lips.

"Was that worth the extra money, Sam?"

"I'm trying to decide. How would you like to partake in a little fantasy?"

"That depends on what your *fantasy* is." Belle was caught up in the moment and failed to read the subtle change in his expression.

"I want you on the floor—on your hands and knees."

The smile left Belle's face in an instant when she finally saw the glazed look in his eyes. "Look, Sam, I don't go for anything out of the ordinary. If you'd like to go to the bed, we can have some fun there, but the floor, and on my knees, is not an option. I don't run that kind of place." A shiver of fear ran up her spine as she watched his features hardened with rage.

He bounded from the chair and snatched her arm. "I don't give a shit what kind of place you run. You see that money on the table? I paid for you fair and square—now I expect to get my money's worth."

"You're hurting me!" She struggled fiercely against his steely grasp, then her own words became as acidic as his. "I think you had better leave and take your money with you!"

"Well now, Belle, I don't think you're in any position to be making demands, do you?" His glittering eyes swept the length of her body.

Belle wrenched her arm free of his hold and lunged for the door. She realized too late that he had locked it behind him. Her frantic fingers fought with the latch, and Samuel grabbed her from behind. She spun away from him, but there was no place to run. She grabbed a nearby lamp and swung it with ferocious intent, but Samuel threw up an arm, knocked the object aside, and pushed Belle roughly against the fabric-covered wall. He hauled back his fist then, and grazed her chin just hard enough to make her more pliable in his arms.

Belle's knees buckled as he dragged her back across the room. His crazed eyes searched wildly for something and, finally, settled on a silken scarf. He pulled a hanky from the dresser drawer next and stuffed it in her mouth, then tied the scarf around her face to keep it in place.

"You bitches are all alike! You flaunt your bodies in front of us until we can't stand it anymore, then you tell us no! Well, you little slut, that's not going to happen tonight!" He laughed into Belle's face and, when he saw the fear in her wide eyes, slapped her once more. The snap of her head, as it whipped to one side, excited him further.

Pulling her arms up tight behind her, Samuel shoved her toward the bar. He bent her body forward and slammed her face down onto the hard surface. Her muffled whimper was music to his ears as he loosened the front of his pants with his free hand and forced himself into her.

"How do you like it this way, bitch? I paid you for this, and now I'm getting my money's worth! See how it works?" Samuel increased the pressure on her head, and her muted sobs released tears on the bar. The power of his thrusts increased, until he felt himself finally reach a pinnacle.

Belle slid to the floor when he stepped back, pulled his pants together at the waist and reached for his hat. He nudged her with the toe of his boot, then stared down into her pale face.

"Thanks for the good time, Belle. Maybe I'll come back some time and we can do it again." He scooped up the pile of money on the table and returned it to his pocket before he sauntered to the door.

Belle heard the lock click shut, but was unable to find the strength to run after him and have one of her employees stop his retreat. Instead, she just lay on the floor, with tears flowing down her cheeks.

Fifteen minutes passed before she eased her bruised body to a sitting position and picked at the knot in the scarf. Spitting out the hanky, her gaze fell to the blood that was mixed in with her saliva. She reached for her dressing gown then, and covered her body before using the chair as support to help her stand.

Her trembling hand reached for the still-full whiskey glass and Belle sipped, then spit into a bowl. Tears tumbled down her cheeks again as she gasped for air.

He said his name was Sam, which meant that she needed to get to Cole. She needed to tell him that the devil from his sister-in-law's past was back.

Cole stood in the paddock, brushing Janie's little pinto. His niece had extracted a promise earlier that he would tend to the animal, then she left with Clancey to spend the day at Carrie and Steve's clinic.

When the sound of a carriage rolling up the drive reached his ears, he shouldered the pony out of the way, walked to the fence, and watched as the buggy pulled to a stop at the end of the wooden walkway that led to the house. He squinted into the sun, and then his eyes widened in recognition when an all too familiar woman stepped from the conveyance.

"What the hell is she doing here?" he mumbled his thoughts aloud, hooked the brush on the fence, and hurried toward the house.

Belle was halfway up the sidewalk before she heard Cole call out her name. She waited for him to approach, but could not meet his gaze. Now that she was there, she was not so sure it was the right thing to do. She would tell him about Samuel Fontaine, and then climb into the carriage for the long trip back to Duluth.

Cole acknowledged the driver—he had seen him at Belle's place on more than one occasion. Rounding the buggy, he approached her with a guarded look stamped on his face.

"Belle, what are you doing here?" She lifted her face to look at him, and Cole's eyes widened in shock when he saw her bruised and swollen jaw. "My God, what happened to you?"

She placed a hand on his arm and found the words she had practiced all the way to the ranch. "Cole, I had a run in with a customer last night. It wasn't until he left that I realized there was a very good possibility he was this Samuel Fontaine you warned me about."

He raised her chin with his gloved hand and examined her bruises again. Anger ballooned in his chest. "Jesus Christ, Belle, did he do this to you? I told you, honey, to watch for him and not let him near any of you!"

Her normally carefree attitude was absent when she looked into the eyes of the gentle man before her. "I know you did, Cole, but the man who was at the house last night was clean shaven, with close cropped hair, and elegantly dressed. He didn't look anything like a hunted man on the run! You said he had blond hair though, and this man did. When I asked his name, he said to call him Sam. He's sick, Cole, just like you said he was. He came up to my room, and..." She held her breath for a moment, then the rest of the words came out in a rush. "You know what I do for a living, Cole, but he hit me, and then he...he raped me. You believe me, don't you? There's a difference, Cole! This man is evil!" Her voice rose as she struggled for the words to explain what happened.

Cole pulled her into his protective embrace, rubbed her back in soothing circles, and kissed the soft tuft of hair that rested against his cheek. "Shhh, Belle. It's okay. I believe you."

Her words were little more than muffled tones against his chest as she continued. "I know I shouldn't have come here, but I couldn't send anyone else to tell you. I needed to know you believe me. I'm sure it was him! I needed to warn you, so he can't hurt anyone else."

"Cole? Is everything all right?" He jumped at the sound of Emma's voice and turned to find her standing at the top of the porch steps. He dropped his arms from around Belle in guilty reaction, and the woman stepped back quickly.

How in hell am I going to introduce her to Emma? The two women came from completely different worlds and were unfortunate enough to be connected by a monster who hurt them both.

"Uh...Emma, this is Belle Andrews, from Duluth. She's been a...friend of mine for a long time. Belle, this is my sister-in-law, Emma."

Belle's startled gaze rested on the beautiful woman before her—a woman who was heavy with child. She could see now why the Wilkins men thought so highly of her. She was soft spoken and one of the loveliest creatures Belle had ever encountered.

"Hello, Mrs. Wilkins. It's nice to finally meet you. I've heard a lot of good things about you." Belle glanced sidelong at Cole, at a loss as to what else to say. *I should have never come to their ranch.*

"It's nice to meet you. Miss Andrews, is it? If you've come all the way from Duluth, I must apologize for Cole not asking you in." Emma stepped back and indicated the front door. "Please, do come in, where the two of you can conduct your business in comfort."

Belle blanched at the invitation. If anyone ever found out that Emma was entertaining one of the local whores, she would never live it down. Before Cole could utter a response, Belle spoke up quickly.

"Thank you very much for the invitation, Mrs. Wilkins—"

"Please, call me Emma."

"Emma...but I have to return to Duluth and really must be on my way."

"Nonsense! May I call you Belle?" Emma watched as the other woman nodded hesitantly. "Belle, I would never forgive myself if I allowed you to climb back in that carriage and make the long trip to Duluth without giving you some sort of refreshment."

Belle decided to put an end to both her and Cole's suffering, despite the fact that she felt drawn to the young woman on the steps—a woman she wished to know better. Her background though, created a closed door that would never be open to her.

"Emma, I really don't think you understand. My line of...work...does not permit me to socialize with a proper lady like yourself."

A gentle smile touched Emma's lips as she glanced down at the flustered woman. "Belle, I understand perfectly what your *line of work* is. It's written boldly across the side of your carriage." Emma indicated the name "*Belle's Pleasure Palace*," which was written across the door of the buggy in embossed lettering. She had passed the establishment more than once while in the city. "You're Cole's friend, and that's good enough for me. Now, please come in and rest before you begin your long journey back to Duluth."

Emma turned, walked into the house, and waited just inside the door as Cole took Belle's arm and led her up the stairs. When they were seated in the library, Emma poured the astounded woman a cup of tea, then settled herself comfortably in the big chair across from her and Cole.

"Excuse me for lumbering around, Belle. I don't seem to be moving as fast as I used to." She rolled her eyes suddenly at her own boldness. "And, here I am forcing my company on the two of you without even asking if you would like to be alone."

Belle perched uncomfortably on the edge of the sofa and hurried to assure Emma that her presence in the room was fine. "This is your home, Mrs. Wilkins, and I have already discussed my business with Cole."

"Do you mind my asking why you would make the trip all the way up here?" Emma saw the pair exchange a quick glance. "I'm sorry to be so blunt, but I have an uncanny feeling it's not good. I would like to know about anything that concerns this family."

Belle watched quietly as Cole moved to hunker down before Emma and take her hands gently in his. "Belle came to warn us about something, honey." He took a deep breath and saw shades of fear flicker in his sister-in-law's eyes. "She's certain that Samuel Fontaine was in her establishment last night." Emma's face paled before his eyes and he felt the trembling of her hands in his. "Tyler, Trevor and I always thought he might come back, but now that we've been warned, we'll be on guard until he's caught."

Emma swallowed convulsively, squeezed Cole's hand, and then looked at the woman across from her. "Did he do that to your face?"

Belle nodded.

Emma's chin quivered when she turned her gaze back to Cole. "He's come back for me, Cole! I know it! We can't let him on the ranch!" Her entire body trembled now with fear.

"Emma, it's okay. Don't get yourself in a tizzy. We've never let our guard down. Either Tyler, Trevor, or I are always here with you..."

The truth of his statement filtered through the shock waves that assailed her mind. Since Samuel's assault, one of the men was always around—and she had not realized it until now.

"We'll tell Tyler and Trevor as soon as they get home, Em, and we'll watch for him. We won't let him hurt you again."

Belle sat quietly by, horrified by what Samuel must have put this woman through. Tyler's wife physically shook with fear.

Emma looked at the other woman with a feeling of kinship. They had both suffered at the hands of an evil man and, as much as she wanted Cole to remain by her side until Tyler came home, her need to speak privately with Belle outweighed her fear.

She looked at Cole again. "Could you leave Belle and me alone for a short while, so we can talk?"

"Sure, Em." He stood. "I'll be right outside on the porch. If you need anything, just holler, okay?"

Emma smiled her gratitude, although rather shakily, and Cole left the room quietly. The door clicked shut behind him.

"Mrs...Emma..." Belle stumbled over her words, "I'm sorry to have put you in this position. If word gets out that you invited me into your home, I guarantee you will be shunned by polite society."

"That doesn't bother me in the least, Belle."

The older woman sat forward and met Emma's gaze directly. "I want you to know something." She was silent for a moment as she chose her words with care. "There are those who would classify me as a *fallen woman*, but I only do what I have to in order to survive. Last night, it wasn't like that. Samuel Fontaine forced himself on me crudely."

"I know he did, Belle. Samuel takes whatever he wants."

"Do you mean to say that you actually believe me?" The tone of Belle's voice made it obvious that she was stunned by Emma's trust.

Emma swallowed to wet her suddenly dry throat and tried to shake off the feeling of descending doom. "I know what he's capable of, Belle, and yes. I believe you."

The woman across from her, dressed in the bright, flashy clothes of her profession, stared back in surprise. "Not very many women in your position would be so understanding."

Emma shrugged. "This is a harsh part of the country for anybody to live in, let alone a woman all by herself. As I see it, Belle, the only difference between you and I is that I get a home and security for my favors. You get cold, hard cash."

Belle could not help but to laugh softly. "Now *that's* a conclusion you don't hear from a gentle-born woman every day."

"I'm just the luckier of the two of us, is all. I have a man who loves me probably more than I'll ever realize. You have your favorites, and I suspect Cole must number high on that list."

Belle ducked her head, surprised at the heat that spread across her cheeks. She could not believe that she was sitting in a fancy home, conversing with a fine lady about such a subject. She lifted her blue eyes and smiled at the pregnant woman seated across from her.

"Cole is special, but I know nothing could ever come of it, even though I've known him for quite some time." She lifted her shoulders in a small shrug. "It's what I do for a living." Her gaze encompassed the room in one sweeping glance. *I wonder if I could ever have anything close to this.* "You know, Emma, since my encounter last night, the thought of closing the business and just leaving town sounds very appealing. I have a fair amount of money at my disposal. Maybe I could start a new life where no one knows my past."

At the moment, the idea sounded good to Emma, too. She would like nothing more than to just pack up Tyler and Janie and run away. The thought of Samuel lurking somewhere nearby filled her heart with fear.

Belle studied the other woman surreptitiously, and finally found the courage to ask the question that occupied both their minds. "Was it awful for you?"

Emma knew exactly what she meant. She rose from the chair slowly, rubbed her lower back unconsciously, and crossed to the window.

"Tyler's sister once told me that what I went through was something no woman should ever have to experience. To be so degraded is almost unfathomable." She hesitated, and then made the decision to bare her soul. "I have never told anybody this, but that first week after it happened, I wanted to die. I could not convince myself I had anything to live for. I had lost my baby and was sure my husband would never want me again. The thought of everyone knowing how soiled I'd become was humiliating. I think I would have found a way to end it all if it hadn't been for this family. It took them a while, but they discovered a way to help me heal."

Emma closed her eyes as the memory of that awful day invaded her thoughts. "Samuel took something from me that he had no right to take—but Tyler gave it back tenfold. I decided then, that I would not let that monster rule my life or the lives of the people who love me." She turned a frightened gaze in Belle's direction. "I have fought every day to regain my former life, but now, knowing

Samuel is close, I'm not so sure I'm strong enough to withstand another encounter. I'm frightened and numb at the same time."

Belle pushed herself up from the sofa and crossed to stand beside Emma when she saw the other woman wipe at the tears on her cheeks. She reached out a tentative hand and placed it on the other woman's shoulder. "You can do it, Emma. Don't let that evil bastard take away what you've worked so hard to regain! You may not believe me, because we've hardly known each other an hour, but I admire you. It takes one helluva strong lady to rise above what Samuel did to you a year ago."

"But it's always there, Belle. The possibility that he might come back was always lurking in the back of my mind."

"Well, you've been warned. Do you honestly think these Wilkins men will let him get anywhere near you? You've got their brute power and your own strength of character to see you through." She laughed suddenly. "Just how many women in your position would welcome their brother-in-law's *mistress of the evening* into their home, just because they felt it would be unmannerly not to? Emma, you are the first real lady to ever treat me with any amount of dignity. I wasn't so sure earlier that I did the right thing by coming here, but I'm glad now that I did. If I hadn't, I would've never met you."

Emma turned to face her. "You're welcome on this ranch anytime you want to visit, Belle."

"I know that now, but it'll never happen again. Cole needs to find a woman he can share a life with; someone without a past that will haunt him the rest of his life. I care for him too much to ever let that happen."

Somehow, Emma knew she spoke the truth, no matter how hard it was to understand.

Belle reached out a gloved hand. "Mrs. Wilkins, it's been an honor meeting you. The hour is getting late though, and I need to be on my way. You stay strong. Your husband will know shortly about Samuel's return, and he'll keep you safe."

Emma ignored the outstretched hand and, instead, hugged Belle close. She could not help but wonder if this would be the last time their paths would cross.

"Do what you said, Belle," she whispered fervently. "Leave the city. Don't ever put yourself in the position to be hurt again like you were last night."

"I'll think about it." She smiled. "Goodbye, Mrs. Wilkins. Trust in yourself and the life you have. You've earned it." Belle squeezed her hand then, and left the room, and Emma watched through the window as Cole handed her up into the carriage after a farewell embrace.

The front door opened and closed a moment later, and Emma listened to his footsteps grow louder as he approached the library. She felt his presence in the room behind her.

"Em? Are you all right?"

"I don't know, Cole." She turned and his heart leapt at the sickly pallor of her face and the fear in her eyes. "What if he comes back for me? I know that's what he's planning." She covered her face with her hands then, unable to control the burgeoning fear any longer.

Cole bolted across the room and pulled her against his chest just as a hoarse sob burst forth.

"He's coming for me, Cole!"

He held her gently, knowing she was reliving the awful experience in her mind. "We'll keep you safe, Em. Everything will be fine."

He held her in his protective embrace until Tyler discovered them a few minutes later and rushed through the open doorway. "Cole? Emma? What's happened?"

Emma ran into her husband's outstretched arms. "He's back, Tyler, and he's going to find me!" She wrapped her arms around his waist and clung to him in desperation.

"Who's back?" Tyler had already answered the question in his own mind though, and he could almost smell his wife's fear. His eyes moved to Cole for confirmation.

"Belle just left, Ty. She came here to tell me that a man fitting Samuel's description showed up at her place last night. He roughed her up and...forced her to have sex with him. She wanted us to be on the alert."

Tyler closed his eyes above his wife's head and quickly organized his thoughts. He had known the possibility that Fontaine would return for either him or Emma was good, but now the threat was real. His mind raced with ways to protect her. Was Emma too far along in her pregnancy to send her away from the ranch? If so, they would have to be extra vigilant—and they would have to be prepared if Fontaine snuck onto the property.

Tyler rubbed Emma's back to calm her, then spoke to her firmly. "It's going to be all right. You have to believe that we'll get him if he shows up here." He lifted her chin and met her gaze with a resolute expression. "I told you that I would never let him hurt you again."

"But how are you going to stop him if he's determined to hurt us? He's crazy, Tyler!"

"I promised that I would keep you safe, honey, and I plan on keeping that promise. Let me work out the details, and you just worry about keeping the baby and yourself healthy." His gaze moved from his wife to his brother. "Cole, find Trevor and bring him back to the house. I left him down at the barn. I'm going to take Emma upstairs and see that she lays down for a while."

Cole sprinted from the room to do his brother's bidding.

Tyler tucked the blankets around Emma's trembling body, then sat beside her on the bed. "I want you to rest. We'll figure out the details. We've got a jump on him, Em. We know he's here, and that gives us the advantage."

"You're going to need more than that, Tyler. He fooled us once—now he's had over a year to plan his revenge."

He bounded off the bed again and stalked across the room. "And I told you that I would keep you safe! He'll have to get through me, and Cole, and Trevor, and there is no way in hell that we're going to let him do that!" His voice lowered with an ominous certainty. "It's our turn now."

Emma scrambled from the bed and yanked on his arm firmly, until he turned to look at her. "Promise me that you won't do anything foolish, Tyler. Evening the score with him is not worth your life! Let the authorities deal with him." She tugged on his arm again. "Promise me!"

Tyler acknowledged her fear and admitted, however grudgingly, that she was right. Evening the score was not worth his life, but he would do whatever was necessary to save hers. No matter what it took, he would not let Samuel near her.

He gathered her into his arms. "I won't do anything foolish, Em." He walked her back to the bed and tucked her under the covers—again. "You rest now. I've got to go talk to Cole and Trevor." He kissed her, then squeezed her hand. "If you need anything, I'll be right downstairs. I'm not going to leave the house."

After he left to find his brothers, Emma lay staring at the ceiling. The baby moved inside of her, and she covered her swollen abdomen with both hands. A feeling of doom had hung over her like a thundercloud since the day she announced she was pregnant. She had tried, for all those months, to shrug off the sense of foreboding, but now, with Samuel Fontaine back in their world, everything was about to come crashing down around her.

She rolled onto her side and unconsciously curled up to protect the child within her. Her blank stare was centered on the ashes in the fireplace, and her mind chanted a single name—Samuel. The devil was coming for her.

"I can't believe the son of a bitch has the nerve to show up in the area again!" Trevor paced the room like a caged animal, remembering only too well their last encounter with Samuel Fontaine. He felt sick.

Cole sat in the chair, silently observing his two brothers as they moved around the room, speaking of what needed to be done. He wanted the opportunity to wrap his fingers around Fontaine's neck and choke the life out of him—and he wanted to do it slowly. He had two women to avenge now.

He brought his attention back to what Tyler was saying.

"I want every man on this ranch to carry a loaded gun with him at all times. We need to stay within eyesight of the house—and one of us needs to be within these four walls at all times. If he's going to make a move, it'll be soon."

"Ty, you couldn't get the two of us to leave now if you tried." Cole stood and walked to the liquor cabinet and splashed some whiskey into a glass. "We're going to get the bastard this time."

Tyler rubbed the back of his neck in agitation and heaved a weary sigh. "Dammit! Emma is too far along to move her somewhere safe. I thought about Carrie and Steve's, but too many people would know she was there."

"She wouldn't leave here anyway, Ty, not without you." Trevor dropped into a chair and met his older brother's gaze. "We've got to come up with another plan."

"I know she won't leave, but what else can we do?" Tyler rubbed his forehead in frustration. "I guess the bottom line is that, actually, I feel better having her here. I don't want to trust her safety to just anybody and, with the two of you here, I know she'll be safe—even if it is like hanging her out as bait." He started for the door. "I'm going to send Dougan to Carrie's with a message and ask her and Steve to keep Janie for a bit longer. She was supposed to come home tonight, but I'll feel better if we don't expose her to all this—plus I don't know what Samuel would do if he ever got his hands on her." Tyler's stomach churned with the mere thought as he paused in the doorway. He turned back to face his brothers, and his determined eyes bore into them. "We have to make sure he doesn't get to Emma. No matter what it takes, we have to make sure."

The family tried to carry on as if everything was normal. They waited anxiously for the births of the new foals, and Emma insisted on visiting the barn every morning to check on Bonnie. One of the men always accompanied her, yet still she could not resist the urge to continually look over her shoulder. As the first week drew to a close, her nerves were stretched taut and the strain started to show, not only on her face, but on the faces of everyone at the ranch. Mamie and Katy kept a rifle in the kitchen at all times, and Cole gave them each a small pistol to carry in their apron pockets when they were away from the house.

Janie continued to stay with Carrie and Steve, but, after four nights of sleeping in a strange bed, the little girl's imagination took over. She started having nightmares and, knowing that the child was simply terrified about what was going on at home, Emma insisted that she be returned to them.

"I don't care, Tyler!" She paced before him as fast as her pregnant body would allow. He sat on the bed and let her rant. "Do you think it's any healthier for her to be experiencing the terror she is every night? I want her home, Tyler, and I want our lives to get back to normal! I'm sick of feeling the hair stand up on the back of my neck every time I step out onto the porch! I'm sick of looking over my shoulder every other step to make sure he's not there! And I'm sick of letting that bastard rule my every waking moment!"

"Emma, calm down," Tyler's voice was composed, almost patronizing. "I still feel it's for the best that Janie stay away for now. If Samuel does show up, I don't want to have to worry about her, too."

"So, what are we going to do, Tyler? Live in fear for the rest of our lives and deprive Janie of the right to live in her own home?" She moved to sit beside him on the bed and laid her hand over his balled fist. "You've got every man on this ranch alerted and guns all over the place! What do we do if a month goes by, or a *year,* and nothing happens? We don't even know for certain if it *was* Samuel at Belle's place. Are you going to exile your daughter forever?"

Tyler released a sigh that echoed his doubt. "All right, Em. I'll send a message to Carrie's and have them bring her home." He cupped her face with his palms and pressed a kiss to her lips. "I'm just trying to be careful, honey. We know what Samuel's capable of, and I'm just trying to keep the two of you safe."

She leaned her head against his strong shoulder, and his arm came around her. "I know, Tyler. I'm sorry for yelling at you, but I'm at my wit's end. I just want this whole thing to end." She tipped her head to drop a kiss on his neck. "Thank you for bringing Janie home. We'll watch her like hawks. I promise."

He rested his chin on top of her head, and reveled in the silky softness of her hair. Emma was so fragile. In less than a month's time, he would be a father again, and the love he felt for her overwhelmed him.

"I'll talk to Cole and Trevor about Janie coming home."

Samuel stared at his reflection in the hotel room mirror and fingered the jagged scar that ran down his cheek. Even after more than a year, it was still painfully visible. *She did this to me. She marked me for life...*

Samuel took a pull from the neck of a whiskey bottle, then suddenly he swung it into the mirror and watched as shards of glass exploded across the top of the dresser. The spilled liquid wound a lazy course through the pieces of broken glass until it reached the edge of the chest of drawers and dripped to the floor.

That's how I'll kill you, Emma. Slowly. Your life will fade away like drops from a spilled whiskey bottle. And, once your cowboy becomes aware of what happened to his precious little bitch, I'll kill him, too.

He would move on then. He was tired of hiding out and only frequenting places where he would not be recognized. He wanted his life back—the life of a powerful businessman—a life he deserved.

Samuel strutted to the open bag on the bed and ran his hand across the large wads of money inside. The only good thing about being stuck in Duluth was the fact that he had hit a lucky streak. He was set to move on now, without a care in the world.

Maybe I'll travel west, he mused. *It doesn't matter where I go, though. All I have to do is tie up a few loose ends, and then I'm free as a bird.*

Samuel crossed to the window and pushed the curtain aside to peer at the bustling street below. It would be dark soon, and he could leave the rented room again. In the morning, he would finalize his plans. He had been watching the Wilkins ranch, living in the woods for a few days at a time, and then returning to the city to think. As far as he could see, he had only one problem. Tyler and the other men on the spread never left sight of the house and, during the infrequent times that Emma did exit the dwelling, one of them was always at her side.

He smiled suddenly. She was pregnant again. *Very* pregnant. *Well, Emma my dear, I hate to break the news, but this one isn't going to be born, either.*

Samuel knew the layout of the ranch like the back of his hand, and he knew Emma's daily routine even better. Still, the frustration was beginning to mount. He could almost taste her sweet flesh on his lips, and he could feel the stickiness of her blood on his hands. He had to have her one last time, and then he would make sure that he finished the job.

Samuel let the curtain drop as he turned his gaze back into the room. He just had to be patient. Eventually, someone would make the fatal mistake of leaving her alone, and then Emma would again feel his wrath—an event that would end in her death.

"This time, Emma, you *will* get what you deserve."

Chapter Twenty-Six

Steven snapped his bag shut and smiled at his patient. "I hope you have everything ready for the baby, Em. My guess is that you have only about two to three weeks left. How does that sound?"

Emma moved her legs over the edge of the bed with some difficulty, pushed herself upright with her arms, and threw him a scornful look, followed by a half-hearted smile. "I think it's going to be the longest two weeks of my life. I feel like I've been pregnant forever."

He chuckled as he took her arm and led her to one of the chairs before the fireplace. "You've done remarkably well. You should be proud of yourself." He gave her shoulder a quick squeeze. "I want to talk to you about something. Do you have a minute?"

She waved her arm at the expansive space around her. "I don't think I'm going anywhere. Lately, I haven't been allowed to do much of anything. I'm stuck in this house all the time."

The physician sat down in the chair next to her, and his face sobered into what Emma had come to call his 'Dr. Steve' expression. Her green eyes narrowed. "I don't like the look on your face, Steven. Is there something you're not telling me?"

"Everything's fine as far as the baby goes. It's your emotional state in the last week that has me a little concerned. You're nervous and edgy and snapping at the people who love you. I know the situation around here has been nerve wracking, to put it mildly, but, Em, you've got to calm down. Number one, it's not good for the baby and, number two, Tyler is just trying to keep you safe. He loves you and keeping you so closeted is the only way he knows to assure that Samuel won't get to you."

She looked at her hands, where they lay clasped on top of her swollen abdomen, and sighed. "So, he's been talking to you?"

"Of course he has! I can see the strain on both your faces every time I walk into the house. The two of you should be happy right now, Emma, regardless of the Samuel issue. You'll be sharing the birth of your first child soon, and it's going to be a momentous occasion for this entire family. Give Tyler a little leeway—along with Trevor and Cole. They're just trying to protect you. Accept their strategy and concern in this matter. It's their way of trying to control the situation."

Emma pinched the bridge of her nose and closed her eyes as she considered Steve's words. With a heavy sigh, she raised her eyes to his again. "How come whenever you tell me something, Steven, it makes so much sense?"

"Because I'm always right." He grinned, then patted her knee and helped her stand. "Come on, I'm sure they're all waiting downstairs for dinner. Since Carrie and I got married, I miss Mamie's good home cooking. I can't wait to eat!"

Emma actually laughed—the first real laugh to leave her lips since Samuel Fontaine resurfaced. "You'd better not let Carrie hear you say that!" she exclaimed, then thinking of the young couple's own announcement a few months earlier, she squeezed his hand. "And, when she reaches the end of her pregnancy, I hope you'll be as understanding with her as you have been with me."

"Well, my dear, another four months will tell the tale, won't it?"

They walked down the steps arm in arm to find Tyler waiting at the bottom with a strained smile on his face. Emma took his hand and let Steve continue alone to the dining room.

"Can I talk to you for a minute before we go in, Tyler?" He nodded, and she pulled him down to sit on a small bench near the front door. "I want to apologize for how I've been acting lately. Steven pointed out a few things that I've lost sight of."

"No apologies are necessary." He reached up to caress her soft cheek. "If anyone should be saying they're sorry, it's me. I've had you under house arrest for the last week, but it's only because I love you so much. You know that, don't you?"

"Of course I do. I'm not going to fight you or your brothers anymore, and you no longer have to stay by my side every minute, because I promise to follow the rules you've laid down. Does that make you feel better?"

His hand moved to her chin, and he lifted it gently so she could receive his kiss. "Yes, it does. Now, let's go join the others and have a little fun tonight. I think everyone deserves it. It's been far too somber around here."

"Well, I don't know about anyone else, but I can't wait for my new niece or nephew to be born!" Trevor pushed his chair away from the dinner table and vigorously rubbed his hands together. "It's going to be great having a baby around again."

"You'd think *you* were the proud father!" Cole shook his head with a wry smile, and his statement elicited laughter from everyone at the table.

"Hell, I *feel* like an expectant father. Between Emma and Carrie and the mares foaling any day, it's going to be a busy place."

The two pregnant women exchanged astounded glances, and Carrie spoke up immediately. "You can say anything you want about our pregnancies, Trevor, but, please, not in the same breath with the horses! You make Emma and me sound like a couple of brood mares!"

Trevor's eyes widened in stunned realization, and his mouth opened, but no words were forthcoming. Surprisingly, his cheeks tinged scarlet, and the group burst into laughter.

Clancey entered the dining room through the kitchen entrance a second later, with his hat in his hands and an excited look on his face. "Excuse me for interrupting you, folks. I thought you'd want to know that Bonnie has been laboring for nigh on to an hour now. If you all want to witness the birth of the first Lakota Pines riding horse, you'd better come quick! There's a good possibility that the foal will be here before the sun sets."

Instant confusion reigned as everyone rose from the table at once. The events of the past year were finally coming to fruition, and their new future was about to begin. Tyler helped Emma to her feet, and she squeezed his hand.

"You all hurry on down to the barn. I'm sure Carrie wouldn't mind tagging along with me at a *much* slower pace."

"No way, Emma. I'll wait for you. After all, it's your horse that's about to foal."

"Oh, don't be silly! You and your brothers have dreamed about this moment your entire life! If any of you miss the birth, I'll feel awful. Go now. I'll catch up shortly. Besides, I left my shawl in the living room, and I have to get it; it's a little chilly out there." Her husband remained rooted to the spot, and Emma placed one hand on her hip and pointed at the door with the other. "Tyler, go! We'll be fine!"

The doubtful dip of his eyebrows finally gave way to a wide grin. "Okay, but if you're not there in five minutes, I'm gonna come looking for you." He dropped a quick peck on her cheek, hesitated for a second more, then left with the other men through the kitchen door.

Emma laughed as she turned to Carrie. "He looks as excited as he did the day I told him *we* were going to have a baby!" She reached for her stepdaughter's hand. "Come on, Janie. Grab your coat and we'll be on our way!"

They walked into the living room, and Emma picked up her woolen shawl, where it lay over the back of a chair. Janie stopped short though, when they reached the front door.

"I've gotta get Whizzer! Mamie made me put him in my room before supper. Please, Emma, will you wait? He wants to see the new baby horse, too!"

"All right, hurry up, honey. We'll wait on the porch. Run fast now. We don't want to miss anything!" Emma smiled after the little girl as she raced to the second floor, then she and Carrie stepped outside.

Emma passed through the doorway first. A shriek left her throat a moment later when a hand snaked out, grabbed her arm, and jerked her to the left of the entrance. Carrie raced through the open door, her eyes wide with alarm.

"Run, Carrie!" Emma screamed.

Her sister-in-law kept coming and swung ferociously at the man who held Emma in an iron grip—a man she knew must be Samuel Fontaine. His animalistic growl preceded the lunge that sent Emma sprawling to the porch and, a second later, his clenched fist connected with Carrie's jaw. She spun backwards and dropped unconscious to the floor.

Emma lumbered to her feet and ran for the steps, then cried out in pain when Samuel twisted his fingers in her hair. He yanked her back against his body, then wrapped one arm around her waist, just above her bulging abdomen, as his other hand covered her mouth to muffle her screams.

Samuel never said a word as he dragged her to the edge of the porch. His darting gaze searched the beginning shadows of twilight for any sign that her screams had alerted someone to his presence. Seeing no one, he hauled her down the side steps and in the direction of the thick forest that skirted the yard.

Emma stumbled along with him and, all the while, fought to remove the clammy hand from her mouth.

"Stop it, bitch!" Samuel hissed. "They won't hear you anyway! They're all in the barn tending to their precious horses!"

Emma reached over her shoulder and her hands clawed at his face. Samuel changed her position, forced the flailing arms to her sides, and tightened his grip around her waist with a jerk. "I said *stop it!*" Her muffled screams met his ears, and he squeezed his hand tighter over her mouth. He was almost to the trees. Ten more feet and they would be out of sight.

Janie cracked open the door to her room, then paused when a scream pierced the air. "Emma must be having her baby!" she breathed.

Whizzer whined loudly on the other side of the wooden barrier, stuck his snout into the opening and scratched furiously at the floor. Janie pushed at the dog's head, attempting to shove him back into her room as another scream filtered up from downstairs.

"Whizzer, *stay*! Mamie will take her broom to you if you're running around and in the way. Emma's having her baby!" The dog's superior weight was too much for the little girl and, once again, he nudged his nose into the space between the door and the jamb. "*Whizzer*! *No!*"

The dog gave one last, tremendous shove, and Janie landed on her backside as he bounded into the hallway and headed down the steps.

The little girl ran after him, almost tripping over her own feet in her haste. "Whizzer, come back!" She followed the dog across the living room and through the open doorway, then stopped dead when she saw her Aunt Carrie lying on the porch.

"Carrie! Carrie!" Janie fell to her knees and shook her aunt's unconscious body. The woman remained unresponsive. "Where's Emma, Auntie Carrie?" Tears of fright welled in the corners of her eyes, then streamed down her cheeks.

The dog sniffed at the inert woman and, with his nose still to the ground, started across the length of the porch. Janie jumped up to follow him. She grabbed at the loose skin on the animal's neck, struggling to hold him back, until her frantic gaze settled on the blond-haired man who dragged Emma into the thick brush at the edge of the yard.

Daddy! I've got to get Daddy to help Emma!

A moan behind her caused Janie to whirl. Carrie was struggling to sit up, and the little girl raced back to drop to her knees beside her.

"Auntie Carrie, I'm scared! A man took Emma into the woods!"

The older woman swayed with the dizziness that assailed her, and her face paled to a sickly pallor. Carrie sagged onto her side again, but reached out with a shaky hand to grab Janie's arm and pull her close. "Janie...run to the barn. Tell...get your dad...Samuel! Run!"

Janie jumped up and raced toward the barn.

The five men gathered around the laboring horse, where she lay on her side in a huge stall. They rubbed the pregnant mare with gunnysacks in an attempt to calm her as contractions rippled across her swollen belly.

Tyler's dark head snapped up when Janie's frantic screams assaulted his ears. "What the hell—"

He tripped over Trevor's leg in his frenzied attempt to get around him and out of the stall, then met his daughter as she tore through the open doors with the yapping dog at her heels.

"Janie!"

The terrified little girl flew into his arms, and a sick feeling curled in Tyler's belly. He held her clinging body away from his until he was able to see into her face. "Janie! Look at me—tell me what's wrong!"

"It's Auntie Carrie and Emma!" she panted between sobs. "Auntie Carrie said to run get you! She's hurt! She said to tell you...Samuel." Janie clutched at her father's shirt sleeves. "I saw a man take Emma in the woods, where you said I couldn't go! Auntie Carrie is laying on the porch!"

Tyler took off at a dead run for the house, and his brain registered the sound of boots pounding the dirt behind him. He leapt up onto the porch, ran to his sister, and dropped to the planking beside her.

"Carrie! Jesus Christ, where is she? Are you hurt?"

"Tyler, go! I'll be all right." A sob caught in her throat. "I don't know where he took her, but you can't let him get away!"

"Tyler!" Cole bounded onto the porch. "Janie said he took her into the woods out front! Take the dog. Maybe he'll pick up their trail. We've got about a half an hour before we won't be able to see our hands in front of our faces. We'll get guns and be right behind you!"

Tyler scrambled to his feet, dashed to the edge of the porch, and leapt into the growing darkness. In a heartbeat, he was racing across the yard toward the treeline. The dog ran along side him. "Whizzer! Find Emma! Go boy!" He chanced a quick glance over his shoulder to see Trevor following close on his heels, then crashed through the brush as he tried to keep up with the dog.

Tree branches whipped at Emma's face and arms as Samuel dragged her ever deeper into the woods. She was helpless now, with her arms pinned next to her body, and terror was the only thing that kept her alert.

It was happening again, but Emma knew beyond a doubt that she would not wake up in the master bedroom this time, with Tyler at her side. No. If Samuel Fontaine had his way, this would be her last night on earth. The eerie sensation she could not shake all these months came at her full force now, and Emma stifled a sob when she realized that she would never hold her child or grow old with Tyler.

Samuel's labored breathing sent a shiver down her spine, and Emma was amazed that he could keep going. It was his insanity that bore her weight and his muttered curses, as he fought the underbrush, that convinced him his cause was just.

They entered a clearing, and he shoved her forward with vicious intent. Emma flung her arms out in an attempt to break the pitching fall. Her hands collided with the pine needle-covered ground and she rolled onto her side, then heaved her ungainly body up again. She had not taken two steps when Samuel's arms encircled her burgeoning waist, hurled her to the ground once more, and rolled her onto her back. He dropped spread eagle across her thighs to pin her body to the earth, and a sweaty hand clamped over her mouth. A knife materialized from inside his boot a moment later, and he held it only inches from her face.

"Shut up or I'll cut you."

Emma blinked away panic-born tears and stared up at him through wide eyes as her heart thundered in her chest. She let her arms fall back to the hard ground, then slowly nodded her head in ascent—and never took her eyes from the gleaming blade. A breathless moment passed before Samuel pulled his hand from her mouth, leaving it in close proximity in case she screamed.

"You know this is your last day on earth, don't you?"

Emma squeezed her eyes shut when he confirmed her earlier thoughts, and stubbornly refused to answer. *Tyler, where are you!*

"It's over, Emma. I finally have the upper hand. All those years of you taking the spotlight in Evan's eyes are done. And, no matter what you say, I know it's your fault that I lost everything I once held dear. The last year of my life has been hell, Emma, and it's time you pay. You should also know that, when I'm through with you, I'm going to kill your husband."

Her eyes flew open and she could hold her silence no longer. "I won't plead for my life, Samuel. I'm too tired to fight you any longer. But I will plead for Tyler's. He's done nothing! Kill me if you feel you must, but let him live. Please!"

"The faithful wife right up until the end, aren't you? Well, I hate to tell you this, Emma, but your pleas don't mean shit to me! Do you think I want that bastard hunting me for the rest of my life? No, Emma, I don't think so."

"Please, Samuel, don't do this! I beg of you!"

"Now, this is a real tender scene, don't you think, Emma? Here you are, pleading for his life and not even worrying about your own welfare or that of your child." He chuckled softly. "I've waited so long for this day."

He jammed the knife into the ground next to her head, and his laugh deepened when he saw the growing terror in her widening eyes. His hands moved to encircle her neck. "You'll go slowly, Emma. I want you to suffer as I have this past year—breath by agonizing breath. My only regret is that I don't have the time to screw you again." He lowered his head to press a fetid kiss to her lips, and Emma felt the bile rise in her throat. "You were good, Emma, but you weren't the best."

The pressure on her throat increased, and Emma struggled for one last breath—enough for one more scream—before his torturous fingers slowly squeezed the air from her body. She was aware of Samuel's weight on her legs and, as black spots danced before her eyes, she heard the wolf's mournful cry again amidst a dog's angry growl.

Suddenly, the burden was lifted from her body. She gasped for air and her eyes widened first in relief, then in horror when she witnessed Tyler fling his body onto Samuel's, raise his fist and smash it into the other man's face. His teeth clenched as he hissed out an oath.

"You son of a bitch!"

Tyler's fist slammed into Samuel's jaw again, and Emma crawled out of the way. She watched with shock-filled eyes as her husband beat the life from the man who had caused them both so much pain and cringed when the sound of crunching bones flooded her dazed senses. She was not sure if the noise came from Samuel's face or Tyler's hand.

Another scream left her lips when her attacker wedged his knee between them suddenly, and pushed Tyler up and away. Both men scrambled to their feet, and their chests heaved as they eyed each other murderously across the small clearing. Blood poured from Samuel's broken nose, and he spit another red stream from his mouth just before an insane smile touched his lips. He circled his opponent slowly.

"I must say I'm impressed, Wilkins, but your...interference served only to make me change my plans. Now, I'll just have to kill you first and take care of your whore later," he taunted. "Not that this new plan doesn't have its advantages. With you out of the way, I'll have time to screw the shit out of your wife again before I kill her!"

Tyler rammed the unsuspecting Samuel in the abdomen. The force of his rage sent both men tumbling to the ground again, and Tyler delivered blow after blow into Samuel's writhing body. Bones crunched, and still it was not enough. He squared his fist, pulled the other man up by his shirt, beat him back to the ground, then started the process over again.

Emma's sobs finally filtered through the red haze of fury that clouded his brain—just as he pulled Samuel upright again and drew his fist back for the death blow.

"Tyler! Stop!" she choked out. "You'll kill him!"

Her frantic words sobered him like a blast of cold air. His bloodied hand froze in mid-air. He turned his head and, for the first time, saw Trevor holding his wife's struggling body in an attempt to keep her from a headlong flight in their direction.

"Let it go, Ty," his brother murmured. "Let the authorities hang him."

"Tyler, please!" Emma sobbed. "Having his blood on your hands isn't worth it. It's over! Please, Tyler, you have to stop!"

Tyler's chest rose and fell with heavy breaths and his heart pumped madly. He stared down at the limp and barely conscious man beneath him and, still, he wanted to kill him. He wanted to do it for Emma and for all the pain he had caused her. He wanted to kill him for all the agony she suffered after the rape, and he wanted to kill him to avenge her scarred heart.

Instead, he let go of Samuel's shirt and watched through lifeless eyes as his drooping body crumpled to the ground. He hung his head then, and listened to the breeze rustle through the treetops. It was over.

Tyler stood slowly, then staggered toward his wife, and Trevor ran a shaky hand through his hair before he dropped his chin to his chest in relief. Tears streamed down Emma's cheeks as Tyler pulled her into the safety of his embrace.

"Christ—," he whispered against her hair with labored breaths. "I didn't think I'd find you in time."

She leaned back in his arms and ran trembling fingers over his bruised face. "But you did. You found me, and it's finally over."

He dropped his forehead to rest against hers, and breathed in the scent of the woman he loved more than life itself. Emma's eyes fluttered shut as she pulled his head down into the hollow of her neck and kissed his hair, then she gently rocked him as she would a babe.

She opened her eyes again a moment later and they widened in horror. Samuel lay on his side now, and pointed a small derringer at Tyler's back. In the space of a split second, she screamed and a shot rang out in the clearing. Emma braced herself, waiting for Tyler's weight to fall forward. Instead, Samuel Fontaine's body pitched backward to the ground.

Tyler spun to find Cole standing at the edge of the clearing. He lowered a smoking rifle from his shoulder. The youngest brother never took his eyes from Samuel's body as he trudged forward, then stared blankly at the man who had attempted to take so much from them all. Finally, he dropped to one knee, pressed steady fingers to the other man's neck and assured himself that Samuel Fontaine was finally dead.

"I had a bead on him before he ever took the gun from his pocket." Rising again, he faced Emma and Tyler. "I wasn't going to let him walk away again, Emma. He just made it easier for me to pull the trigger. He tried to kill both of you and, for that, he lost his right to be judged in a court of law."

He met Tyler's gaze then, and the two men came together in a fierce embrace.

"Thank you," Tyler whispered.

Cole was beyond further words, and just clung to his older brother tightly.

"Tyler..."

He turned at the peculiar timber of Emma's voice, then caught her when she fell against him. "Emma!"

"The baby..." She winced as she doubled over in pain, and Tyler gripped her tighter. "It hurts—"

"Jesus, she's in labor!" He eased her into the cradle of his arms. "It's okay, honey. We'll get you to the house."

He was already heading in that direction, with Cole and Trevor breaking a trail through the thick underbrush.

Tyler burst through the front door, with Emma in his arms, and hollered for Steven. The doctor sat beside his wife, who lay on the sofa with a rag pressed to her swollen jaw. Dougan stood a short distance away, next to Katy and Mamie, with a shotgun in his arms.

"Steve! The baby's coming!"

Emma gritted her teeth with yet another contraction, Tyler's features were ashen with panic beneath the bruises and cuts.

"Get her upstairs, Ty." The other man started up the steps as the doctor ran back to his wife, while issuing an order to Katy. "Get some linens and bring them up to the bedroom—I'll be right behind you." The housekeeper hurried to do his bidding as Steven dropped to a knee beside his wife and took her hand gently in his. "Carrie, are you going to be all right?"

"I'm fine, Steve. You need to help Emma. Dougan is here with a rifle."

"He won't need it." Cole uttered the words from where he stood in the open doorway, with his own gun in his hands. "It's over. I sent one of the men for the sheriff. Samuel Fontaine is dead." He stared at the young doctor with an unspoken message in his eyes.

Steven nodded his understanding, then squeezed Carrie's hand. "I'll be down as soon as I can." He stood then, and raced for the steps.

Emma was in the middle of another contraction when the doctor entered the master bedroom. Tyler looked scared to death. Drawing a deep breath, Steven crossed to the bed.

"Breathe, Emma. Don't fight it."

"Steven, it's awful!"

"Come on, Em, you can do it. Just remember what I told you." He watched as she took a deep breath, and then released it in a slow, measured exhale. "That's it, try and relax now. You need to rest between contractions."

He rolled up his sleeves and, when Katy entered with the linens, motioned for her to help him place the sheets beneath Emma's body. Steven glanced at Tyler over his shoulder. "All right, Ty, I'm going to leave you in charge of getting her out of that dress and into a nightgown while I sterilize my instruments."

Tyler dragged his eyes from his wife's pale face, then grabbed his friend's arm and hauled him away from the bed. "Is she going to be all right?" he whispered. "Isn't it too early?"

Steven smiled. "She's close enough, Ty. After the ordeal tonight, I would have been surprised if she didn't go into labor."

"You two can quit talking about me now," Emma reprimanded with a half smile that turned into a grimace when an even stronger contraction ripped through her body.

The two men were spurred into action. Steven left to run downstairs, and Tyler pulled a dresser drawer open. He ruffled through his wife's underthings until he heard her exasperated voice from across the room.

"Tyler, just take the one on top!"

He grabbed a frilly pink nightgown, rushed back to the bed and helped her to sit up. "Is it very bad, Em? Christ—" His hands stilled when his gaze met hers, and she heard the catch in his voice. "I thought I was going to lose you tonight."

No other words would come, and Emma reached out to gently run her fingers over the cuts and bruises on his cheek. "But you didn't. It really is over, Tyler. He's finally out of our lives."

Emma groaned and reached for his hand as the pain started again. They sat through it together and, when the contraction subsided, Tyler helped her remove her dress and put on the nightgown. He laid her back against the pillow gently and covered her with a light blanket. Suddenly, she stiffened on the bed and raised her knees.

"Tyler, the baby's coming!" she panted out.

He raced across the room and reached for the doorknob just as Steven entered the suite. "Christ, she wants to push already!"

Steven rushed to the bed and pulled the blanket up and over her knees. Emma's head lolled on the pillow and she grimaced in pain.

"I...need to...it's coming!

Tyler stepped away from the bed and, when Emma opened her eyes, she saw the worried expression on his face.

"Tyler, don't go, please! I need you!"

Steven could only shake his head at how fast the labor was progressing. He could see the top of the baby's head already. Tyler sat beside his wife, and Steven began issuing orders. No longer was he the friend. He was a doctor ready to bring a new life into the world—a life that was coming fast.

"Ty, get behind Emma's back. When I give you the word, help her sit up. Now, Emma, listen to me. You can't push until I tell you. When the time comes though, Tyler will help you sit up, then bear down like we talked about."

"I can't do it, Steven...it hurts too much!" Her eyes were wide with fear.

"Yes, you can, honey!" He watched her face tense again with the pain that spread from deep inside her body and culminated across the top of her abdomen. "Don't push yet, Emma."

"I have to!"

"Well, you can't. Breath!"

The contraction subsided, and so did another and another. Steven checked her progress. "All right, honey. On the next contraction, I want you to push."

"Okay," she squeaked. The next pain gripped her less than a minute later.

"Okay, Tyler, time to help us out!"

Emma felt Tyler's hands on her shoulders. He pushed her up and braced her with his chest. "Come on, honey, you can do this!"

Emma took a deep breath, gritted her teeth, and bore down. The pressure was tremendous, and she felt the baby slip forward slightly.

"That's it, Emma, you're doing great!" Steven's hands were busy beneath the blanket. "Keep pushing! Come on, push...push! Don't stop until you feel the contraction slow."

The pain diminished, and she let out a moan as she fell back against Tyler's chest. Her forehead was damp with beads of perspiration. Emma was consumed with pain and joy, all at the same time. She could feel her child trying to enter the world. It would be over soon.

Tyler kissed the top of her head and murmured words of encouragement. "I'm so proud of you, Emma. Rest now, honey. Breathe, like Steven said." He grabbed her flailing hand and held it firmly until another wave of pain took her again. She panted, squeezed her eyelids tightly shut, and listened as Steven coached her once more.

"Oh, God...Steve!"

"Bear down, Emma! Now! Come on, honey, you're almost done!" He could feel her straining as he held the baby's head in one hand and guided the emerging shoulder with the other. Suddenly, the child slipped into his hands. Emma fell back against Tyler again, and perspiration dotted both their faces.

A lusty cry filled the room, and Tyler hugged her from behind. "You did it, Em! Honey, you did it!"

She glanced down at Steven and strained to see the infant. She was greeted by the huge smile on her friend's face. "Well, Dr. Adams, are you going to keep us in suspense?"

Both husband and wife waited breathlessly as he lifted the child into their line of vision. "Emma, Tyler, I would like you to meet your new son." He gazed at the tiny baby in his hands. "And, Master Wilkins, these two fine people are your parents."

The newborn wailed, his arms and legs as stiff as boards, as Steve reached for a small blanket. The doctor wrapped the new life gently in the swaddling cloth before handing him to his mother.

Emma fell in love. She cradled the baby close against her breast, then counted ten perfect fingers. She turned her head to look up at Tyler, her eyes filled with a soft and gentle wonder. "Look what we created," she whispered softly. "Isn't he beautiful?"

Tyler rested his chin on her shoulder and gazed at his son in amazement. "He sure is, honey. As beautiful as his mother."

Steven let the new parents coo over their new son as relief flooded his body at how the evening had turned out. A madman had tried to take Emma's life and, in payment, lost his own. God saw fit to ease the tragedy though, by allowing a baby to be born into this family that had suffered so much pain. He watched his friends, then a shiver of anticipation ran up his spine when he thought about his own child, who would be born in a few months' time. *Thank you, God, for watching over Carrie.*

"Ty, how would you like to introduce your new son to the rest of the family? I'm sure by all the commotion he created, they know he's here. Emma and I still have a little work to do."

Tyler moved to sit on the edge of the bed again, and Emma handed him the small bundle. He looked down into the small, wrinkled face, and remembered how he felt when he held Janie for the first time.

I hope you're looking down, Sara. I hope you can see what I've accomplished. I did it!

The pieces had finally come together to create a whole. He had found happiness and contentment again, things he once thought would forever be out of his reach, and he had found them in the arms of the precious woman next to him. Tyler knew in his heart that Sara would approve.

The gentle touch of Emma's hand upon his arm brought Tyler's gaze to hers once more. Her green eyes sparkled with unshed tears. She smiled softly. "She knows, Tyler, I can feel it. Sara is happy for you; happy for us."

He was speechless. She understood him only too well, sometimes better than he did himself. She had never given up on them, and he would be eternally grateful for her persistence. Finally, he found his voice.

"I'm sure Janie is waiting none too patiently to see her new brother. As soon as Steven is finished and comes down, I'll bring her back up to see you." He looked at her, and his eyes glistened as he kissed her warm lips. "I love you, Mrs. Wilkins. Thank you for my son."

Tyler walked up to the waiting group at the bottom of the steps and proudly presented his son to the rest of the family. Father and daughter exchanged smiles, and Tyler saw the excitement that was ready to bubble over. He stooped before her.

"Look at your new brother, honey."

The little girl reached out gently to take a small hand in hers. The baby grasped her finger and clung tightly, and Janie's smile deepened.

"Oh, Daddy, he's so cute! I'm a big sister now, aren't I?"

"That you are, honey."

"Can I hold him?"

"Not until he's had a bath and is all cozy and warm," Mamie insisted as she moved to take the child from Tyler and nestle him against her large bosom.

"Can I go see Mama, then?"

Janie's big eyes, so much like Sara's, met his again when she asked the question, and Tyler felt his heart open wide at the simple term that rolled so easily off her tongue.

"Uncle Steve will let us know in a few minutes when we can go up. Your...Mama wants to see you too."

"Tyla?" Mamie spoke up softly, "I got somethin' I wants you to rememba'. We've had our past, and all the tomorrows in our future we'll be meetin' shortly. But today is what we need to be thinkin' of. This small babe be your silva linin' we talked about. You jes' grab the thread and keep on pullin'!"

Tyler could only embrace her soft shoulders; no words were necessary.

Steven descended the stairs a short time later, much to Janie's relief, and announced that Emma was ready for visitors. Tyler now nestled a clean and cuddly baby in his arms, and he took his daughter's hand and they made their careful way up the steps.

Emma sat in the bed, her arms outstretched, and Janie ran to her side. Tyler followed with their son, and the new family talked quietly about their future—a future that looked brighter than it ever had before.

Late into the night, Emma lay in the bed with her son at her breast. Her gentle gaze rested on her husband where he lay stretched out beside her. Light from the fire flickered across his muscled shoulders.

Tyler looked up and a small grin tugged at the corners of is mouth. "You're staring again—what's on your mind?"

A happy sigh left Emma's lips. She reached for his hand and, bringing it to her lips, pressed a kiss to his bruised knuckles. Her emerald eyes sparkled in the semi-darkness. "You've given me so much, Tyler. I've spent most of my life following a completely different course—a course that should in no way have met with yours. How is it that I was lucky enough to finally have our paths cross and find you standing there waiting for me?"

He smiled at her question and could not help but reach out to caress the soft shoulder that peeked at him above the covers. She had called him her shelter in the night, and he had never forgotten those words. Many times, he wondered if she even realized how her mere presence had healed him and given him hope—that, in effect, she was *his* shelter.

"I think we were destined to find one another, honey. When I was at the darkest point in my life and just trying to get from one day to the next, you burst through the door of your father's study and my life was forever changed. You dominated my every waking thought. You made me realize that I could have a life after Sara's death; that maybe I *could* be happy again." He gazed directly into the depths of her green eyes. "Do you know what you've done for Janie and me? Trevor told me once that you brought the sunshine back into this house, and he was right. You're my ray of sunshine, Emma, and I'll never stop loving you."

He pulled her close then, and, with their son nestled between them, they drifted off, never to be lost in the loneliness of the night again.

Epilogue

Emma opened her eyes to greet the new day. She immediately rolled onto her side to look at her son, where he lay in a small cradle next to the bed. Tyler peered over her shoulder and chuckled at the sight of the tiny fists that flailed in the air above him.

"I think someone's going to start hollerin' real quick if his mama doesn't feed him."

"Isn't he the sweetest thing you ever saw?" Emma's infatuation with the baby was evident in the expression in her eyes. "A new little life ready to meet the day," she mused.

She watched quietly as Tyler climbed from the bed and tenderly cradled their son before handing him into her care.

"I'll get some clean napkins so we can get him changed."

Emma smiled. Tyler was not like most fathers. He was confident in handling his infant son and ready to help at every turn.

Holding her child close, Emma mused about what life had offered her in such a short space of time. A loving husband, a family she cherished, a beautiful home and, now, a baby to call her own. A small, contented sigh escaped her lips as she watched Tyler pull on his pants and move about the room. Suddenly, she gasped.

Tyler whirled and, seeing the confusion in her eyes, he rushed to her side. His heart pounded a rapid beat against his ribs. "Em, what is it?"

"I forgot about Bonnie! Did she foal last night?"

His mouth dropped open with her words, then he rolled his eyes heavenward, placed a hand over his heart and fell across the end of the bed. "Jeez,

Em! You scared me half to death!"

She giggled at his antics and nudged him with her toe. "Well, did she?"

Tyler pushed himself up on an elbow and flashed her an incorrigible grin.

Emma's heart quickened as her gaze caressed his handsome face and dark, tousled hair. "You're smiling, Tyler."

"I'm pleased to tell you that Bonnie is also the proud mother of a little filly as jet black as her father. When I came back up last night with the news, you were finally sleeping, and I didn't have the heart to wake you." He rolled onto his knees, straddled her body and, bracing himself with his arms, leaned down to give her a quick peck on the cheek. "Double congratulations to you, Mrs. Wilkins. Your dream of having your own business has finally come true."

"What do you mean, *my* dream? It was you and your brothers who never gave up and made this whole thing come to be."

He lifted his knee over her carefully, rolled off the bed and pulled on a shirt. "And who deserves the credit, my dear, is inconsequential. We're on our way. Last night, we became true horse breeders! In fact, I think I'll run downstairs and check on everything. I'll be back up shortly." He gave both her and the baby a kiss and left the room with a happy whistle as he buttoned up his shirt.

That afternoon, Tyler peeked into the bedroom to find Emma sitting against the headboard, reading a book. Their son slept next to her, his tiny mouth open in slumber. Janie laid beside him and could still do nothing but stare at the small person who was her new brother. Tyler chuckled when the baby's little mouth puckered slightly, then the newborn turned his head and nestled comfortably against Emma's body once more.

Tyler crossed to the bed and, without a word, bent to scoop Emma into his arms and lift her carefully from the bed.

"Tyler! What are you doing?"

"Shhh. I've got something to show you." He carried her to the window. "Look down there, Em," he whispered.

She leaned forward slightly and peered into the yard. Trevor and Cole stood beside Bonnie and, seeing her in the window, they smiled and waved up to her. The tears burned behind Emma's eyelids when a small, black foal took one tentative step, and then another, and finally emerged from behind the mare. Her wisp of a tail swung back and forth in the cool air, then she leapt to one side, almost lost her balance, and repeated the maneuver again with more confidence.

Emma squeezed her husband's arm, but never took her eyes from the group assembled below. "Oh my God, Tyler, she's beautiful! It's your dream finally come true!"

"No, Emma, it's *our* dream finally come true. We're in this together." He leaned forward to gaze out the window himself, then cocked a dark eyebrow in her direction. "You know, we have to decide on two names now. Have you thought of one for the baby?"

She nodded, but her eyes were still glued to the small filly, who took a few faltering steps from its mother's side before rushing back in panic. Emma's features softened when she glanced back at her husband.

"I thought about it all morning. That tiny foal is part of our future, Tyler, and so is Bonnie. The other part is those two beautiful children across the room. In honor of our *past* though, I would like to name the baby after your father." She raised a playful eyebrow. "Thomas Lakota Wilkins. How does that sound to you?"

Tyler dropped a kiss on her lips, and she watched his green eyes take on a mischievous sparkle. "I think it's perfect, Em."

"Has anyone thought of a name for that little one down there?" She moved her gaze back to the window.

"Yup. Trevor and Cole wanted me to run it by you though, and see what you think."

"Well?"

"How does Spirit of Lakota sound to you?"

Her laughter tinkled across the room, and she nodded her head. "As you just said, Tyler, I think it's perfect!"

The grin widened across his face, and Emma pressed a kiss to his lips before her gaze dropped to the small wooden loon that sat on the sill next to the statue of the Indian. Years later, Emma would still swear that she saw it smile in just the quick blink of an eye.

Her gaze lifted to the window once more, and Emma's eyes sparkled with happiness as she watched the little filly prance about the yard with increasing confidence. Neither she nor Tyler noticed the small Indian children who danced among the trees in the distance, flitting in and out of the shadows as they played their childhood games.

The loon sang out to the drumbeat, and a young Indian brave, with a gray wolf by his side, crossed the field. The frolicking children called out to him and he quickened his pace. Looking heavenward with a smile, he gave thanks. He was home. His long journey was over.

Following is an excerpt from:

Keeper of the Dream

Second novel in the "Keeper" Trilogy
By Kim Mattson

Due for release in April, 2003

"Keeper of the Dream"
Kim Mattson

Cole arrived back at the ranch late in the afternoon and immediately searched out Emma. He delivered the medicine Carrie provided for little Sara, then went to find August to fix what happened between them the night before.

He had battled with himself during the entire ride home over how to make amends. He would not apologize for kissing her; for a moment, she had enjoyed the tender caress as much as he. He *would* plead her forgiveness, however, for anything he might have done to make August feel unworthy of him. To the best of his knowledge, Cole had never spoken ill of the Sioux people. She took his words out of context and that misguided notion was what he needed to fix first; he needed to assure August that the difference in their ancestries meant nothing to him or his family.

Cole's eyebrows rose in surprise when both Tyler and Emma jumped from their chairs when he entered the house through the kitchen door.

"Thank goodness you're home!"

Cole immediately detected the alarm in Emma's voice. "I've got the medicine. How's Sara? Is she worse?"

Emma's expression changed from worry to confusion in the space of a split-second, and then she realized that Cole thought she was upset about her daughter.

"Oh, no, Sara's fine. It's August."

Cole features paled at her words, and he looked from one to the other. "What happened?"

Emma wrung her hands and glanced at her husband. Tyler, in turn, squeezed her shoulder before moving his gaze back to his brother.

"Did something happen between you and August? She left—"

"What do you mean she left?" Cole's stomach lurched. He had lost his chance.

"August came downstairs this morning dressed in the deerskin clothes she arrived in. She returned all of Emma's items; the dresses, the shoes, everything, and thanked her for the loan. When Emma argued that the clothes now belonged to her, August said she had forgotten she was a Sioux Indian and it would be best for all of us to remember that. According to Clancey, she took Joe from his stall an hour later and left the ranch."

"You let her go?" Cole exploded. "Why didn't you stop her!"

"August is not our prisoner," Emma stated. "She's always been welcome to ride any horse on the ranch and to come and go as she pleases. She was gone before we knew it."

Cole turned on booted heel and headed for the closed door.

"Cole, wait!" Emma ran after her retreating brother-in-law and grasped his arm. "It wasn't until after she left the ranch that I realized she might not be coming back. Why else would she return all the things we gave her?"

Cole ignored his sister-in-law's last statement. "I'm going to look for her. How long has she been gone?" In his mind, Cole was already picturing the numerous spots they had visited since her arrival, as well as calculating how long it would take him to reach the farthest one out.

"About four hours," Emma and Tyler answered his question in unison.

Cole paused to nod in their direction, and their worried expressions told him that they were both more concerned than they portrayed.

"I don't think she left for good. August wouldn't steal my horse. I'll be back when I find her."

Cole saddled Spirit, refusing to let the knowledge of August's past stop him from seeking and claiming what he had wanted for so long. He was not sure where to search for her, or how long it would take to find her, but by the end of the day, he would take her in his arms and tell her of his love. He would bare his soul if that was what it took to make her stay. The mere fact that she took his horse showed that she intended to return. August carried too much honor to steal what belonged to him. No, she was somewhere close by, and he would find her.

Two hours later found Cole frustrated, weary, and beginning to doubt his earlier faith. Maybe he was wrong in assuming that she would not take what belonged to him. If she was desperate enough, she might run.

Where in hell is she?

Cole left the little-used road and turned Spirit onto a narrow, insignificant trail. He had not ridden this area in years and closely watched the landmarks for his return. The winding path snaked its way downward through a thick, shaded mass of Norway pines, and then suddenly sunlight broke through the branches. The horse stepped into a small field at the base of the hill, and the hair on the back of his neck stood on end with the wave of dark familiarity that washed over him. The treeless expanse that stretched before him was the same landscape he had seen in the twilight of his dreams. He kicked Spirit into a gallop.

Cole's blood pumped madly. He had ridden this hillside in the dream, with Spirit straining beneath him to reach the summit. This time, however, Cole knew deep in his heart that he would reach the top and, when he did, she would be there waiting for him. August was the mysterious woman of his dreams, and she was waiting...

The land itself reached out to him and time stood still as man and horse crested the ridge. Cole hauled back on the reins, and Spirit reared up on hind legs as her master's eyes frantically searched the broad expanse for the woman he knew beyond a doubt would be standing in the field.

August was there—one with the backdrop of the approaching night. Cole slid from the horse's back and, never taking his eyes from the woman he wanted more than life itself, let the reins slip through his fingers. He strode purposely toward her.

August's face was unreadable. She stood proudly; frightened, yet defiant; wanting, but not asking. Not until Cole stopped before her and reached out a tentative hand did August's lids drop to hide the desire in her eyes. Her lips silently mouthed the word 'no.'

"August..." The single word was a quiet plea.

"We cannot-"

"You want this as much as I do, August. You kissed me back last night. You want me as much as I want you—I think I've always wanted you."

The whisper of his words brushed her soft cheek like gentle fingertips. He stepped closer and the air rushed from August's lungs. The feeling of betrayal toward her own kind was nothing compared to the treachery that her body yielded now. Every beat of her heart reached out to the man before her, but still August fought her need. She turned to run; if he touched her, all would be lost.

Cole's strong fingers grasped her arm. August would never know if it was his physical strength that pulled her back, or if her bursting heart demanded that she cling to the man she had struggled so desperately not to love. She was past caring when he pulled her into his embrace.

She met his lips with unbridled passion; not as a woman haunted by the life she had led thus far, but rather as a woman who had discovered the one person who could own her very soul. Everything was forgotten; the angry words, their different ways of life, the problems that were sure to plague their future. None of that mattered as his mouth tormented hers and he pulled her closer.

They dropped to the ground as one, each aware only of the feel of the other. Cole dragged August across his chest, and a moan escaped from somewhere deep within her when his hands moved to grip her firm bottom and pull her closer. She was finally in his arms, and never would he let her go again. His lips left hers momentarily as he rolled her onto her back, and his fiery gaze pinned her to the ground.

"I knew you would come," she breathed. "In some unspoken way, I knew, and I cannot fight you any longer."

Cole's head dipped slightly and his lips trailed small kisses from her earlobe to the base of her throat, pausing at the rise of her breast and the frenzied beat of her heart.

"Then don't," he whispered. "Just love me, August. That's all I ask."

"It can never be."

"It can be all that we want it to be." Cole coaxed her mouth open once more, and August fought the searing kiss. She pulled her lips away to search the flaming depths of passion she found in his eyes.

"We can only live for now, Cole. There can never be anything more—"

"No, August. It can be forever. Just you and me, forever. I can never let you go now."

A small, poignant sigh escaped her lips. He was wrong, but she could fight the battle he waged no longer. Her answer came in the form of a gentle kiss...

ORDER A PORT TOWN PUBLISHING TITLE BY MAIL USING THE FORM ON THE FOLLOWING PAGE AND RECEIVE $1.00 OFF <u>EACH</u> TITLE ORDERED!

Mail the form along with your personal check or Money Order to
Port Town Publishing, 1106 N. 8th Street, Superior, WI 54880
www.porttownpublishing.bigstep.com
Email: PortTownPublish@aol.com

PORT TOWN PUBLISHING TITLES/PRICES
(Indicate number of copies desired in the space provided)
Synopsis/Excerpt from each title available on our website.

Historical Romance
_____ Fiery Surrender - $9.95
_____ Hannah's Promise - $7.95
_____ Heartstrings - $7.95
_____ Keeper of the Spirit - $9.95

Contemporary Romance
_____ Tender Persuasion - $9.95
_____ Never Say Never - $9.95
_____ VetCop - $7.95

Time-Travel Romance
_____ Charmed Passage - $9.95
_____ Destined Passage - $10.95
_____ Wagons To The Past - $8.95

Science Fiction
_____ S-4, Roswell Was Only....

Romantic Suspense
_____ Van Winkle Bride - $7.95
_____ Bury The Past - $10.95

Mystery-Thriller
_____ Stigma - $12.95

Horror
_____ The Hunger - $8.95

Poetry
_____ Dori Dreamer's Dreams - $9.95

Anthologies
_____ Fourteen Pieces of Gold - $9.95

Please ship my order to:

NAME: _____

ADDRESS: _____

CITY/STATE/ZIP: _____

PHONE:_____ _____EMAIL ADDRESS: _____

CALCULATE YOUR ORDER:
Combined cost of all books ordered: _____
Minus $1.00 PER TITLE: − _____
Sub-Total: _____
Tax (WI Residents Only): _____
Shipping (See Table Below):   + _____

TOTAL ENCLOSED: _____

Shipping Rates (Via U.S. Priority Mail):

1 Book	2 Books	3 Books	4 Books	5 Books	6 Books	7 Books	8 Books
$4.00	$7.50	$7.00	$6.50	$6.00	$5.50	$5.00	$4.50